Light of the Enkeli

Jazmin Loera

Dedicated to those in search of the Lighthouse.

Light of the Enkeli

PROLOGUE

It was a timeless drive. What was only six hours felt like years and seconds at the same time. I was in the passenger's seat with the view of the coast at my right and music playing not nearly loud enough, still in disbelief. Leon continued to change the radio station in search of the right song, though we both knew no song could ease our nerves. We settled for silence. It was more comfortable for us to relax in silence than for us to make small talk. Moving away from home wasn't something we had planned to suddenly do, but when an opportunity struck, we took it.

"I know we are a short drive from home, and we can drive back as often as we want. It's just something about this move makes it feel further than a short drive," I said, breaking the silence. "What are you going to miss the most?"

"Hmm," he thought for a moment before he looked at me, "to be honest, Lucy, I haven't thought too much into it. I just know it's something we have to do. I feel it." His voice was automatic, more focused on the road than our conversation.

His response was exactly what I had expected it to be because my feelings were parallel to his. Moving and living away from home was what I always knew I needed to do, it was also something I thought would never actually happen. The energy of the car suddenly changed, both of us submerged in our own thoughts.

"Not like that time we were eleven, and you *felt* it would be a genius idea to get all the boys to wear high heels trick-or-treating?" I laughed and nudged his arm.

He side-eyed me and caught on, "I give you ladies props on that. I don't know how you do it all the time. Besides, I looked good in them, and they were boots, not heels." His smile was genuine.

"It's the same thing. They were heeled boots. What was worse is they were moms!" It was strange of me to bring her up. We both never talk about her, he seemed unaffected by my slip up. "I didn't even fit in her shoes. They were too small for me."

"That's because you have giant feet!" He said.

We continued to reminisce over our favorite memories, fun camping trips with our best friends, and family gatherings at our dad's house on the lake where we grew up. Mostly we reminisced about times where it was just the two of us. It was fun to remember things through each other, though it also made me unsure about moving away from our dad.

Although we had almost everything someone could possibly want, there was always something missing. I didn't know exactly what it was. I did know moving away was what we had to do to find out.

"We are making the right choice. We are following our path," Leon recited, commenting on my thoughts like he usually does. In saying so, he was also answering his own self-doubt, convincing himself we were making the right choice. I understood. We were leaving our loved ones and our dad behind. Our dad, our home, and our safe place.

The last hour of the drive could have been minutes before we arrived at our new house, a two-bedroom bungalow surrounded by fruit trees, giant Willow trees, with a few oak and pine trees bordering the perimeter. Vines climbed the fence of the yard making it impossible to see through. As I looked around, I noticed the property could have been a chunk of home airlifted and placed in the city's outskirts. I didn't know how Leon found this place. I had been browsing for months to find a house with everything on our checklist while staying within our budget. I told him I was having a hard time finding a home for us, and less than three hours later, he had not only found a place but had signed the lease and said we could move by our eighteenth birthday at the end of the week.

There we were, on that same Saturday, moving into a house we would be calling home for as long as we needed it to be. We pulled into the long driveway, and although I had never been here before, I felt a tinge of familiarity. Deja vu. Before the car was turned off, I knew inside there was a stone fireplace with different engraved insignias. I also knew there were blackberry vines around the arched back door and strawberry bushes along the back walkway. I turned to tell Leon, only he held his finger up. He reached for his phone and pulled it out of his back pocket before I could speak. I knew it was our dad who was calling.

We stepped out of the car and into a chapter of our lives that would change everything. We just didn't know it yet.

1

Sweat dripped down my nose and fell on the top of my hand. I couldn't tell whether it was from the heat or the work I had been doing. Perhaps it was both. The same repetitive motions for weeks have made me a machine, and I worked faster than ever. The insulation was almost entirely installed. After today the only room that needed insulation was the bedroom. The rest of my new house started to look more like a home and less like the skeleton of the barn it had once been.

My muscles ached. Every time my body had grown used to the motions of a specific movement, that project would end, and a new one would begin. There wasn't much room for rest if I wanted to be finished by winter. If I'm not finished, the rain would slow down the build and double whatever time was left. In reality, no rush was necessary, no rush at all. The home I have been living in for the last few months had been precisely what I needed. It was on the property I inherited, a small gran-ny flat on the other side of the lake from where my dad lives and where I grew up in Shadow Rock. On the same property was an old, well-kept barn. I was turning the barn into my new home.

My palms were sweaty when the hammer slipped from my grip and instantly sent shooting pain from the top of my foot to my ankle.

I give up for today. I thought to myself and held my breath along with the pain.

I sat in place and untied the laces of my old work boots. Thankful to have been wearing them even though I despise them most of the time. I would prefer to be barefoot but quickly learned to wear them after stepping on a rusty nail.

The familiar brush of a gentle beast rubbed my back, and the sound of a low whimper echoed throughout the barn.

"I'm okay, boy," I lied.

Kona laid on his stomach and pawed my foot. My body tightened and my face fell. Kona nudged for me to stand up and put his head under my arm. His body tensed, his eyes looked blank, ears moved forward, and he howled so loud I had to cover my ears. I heard footsteps on the deck. Kona knew someone was here, yet he was still at ease. This could mean one thing.

Leon.

"I already know you hurt yourself, Lucy. I don't even have to go up there to know," Leon said. His footsteps continued up the spiral staircase.

"Zip it," I said.

The sound of plastic wavered over my head.

"Dried mangos, my favorite. Thanks." I snatched them from his hand and opened the bag, immediately taking a bite.

He smiled and walked over to my foot.

"Hammer?" He asked.

I should have known.

"How do you always know?" I couldn't hide the irritation in my voice.

"How do *you* always know?" He waited a few seconds. "We're twins. Some things we can't hide. The hammer right next to your foot might have given it away, just saying."

We both laughed. It wasn't just Leon knowing what hit me. It was him showing up at the exact moment I needed him. I should be used to it by now, I do the same thing, but it still surprises me. As much as I try to keep to myself, it seems we are always connected.

He helped me up and gave me a piggyback ride down the narrow staircase. Kona followed.

"Why are you here? You said you wouldn't come till Friday," I asked.

"I was going to wait, but I had a feeling I should come see you. I knew you would be bitter about me coming, so I didn't come empty-handed. I brought groceries," he said, gesturing towards outside. We both walked to his Jeep.

"Fine. But you have to stay and hang out for a few. You keep dropping by and leaving right after. It's annoying," I said.

He looked at me, a flash of emotion in his eyes, and then he smiled right after.

He was hiding something.

"Sorry, I've been busy helping Dad. He seems to need more help lately." Leon tapped his leg.

Guilt stung more than the pain in my foot. Our dad's physical health has been deteriorating, affecting his leg more than anything else. He now permanently has a cane at his side and a smile that doesn't reach his eyes.

I hadn't realized how late in the day it was. The sun would be setting in an hour.

"How is he?" I asked.

He took a deep breath and looked across the lake directly at our childhood home.

"You'd know if you drove the five minutes to his house or if you walked your giant dog to our home."

Kona grumbled at Leon in defense of us both.

I looked away and rolled my eyes, grabbed a few bags of groceries from the back of his Jeep, and walked into my tiny flat. Leon and Kona trailed close behind.

"It's not because I don't want to go visit. The time just flies by, and before I know it, the day is over. I'm too exhausted to do anything but eat a bowl of cereal and read a book or watch trash tv. Being there for him isn't the easiest for me right now." I couldn't look him in the eyes, so I focused on putting the groceries away.

"It isn't easy for me either, Luc, but one of us has to do it," his words stung, but he called me by his nickname for me to ease the blow. He wasn't trying to be hurtful, just honest.

I looked up at him, my face too warm from the rush.

"He is going through more than we know right now. I don't know exactly what it is, but he's been meeting up with his brothers more than usual. He says it's for work, but I know it is more than that. He steps out at night and looks this way, you light your fireplace every night. He sees the smoke. It's his way of knowing you're okay." Leon's concern wrinkled his forehead.

I didn't notice I lit a fire every night.

"Our birthday is never easy for him, as much as he tries to hide it. It's only a few weeks away," I said, as I took another bite of dried mango.

"I guess." He looked out of the front window in the distance, "he's been trying. He has been out rowing the boat every morning and picked up woodworking again. Said he learned a lot from your neighbor."

"My neighbor?" I thought about the only other house on this side of the lake. "I've never talked to him before."

"I find that hard to believe. Anyways, what's for dinner?" He said.

"Spaghetti Bolognese. I haven't had pasta since the last time you brought groceries. That was forever-ago," I said. My mouth watered at the thought.

"Lucy, I brought you groceries last week, and the week before, and the week before," he said and looked at me.

We laughed, thankful to have a change of subject. Leon smiled, but it didn't reach his eyes, and I could see a shadow of our dad on his face. He knew more than he was willing to talk about.

Leon doesn't like to be pushed. I thought about pushing him with this, asking him more about our dad, but that would be selfish. He would talk when he was ready, just like I would. We tend to go through similar situations at the same time. I know I had more on my plate than I was willing to admit. I had things I didn't want him to know yet, and it was only because I didn't know what it was exactly. I just felt different.

The sun had gone down, and we were in the middle of a horror film, stomachs full and satisfied. The last few months have been a series of events I never would have expected. Us graduating college and moving back home to be closer to our dad. We knew we wanted to come back one day. I just never thought the day would come so soon. Now that we are back home, some things had started back up again, the way they did before we left. Things that only happened here.

In the middle of the second movie, I found myself watching him instead of the film. He was my twin, my exact same age, but his soul felt younger and lighter. Even his features were much lighter than mine. His skin was tan but still shades lighter than my own. His eyes are hazel, where mine were dark brown. He towered over me, a solid foot taller than me. Everyone has always said how much we look alike, though I knew it was more because of our mannerisms than our appearance.

Leon has always been so laid back and cool. He always knew how to live and go with the flow. Somehow everything always worked out in his favor. Leon made life seem easy, and I have always admired his effortless way of just being himself, honest and open.

I don't know why I hadn't noticed when he first arrived. I thought he was just worried about the hammer falling on my foot, but this was something else. The look on Leon's face, his eyes were on the small tv, but his head was somewhere else, just like mine. His forehead wrinkled, and he was biting his nails, struggling with something. Worry deep on his mind. His hair was getting long for him. The longest parts brushed his shoulders, the gold coming through the ends of his brown hair. He has been surfing. The salt always dyed his hair streaks of golden brown. Even his thin lips were flakey from too much sun.

Leon surfs daily, but he never stayed out all day unless something is on his mind.

He sensed my unease and looked directly at me. Some call it twin telepathy. I call it Leon being Leon.

"Stop," he said.

"What's going on?" I ask, my voice flat.

"What do you mean?" His face didn't give anything away.

"Leon, what's going on? We are twins. I can feel it," I said.

He got up, pushing my feet from his lap.

"You always say that. Nothing is going on. Like you said, our birthday is coming up. It's a tough day for us," he said.

He reached for his keys, pat Kona on the head before walking out of the door. I followed him, immediately wrapping my arms around myself. The chill in the night air was too cold for the upcoming summer.

"Leon," I said.

"Lucy, I'm fine. Everything is good right now. You're reading too much into things like always. We are twins, I can feel it. Love you," he said, mocking me.

"Love you, too. Jerk."

He smiled and got into his car. I watched him drive off, disappearing into the trees.

Maybe I had been reading into things too much lately.

Maybe he was lying.

After Leon left, I took a shower and cleaned the small kitchen. One of the downsides to living in the middle of the forest is all the bugs you get from leaving food out for too long. Luckily my house was small, a little granny flat studio-like home. All that was in here was my sofa bed, a rug, a small coffee table, a small round table with four chairs, a tiny bathroom with an armoire just outside of it where I kept all of my clothes and linens, and a small kitchen in the corner of the room. A simple and comfortable place, perfect for me now and precisely what I needed.

I fed Kona, lying on the rug in front of the lit fireplace, waiting for me to make the bed. I laid out my sofa bed and got it ready. Before I could finish flattening out the comforter, Kona came with his fluffy blue blanket in his mouth for me to put it on his spot in bed. When he was a puppy, I had gotten him this blanket for comfort. Now I lay it down on the bed to contain his long coarse black fur from getting everywhere.

"Good boy, Kona." I rubbed his head.

We laid in bed, and I braided my waist-long brown hair before I reached for my sketchbook to sort out my thoughts and wind down for the night. Kona had grown rapidly the last few months. He was almost a year old and seemed to still be growing. When he first showed up in my life it was a surprise. Literally, Leon and I were living in the city, and I woke up one day to find a tiny five-pound black ball of fur underneath the coffee table all by himself. We didn't know how he got there, all of our doors and windows had been shut and we had no idea how he appeared, but he did. Immediately I knew he was a part of me. I needed him. He'd grown to be over a hundred pounds. His fur is still all black except for the silver fur on his paws and around his mouth. Leon had always made fun of me, saying I couldn't keep a wolf as a pet, and called Kona a wolf dog.

Kona was huge, and so was his personality. He picked up everything

I taught him, from being housebroken to understanding what I say. He has even caught a few fish in the lake. Luckily, we have tons of land here where he can let his energy out. Though he's never been destructive like most puppies, he does require tons of activity, but he is good at entertaining himself. He is well trained and obedient, a little overprotective but always obedient.

I looked down to see Kona in my drawing, nothing new. What was new was the symbol in the background. It could be an old family crest of some sort, one I have probably seen before in one of these old houses around the lake. I knew it was nothing more than doodles. This was what happened when I spaced out and would draw or paint. Sometimes it was a view of the scenery, sometimes random symbols or places, things I had never seen before or places I have never gone. Not while I was awake, at least.

Ring ring ring.

Alika, a friend since before I could remember, called before the sun was completely up. She knew to call at a time where I thought it could only be an emergency. It wasn't. She had been planning a birthday party for Leon and me at our favorite beach and wanted to let me know weeks beforehand so I wouldn't have an excuse to not go. She talked about our loved ones and express how they were looking forward to seeing me. I found my thoughts wandering in any direction except our conversation. An echo of my voice repeated generic responses until an hour had passed, and I had an excuse to hang up the phone.

The sun was out, and I was ready to start my day. I peeled my warmth off of my body and was hit by unexpected soreness. My foot was especially sore and bruised. After months of manual labor, my body was stronger than ever but still getting used to being pushed to its limits. Perhaps manual labor isn't something you ever truly get used to. Building my home was the single most efficient way to spend my time as of lately. It gave me a reason to keep my phone out of reach, not answering anyone who would call, and reason to skip out on invitations without completely blowing someone off. This is exactly what I had been doing lately, skipping events and blowing everyone off. Telling myself, I was too busy being productive selfishly made me feel better, even if it was a lie.

Kona pawed at the front door, ready to go out per his morning routine. I walk the few short steps from my sofa bed to the front door and let him out, stepping out onto the porch to get a breath of fresh morning dew from the lake. He ran straight towards the tree line next to the water. Already I knew it was going to be a beautiful day. The clouds were few and the air fresh. Perfect for a day under the sun.

My morning routine has been the same every day for the last four months. Wake up, let him out, get ready for my day, review blueprints and my building schedule while eating my breakfast. Which today happens to be a bowl of oatmeal and an apple with a cup of warm tea. My small round wooden table was full of sample materials and blueprints of my new house. I had to hold my bowl of oatmeal with a tea towel because it wouldn't fit on the table.

The familiar sound of a truck driving through the gravel echoed through the room, followed by thirty minutes of silence and then the customary wood cutting and hammering. It was Talan. He has taken up an "easy project" in converting the old barn into my new home. I have been an extra pair of hands instead of the other way around. I grew up helping my dad build homes and work on projects around the house. This project has been nothing new to me.

He continued to work outside while I finished getting ready for my day. No makeup, loads of sunscreen, my long hair pulled back into my baseball cap, a t-shirt, and jeans with my work boots. Extra thankful to put them on today after yesterday's mishap.

Kona barked in the distance multiple times. It is a playful bark. He's having fun, which reminds me to fill his bowl up with food and get him fresh water. I add a few scraps of leftover chicken to his bowl and a carrot on the side to help brush his vast teeth and head out the door. I looked towards the lake on my left where Kona was barking, either playing with ducks again, fish, or both.

The patio is still damp from the morning dew though the morning dew is gone and replaced by a fresh breeze and a warm day. The fresh air eliminates the small amount of anxiety I felt after my phone call from Alika, putting the beach day away in the future where it belongs.

Something looked different. The dirt on the floor now had a black pebbled path leading from my flat to the barn's front door. The way the pebbles shined in the sun made them look wet. I had to touch them just to make sure they were not. It was beautiful.

"Leon came early this morning. He called me and said he was going to do this before he headed out with your dad." Talan's deep voice carried from the short distance.

"Good morning," I said, quickly making eye contact with him before looking back down at the pebbles.

"Have you met your neighbor?" Talan asked as he looked over towards my neighbor's house.

"Neighbor? I always forget there is even a house there. Why?" I said.

"Just asking, Leon mentioned him this morning. I was only wondering if you ever talked to him." He eyeballed the house. It wasn't much bigger than my flat, I could tell it had a bedroom and a garage. Whoever lived there always had the garage door open during the day.

"Never." My voice trailed at the thought of Leon and how he acted yesterday. I hope he is okay. He asked me about my neighbor yesterday too.

"Are you okay?" He asked.

"Yeah, why?" I looked back up at him.

He observed me for a minute before jumping a few feet down from the barn's porch to the floor and walked closer to me.

I could see questions in his eyes. He opened his mouth to talk and immediately closed it again.

"You know you can talk to me, right?" He said.

Everything in me knew I could, I nodded.

"How about a date then?" He laughed. I knew he was half kidding.

"Ha. Very funny. Let's get to work," I said as I tried my best not to roll my eyes.

The rest of the day went smoothly, I didn't drop any tools on my feet, just a new blister on my hand, but I would rather have a blister over a broken toe. The barn was almost done and began to feel more and more like home. The flat was perfect, but it wasn't entirely me. It was built in the late 1800s and untouched before I moved in, looking and smelling the part. It was cozy and beautiful in its own way, and I am thankful to have had it as a place to live and a place to call home. It just felt as if it was made for someone else. It still felt like home, but more of the way home feels when it's a family member's house. Feeling comfortable there and welcome to stay as long as you like, but it isn't quite the same as having your own. The barn was larger but not by much. The whole space was open except for the bedroom and bathroom. Outside of my bedroom door was a spiral staircase leading up to the loft, which would be my library and art space. It also had a larger kitchen with an island, an area for a small table opening up to a living room with large windows and sliding doors looking out onto the lake. Right outside of the sliding doors was a deck and a two-lane lap pool, which is currently just a hole in the ground. The whole idea of restoring and adding original pieces similar to the flat filled me with several different emotions because I would soon be living here.

We were still working on getting it to a point where it would be livable, but I can't do all of the work myself. Days like today when Talan comes, he does all of the work I don't know how to do. Leon also comes by to help and sometimes brings another friend of ours, Dario. They all, somehow, do work much quicker than I can. Something that would take me a week would take them a day.

Other than seeing those three, I don't see anyone. Not even my dad. Since we moved home a few months ago, I haven't felt like myself. I knew we would be coming home eventually. I just thought we would both be living with our dad. I majored in art, Leon majored in business.

The school hosted an art show, one of my favorite teachers had me submit a few pieces, and the following week I received a check for much more than they were worth. They were canvas paintings, doodles as I would call them. All of a place close to home called the Bloom. It was just enough money to convert the barn into a house and have a year, if I budgeted, to figure out what I wanted to do from there. I repeatedly tried to contact the person who purchased them to give the money back. I would rather just give them the art, flattered they wanted it at all. They were anonymous and untraceable. Someone who I don't know has a collection of my art on their walls.

Kona barked and nudged my shoulder with his head bringing me back to the now. I had been sitting on the porch stairs of the flat, watching the sun go down over the lake. It was setting right above my dad's house.

He nudged me again. Only this time, I could tell it was to let him go inside.

"What's going on, boy?" I asked him and pet the space between his ears.

Kona pawed the door and let out a low whimper. This wasn't like him. Usually, he wanted to stay outside until I made him go inside for the night. He must have been tired.

"Okay, I'll feed you, shower, feed me and make our bed. Deal?" I said.

He barked once. I was convinced he knew what I was saying.

As soon as I walked into the flat, I felt the urge to shut and lock the door behind me, not sure why. It could have been from the long day or from Kona's rush to come inside. I took a few deep breaths, not letting anxiety get the best of me.

I fed Kona and gave him fresh water before getting into the shower.

The water ran down my body into the drain, taking with it a layer of dirt, a hard day's work, unease, and the dismissal of Talan's date offer. It haunts me every time he asks. Which is often.

I hopped out of the shower, put on an oversized t-shirt, shorts, and brushed my hair. It grew fast and was now hitting my hips, a dark brown curtain of straight hair. I rushed a quick loose braid while I walked over to the kitchen.

"What should I cook?" I mumbled, though I already knew the answer.

I was too tired to cook. A sandwich and a bowl of grapes would have to do.

Kona barked at me to make the bed as he pawed the corner of the couch.

"You're just extra needy and demanding today, aren't you?" I said.

Nonetheless, I did as he asked. I placed a few logs in the fireplace, started the fire, put an old musical on my tv, got my food and a glass of water, then laid down. I itched for my sketchbook, still a little uneasy for some reason. The only way I could let it out was on paper.

I took bites of my sandwich between the strokes of my pencil. Feeling more and more enveloped on the page than I did in real life until there was hardly any white on the page left. A spiral of thoughts and replays of conversations until I yawned, breaking the trance.

It was after midnight when I finally got up to stretch and refill my glass of water. I stood at the sink and drank my water as I looked around my home. It was everything I needed it to be, made of wood, so simple and clean, my own little timeless bubble. It was easy to forget all of the strong, intricate carvings on the doorways, windowsills, and beams because every house on the lake had them. The more I look at them, the more beautiful they get. As a kid, I didn't see their beauty, now it is all I see. I placed the cup in the sink and walk back to bed.

That's when I felt it, a chill up my spine. At that moment, Kona jumped up to stand on all fours on the bed. His hair was standing up, and he let out a low growl, displaying his sharp teeth.

"Kona, relax. You just had a bad dream," I said, trying to settle him down. He continued to stand there, no longer growling, but he was still uneasy and not breaking eye contact with whatever it was he was staring at. I looked in the same direction as him. He was growling outside of the window above the sink. Right where I was just standing. I looked outside of the window from this distance and could barely see a thing. An abyss of black led me to believe he was barking at moving trees or a shadow from one of the trees.

I looked out of the front window on the opposite side of the room and saw the shadow of my new house, softly lit by my neighbor's porch light. His house looked warm, his front porch was larger than mine. The light was dim but still illuminated all around the three houses. Something moved on his porch, squinting my eyes so I could get a better view, and found him sitting on a hammock reading a book. It was nice to know I wasn't the only one who was up at all hours of the night.

I got back in bed and laid down, putting my sketch pad on the floor next to the bed, closing it, and my brain off with it. I turned over to see Kona lying down again, only he was not in his usual position. He laid his head on his front paws, and he still stared out of the back window.

"You are one weird dog. Now come over here. You're creeping me out," I said softly, reaching out for him. He turned his head to look at me, then back again to look out of the window, and took a deep breath. After a moment, he decided to lick my face once and lay down. This time he was closer than usual with his head on my pillow instead of next to the edge of the bed where I had trained him to lay. I didn't move him. I still had the chill on my spine. I pat the space between his ears, and we both drifted off to sleep. Dreaming of shadows, darkness, and a spiral of secrets.

2

"Kona!" I called out to him several times with no response.

My worry grew each time I called out for him. The louder I yelled without response, the more I fed my fear. I climbed down the ladder in the barn and walked outside when he sprung out of my neighbor's garage. He ran towards me and jumped on me the way he does every time he hasn't seen me for over five minutes. I turned back towards the garage of my neighbor's house. He smiled and waved in the distance. He walked back inside of his garage before I could wave back.

"Kona, you can't just leave and go wherever you want. We don't know him. Stay close to me," I said.

I stared at him for a few seconds before I gave him a pat on the head. His eyes drooped, and his ears fell. He walked to the back deck of the barn in the shade and stayed there for the remainder of the day until it was time to go in for dinner.

"Want some food?" I said to wake him up. He lazily got to his feet, sprinted to the door of the flat, and jumped over the five stairs in one stride.

There were still about two hours of sunlight left, and after having Leon over yesterday, I realized I needed to go see our dad. It'll take about forty-five minutes if we walk, especially since Kona likes to stop and smell everything.

I quickly showered, put on a pair of comfortable jeans, a sweater, and some shoes then headed out. Kona never needed a leash. He stayed close most of the time. If he was too far for me to see, I only had to call out for him, and he would make his way back. We stopped at my car to get a flashlight from the trunk in case we stayed past sundown.

The trail to my dad's house was a familiar one. The surroundings of the lake were all almost identical. We were in the middle of a forest filled with an assortment of giant firs. The trail was narrow but wide enough for a car to get through, but just barely. The trees blew in the wind, and on certain days when the wind blew strong, it sounded of airplanes flying overhead. The trees were the largest trees I had ever seen. Some were over two-hundred-fifty feet and made up the entire forest. You would also find at random a pepper tree and an occasional willow. It was always strange the types of trees that grew here. There were plenty of streams going from the lake to a nearby river and into the ocean. There was a stream behind my flat, and on quiet nights, I could hear the water making its course.

Along this trail, just under halfway to my dad's house, was a cluster of a wild orchard you wouldn't guess to be there. Short apple trees of all colors, pygmy orange and grapefruit trees. A random row of grapevines and a blood-red plum tree. Two large trees were much taller than the rest, a peach tree and a walnut tree. Along the base of the trees was a mix of berries and vegetables. Raspberries and blackberries intertwined with each other. An abundance of blueberry bushes blossomed on the base of the walnut tree, and strawberries grew, covering most of the remainder of the floor. Tomato vines were randomly on the far side, next to a chili plant and assorted squash. I could only see one pumpkin, but I was sure there were more if I were to look closer at the other end of the orchard.

There was also what came with them, naturally. Birds, bees, mice, and squirrels climbed the trees. I have also seen raccoons and deer when I would come as a child.

One thing that was always here at any given time was the butterflies and hummingbirds. Every shade of butterfly imaginable, every color combination, and every size, all here in one place. The hummingbirds seemed to dance with the way of the land, knowing every leaf and every branch.

The wildflowers grew high enough for my hands to brush them as I walked. When I was a child, I would tell my dad and Leon not to pick them. I always thought flowers were much more beautiful when they were in the ground.

The vines grew to the treetops, making their way from one tree to another, a natural canopy. Most of them were jasmines and smelled refreshing. Every once in a while, you'd get a good breeze with the scent of wild lavender and moss. It smelled of home.

My dad would always tell me all of the fruit and flowers bloomed just for me. I had always been fascinated by the colors and smells. There was nothing else I could compare it to. Leon and I used to come here to play as kids, going home hours later with berry-stained fingers and clothes and our bellies full. As I looked around, I realized just how much I have missed it here. It was full of memories and simpler times. This felt like home.

The more I looked, it seemed as if nobody had walked through here in years. There was barely a trail left to walk through without stepping on some sort of plant. If it weren't for Kona leading the way and moving the greenery aside, I would have tripped and fallen multiple times by now. The strawberries smelled too good to pass up, so I picked a few. They were bigger than my fists, the size of large apples. I tossed one to Kona, and he swallowed it whole.

"You're one crazy beast. You're going to choke one of these days," I laughed.

He turned his head around and looked me straight in the eye with his mouth open and his giant dog smile. I swear he knew what I was saying, especially right now. Even when he ignored me, I am positive it was his intention to do so.

The first bite of strawberry was an immediate flashback of my childhood as the juice of the strawberry dripped down my face.

I took a step forward, and a root caught my foot before the ground did. With absolutely zero grace, my face hit the floor and, thankfully, landed on a thick bed of moss. Surprised it didn't hurt as much as I thought it would.

Kona's face was at mine as soon as I looked up. He let out a whimper as he pawed my back. His brows were up, and the black space between his ears was narrow. I kissed his face and hugged his thick neck to let him know I was okay. The tension left his body, and his tail lifted from between his legs.

My body ached when I tried to get up, so I rolled over and laid on my back. The sky was beautiful, a cotton candy sunset full of clouds of different colors. The trees were high. As the wind blew through the leaves, it made a soothing whistling sound. The birds chirped and sang in perfect harmony along with it while the butterflies danced to the song. Some were so close I could touch them if I extended my arm.

My eyes followed the only white butterfly and watched as it landed at the base of the thick pine tree, directly at the center of a carving I had not seen here before. I turned over back to my stomach to fully see it. The engraving had a circular pattern, detailed so finely, and looked as if someone had put hours into it, maybe even days. The butterfly was directly in the middle, perfectly centered as if it knew just by being there it was adding to the beauty of the carving.

A tinge of familiarity swept over me, and I felt like I had seen it before, but I couldn't remember where.

I inched closer to the carving, doing my best at an army crawl when Kona shoved me in the opposite direction. He barked and continued to walk down the path towards my dad's house without breaking eye contact.

"I get it. We're going now before it gets too dark," I said.

My oversized dog had scolded me. I knew it was strange that I talked aloud to my dog so often. Then Kona does something to validate my words, and I realize he does understand me most of the time.

We walked through the trail another twenty minutes before the trees began to thin out. We were almost there. The lake was glassy and untouched. It was much easier to see as we approached this side of the lake because there were no trees between the trail and the water. Along the path leading here were patches of high brush and thick trees, making it difficult to see the water.

I always knew I took home for granted. This was the most beautiful lake I had ever laid my eyes on. The water was deep turquoise blue, clean with colorful rocks throughout, except for the black stones at the bottom of specific areas. The same black stones Leon had put as the walkway from the flat to the barn. The fish were camouflaged with the rocks, some more colorful than others.

Even at its deepest of seventy-five feet, the water was so clear you could see straight to the bottom. Similar to a magnifying glass when looking from above, you'd never know its actual depth unless you were swimming in it.

I could see my dad was on the lake paddle boarding close to the dock where Leon was sitting with his feet in the water as they talked.

Kona sprinted straight to the dock to see Leon.

"I thought you said you had plans to cook dinner with this old guy?"

I said as I passed my dad's neighbor's house.

It was the last house on this side of the lake and the only house on the entire lake completely fenced off. It always looked creepy because we never knew who lived there. Every now and then, we would see smoke coming out of the chimney. Other than that, it had been vacant as far as we knew. It no longer felt as creepy, just another part of what made home, home.

Leon and my dad looked my way, then at each other, then back at me. Leon was the first to shrug off his look and met me at the shoreline by the dock. He picked me up and threw me over his shoulder, pretending to throw me into the clear water. Our laughs echoed over the lake.

Our dad took his time as he pulled the paddleboard out of the water and began to make his way over to me. I forgot how slow he was without his cane.

Leon still hadn't put me down. He walked over to the house with me slung over his shoulder and our dad alongside him.

"You can put me down now," I said.

There was no use in fighting or struggling. My body hung limp against his. He always does this.

"Not yet." He took the last few steps and gently put me down on the porch.

Our dad reached the porch a few moments later when he pulled me in for a hug and reached for his cane at the top of the stairs. I forgot how warm my dad was, and for the first time in weeks, I can breathe deeply and fully. His warmth etched at the lingering coldness of the previous night.

"There's my little Luc. I have been waiting for you to come see me. Now that you are here, do you want to help with dinner?" My dad said.

"I'll do whatever you want except the dishes. Leon has to do them." I spoke in Leon's direction.

He laughed. "Like you have ever done them. Anyway, we all knew

I was going to do them. Some things just don't change."

We all laughed together. Leon sat on a barstool at the island in the kitchen while I got to work cutting the vegetables and our dad started with everything else we would need for dinner.

Once I had finished cutting the broccoli, I handed over the stem to Leon for him to snack on. As soon as he took the first bite, a familiar padding sound inched close. Kona was waiting for Leon to share. He always shared what he was eating with Kona.

"She gave this to me because I am her favorite," Leon said to Kona, who had let out a half bark, half whiney growl in response.

Kona looked at me.

"The both of you need to stop bickering. We all know that I am her favorite," our dad said, causing us to laugh.

"What are we cooking anyway?" I ask and tossed Kona a piece of carrot.

"Steak with veggies and baked potatoes. For dessert, we have fresh baked cookies. Your neighbor brought them over first thing this morning. Said he made them from scratch," my dad said without taking his eyes off of me.

"Luc, you're going to love 'em," Leon chimed in.

"You both know cookies are my weakness." My voice was too excited, unable to hide their awkwardness.

They both looked at each other with expressions challenging to read and convinced me momentarily that Leon wasn't talking about the cookies. Still, I had no idea who my neighbor was.

We talked and laughed as we cooked dinner. When it was finished, we all served ourselves and sat at the wooden table. Kona laid under the table, waiting for one of us to feed him any sort of scraps, which we all did.

"Thanks for dinner," I said through a forkful of potato.

"Any time, my little Light," my dad said. He smiled. Leon looked at me and smiled too.

Our dad hasn't called me that since before I moved away. It was always my favorite nickname from him. My brother always called me Luc, pronounced like Luke. Our dad called me his little Light, Luc, Luca, Lulu, Lua. Mostly everyone else I knew just called me Lucy.

Throughout dinner, we talked about everything and nothing at all. I asked about my dad's newfound love for woodworking. Leon even started in on it, and they have made some beautiful pieces, mostly furniture. My old room was upstairs, and they made a swinging chair up on the balcony outside of my room. They talked about upgrades they made to the house. They updated me on our cousins and my uncles. I, naturally, turned my head to look at the wall of pictures to my right in the living room. It was full of memories. I have ten cousins, all of which are boys, and three uncles. I have no living aunts and no girl cousins. I am the only girl and the youngest of them all, Leon was minutes older than me, but he has always insisted I am his baby sister. Nobody has ever gotten remarried or had long-term relationships or anything of the sort. My mother died giving birth to me, Leon was born first, and our mother was okay. As soon as I was out of the womb, my mother's heart stopped beating with my first breath.

As for my aunts, they all died in freak accidents. My aunt Claire married my uncle Colton and had three sons, Chris, Charles, and Cameron. Aunt Claire was stung by a bee and didn't know she was allergic. She died on the way to the hospital.

Aunt Serena was married to my Uncle Silas. They had three sons as well, Sawyer, Sean, and Sanford. She was struck by lightning twice, not making it past the second strike.

The only one I have ever known was my Aunt Millie. She had a tree fall on her and died. I was four years old when she passed away. She was the sweetest lady. She was married to my uncle Mikael, and they had four sons together, Mateo, Max, Mike, and Marcus.

Every uncle married a woman with the same first initial and named their sons with the same initial. Even my dad, Leo, married my mom Lola and had Leon and me, Lucy.

"LUC!" Leon said to get my attention as he clapped his hands once.

"Sorry, I was daydreaming."

"Can I take your plate?" Leon said. I gave him my plate and looked outside. It was way past sundown. Our dad stood up with the help of his cane and sat on a barstool on the island, making conversation with Leon while he did dishes. It was time for me to go home. I was getting tired.

They both read the expression on my face when my dad asked something that surprised me, "Do you want to stay the night? Your room is the same as it was when you left. But I know Leon wouldn't mind taking you home if you didn't want to stay."

I almost made up a lame excuse for why I needed to go home, but the look on their faces made me change my mind. Something about the concerned look in their eyes made me nod in acceptance instead.

My old room upstairs was exactly the way I had left it. Kona ran in and jumped on the bed before I had even stepped foot inside. Somehow, he knew we were staying the night. My old white floral quilt was on the bed and smelt of fresh detergent. Twinkle lights still bordered the perimeter of the room. All of my colorful paintings from when I could pick up a brush in one place covering the north wall till recently. In the middle of the wall in a heart shape were polaroid pictures I had accumulated throughout the years.

It would have made sense for my dad to have changed the room a little, taken some of this down, and made it into a room he could use. I was glad he didn't. It was a glimpse of the person I used to be. I was a girl who wanted to soak up the world. I wanted to fill up my life with colors and knowledge. I thought I knew so much. As the days away from home went on, I realized there was more hidden in the shadows of my dreams. Whatever that meant.

I walked out onto the balcony just outside my room and picked up a folded blanket on the way. The old hammock was still out there. It was right next to the beautiful hanging chair my dad crafted.

I laid on the hammock and covered myself to keep the chill of the night at bay. It truly was a beautiful night. The soft wind was blowing through the trees, filling the air of the balcony with fresh scents of the forest. I could smell the wild night-blooming jasmines that grew just under the balcony. This view was much different than on the other side of the house. This was the side where the trees were, opposite the lake, though I could still hear the wind rippling over the water. The full moon illuminated the tops of the trees and all that belonged underneath.

"How's the house coming along? I heard from your neighbor, Clay, you've been working hard." My dad's voice carried through the doorway of my room.

"It's, well, going. I just want to move in already. So I can finally see what it will look like when it is all finished. You should come by sometime. You'd be proud of me." I purposely made my voice a pitch higher than normal as I tried, and failed, to hide the disappointment I felt because he hadn't gone to see it.

"I will visit soon, my Little Light, soon." His voice was full of a broken promise. He didn't want to go visit me and I didn't know why.

"This moon, nights like tonight remind me of when you and Leon were children, about ten years old. Do you remember? We'd come out here and bring blankets. You two would always talk about the future and your dreams. They were so big, you wanted to be an artist and a boat builder and own a dog farm so you could tell your dreams to them and paint portraits of them." My dad said as he walked over and sat on the hanging wooden chair.

"And I wanted to be a warrior, a cowboy, and a surfer," Leon chimed in from his room. I didn't know he was listening. He opened his door to the balcony and walked out towards us, laying on the hammock with me. I lifted the blanket so he could get under.

"With your birthdays coming up, I've been thinking of how much has changed. I'm proud of you both. You two take care of each other and listen to one another. Your mom is proud," our dad said.

We didn't respond, dad always talked about our mom as though she was still with us. I haven't met her, but through him, I do know her. We laid there in silence, looking at the stars. We could have been ten years old again, and the feeling felt the same. Almost as if we had never left. Almost.

3

"Luc! LUC!"

I screamed and jumped out of bed.

"Woah, relax! It's me! Relax!" Leon said. I hadn't seen him in a week since I stayed the night.

His arms were out in front of him with his palms facing me, taming a wild beast, half true since Kona was also alarmed.

"Jeez, Leon! You could have called instead of showing up before the sun did!" I yelled and threw a pillow at him. I hated being woken up.

"Lucy. It's already eight, I figured you would try to skip out today, so I thought I would come to get you before you made an excuse not to go," he said with a smile and tossed me a bagel.

I stared at him through a bite of bagel, my face blank.

He caught on, "today… the beach day Alika has been planning for us for our birthday even though it is in a couple of days. You have to come."

"Oh shoot. I know, I know. Thanks for waking me up. I'll be ready soon," I said through another mouthful of bagel.

When Alika first told me she was planning a beach day, I was not looking forward to it, but between the days of isolation and my visit home, that changed. I had been home for months and hadn't reached out to any friends or family members at all, just Leon and Talan, who had come to help out with my house. I reminded myself to thank Alika later.

I finished getting ready and decided a colorful bikini, jean shorts, and a cozy white tee with my hair down would have to do. It made no sense to do my hair or makeup when I would be in and out of the water all day. We walked out of my house and got in Leon's black jeep. Kona leaped into the middle of the back seat and with his head between Leon and me.

I was always scared to ride in this car because Leon took the doors off and drove like a wild man. Today, it didn't feel scary. It felt free.

My mind wandered.

Leon had been over more often and for extended periods since my visit home. He's been over to help me with my new home when he isn't working with our dad for movie nights and dinner a few times. The distance we've had the last few months has almost completely dissipated, but I knew there was still something he wasn't telling me.

Since that night when my dad mentioned him, I don't know if I have just been paying more attention to him or if he had always watched me, but I noticed my neighbor, Clay, looking at me every now and then. When I work on the barn or go outside for walks with Kona, swim in the lake on a warm day, I look over, and I see him, never too far. At first, I would pretend like I didn't notice him and continued with whatever I was doing. Kona disappeared a few times, and I would call out for him to find him running out of Clay's garage. It gave me more reason to look towards his house and acknowledge him when he was looking at me, which he was often. From a distance, I could see him smirk or wink. He wanted me to know he was watching me. It wasn't in a weird or uncomfortable way. It was in a way that made my stomach tingle. I was equally intrigued as I was annoyed, more with myself for not introducing myself.

I didn't notice how handsome he was before. Whenever I made eye contact with him from afar, I would see something I didn't see before. Like his sandy brown hair and the way it started to curl as it grew out and framed his perfect square jawline, it was so distinct I could see it from a distance.

There were two occasions where I had mustered up the courage to go knock on his door, and both times he was not home. The first time was two days after I went back home, Kona growled at the window at night again, and I went to ask Clay if he had seen anything around my house since he stays out on the porch late. Most likely, it was an animal, but I just wanted some sort of comfort, or maybe I needed an excuse to meet him.

It had been a week since the second time I attempted to meet him, and I had zero intentions of going back. If he wanted to meet me, he would have introduced himself by now.

My mind snapped back to the present with the first smell of sea salt in the air. We rode twenty minutes to the beach on the old bumpy dirt road through giant trees. We had our old road trip playlist on. We used to listen to it with the volume as high as possible. My hair was wild in the wind while we sang "Jump" by Van Halen as loud as we could. I stretched my arm out to feel the ocean in the air as it got closer. The air was different when the ocean was near.

We were there when the tree line ended, and the cliffs started. The cliffs were between ten and fifteen feet high. Some parts you could jump straight into the deep water, and others were stretch areas of sand to make miles and miles of pockets of sandy beaches.

The beach we would go to has been the same since we were kids. Marked by four oak trees twisted together to become one. I had never seen anything like it anywhere else before. They were braided and intertwined the way they twisted up. We drove right past the tree and parked on the cliff. By the look of the number of cars already parked, we were the last ones here.

I picked up my canvas beach bag and waited for Kona to get out before I walked down the makeshift trail. Kona ran down the path and barked before I could see anyone. The trail from the top of the cliff to the bottom of the ridge where the sand began was sandy and steep, lined with bushes that only grew near the ocean. When I walked to the cliff's edge to head down the short trail, everyone started whistling and cheering for us. Leon raised both of his hands and yelled out to them. He leaped and ran down the trail and was tackled by three of his four closest friends, Dario, Talan, and Fazi.

Dario was as strong and tall as they come, his body was that of a titan, his loyalty had no limits, and he had the most perfect ebony skin.

Fazi, on the other hand, was quite the opposite. He was short, chubby, had orangey-red hair, a body full of freckles, and was so funny he could make even the most bitter person laugh.

Talan was blond, well over six feet tall, the same height as Leon, with broad shoulders, perfect blue eyes, and bold lips. He was the closest to me of them all. I always felt it was because he was the most like Leon. He was warm and outgoing and always made more of an effort than the others to include me.

When the guys had finished saying their hellos to Leon, they came to greet me. Dario was the first to reach me with his perfect white smile and deep voice.

"Lucy, you've been a stranger. It's nice having you back." He picked me up and spun me around in a bear hug, the way he always had, and like the gentleman he was, he took my bag and placed it on one of the fold-up beach chairs.

Fazi reached me next, and we did the special handshake we made in second grade after we were paired up for a project.

"My girl! Hope you're hungry because I brought enough food to feed a small country. Or enough to feed your," Fazi paused for a moment as he looked over at Kona, "dog."

Everyone within earshot laughed, and I heard Fazi apologize to Kona as he walked towards him. If I didn't know any better, I'd think he was scared of him.

Talan reached for my hands and held me at arm's length piercing me with his blue eyes. A whirlwind of a second passed, and he had spun me around and dipped me.

"Hi." Was all he said before I was back on my feet and ran off to catch up with the rest of the boys, including Kona, towards the water.

I walked to the canopy where a table was being set up by my closest friends, Alika and Omala. The three of us gathered for a group hug, and I could feel them smiling as big as I was. Omala has always been the most welcoming of us three. She was never one to judge. She was tiny with a sweet voice, long straight jet-black hair, and caramel skin. She's sharp and quick with words. The definition of a human encyclopedia, she knows everything.

Alika was the reverse in many ways. She had big curly auburn hair and the attitude to go with it. She was always jumping to conclusions and had a firecracker light about her. Her loyalty paralleled Dario's, a true friend. Her dark green eyes and freckles matched her hair. She was a force, and that was precisely how she greeted me.

"Here is the lady we have all been waiting to see. I knew you would come, Leon was saying he wasn't sure you'd make it, but I knew you would," Alika said as she pulled us in for another hug.

"Finally, we are all together again!" She said.

I was finally home.

As the day went on, I was surprised as more people continued to show up. Friends who I haven't seen in years and almost all of our family. My dad even showed up shortly after us for a couple of hours but left right after we all sang happy birthday to Leon and me. We made small talk. Leon told stories about living in the city. It had been years since I enjoyed myself like this, with these people, the people who love us the most.

My toes were in the sand, and my skin was warm from a day's sun. I looked around and my heart was full at this very moment. All of the memories I have on this beach with these people surfaced. We were lucky to have each other. I was fortunate to have them.

"Would you rather eat pizza or tacos for the rest of your life?" Fazi asked aloud as he bit into a burger.

"Tacos. Definitely tacos," Talan said.

"Pizza. Definitely pizza," Alika said as she looked over at Talan, who was sitting next to her. She was always picking at him, even if it meant arguing over pizza and tacos. For being so strong and sure of herself, she melted around Talan.

"Omala?" Asked Fazi.

"Pizza with tacos on it," she said as she gave Alika a look.

"Lucy, pizza or tacos?" Fazi asked.

"Let's ask Kona. Kona, pizza or tacos?" Kona was lying next to me on my large beach blanket. He let out a low whimper.

"I can't pick either." We all laughed at Kona's response. Fazi tossed Kona the rest of his burger and knelt down to pet him on the head.

"I'll feed you, so you don't eat me. Do we have a deal?" Fazi told Kona, who replied with a bark.

We all ate a burger, fruit, and chips for dinner as we continued our conversation. I gave Kona some fruit and hamburger patties. He inhaled them before running back to the water. Leon and Dario began to make their way in from surfing, and Kona met them halfway in the water. He jumped on Leon's surfboard, and they rode the whitewash to the shore together. Kona shook off and laid next to my blanket in the warm sand.

I got up to make burgers for them as they set their boards down and dried off.

"I'll start the fire right now. The sun is almost set and-" Leon's voice cut off. I turned around to see where he was going. He was walking towards the bottom of the ridge, where the path from the cliff met the sand.

Emma.

Emma is the fourth of Leon's closest friends and the closest thing Leon has ever had to a brother, the closest person he has next to me. His name was Emmanicko, but we call him Emma. I haven't seen him in a long while. Emma always rolled with the tides, coming and going to whatever served him best. The look on Leon's face told it all.

"Brother." They said in unison when they were close enough. They shook their right hands while they put their other hand on each other's shoulder and their foreheads together.

Emma greeted everyone else and hugged me extra tight before helping Leon start the fire. He wore his usual beanie to cover his short black hair and a hoodie with rolled-up jeans. As he talked to Leon, his cute big happy smile was infectious and made everyone else smile. His dark eyes told a different story. He has always been a humorous person, always in the moment, and made everyone laugh, but there was always something in his eyes that most people didn't notice. Something inside of me told me he was struggling with something. Perhaps that was why he stayed away more as we got older. He had demons to face.

I stood next to Leon and noticed they were the same height though Emma seemed smaller. Maybe it was the way he let Leon take the lead all the time.

Once the fire had been started, we sat around the sand on our blankets or beach chairs. The sky was a rich blue, and the clouds were glowing purple and pink like they do right before a perfect sunset. The crash of the waves was a neon blue with the sun on the horizon shining through the waves.

I had just put on my sweatshirt over my bikini and sat down when Emma yelled, "last one in the water has to run around the beach naked!"

That sets all of us off. As soon as I got to my feet, Talan pushed me back into the sand and winks at me as he ran towards the water. I scramble to run as fast as I could while taking my sweatshirt off. Luckily, I didn't come in last. Fazi did, naturally. Instead of running around naked, he took off his swim trunks and swung them over his head, jumping in the water to skinny dip. Grossing all of us out but making us laugh, nonetheless. We all closed our eyes and turned towards the waves. He stopped when he was waist-deep to put his shorts back on, the water too clear for him to go commando.

We swam out past where the break of the waves had been even though they slowed down. The water was around twenty feet deep. I could still easily see the ocean floor. There was not one fish in sight. When I turned towards the shore, there were no waves suddenly, just a glassy calm beach. We all splashed around and played games that we would play as kids. Marco Polo was first with Fazi being it because he was the last to get in the water. My favorite game was when we all swam to the bottom of the ocean and sat in the sand. Whoever lasted the longest won.

I felt a hand in mine, it was Leon. I felt my other hand automatically reach out for someone else's. It found Tre's. We continued to connect hands until we formed a circle facing outwards. We kicked our feet up to stay afloat as we laid on our backs and relaxed, floating in unison. We extended our arms with our heads in the circle and our bodies floating on the outside. At that very moment, we became one. All of us looked up as the stars began to shine through the many colors of the sunset. It felt magical, and I was able to breathe, really deep breaths, safe and warm. The sound of the ocean muted out all thoughts.

Something shifted. A sort of click inside of my body made me lift my head up, letting go of the circle. I looked back at the sand where the cliff starts, and the trail began. Clay, my neighbor, stood there with his surfboard in the sand and his wetsuit half off, looking out at us.

We locked eyes. Even in this distance, I knew he could see me. I felt it. Everyone in the circle breaks when I let go. They started another game.

What am I going to say? I thought to myself. I don't want to sound crazy, but I knew he had mentioned me to my dad a few times, and Kona was always at his house. He watches me, and when I would knock on his front door, he was never there. So, this was my chance, and I wouldn't back down.

I continued to lock eyes with him, and without breaking my gaze, I swam all the way to shore. He was still drying off, and as I grew closer to him, I could see he had a smirk. It was annoying because his smirk only grew the closer I became until it was an ear-to-ear smile, and at that moment, I knew I needed to know him.

It wasn't about his smile. It was about his silence and his absence. He was familiar when I never met him before. Something about him compelled me.

He was less than three feet in front of me.

I spoke before he could say anything. "It is either you come with me to meet my friends and family now, or you go home, shower, get comfortable, and I'll meet you there in a few hours. Which one?"

I was surprised at how calm my voice sounded when on the inside, I could have been screaming.

His smile became a secret.

"I'll see you in a few hours."

I almost knocked on Clay's door when I glanced down and realized I wasn't wearing any shoes. Kona had followed me and instinctively stayed behind me, blocking me from turning around and going down the porch stairs back to my house. He knew I would run back home and stay there if he didn't block the way. Kona wanted me to meet Clay, too. He looked up at me, licked the air, and smiled. He stayed smiling.

A few hours had gone by since Clay left the beach, and it was well past sundown when we said our goodbyes. I was in a hurry to get home, and Leon knew. He looked at me to peep my thoughts the way only he could. When we left the beach, he drove faster than usual. He wanted me to meet Clay.

When I got home, I showered quickly and slipped on some clothes while brushing my teeth and tangled hair. I had to rinse Kona off too, he had gallons of sand in his thick black fur.

"You suck, Kona, but thanks for being here," I whispered as I turned back towards the door.

Talking to him eased my nerves. I knelt down to pet him, and he ran past me and straight into Clay's house. Clay stood there with the same smirk he had on earlier as he leaned against the doorway.

He was handsome.

Meanwhile, I was standing there with crispy skin after a day's sun, in my old pajamas, with wet hair, barefoot.

"I was waiting for you to knock for about five minutes but decided it would be more entertaining to watch you from the window instead. You really shouldn't be walking around barefoot, you know," Clay said sarcastically while he opened the door to let me in. I looked down and smiled when I noticed he was barefoot, too.

I took a few steps in, and Kona was already on the couch, sitting down comfortably on a blanket as if he had been here for hours just waiting for me to come over.

"Oh no. I'm so sorry about Kona! He really has made himself at home," I said. I motioned for Kona to get off the couch.

Clay sat next to him and placed a hand on Kona's head.

"He comes over every day since you two have moved here. I brought out this old blanket and told him he could have it, even though he made it his before I offered," Clay said, "my door is always unlocked, and he figured out how to open it. I come home and find him in here sometimes."

He pets Kona, fluffing his fur. He cared for him. My nerves ease to half of what they were. Kona usually had no desire to be around anyone except me since the day he appeared in my life.

"Okay," I said.

"Why are you always watching me? Or why are you always close by? I mean, I know we're neighbors, but still. You never even stop to talk to me. You are a stranger to me, and my dog is literally at home here. It's weird." I didn't realize I was talking until I had finished blurting out my rehearsed speech.

As I waited for his response, I realized I had never actually been nervous around a man or had any interest in getting to know anyone on a different level. Yet, Clay had something about him, something I couldn't place.

He relaxed some and didn't change his position, still leaned against the back of the couch petting Kona.

"You can sit down if you'd like," he said, mystery smirk still intact.

I was still standing awkwardly by the door. I walked to the single sofa to his right and sat down. I didn't let go of the question, and I raised my brow for him to speak.

"You are good with tools. You know what you are doing when you are building, and I am a woodworker. I pay attention to skill. I admire your ways of working with what you've got." He chuckled to himself, "Today, I ran into a mutual friend of ours, Emma. He invited me to surf north of the beach where you all were. I gave him a ride to go see you all. Last, I give Kona scraps."

"How do you know Emma?" Was what came out of my mouth,

unsure why I asked.

"We met on the water years ago and have been surfing ever since. We are swell chasers. We like a challenge. North of where you were, there were waves double overhead," he said.

Embarrassment flushed through my body. I read into every small and insignificant thing he did and made it into something more in my head. I hadn't known what I was expecting, but I knew it wasn't this.

"I always jump to conclusions. Well, that's hilarious. And embarrassing." I said to myself a little too loud.

"Sorry to bug you," I said.

Only this time, I was talking to him.

I stood up and called out for Kona to come, but he didn't budge. He had selective hearing.

"Movie and cookies?" He said as he tossed me a fluffy knit blanket.

I wanted to get Kona and leave. I also wanted to stay. So instead of my usual no thank you speech, "Chocolate chip and it's a deal," came out instead.

It wasn't like me to want to be around one person in particular, but something about Clay was familiar. That was the only way to put it. His voice, tone, and body carried out a different feel. I also felt he wasn't the type of person to ask many questions. We watched a movie and ate cookies without any sort of conversation other than movie commentary for the rest of the night.

Being here felt normal, like I was hanging out with an old friend.

Clay ended up falling asleep before the movie was over. I got up quietly and picked Kona up off of Clay's lap and carried my big baby home. I was surprised I could still do so. I laid down on my bed with Kona on his blanket at my feet and for the first time in years, slept through the night.

That's when the dreams started.

4

The sun was warm on my cool skin. I was almost dry after my swim. The sound of the waves soothed me despite the danger within our village. The smell of the ocean was enlightening.

All of the hairs on my body suddenly stood up. There was a loud, piercing scream from a young woman in the distance.

They're in search of something they like to call hags. Hags are a good cover-up for my people. We are witches among the Lemurian's, but we can do much more than they believe. They were looking in the wrong places and for the wrong things. We used it to our advantage.

I began the commute through to the other side of the village to my home.

I wondered how many checkpoints and guards I would pass today. Would today be the day, my last day? If death didn't meet me today, who would it be?

I was hopeful they would not capture anybody else, even through the screams.

I passed the first small group of huts. When I broke past them, I arrived at the blue stone bridge. There was a checkpoint before I could cross at the opening. If I turned around at this point or tried to go another way, the guards would follow me as I *was already within their peripheral. In the corner of my eye, I caught movement by the water next to the bridge. A boy no older than five years of age sat at the water's edge, throwing rocks into the white rapids, glaring at the other side. I waved at the guards who were preoccupied with other villagers attempting to cross the bridge and walked down the rocks towards the river where the boy was. He looked up at me, and I saw terror in his eyes. Unable to hide his fear, the only reason he would be afraid is if he had something to hide.*

He was like me.

"Are you unable to cross the bridge?" I asked him, gesturing with my head towards the guards.

He looked at me and didn't move. I gave him an energy wave of trust, an invisible fog moving towards him. His face went from terror to trust in a moment. He felt it. He knew I was like him.

"They will catch me. I want to go home," he said after a moment.

The water was white as it rushed towards the river mouth, where it greeted the ocean a mile west. Under the white, you could get glimpses of dark water. There was no light getting past the surface. The water was a reflection of our times, full of danger.

I looked up behind me to the bridge to gauge the situation. Five guards were now preoccupied with dozens of people who were attempting to cross the bridge. Each one had to be tested individually. It would buy us some time. Or so I thought. At that moment, the guard closest to us made eye contact with me. He turned toward us and made his way down the rocks.

I felt myself automatically adjusting my body. I stood up straighter than I had already been. I relaxed my shoulders and took a few deep breaths, my eyes squinted, and I pointed my chin down the slightest.

Flattery.

I felt the energy, the wave of fog returned, only this time it was filled with excitement. I would make the guard want to impress me. He wouldn't see more than my beauty. It was what most humans would see anyways. This should be easy enough, he was about the same age as my physical body appeared, and he was handsome.

He knew it, too.

The fog touched him just before he approached us. I could tell by the smile on his face and the way his hand fell from his sword on its holster.

"My lady," he bowed, "You two need to go through the checkpoint. It is law."

"I was headed that way when I saw this handsome young man. He is trying to get over his fear of water. I could not leave him here to face his fears alone, now could I? What kind of woman would I be if I left this poor child alone?" Concern in my voice with one arm around the boy and the other over my heart as if I was trying to catch my breath.

"Where is his mother?" He asked. I knew my fog was still working, or else he would have already taken us to the bridge.

He looked at the boy and gestured for him to speak.

The boy looked up at him and said, "My mother is at home with my younger siblings, she asked me to go to the market for a loaf of bread, but I came here instead. I heard the screaming and saw the woman," he pointed up to the center of the bridge where a body hung. "The water scares me. Crossing the bridge with her hanging there scares me more."

The little boy was a good liar. Our people don't fear water. He was also clever by using a child's innocence against the guard. Our kind does not think like children even as a child.

"One test and you two can stay down here. Do we have a deal?" The guard said.

CLAP!

He abruptly clapped before we had a chance to answer. Neither of us flinched. The guard looked at both of us. We failed the test. One thing they knew about us was that we don't carry much fear. A clap is just a sound to us.

"It must be the water covering up the sound. There is no way both of you are hags. You two get home. We do not want them harming either one of you," he said as he turned and walked up the rocks where he was stationed but not before turning around and looking at me for an extra second. It worked. My charm worked.

"Can you swim?" I asked the boy.

"Yes," he replied.

He looked at the water and then back at me, waiting for me to help. We could make it across, but we would be winded and dragged down to the river mouth.

I will fix it.

"Water, I call to you. We need safe passage, you know why. Clear, calm water is what I ask. Please help us cross your waters safely," I whispered.

My eyes weren't open yet, and I could already feel mist on my face. The water turned clear and almost illuminated a soft turquoise path straight to the other side. It was calm, and the temperature of the water rose a few degrees, inviting us in. I looked up at the bridge to see if anyone could see what was going on. They all looked directly at the water and noticed nothing.

The little boy tugged at my arm, closed his eyes, and took a deep breath. When he opened his eyes, he looked at me and said, "I am ready."

"I know you can swim, but it would be helpful for me and for water if you held on to my shoulders and kicked your feet. Can you do that for us?" I asked.

He nodded.

I bent down, and he climbed on my back, his grip tight. If I was human, it would cause pain. I walked into the water and could feel the current when the water reached my waist. Only the current we were on was not going with the rest of the water down to the ocean. This current started at my feet and directed us across the water to the opposite side of the river under the bridge. I continued to walk in the water until I could no longer feel the bed of the lake. The water kept us afloat and carefully carried us across. The boy let go a little. I turned to look at his face, and he was gleaming, his little teeth fully exposed in an ear-to-ear smile.

Behind him was the regular current erasing any trace of us, and the darker water with white surface had returned. A storm beneath the surface. The water in front of us remained turquoise and warm. When I could touch the floor, I felt the water had begun to cool. The moment I was knee-deep and safe, the water had returned to normal.

"Thank you for safe passage," I whispered to water. I felt a slight temperature change, waters way of saying you're welcome.

"My mother doesn't let me use it," the little boy said when I put him down on the rocky shore.

"Your mother is a smart woman. It is a dangerous time for our kind right now. There will be a time for you, now isn't it," I said.

He smiled at me and turned to run up the rocks. He was just barely within earshot when he turned to me.

"Use the wood to find your way." He looked to his side. He was listening though nobody was next to him, "I will not tell her that-," he looked to his side again, and I realized he wasn't talking to me. "No... Okay, I can say that."

"Find balance between the one who drinks blood and the one who protects it," he said and ran towards the market.

I wondered what the boy meant and who he was speaking to. I would remember it. His gifts were in tune if he could easily hear them, whoever it was he was speaking to.

I was still in my swim clothes as I made my way up through the market to go home. The smooth pebbled path was soft on my bare feet, unlike the sharp rocks by the river. Vendors were selling fruit, beans, woven goods, moccasins for the upcoming summer. A little girl was brushing her hair and asked her father to braid it for her. I smiled at her and continued to walk home.

The jingling sound of my coin pouch was absent. I left it at the fruit stand. I turned around retrieve it and saw the guard from the bridge. He was heading towards me. He held his hand up, and I could see he had my coin pouch in his hands.

He extended his arm to me and handed it over.

"I am Rowan of house Tronlago," he said.

I knew I needed to charm him with beauty again. I immediately felt the warmth rush over my body, "I am Adelaide." I bowed my head, his house of higher rank than mine.

"May I walk you home? You live in the grasslands, am I wrong?" He asked.

"You are not," I said as I bowed my head in acceptance.

We walked, and with every word that left my mouth, I made sure to use charm and sweetness. Every gesture I made that caught his eye was made with intent.

That is when I saw it. A vision flashed. Rowan will fall in love with me and learn who I am. He will still love me. He will keep my secret. In turn, I will fall in *love with him. But there was also something there I could not see.*

He could not find out soon, he could not enter my home, or he would find out my truth.

We approached my home in the grasslands, an adobe home connected to other adobe homes, thankfully my wooden door was hinged correctly, and the curtains of the hut were closed. I closed them before I left.

"Thank you for walking me this far. I must change out of my wet clothes. I will be seeing you around." I bowed and went inside before he had any chance to oppose.

My white lace dress hung over the chair in the corner, the herbs hung next to the large chiminea in the corner, and the woven blankets were on the floor where I sleep next to the built-in adobe fireplace. I placed the mangoes and the rest of my fruit in a basket on a bench under the dried herbs.

Some will never know. This is a true witch's den.

I woke up, unable to move. Stuck in place, all I could do was breathe and look around. I knew better than to open my eyes. This would happen to me as a child. When I opened my eyes, I would see things other people only see in scary movies.

Waking nightmares. So, I left my eyes shut.

A laugh filled the air. Not one I want to remember. It was hoarse and deep and gave my entire body chills.

Instead, I focused on the thought of a candle. A light so bright it could fill any dark room. Only brightness and white walls. I placed myself in there.

My paralysis lifted.

I moved my hand, then my head.

I reached for my phone to message Leon. I type out what had happened, and before I could finish, I received a message from him.

It happened again.

5

I woke up after falling back to sleep and could still smell the dried lavender and sage. I could still feel the life of Adelaide. I took a few deep breaths and stared at the wooden ceiling. Kona moved closer, sensing I had woken up. I reached over and stretched my body, and my hand hits my notepad. Immediately I picked it up and wrote down my dream. I knew it was a dream I had to write down.

This wasn't a whimsical dream or a dream where I had influence. It was a dream-like I would have before. When I was younger and lived at my dad's house, I would have these dreams. It was vivid, and I still felt every emotion of Adelaide's.

The sun was barely rising, and part of the sky was still dark. Though I had only slept for a few hours, I feel as if I had been sleeping for a week. I didn't want to get up, but I could no longer lay down.

As I got ready for my day, I felt a little different. My skin felt soft from the beach yesterday, and my cheeks were sore from a day full of smiles and laughs. I felt refreshed.

A rush of memory came to the surface as I remembered last night at Clay's house. I was surprised my dreams weren't of his cookies. I wish I had one of those this morning instead of my bowl of cereal.

When I opened my front door, Kona leaped from the porch to the dirt and rushed off towards the lake like he always does, never going too far. I took a step out, and my foot hit something, a brown paper lunch bag. I picked it up, and to my surprise, my wish had come true. It was a giant chocolate chip cookie, Clay's chocolate chip cookie. It was like he had read my mind.

I walked down the stairs to the dark pebble trail and head towards the barn. I smiled a smile too big for it being this early in the morning as I chewed a mouthful of cookie. I now understood what my dad and Leon were talking about. These cookies were dreamy. Clay wasn't half bad either. Thoughts about last night surfaced and how familiar he felt as if I had known him for much longer than an evening.

I walked around to the back porch of the barn to gather the materials I needed when I heard footsteps coming from inside the house. I turned around to find Clay standing at the bottom of the spiral staircase. He had a toolbox in one hand and a half-eaten apple in the other.

"I added a few touches. Hope you don't mind. All of the exposed wood was too tempting for me to leave alone," he said. He stood up straight, pride dripping from his pores.

I looked around, awestruck. There were wood carvings in the wood beams and door frames almost identical to those in the other houses around the lake. Some were similar to the ones in the granny flat. I walked around the rest of the house, drawn to the pillar in the center of the house. It extended from the very bottom of the house to the very top of the loft. I looked at the bottom and saw a circular symbol. I knelt down to get a closer look and immediately knew I had seen it before, unsure where.

"Clay, what is this?" I asked.

"There is an old legend passed down from generation to generation around the lake. There is a carving identical to this one. The only difference between this one and the real one is, the real one is said to have been carved from the other side of the tree," he said.

"The other side of the tree? What do you mean?" I asked as I got closer to the carving.

"The inside of the tree," he said as he looked at me, half expecting me to know.

I looked at him, then back at the carving. I touched it with both hands and dismissed the idea of the legend. The details of this should have taken weeks, I left his house late last night, and he was asleep. If he had woken up right after I had left, that would have given him a maximum of nine hours to do all of this. There was no way.

"You only had a few hours to work on this," I gestured towards every carving, "it should have taken you a lot longer than a night. Every detail is incredible."

"I had help," he said.

He let out a low whistle. Kona ran his way in.

"Kona? My wonky wolf-dog helped you carve all of this?" I laughed.

"Yes, but not exactly. After you two left last night, I woke up to get some water and couldn't go back to sleep. I headed out to get some fresh air on my hammock with a book when I spotted Kona looking at me through your window. He opened the door and walked towards the road, then towards me. I ended up with my toolbox instead of my book and came inside. It truly is a beautiful place. I had maintained it throughout the years in my spare time. When you purchased it and I found out you were going to turn it into a home, I was relieved you weren't going to knock it down. I thought I'd give it some touches to make it feel more like home, and Kona kept me company while I worked. It looks harder than it is. I've been doing this my whole life," he said.

"A whole what, twenty-seven, twenty-eight years, max? There was no way you did this overnight," I said.

"Somewhere around there," he chuckled when I mentioned his age. "Want to watch? I have one more to do on top of the stairs."

I nodded and followed him up the spiral stairs. He pulled out a tool from his toolbox and got to work. I watched him closely. Every motion he made was swift. If I blinked for too long, I felt like I'd miss it. Ten minutes later, he put the tool away in his toolbox, sands a part of the carving then was done. He let out a heavy blow to blow off the remaining sawdust. It was much more detailed than I had imagined.

"Wow, just like that?" I said.

I got closer to examine his work.

"Just like that," he smiled. I felt his eyes on me.

It was a hummingbird. A perfectly carved hummingbird. It looked more like a picture and less of a carving. It even had grooves in each tiny feather, and there were hundreds of feathers.

"How do I not believe you did that so fast when I just watched you?" I said as I observed the bird.

He smiled. This was new. He seemed confident in himself usually, but he liked compliments. I made a mental note.

"I have to head to town. Need anything?" He asked.

"That depends," I said.

"On what?"

"If you have more chocolate chip cookies," I said, making eye contact with him.

He smiled.

Kona sneezed, and something changed.

"I have to go." His response was short.

All of the playful energy in the room was sucked out with those four words. Clay turned and waved and was out of the front door before I could say thank you.

My phone rang from the bottom of the ladder. I climbed down to see who was calling to see if I should answer or not.

It was my dad. If I didn't answer he would keep calling or send Leon over to check on me.

"Hi, Dad," I said.

I laid on the barn floor, completely drained.

What time was it? I asked myself.

"Lucy. Are you okay over there? I didn't see smoke from your chimney last night," he was worried.

"I'm fine. I went over to a friend's house after the beach last night to watch a movie. Nothing to worry about," I said.

"A friend?" He pushed.

"Yes, well, it was just my neighbor," I said and immediately filled with regret.

"Your neighbor? Clay?" His pitch went up an octave.

"Yes, Clay. I will make sure to put the fire on from here on out, so you don't have to worry. I really do have to go, dad. I'm in the middle of something here," I lied.

"I love you, Lucy," he said.

"Love you, too."

I hung up.

I looked at my watch to check the time and couldn't believe it was five o'clock. Exhaustion hit me like a bucket of ice as I stayed lying on the wooden floor. I was covered in dust and sweat, and I was hungry. I could fall asleep right here if I wasn't so hungry. But hunger won and made getting up easier than I thought it would be. I guess the thought of being able to eat was greater than my exhaustion. Time flew by today. I didn't even eat my lunch. I walked down the spiral staircase and eyed the new hummingbird at the top. When I got to the bottom, I glanced down at the circular carving. I knew I had seen it somewhere before and knew it would bother me until I could remember where.

"Kona!" I yelled out for him and heard a bark in the distance.

He broke my gaze when I saw him run through the back door dripping wet.

"Were you in the lake again?" I asked.

He shook his big wolf-dog body, and I was soaked.

"Let's get home and get cleaned up. I am starving. Do you want food?"

Kona licked his face and smiled up at me. I already knew the answer. I walked out of the front doorway onto the small deck. To the left was Clay's house, to the right was my flat and straight ahead was an open area leading to the forest.

I peeked over to Clay's house and could see him lying on his front hammock. He was asleep. He had a book on his chest, and his face was relaxed.

I walked down the steps and made my way to my tiny home. The dark pebbled path was a nice contrast to all of the wood and greenery. The sky was beginning to change color, the sunset was just a few short hours away, and the dew from the lake was nice and refreshing.

The flat was cozy. As I looked at it from the outside, I could tell it was tiny and old but well kept. When I opened the door, it creaked, and a rush went over me. It was a combination of the smell, the lake, the way the sun would hit the trees. All of it made it feel like home. The things I would take for granted as I grew up are the same things that made me move back. I felt safe here.

My body mechanically took over as soon as my foot hit the old wood floor inside. I took off my work boots and placed them next to the door. I took my hair tie out and let my straight hair fall, brushing my waist.

"What should I make for dinner?" I said aloud.

"Pasta!" I answered.

A day like today called for something heavy. Before I started cooking, I took a long and hot shower. Brushed my hair and put on some pajamas, a pair of shorts, and an oversized t-shirt.

"Pasta time!" I told Kona.

I boiled the noodles, cut the vegetables, made fresh Bolognese sauce, and put the garlic bread in the oven. Making sure to take my time to make something I would enjoy. When all was done, I made two plates instead of one. I quickly started the fire so my dad wouldn't call me to check on me and placed the food on a tray before heading out of the door. Kona followed close behind. I walked the dark pebbled path, which was now shining a deep purple from the reflection of the predominantly pink and purple sunset with hints of yellow and orange.

I climbed the steps, crossed the porch, and knocked on the door. The light flickered on from inside.

"Hey," Clay said as he opened the door with one arm at the top of the door. His body leaned against it. He was only wearing shorts, and I tried my best to not look down.

"I made you dinner to thank you for the carvings," I said as I raised the tray a little.

He smirked and stepped aside, opening the door for me to come in.

The moment I walked inside, I realized he was asleep. The air was still. There was a blanket on the couch.

"I am sorry, I didn't know you were asleep. I'll leave this here. You can eat it when you wake up," I said, turning around.

"No, don't worry about it. I was going to get up now anyway," Clay said.

I sat on the same single sofa I sat on last night and put the tray of food on the coffee table. He was slowly walking towards the other side of the room where the fireplace was. He rubbed his eyes and ran his fingers through his light brown hair brushing it out of his face. He stretched his bare arms and torso before he crouched down and started the fire. He had beads of sweat on his forehead.

"Will you excuse me for a moment?" He asked quietly.

I nodded, and he went into a door that I assumed was his room. I turned back towards the food and set up the plates so we could eat. The remote was on the arm of the sofa next to where Kona was lying. I clicked the tv on, and the first thing that came on was music. Jazz, a refreshing sound. I left it on.

Clay turned on the water from the bathroom, and I could hear splashing. He came out, wiping his face with a small towel, and put his shirt on as he walked towards the open kitchen behind the couch.

"Water, coconut water, or beer?" He asked.

"Water is fine. Thanks," I said.

"That smells great," he said.

"It is. If you like pasta, you'll like this. My dad always made his own version of Bolognese growing up. I use his recipe but put more veggies in it. I picked them fresh from the patch of fruits and vegetables on the trail to the other side of the lake," I said, speaking of the Bloom.

He looked at me, his face full of questions.

"I do not know what you're talking about. I walk the lake all the time, and never have I seen a patch of anything other than random wild berries," he said as he picked up his plate and sat on the sofa.

"Really? You can't miss it. Walk down the path that goes to my dad's, and you walk right through it. Literally, it's a weird patch of trees that seem like they don't belong, different kinds of citrus trees, strawberries everywhere. There are apple trees, squash, melons, different kinds of peppers. Even onions sometimes." I paused to take my first bite.

"Okay," he laughed.

"What?" I asked.

"Nothing," he said through a bite of garlic bread. "Did you get the bread from there, too?"

"You really don't believe me?" I asked.

If he has ever walked around the lake, he would see it. I wondered if there was another trail I didn't know about.

"If you say it is there, then it is. I must miss it every time, but maybe I am not looking in the right places, or maybe it is seasonal," he said, half-joking.

I couldn't tell if he believed me or not.

"I will take you. Next time I go to my dad's house or need more fruits and vegetables. I'll see if you have time to go. Deal?" I asked.

"Deal," Clay smiled with his eyes through a mouth full of pasta.

His eyes looked greener today. They were dark forest green, or were they blue? I couldn't see clearly. He gazed into the distance when I realized he was thinking heavily about something.

"Are you okay?" I asked.

"What makes you ask that?" He blinked a few times and maintained eye contact while he bit into his garlic bread.

"Your eyes are-" I took a deep breath as I tried to find the right word, "-busy."

"Your eyes are dancing."

He smiled, and a piece of me melted.

"I enjoy your company."

Did I just say that out loud? I thought to myself.

"And I had a long day after I left your house this morning. So, thank you for bringing dinner. I needed it," he said. I was thankful he grazed over my comment.

"I always make too much food. I was used to cooking for my dad and Leon. He stops by for dinner. Otherwise, it goes to wa-,"

"If you made an oath or a promise, do you think the timing matters? Would you have to fulfill the promise as soon as you could or when the time was right?" Clay interrupted me, our playful conversation dove in a different direction.

"I think, if it were me, it would depend on the circumstances and the situation," I said.

A minute of silence goes by. When I looked over at him, he was looking deep into the fire.

I continued, "We met yesterday, and you are easy for me to understand. Not necessarily easy for me to read, but I understand you. Correct me if I am wrong, but you don't seem like the kind of person who doesn't know what to do. You know what to do by following what feels right. Trust yourself."

"I was with Emma earlier. He said with this situation to wait until the time is right. That even though it is my promise, it isn't my place." He brought up Emma, and it made me wonder what he was talking about. I knew Emma wasn't always on the straight and narrow path. "I guess I'll sleep on it. I still have cookies. Want some?"

He got up and walked to the kitchen.

"I would love some." I wasn't ready to let it go, "Emma? When Leon feels stuck or needs to talk, he goes to Emma, too. I would take his word for it."

Clay's back was to me as he faced the open refrigerator, and I could visibly see his muscles relax through his shirt. He put his head down and took a deep breath.

"Thank you," he said.

He walked towards me, a plate of cookies in hand, and I looked him up and down. He was built like a sculpture of a God. Bodies like his don't look like they eat pasta. His body was lean and muscular. He was light on his feet, too. These old wooden floors creek easily, and he never made a sound.

I swallowed and my cheeks flushed.

"Movie?" He asked.

"As long as you choose it," I said.

He extended his arm with the plate of cookies towards me, offering me one before placing the plate on the coffee table.

Kona jumped from the floor to the sofa on the blanket Clay had laid out for him. He put his head on Clay's lap and looked at Clay, then at me before closing his eyes.

He watched the movie and made comments referring to it. I wasn't paying close attention to the movie. Instead, I thought about how heavy his secrets were. A burden so heavy his body was tense from the weight of it. I also thought Emma and him were just surfing buddies, not the type of friends who hung out and had deep conversations about dark secrets or oaths or promises or whatever it was Clay had said. Maybe that's why we connected so well. We were both trying to figure ourselves out.

I didn't know I fell asleep until I felt the mist from the lake on my face. My body was moving.

I was being carried.

I was warm.

Why was I warm?

I rested my head and almost fell back to sleep.

Clay.

He smelled nice, like pine tree and man. He was warm. My head laid on his chest as he was carrying me to my flat. Kona padded ahead of us.

"I can walk myself home," I said, slightly embarrassed.

He smiled and looked down at me, "you aren't wearing shoes."

I looked at my bare feet. I always forgot to wear shoes. I laid my head back on his chest, giving in to my tiredness. Somehow this didn't feel awkward. He felt like he has always been here, always been a part of my life.

Clay climbed up the few stairs to my front porch and put me down at my front door. He wasn't winded even the slightest from carrying me.

"Thank you for dinner, and thank you for your words," he said.

I smiled, "Goodnight."

I closed the door behind me.

I took a step inside and immediately reached out and opened the door again.

"Clay? Do you ever have strange dreams about things that aren't real but feel like it?" I asked.

He thought for a moment, choosing his words carefully before saying, "Usually, when we have those dreams, it is a sign to pay attention. What was your dream about?"

"It sounds pretty dumb when I say it out loud. It was this place. There was magic. Witchcraft of some sort. A lady named Adel-" I cut myself off, "-and as I say it out loud, I realize it was just a dream. Have a good night."

His face was intrigued just before I shut the door. I sounded crazy. His face had changed. He was eager to hear my dream. He does like books, after all. I watched him through the window as he walked back over to his house. I laughed because he was barefoot too.

I put a few more logs in the fireplace then Kona and I went straight to bed. My body was still warm, and as I inhaled, I smelled Clay. Just before falling asleep, I smelled herbs, lavender, sage, man, and pine.

6

I woke up to a bright light shining through the window. The sun would be rising within the next couple of hours. This light was more promising than the sun. It was an illuminated fog.

An old carved wooden chair was under the front window in the corner of the room where the mist rested, a beautiful iridescent glow.

My body began to feel warm, my cheeks were getting hot, and my palms grew sweaty. I was surprised Kona wasn't barking at it, still asleep beside me.

The fog changed, making up a form. I sat up more to get a better look.

Bliss overcame my entire being. The form becomes a man. He was still glowing but was now visible. He was bald and beautiful with a bold face. I looked at his body. He wasn't wearing a shirt but, he was wearing some type of shorts. Natural material and looked like an old unfinished suede. His body was built like a warrior. His legs were trunks, his feet bare. He held one hand up, I realized he was holding something.

A staff?

No. I looked closer.

A spear.

When I looked back at him, he smiled, the purest *warm smile. I felt it. It was then that I realized he was covered in scars. They were shiny, almost glowing, and covered him from his bald head to his bare feet. Hundreds of scars covered his body. Though it didn't make him look scary, it made him look strong.*

He was lethal. He was someone some people should be terrified of. He was someone pure and full of Light.

"Who are you?" I needed to know.

He smiled, displaying a perfect radiant set of teeth. He rolled his shoulders and sat up straighter, if that was even possible. He put his head down, and when he looked up and sat up, a wave of light beamed *from behind him.*

Wings. He had wings.

My face must have been ridiculous because he let out a silent laugh.

Michael, the name suddenly in my head.

His wings were every part as magical as he was. Joy pierced my soul. I have never felt anything like this. Ever.

He drifted off, turning to mist again, then to nothing.

I laid my head back *down and drifted back to sleep.*

I opened my eyes, and my alarm went off shortly after. The sun wasn't out yet, but the sky was showing signs it would soon. I had about half an hour before Leon wakes up, naturally, unless he was already up. Nonetheless, I rushed to get ready, hoping he would still be asleep when I got there.

"Kona, want some food?" I filled his food and water bowls and hopped in the shower. Less than five minutes later, I was out. Quickly brushed my hair and teeth, put on sunscreen and lotion because a day like today calls for it. I walked to my closet, an armoire and a dresser in the living room corner next to the bathroom, slipped into a bikini, jean shorts, and a tee-shirt. I grab a small crossbody bag and pack spare clothes. I got a granola bar for the road and my keys and was out of the door within fifteen minutes of waking up.

As I stepped out of the door, something felt different. I wasn't sure if it was because it was our birthday or from the excitement for the day ahead or what. It just felt different. I took a few deep breaths of the morning air. Slight traces of salt from the ocean lingered.

My old red buggy that I hardly use was parked on the side of my flat. I put the convertible top back so Kona could jump in the back seat. He barely fit if the top wasn't down. We both hopped inside and waited for the car to warm up. I looked over to Clay's house and saw the curtains were closed and the lights were on inside. There was a shadow on the curtain. He was awake. Then I saw another shadow. He had company.

What time did I get home last night? He had company so early in the morning, or did they come over after I left? Did he carry me home because he was expecting someone to come over? I mean, I did just show up at his house unexpectedly. Maybe this was who he was talking about with the oath or promise. Perhaps he was clearing the air. I hoped he felt less conflicted today than he was last night.

The old dirt road to my dad's house never changed, the same trail I always took, one way only. It was narrow, barely wide enough for my car to fit through. I don't know how Leon's Jeep fits through here. When you walked the trail, you wouldn't think a car would fit. I drove past the Bloom and wondered how Clay had never seen it before.

Spur the moment, I pulled over to pick berries. I also picked a few lemons to use for dinner. Walking around here was always so refreshing. I walked towards the center where the largest strawberry patch was and made sure not to step on any berries. They smelled so delicious my mouth watered. Lastly, I picked Leon's favorites, blackberries and raspberries, intertwined on a few trees. This was where I fell last time. I looked down and saw it. The spiral carving. This was the same one that Clay carved in the barn at the bottom of the staircase. He said he has never been here, but I have never seen this anywhere else. This sign must be more common than I thought.

The tomatoes smelled like I wanted to bite into one like an apple. So, I picked a whole vine of them. There was no way I could pass these up.

After a tote bag full of fresh goodies, I walked back to the car and continued to drive, much faster than before if I wanted to get there in time.

The sun was rising. Leon would be up soon.

I pulled over onto my dad's unfenced property and parked next to Leon's Jeep on the side of the house and immediately realize the ground is covered in little black pebbles from the bottom of the lake. The same stones Leon put around my house and trailed around the flat and the barn house. He even made a trail going from both of my houses all the way to the lake and to Clay's house.

I reached for my bags and walked around to the lake side of the house where the porch was and could see the black pebbled trail went all the way to the dock. At least it was smoother than the usual dirt and rocks beneath it.

The neighbor's fence seemed higher than usual, but it was the same height it had always been. The dark wood of the house stood out from the rest of the houses on the lake. It always seemed so empty, even the few days a year when smoke came out of the chimney. Then, like today, there was smoke, but never a face to the house. It was the last house on this side of the lake, and on the other side was just my house and Clay's house. This side of the lake is where all of our friends live and some other neighbors. Together, we made a community, always doing everything together, but nobody ever talked about the last house on the lake.

We hardly ever went to the other side of the lake where I live. Only ever going as far as the Bloom to pick berries.

The porch steps felt steep, five steps up for me and a short leap for Kona before we were at the door. I went inside quietly and could see everything was still off. Leon was still asleep, or else there would be food cooking right now. Not a stir in the air. Perfect.

I set my bag of clothes and the tote full of goodies down on the kitchen table. Rummaging through the pantry for a birthday candle and a cinnamon roll. I lit the candle and placed it in the roll, then headed upstairs. Kona followed close by. He seemed just as excited as I was. Birthdays are always taken for granted. I felt we should be thankful for another year we have with someone, and another year we get to be here.

I opened Leon's door and began to sing, "Happy birthday to us, happy birthday to us, happy birthday Leon and Lucy, happy birthday to us!" I walked over to his bed and sat down.

He rolled over and smiled with his eyes shut, a full smile. He opened his eyes and blew out the candle.

"Happy birthday Luc," he said.

"Good morning, sleepyhead. I thought you'd be up before me. This is like, the fifth time in our whole lives that I've woken up before you," I said, teasing him.

"I've been up late lately. But still wake up earlier than you if you would have woken up at your normal time," he said.

He bit into the cinnamon roll. Three bites, and it was demolished.

"True. Is dad usually awake by now?" I asked.

"He woke me up earlier to tell me he was going for a bike ride. He should be back by now," he said.

"Happy Birthday, you two," our dad says with a smile as he walked in, right on queue.

He gave me a hug and a kiss on the forehead and made his way over to Leon to do the same.

"How was your bike ride this morning?" Leon asked him and gave him a strange look.

"Oh yeah, my bike ride. It was good. Do you guys want pancakes or waffles? Both? I'll make both," he said and walked out of the room.

"That must have been a smooth bike ride. He wasn't sweaty or in pain or winded at all. How has he been? He's limping extra, even with his cane." I was always concerned but never let myself think about it.

"His doctor said he could loosen his joints naturally by going on bike rides and swimming in the lake when it's warm enough. It'll help strengthen his body, but it does take a toll on him," Leon said as he looked towards the door.

"Get ready and head downstairs when you're done. I'm going to go help dad with breakfast." I got up and yanked the blankets off of him and ran towards the door laughing. He threw a pillow at me. It would have knocked me down if Kona didn't jump up and catch it. We both laughed.

"Good boy, Kona. Now let's leave Leon to get ready. Go downstairs." I pointed towards the wooden stairs, and we both went down to the kitchen.

My dad was in the kitchen with his cane parked beside him.

"Need a hand?" I asked.

"Yes, I do. Want to cook breakfast?" He asked with a smile pasted on his face. I knew he was only joking. Breakfast was his masterpiece. He already had the vegetables cut, the eggs and bacon cooking, and he was mixing the waffle batter in the mixer while measuring out the ingredients for pancakes in a separate bowl. The combination smelled delicious. It made my mouth water. I sat in silence on the stool of the island in the kitchen and watched him cook as Kona laid at my feet.

He was making our traditional birthday breakfast. I always wanted waffles, and Leon always wanted pancakes. Our birthday was the only day of the year he would make both. Our dad took the bacon out of the skillet and threw the small cut potatoes along with the vegetables in the bacon grease. He was making a potato hash. He wrapped a piece of bacon in a paper towel and handed it over for me to eat.

"I can't remember the last time I've had bacon," I said.

My mouth melts. My dad smiled and handed me another piece with tongs.

"Have you talked to Clay?" He asked, not making eye contact with me.

"No, not since yesterday," I replied.

"So, you've seen him again? After the night at the beach?" He said. Trying to make it seem like a light conversation, he was bad at pretending. He was fishing for information.

"Yes. A little. He came to say hi for a minute while I was working on the barn," I said, but I wasn't bad at pretending. I wasn't lying, but I wasn't telling the entire truth. I didn't want to tell him I fell asleep at his house last night, and he carried me home. When he talked about Clay, he had a sort of secret behind his words. My dad said his name louder than the rest of the words he spoke.

"Did you guys talk about anything? Anything specific?" He said, still pretending.

"Nope." I picked apart the bacon.

We made eye contact, and I smiled. He shook his head. He knew he was caught.

"Can't blame a dad for trying," he laughed, letting his breath out.

He seemed more relaxed now.

"Where is my bacon?" Leon said as he sat on the stool next to me.

"In my mouth." I open my mouth to show him a mouth full of half-chewed bacon.

"I'd still eat it," he said.

"How do you always end up being grosser than me when I was the one who did the gross thing?" I said.

"Let's get one thing straight. You will always be grosser than me," Leon said and made all of us laugh.

Our dad was almost done making breakfast, cooking the last of the waffle batter in the waffle maker. I started setting everything up when

I realized I had forgotten about the produce I picked. I walked over to the dining room and returned to the kitchen with the tote of fruits and vegetables.

"I brought fresh berries and some other things. I'll wash the berries so we can eat them with our waffles and pancakes," I said, quickly washing the berries.

"Sweet deal. Did you get these at the market? They smell good, and these strawberries are huge." Leon held one up, comparing it to his fist before he bit into it.

"I got them from the Bloom. You guys never stop to pick anything when you go to or from my house?" I asked.

They both looked at each other. I didn't recognize the look they shared.

"The Bloom. Or that's what we would call it growing up. Remember dad? You would say it only bloomed for me?" They have to know what I was talking about.

"Oh yeah, the Bloom. Must have skipped my mind," Leon said. "Where is it exactly?"

"You have got to be kidding me. You literally drive or walk right past it whenever you go to my house. It is closer to my house than it is from here but not by much. You can't miss it." First Clay, now them? Do they really not pay any attention to anything other than the road?

"I remembered. How often do you go there?" My dad asked.

"At least three times a week. Kona loves it there, so I make it a point to go," I said.

They shared another unreadable expression.

"Be careful with the snakes that have been coming around. You don't want to get bit in the middle of nowhere, or worse, for Kona to get bit, and he is too big for you to carry him if he were to get hurt," my dad said.

"I didn't even think of that. But you're right, I will be more careful."

I set the rest of the food up for my dad, syrup, butter, fruit, and I got cups and drinks along with plates and forks. We made our plates in silence.

"Thanks for breakfast, dad. I need to fuel up for all of the boat action in store for us today!" I said.

Leon perked up. Water sports were his favorite. Anything to do with water was his thing.

"I docked the boat before my bike ride this morning. The tank is full, and I have a fridge full of food to barbecue for dinner. I figured we could come in and eat sandwiches when we got hungry for lunch," my dad said.

Leon grew more excited, "I got a new wakeboard last time I went to town. We have to try it today, Luc!"

"You're on."

As twins, you would think we would be competitive with each other. That is only half true. When it comes to sports or water sports specifically, I am the competitive one. Leon goes along, but we both knew he was more supportive than competitive. With this, in particular, I knew it was because there was no competing with him, anything in the water he excelled in. Not that I was uncoordinated or a lousy swimmer. That's far from it. He was just abnormally strong in the water.

After breakfast, we went straight to the boat. I couldn't remember a birthday of ours we didn't spend on the lake, just us three. Year after year, the warm sun shined on us without a trace of clouds in the sky. But this birthday was different and the same. Somehow it felt much more special. It might have been because it was our first birthday since we moved back home.

You couldn't see the pain in my dad's eyes today. His health had taken a massive turn after we moved. His joints were continuously stiff, and his back always hurt. Some days he couldn't get out of bed, and that wasn't like him. Leon would come back home more often than I would to help him out. But, today, he seemed almost like his old self. He even sat on the innertube and let Leon pull him around with the boat.

A day full of water and sun. We had been at it all day, only a couple of hours left till sunset, and it was time for us to start dinner.

We had docked the boat about an hour ago. I was lying on a paddleboard while Leon was in the water with his arms on the board. He pushed me in circles while our dad talked to us from the dock. He had his feet in the water, leaning back on his hands.

"Twenty-three years ago was the best day of my life. Your mom is happy and brave. She's the light of my life, and she gave me you two. When she took her last breath, she gave you your first," our dad said.

He took a few deeps breaths.

"Why do you always talk about her like she is still here?" It was strange for us to ask about her. I was surprised Leon said anything at all.

"She is. Through you two, especially. I can still feel her around. Lucy, when you talk, I can hear her. When you are in the kitchen, you cook like her. You have her essence in the way you respond to nature. Leon, your eyes are hers. When I look into your eyes, I see her. You move in the water like she did. Your free spirit is from her, too. You two might think she is gone, but I see her every day in both of you. I will never be sad about her passing because she believed anything was possible, even in the darkest of times. Even when you are most down, miracles can happen. She proved that the minute she passed and you two were born. My courageous lion and my light in what was the darkest part of my life." He glowed with pride.

"Thank you for keeping her alive in our eyes," I told him. "We've never asked questions about her. We know nothing of her family or where she came from. Only by piecing bits and pieces together of what you've told us. It's not that you have ever closed yourself off or felt we couldn't ask but asking isn't easy when she isn't here to tell us, and we never wanted to make you feel sad or down or like you weren't enough. You are more than enough."

Leon continued to paddle in circles, and I kept brushing my fingers on the top of the water.

"Your mother was from a tribe. I really didn't know much except her mother was a wise woman, a shaman, and told her to leave the tribe to find me. She said she knew I was the one she was looking for when she laid eyes on me, whatever that meant," he smiled. "I loved her even before I met her. When I first laid eyes on her, the whole world stopped. I guess that's what she meant. I never met her family. As much as I insisted and pushed, she always said that part of her life was behind her."

He explained all of this for the first time, and somehow, this was all information I already knew. I slipped off of the paddleboard and submerged my body into the clear water. It was fresh but warm. When I reached the surface, I decided to float on my back instead of going on the paddleboard.

Leon hopped up on the board, sitting on his ankles, using his hands as paddles as he paddled around me. I looked up at him from the water. I couldn't hear the mumbles he and our dad exchanged. My ears were underwater, their muffled voices and faces with these new expressions that I was starting to see more than I would like. Leon had the same look on his face when he came to visit and brought groceries. Something was going on. He continued to look at me, checking to see if I could still hear him. Something has been going on, and Leon wasn't telling me. I was sure of it. He looked at our neighbor's house and made a comment I couldn't hear.

I picked my head up out of the water and asked, "What about the neighbor?"

"We didn't say anything about the neighbor," my dad said, making eye contact with Leon. "Do you two want to go for another lap around the lake before we dock the boat for the night?"

He changed the subject.

"Yeah, that sounds like a good idea," I said.

There was no point in trying, not with these two. Leon usually told me everything. If there was something he wasn't telling me, then I wasn't supposed to know. It was his burden, not mine.

They both smiled, and my dad slowly got into the boat. Leon jumped off the paddleboard onto the dock, pulling it out of the water and onto the rack so it wouldn't drift. I stayed partially in the water, with my hands on the dock.

Before I could pull myself up, the water temperature began to drop, probably because I stayed still for too long. The wind suddenly picked up, and I looked up to see dark clouds rolling in, faster than I've ever seen clouds move. The ground began to shake, small jolts causing ripples in the lake. I looked up at my dad who was yelling something at me. I couldn't hear him. The wind's speed became too much for my ears. The wind against the tall trees sounded like jets flying overhead. I looked up at Leon and could feel his hands on my wrists. He immediately pulled me up out of the water with so much strength I caught air before my feet hit the dock. When I caught my balance, I looked up at him again. He had fear in his eyes.

Our dad jumped from the boat to the dock without his cane and yelled again, only this time I could hear him.

"Run and get inside as fast as you can!"

We all ran. Barefoot and wet. Over the dock, through the little black pebbled path. As fast as we could. Surprisingly, my dad reached the steps and jumped onto the porch before I did. He opened the door for me to get inside.

One foot reached the first step, and the other just lifted off of the gravel when I felt a firm hand on my arm. It wasn't Leon.

The force of the hand abruptly stopped my body, the weight of my body changed momentum going in the opposite direction, and I slammed directly into Clay's chest.

Where did he come from? I looked directly into his eyes. He was looking up at my dad. They made eye contact, and at that moment, plans changed. My dad jumped over the railing of the porch, landing flat on his feet as if his age and condition weren't hindering his movement.

Clay pulled me away from the house. Leon and our dad trailed our every move until I found myself on the other side of the tall fence outside the dark wood house.

Before I could get to the porch stairs, he grabbed me by my shoulders and bent down a little. inches away, looking me squared in the eyes. "Follow Kona upstairs, make a right and go into the first door on the left. Do not make a sound," his voice was cold.

I didn't have to look at my dad or Leon to know they knew what was going on, unlike me, but I looked at them anyway.

"Go!" Said Clay, eyes pleading.

I did what was told and stepped into the abandoned-not so abandoned house and realized it had the same feel as his house on the other side of the lake. However, this one had more of an essence to it. It was filled with old books and strange pieces of art.

Kona seemed to appear out of nowhere and barked at me to follow him. I did. He knew exactly where to go. Up the stairs, right turn, and he went into the first door on the left.

As soon as my foot crossed the threshold of the doorway, the room became alive. The wood started sprouting vines and leaves, making it smaller but in a way that made me feel safer despite the fear in my heart. The vines were getting more and more intertwined until they formed a nest-like sphere. Flowers and everything grew from them. It was just large enough for Kona and me to fit comfortably.

As soon as the room stopped growing, I found a few small holes where light peaked through. There was only one hole that was clear enough to see through to outside. I was looking through the eye of a needle. Kona whimpered as I got closer to the hole, but he didn't move.

7

I felt the darkness before I saw it. There was someone or *something* on the other side of the fence. My brother, dad, and Clay, in that order, all walked from the porch toward the darkness.

"We don't care why you are here. You are not welcome," my dad said. He sounded bored. I would have believed him if it weren't for every muscle in his body tensing up. He looked strong, bigger somehow, no longer frail.

"Do you take me for a fool, Enkeli? Hand her over, for she isn't yours to keep." The darkness sounded like a man, but not. Ancient, yet still timeless. Its voice was dark and raspy. It was evil. Chills covered my body. I feared they would never go away.

How could this be real? I asked myself.

Leon stood up taller, and with nothing but frustration, he shouted, "It was me! I was born twenty-two years ago today!" He then took a deep breath and calmly said, "Do I look like a woman to you?"

"I mean, it depends on who you ask." Clay winked at my brother and spoke up again, facing darkness through the fence, "You are breaking code by being here. If I have to ask you to leave, you know what that will do. None of us want that. Not even you." Clays voice grew with power through every word he spoke. He also changed, like my dad. He seemed taller. His skin rippled. He looked dangerous.

"I will be around. We all will. Waiting, watching. If there is a girl, and I am sure there is, we will find her. It is only a matter of time." The darkness let out a laugh and growled at the same time just before it vanished altogether.

My body was trembling from the feeling darkness left behind, from hearing its voice.

I felt sick.

Kona had been up and ready to leap down the stairs before the vines returned to their original place within the walls. As soon as darkness, or whatever that thing was, had left, the vines withdrew, leaving an ordinary room behind.

What was going on? Who do I ask? What questions do I ask? I asked myself.

I sat on the floor with my legs crossed in front of me. I put my palms on the floor to the side of me and took a deep breath. Then another, and another until my mind was clear. Only focused on one breath, one at a time. I gathered myself feeling empty and full simultaneously. When I finally stood up, I felt better than I thought I would. I felt strong. I was going to get an explanation today, or there would be hell to pay. I did what I needed to do, what needed to be done, and I walked downstairs to face three people who have been lying to me.

I expected them to be outside because I didn't hear them come inside, though I wasn't really listening. I finally got to the bottom of the dark wood staircase and saw the three of them all in the oversized sitting room on three separate sofas. All of them were on the edge of their seats with their elbows on their knees and their faces in their hands.

I walked in front of them. Leon and our dad looked up at me. Clay didn't move, still looking down.

I waited for someone to say the first word.

"None of this makes sense to me, and it is clear all of you know what is going on. All of my questions *will* be answered, or I *will* follow that thing and find out why it wants me. Clay, how are you here and tied into this? We barely met." I turn to face my brother, "Leon, you are my twin! I know what you are thinking most of the time. How could you keep a secret from me? And for how long?" Leon's face fell. He was pained seeing me this way, upset with him.

I turned to my dad, "I know this secret was kept because of you. So, speak. *Now.*"

I waited for three whole minutes, and I know because I counted. Clay finally looked up and broke the deafening silence.

"If nobody says anything, I am going to tell her everything, and unlike you two," he looked at Leon and my dad separately, "I cannot keep secrets from her. I am bound by oath to be truthful and protect her. If she asks, I answer."

My dad's face didn't flinch. He wasn't going to say anything. Leon was a different story. He looked at me, closed his eyes, and spoke soft and slow, "Lucy, there is no way we could say anything to you that you don't already know. You have always known. When we were younger, you would dream about it and make paintings. Dad was doing the best he could, especially after losing mom. We couldn't lose you too."

"Leon. Why would I ask for an explanation if I knew what was going on?" My voice stripped of emotion.

I turned to Clay.

I could tell this wasn't easy for them by the look on their faces and the tension coursing through the room. There had always been something off about the way we were, not wrong but different. I thought it was because our mother had passed and we were twins. I mean, what dad is a single dad of twins?

Clay looked up and when our eyes met, Deja vu hit me like a punch to the face, and I knew what he was going to say, yet I still needed him to say it.

After a deep breath, he said, "Lucy, your family comes from the descendants of celestial beings. Some call them angels, witches, fairies in some cultures. Though you are none of those. We call them, or you, the Enkeli. Your father's bloodline is the last of its kind."

Inhale, exhale.

I had no recollection of the amount of time in which had passed.

Inhale, exhale.

Nobody said anything after Clay.

Inhale, exhale.

I do not know how I got on the floor, but I was sitting with my eyes closed in the middle of the living space where I was standing.

Inhale, exhale.

I was confused.

Could this be real? *Yes.*

Am I right? *Yes.*

This cannot be real. *It is.*

My own voice answered.

Inhale, exhale.

When I opened my eyes, nobody had moved. Kona was in his spot next to me on the floor. I looked out of the window ahead of me, and it was dark outside. Hours had passed, I closed my eyes again.

Inhale, exhale.

Time passed by.

Inhale, exhale. Inhale, exhale. Inhale, exhale.

"Lucy… Lucy." I felt a hand brush through my hair and another on my shoulder.

"Lucy," a voice said softly.

"Lucy." The hand on my shoulder continued to stroke my arm. I noticed the hand brushing through my hair supported my head more than I realized.

I opened my eyes.

"Lucy, can you hear me?" Leon said my name gently.

I nodded.

"We don't have much time, so I need you to pay attention. We all need you to pay attention." He gestured towards the sofas where Clay and our dad were sitting.

They were still in the same seats, everything the same except for a spread of untouched food on the coffee table.

I looked at our dad first. There was sorrow in his eyes parallel to their firmness. He looked different somehow. I couldn't place it. His eyes were sure. He was sure of me, not worried. He had confidence in me.

I turned to Clay. I didn't know why I heavily dreaded the thought of facing him. When our eyes connected, he leaned forward on the couch and ran his hands through his hair before he leaned back. He grew impatient as he leaned forward again.

"Talk to her," Clay said to Leon. His voice was firmer than I have ever heard it.

My dad stood up, "Give them a minute!" He shouted. It was unlike him to raise his voice.

"We do not have a minute, Leo," Clay said.

His body radiated heat.

My dad stepped closer to Clay, "Then we make one!"

"Leo, we have until sunrise before the council comes. We do not have a minute," Clay remained composed. The heat he radiated was the only indication he was affected.

His skin rippled like it did earlier. My dad looked from Clay to Leon and sat down. He nodded towards Leon before sitting back. Clay reached for his cup of water and an apple before he sat down.

I looked at Leon, naturally.

My voice spoke without my permission, "Leon, this has to come from you, whatever it is. When you talk, I feel your emotions. I see visuals sometimes. I need *you* to tell me what is going on."

"Okay," he took a deep breath. His eyes watered. Though his face didn't change, I could feel his concern.

He was doing his best to stay strong for all of us.

I reached for his hand and stood up, pulling him up with me, "It's okay, brother. I will be okay." I guided him to where he sat before and sat next to him. Clay was to my right, Leon at my left, and our dad was on the sofa to the left.

I lifted my feet onto the sofa to get comfortable and took a few deep breaths before nodding to Leon.

"Your paintings, they are real. All of them," he began.

I open my mouth to speak, and he put his hand up.

"Your paintings are real. Your stories as a child are real. All of it is real. Our family has nothing but men because of a curse. No woman could survive because women born of our lineage are powerful. They have-" he searched for the right word, he took a deep breath and continued, "-gifts. They have light. You have a light inside of you that can throw off the balance of good and evil. The thing that came tonight was a demon. That one, in particular, was patrol, a scout, it'll be back. The rocks at the bottom of the lake are sacred and mute your vibration to them. As long as you're on them or in the lake, you are safe from being detected by them. Demons, the ones who hunt us, are a part of a darkness called Deminio. I'll touch more on that later. Your recent paintings told us what you subconsciously knew. It helped us be able to help you the last few years. You wrote about what started it all and the curse when you were in grade school. We need you to go back to that place in your head when you painted the paintings that sold recently. What were you thinking about? What did you feel as you painted them? We need vital points and some sort of structure. The curse banished all women because they brought light into the world, casting out all evil. The curse ensures the Deminio will always have a place here on earth in this realm. Every girl who is born to this family dies before she could reach a full hour old. Nature now doesn't provide us with women anymore after so many have died. Every woman married into the family still falls under the veil of the curse. They die a tragic death. The only reason you are here is because-"

"Because of you," I finished.

"Yes, because we are twins *and* because mom died giving birth to us. It threw off the balance of energy. We were born within minutes of each other, and mom dying at that moment made a sort of loophole. We were able to conceal you," Leon said.

"Until now," Clay's voice held firm.

He was staring at me through the death glares of Leon and my dad.

"Yes, that is right, until now. Lucy, you have been letting out a signal lately. We all feel it. We think it is because you have been using part of your gifts to build the barn. Even small things like you lifting something too heavy for your human body, but you carry it anyway, or when you sketch or write and tap into those memories. All of it can let out a sort of signal. Your powers start fully manifesting after your twenty-second birthday. You went somewhere else in your dream recently, you know what I'm talking about, and we need to know," my dad said.

I told Clay about the dream, and I also wrote it down.

"I already told Clay I had a dream," I looked over at him, "did you tell them?"

"I told them the dreams started again. You only told me you had a strange dream and nothing more. I could feel it while you had it. What-ever you share with me isn't up to me to report. It is up to you," Clay said.

I told them the dream, staying vague, not going into depth. Just how I was a woman and briefly explained the location and about a Guard, I didn't say his name. They all listened carefully. I could see them exchange looks here and there as they picked out details. Finally able to share what has been going on in my head gave me a sense of relief. For the first time in months, I finally felt like I was where I was supposed to be. I didn't exactly know what all of this meant, and I still had barely touched the surface, but I felt relieved. I had a million questions, but I wasn't in the dark.

When I finished telling them the dream, I had realized by the looks on their faces that there was still so much I was unaware of. The three of them were making eye contact with each other, silent communication. With each new look they gave, it added to the list of questions I already had.

"Wait. What exactly are we? What can we do?" I asked.

"We are called Enkeli. Technically we are a type of angel, or descendants of angels. Not the kind with wings. Those are our ancestors. They are higher in rank than us and always will be. They are the purest of beings and harbor the most light. We are workers of light, Lemurians. We have many gifts. Some of us have been able to bloom full forests, protect and clean an ocean, talk to animals, heal people, change energy, read the emotions of humans, and much more. That being said, it is why we are so few. Men Enkeli are not nearly as powerful as women. We could heal a wound that would otherwise need stitches, where a woman could mend every broken bone with a thought. Men can grow and blossom a tree from a seed, a woman can grow a forest in the same amount of time. Women have a different light in them. The Deminio can't stand against you individually. They'd need an army," the way my dad pieced words together was different. He was having a hard time finding the right words to say.

"I can do all of that on my own?" I asked.

"Technically, you could have a major affinity for something. Like healing, for example. Something specific. Or a strong affinity for water or earth while still being able to do other small things. Some women have been known to have more than one strong power. Some have many small ones. It depends on the person and their lineage," Leon said. I was about to speak when he said, "No, we don't know what yours is."

"You showed signs as a child," Clay said.

He looked at my dad and Leon, pushing them to tell me more when I wondered how he tied into all of this. I looked at him through narrowed eyes.

I got a feeling I needed to talk to him separately. I also realized they were having difficulty reading me. I hadn't been making any facial expressions or moving much, subconsciously not giving anything away. They are unaware of how I feel, not my usual self where I would be more generous with my thoughts. I looked at Leon and could feel his nerves. His face was sad, the same face he'd had for weeks.

"I have to go home. I need to digest this without any influence. I know I need to know much more, but I need some sleep and a clear mind." I got up off of the couch.

Leon understood. Our dad didn't want me to leave though it wasn't his decision to make.

Kona followed me out of the large house. I was in my bikini and had no shoes on. I ran inside of my dad's house and got my bag along with my keys and went back outside.

Clay, Leon, and my dad were all standing on the bottom of the porch stairs.

"I just need some space." I walked down the steps.

Worry was heavy on their faces.

"I'll be okay, I promise. Let me have the rest of the night to myself. I will come back in the morning, and we can sort this out. I love you both," I said.

I gave my brother and dad a hug and reassured them I would be okay and would call if I needed anything.

"You are coming with me," I said to Clay.

He didn't skip a beat. He followed me to my car. Kona ran and jumped into the back seat. Clay and I got in, and I drove through the dark around the lake to our houses. As soon as I parked, I asked Clay to start the fire while I showered. Not another word would be said until I am clean and ready.

I let the hot water run over me. I imagined my body was a water bottle full of dirty water. As the water hit my body, I imagined the water turning clear, eliminating all traces of fog and anything unsettling. I breathed in and out and took deep, cleansing breaths. A few minutes have passed, and it washed away the fog in my head, and I've come to a few realizations. I knew my dad and Leon were protecting me, but why wouldn't they help me instead? Why would they want to keep this a secret? I also knew that weird things happened all the time growing up and was always told it was my imagination. Leon kept this from me, twin telepathy is real with us. He must know how to block me out sometimes.

There is much I do not know. I could feel it.

I also knew this was the beginning of a life I was born to live. I was chosen for this. I know I will have to fight, or I will die. Or worse, I would have to go with the darkness that came for me today.

8

"How would you know?" I asked before I could sit on the couch.

"Know what?" He said.

He laid the floor next to the fire with Kona beside him on the rug.

"That I used to show signs of power as a child," I said.

I covered myself with a fluffy throw blanket and laid my head on the armrest facing them.

"I was there," he said, voice low.

"What do you mean you were there. You are almost my age, and I would remember playing with another kid as a child," I said.

"What I mean is I saw you grow a flower out of the dirt when you were two. Leon picked a flower, and you got sad, so you buried it, you closed your eyes and put your hand over it, and it bloomed through the dirt right then," his voice still soft.

"How old were you? Three? Four? Six? We just met, or so I thought. How do you tie into all of this? Are you also what I am? Enkeli?" I grew anxious with every word and tried my best to hide it, an inner debate on whether or not I could trust him.

"I have looked this age for mostly the entirety of my being. I do not age. Time is different where I come from." He took a deep breath and looked up. He was trying to figure out his words, "I am a Guardian, not Enkeli."

"Like a Guardian Angel?" I asked.

I could taste uncertainty on my tongue.

"No, a Guardian. I am part of what is called the Guard. A warrior force designed to protect Enkeli. When you were born, I was called to protect you," he answered easily.

He didn't second guess his words or hesitate. He was telling the truth, and at that moment, I realized I could trust him.

I looked at him again. I could somehow tell he could sense my ease. I took a deep breath, got off of the couch, and crouched down, sitting on the floor beside him and the fire. Kona was on my left, and Clay was in front of me. The fire crackled on my right.

"Clay, I need you to tell me what I need to know," I said as firmly as my voice allowed. I resisted the urge to reach for his hand.

I tested my theory of him answering every question. He moved from his back to his side, propped himself up on his elbow and looked into me. I could feel the heat of his eyes and his body.

"I am oath-bound to you, Lucy. If you are in danger, I feel it. I know where you are at all times. As a part of the Guard, it is my life's duty and purpose to protect you. If there is something you need to know, I will not hesitate to tell you. I keep no secrets from you," he said.

I was right.

I looked over at the fire for a minute, then back at Clay. He was staring right at me. I felt him reading me. The ease I felt around him from the first time we hung out still remained, though tonight it was more. More emotional, more intense, more concerned, more passionate. Just more.

Clay's eyes gleamed, and I have never noticed before this moment, but now that I have, I don't know why I didn't see them before. I knew his eyes were large almond-shaped, and his lashes were bold and brought out the color. I knew those things. I didn't notice his eyes were different colors. Both hazel and honey in the middle, but one was glowing sage forest green, and the other was turquoise blue. They were breathtaking.

"Your eyes-" I cut myself off. I didn't mean to say it out loud.

He put his head down and let out a laugh.

He looked up at me and said, "The mark of a Guardian. We usually wear contacts around you."

His face changed. He was calm and still hard to read, but his eyes watered.

"Lucy, I *have* to answer your questions. I *have* to protect you. I *have* to be honest with you." He leaned back on the floor and laid on his back, brushing his hands through his hair before placing them on his stomach. His breathing hitched, growing frustrated.

I didn't understand.

"You don't understand? I told you I sense emotions when they're heightened. I sensed confusion," he clarified.

I should be a little creeped out though nothing about him made me uncomfortable. I had no words.

He closed his eyes, "You wouldn't get it. I shouldn't expect you to understand."

I knew it was unfair to ask. If he wants to explain it to me, he would have told me, but I knew if I asked, he would answer. I asked anyway.

"Explain it to me then," I said.

He looked at me, still lying down, and said, "The problem isn't that I have to do anything. I don't mind the obligation or the duty. It is my purpose, what I was created to do. I expected to feel connected to you." He took a deep breath, "The problem is, I *want* to. I *want* to protect you, Lucy. I am unsure whether it is because I am bound to you. Or if… if…"

he struggled to finish, struggled to find the words.

"If what Clay?" I asked. I could feel my heart beating and wondered for a moment if he could hear it too.

"I don't even know how to explain it. I have been training my entire existence to be a warrior, a Guardian. Fear doesn't exist in me. I learned tactics, strategy, strength, and skill. How to use energy, how to read energy, everything necessary to become what I am. I am not supposed to feel anything more. The first time I heard your voice as an adult just a few days ago, the oath shifted, as it does for all Guardians with who they are oath-bound to protect. It strengthened the bond. Then I started seeing other things, you like to be barefoot and feel the earth. You have some sort of weakness for anything with sugar," he laughed. "You become the water when you are in it. Your eyes dance, you can be completely silent, and your eyes dance to the hypnotizing rhythm of your own song. In just days, you have become the center of my gravity. I feel for you when I am not supposed to feel at all." He looked at the ceiling, lying on the floor like stone.

The wheels in my head raced. I have never connected with anyone before, never felt that pull to want to be around someone the way I do with him. From the first day after the beach, he made me feel at home. I have slept full nights since then. Looking back, I knew I was safe. I caught myself thinking of him and wondered when I would see him again.

Is this what it felt like to actually have a connection with someone? More than just a friend kind of connection? I mean, I knew he was handsome. Anyone could see that. But it was more than that. The way he carried himself, the way he talks, even his movements were mesmerizing.

"What is the problem?" Was all I could say.

He sat up, and in one swift move, his hands are on both sides of my face, so large they held the back of my neck too. His face inches from mine, his breath sweet against my face.

I thought he was going to kiss me. Instead, he put his forehead on mine and closed his eyes.

He took a few breaths before saying, "It is forbidden. As Guardians, we cannot decipher whether we feel because of the oath or because of love. Not being able to tell the two apart. We are trained to be a Guardian and nothing more."

There goes that word again, more.

"I feel it, too, Clay. A pull," I whispered.

My hands found their way to his wrists, his hands still on my face. He pulled back just enough to look me in the eyes. I did feel it. At that moment, more than ever, I felt the pull towards him. A part of me knows he must follow the ways of the Guard. I didn't have to ask him to know that, but how can we both feel this and pretend we didn't? How could we pretend it wasn't there?

I looked into his eyes, full of fire, and his hands flushed warm on my face. I nodded, letting him know it was okay.

His mouth found mine. Hard and soft at the same time. A wave took over. I forgot about everything. I forgot about the day, about the night. I forgot about the darkness, about the secrets, about the Guard and the Enkeli.

I have never experienced something like this, not just a kiss but one where everything else stops. The whole world seemed to slow down.

He pulled away, and I opened my eyes to see him smiling at me. Not his full, heart-wrenching ear-to-ear smile, but an uneven half-smile. A smile that was just for me. I was breathing heavily with a smile I've never felt before, pasted on my face.

"Tonight was just the beginning. We haven't touched the surface." I thought he was talking about the kiss. I realized he wasn't when he continued, "You need to get some rest. Tomorrow will be longer and more taxing than today."

Maybe he was talking about both. Clay got up and extended his hand out to help me up. He pulled out my sofa bed and made the bed. Once the bed was made, I looked up at him. I laughed when I saw he was blushing.

"What?" I said.

"Well, now that you know about yourself, and what you are and what I am, or what I am to you, and with the demon coming today," his voice trailed.

"Go on." I gestured for him to continue.

Clay hesitated, "I don't have to sleep on the bed or anything. But I don't want to take any chances of something coming back."

I could tell he was stepping out of his comfort zone.

"Are you asking to stay the night?" I smiled. He was actually embarrassed to ask.

"Yes, I cannot risk it anymore. Most nights, I sleep on your porch. That is why I am always on my porch reading. When I can feel you getting up to look outside, I run to my porch before you could see," his voice changed. He was serious, "Putting aside our moment, I would have insisted either way."

He wasn't shy to ask to stay the night. He was shy about the kiss and then asking after.

"Yes, you can stay." I walked over to the closet next to the bathroom and pulled out a few blankets and a pillow. I tossed it on the floor next to the fireplace at the foot of the bed where we were and where Kona was lying.

Clay's shoulders relaxed, and he smiled in relief. I wouldn't make his duty more difficult by refusing a request as simple as this one. I remembered the way darkness sounded and how I felt, and chills covered my entire body. If he wasn't here, I wouldn't be able to sleep, and I would spiral down a rabbit hole of unknown. I would rather him stay.

My stomach grumbled.

"Are you hungry, too?" I asked. I was as equally tired as I was hungry.

"No, but I do have to run to my place for a quick shower and to get a few things. You eat, and I will be back before you go to sleep. If I am not back by then, I will be soon after," Clay said and walked towards me.

He touched my face, and I instinctively leaned into his touch.

"I'll be back," he said just before he turned around and walked out of the door.

I walked to the kitchen and looked in the refrigerator. All I had the energy to make was a bowl of cereal. I sat on the counter as my feet dangled over the edge and ate. With my first bite came my first moment alone and in came a massive wave of everything, rolling in all at once.

I realized my entire life wasn't what I thought it was. I know there was more. Clay even said so. Before I could overwhelm myself even more, I took a few more bites of cereal and sat on the floor. I crossed my feet in front of me, and I put my palms on the floor to my sides. Kona immediately walked over to me and sat down. I sat up straight and took a few deep breaths.

Inhale. *What should I do?* Exhale.

Inhale. *Where do I go from here?* Exhale.

Inhale. Exhale. Inhale. Exhale.

Words come to me, and I knew what to do. *Trust yourself to know who to trust. Those few will help you get to where you need to be. They will tell you all that you need to know. Follow and trust your path. Every step you take needs to be taken. You will always be right where you are supposed to be. Do not forget.*

The words were my own. The voice in my head was my own. So, instead of overthinking and stressing, I will do what I knew needed to be done.

I took one last deep breath and said thank you aloud before I got up. I walked over to my pantry and got a handful of dried mangoes. These had always made me feel better. I ate them as I filled my water flask with ice-cold water. All things I did as I have always done and reminded myself, I am still me.

That was what was most important, that I remain me and true to my authentic self.

I went to bed and tucked myself in. Kona jumped up to his usual spot and licked my face before he laid down.

Sleep came before I remember closing my eyes.

9

Clay

Clay opened the door to Lucy's house and placed his bag next to the door. He made sure to stay silent and could feel she was asleep. He wasn't particularly loud and was trained to be silent when necessary. The moment he stepped inside, he felt the warmth of her home. Not just from the heat of the fire but the warmth from *her*. The light she has inside of her shined even when she was asleep.

He turned off the light and walked over to the fireplace to put another log in the fire.

Clay looked over at Lucy. His heart raced, but he was calm.

"As ancient as the sun is my bond to you. My strength equally balanced to your brightest Light. My faith parallel to your love. Living to protect you in your entirety, living to conserve the Enkeli, and living to Guard Light at all costs. My oath to you knows no bounds. Living to protect, living to conserve, and living to guard," Clay whispered with his fist over his heart.

The oath he took the day she was born, the day he was called to take his place next to her. Flashbacks surfaced quickly. The night she was born, the ripple it made with the balance and the lengths he had to go to protect her. He created a life for her in a matter of hours. From concealing the lake from the Deminio to all the people who lived on the lake. Changing some out and inserting the council who would be her friends. Everything he did was all for her. It was for the Light.

He walked over to her and softly kissed her on her forehead.

"Goodnight, Lucy."

Clay walked over to his bed on the floor next to the fireplace just a few feet from her and laid down. He wanted to wake her up and give her a rundown of what would happen in the morning. He wanted to prepare her as best he could. He knew he should have informed her instead of letting her know his new ability to feel, but she needed rest more than she needed insight right now.

After all, she was mostly mortal.

For now.

10

"Are you okay?!" Clay asked, his eyes scouted the perimeter. He was looking everywhere but at Lucy, looking for any sign of danger. His face was stone, but his skin was different. It was vibrating or rippling how it did when the demon was near. When he was in his human form she was to his chest, he was already a foot taller than her. When he took his form as a Guardian, he was massive.

When he looked at her, he tried to read her body language and waited for a response.

"I got your note to meet you out here when I was ready. I came out here looking for you when a bird flew close and scared me. I jumped," she said as she held her breath.

He let out a deep breath, and his skin immediately went back to normal, but his height stayed the same. He towered over Lucy.

"We have to go. Everyone is waiting for us," Clay said.

They both walked over to his old red pickup truck, and he opened the passenger door for Lucy to get in. Once she was in, Kona leaped onto the bed of the truck. Clay had already made his way into the driver's seat. Lucy wondered if they would talk about the kiss from last night, but she quickly put that thought aside. At least until Clay mentioned it.

The grove-like trail to the other side of the lake was short. They'd be there in minutes. Lucy looked out the window, enjoying the silence when Clay slammed the breaks and got out of the car.

"Come to Lucy's house... yes... all of you. Now." She thought he was talking to her before he put his phone in his pocket.

"Lucy, how long has this been here?" Clay asked.

"I'm guessing as long as there have been people walking around the lake," she said as she looked down at the trail in front of them.

"Not the trail. This!" He extended his arms towards the Bloom.

All of the colorful flowers smelled so wonderful, even from inside of the truck. The fruits were ripe and ready to be picked. The vines and trees all intertwined so beautifully the way they only did here. She truly had never seen anything like it.

"I told you this was here. Remember?" She said.

"Lucy, answer my question." His body language was different. He was sharp, he was her Guardian.

"Every time I go to my dad's or walk to the other side of the lake, it is here. It was smaller before and seems to have doubled in size over this last spring," she said, still not wholly answering this question.

His face remained unchanged.

She finally answered, "It has been here my entire life. Or for as far back as I could remember."

She got out of the car, and Clay was looking around. He moved vines around, looking at every tree. Lucy didn't quite understand what he was doing or what he was looking for.

"Can you explain to me what is going on inside of your head so I can help you? You might be able to read my mind sometimes, but I can't read yours," Lucy said.

"Lucy, I need you to pay attention, okay?" She nodded at him. He continued, "This is very important. Remember that carving I told you about? The circular one I carved in the center of your house?" Clay was talking slow. He even lowered his head a little to be more leveled with her.

"Yes. What about it?" Lucy said.

"Is that carving here?" Clay asked.

Lucy couldn't read him. She couldn't quite place the emotion she felt from him. He almost seemed scared.

"Yes, it's right over here." Lucy walked Clay over to the carving. She moved a few berry vines for a clear view. Lucy knelt down on the bed of moss and looked at the carving. It was the same one she saw the other day and the same one Clay carved in her house. However, something about this one was a little different. She couldn't pinpoint exactly what it was. It should look identical, but it didn't.

Clay knelt down beside her and touched the carving. He looked at her in disbelief.

"Clay, speak," Lucy demanded.

"Do you know what this is? Do you know at all?" He asked.

She shook her head and tried not to roll her eyes at him.

"Lucy, this carving was carved from the *inside* of the tree. I tried telling you when I worked on the carvings in the barn. I told you this was part of the history of the lake, but it is also a part of yours. When you were born, many of us came together to build a place where you'd be safe-" Clay was cut off by Kona's bark. Kona ran back to the truck and leaped in the back. Something was going on.

He looked at Kona and then looked around. His skin started to do that ripple thing again, "Let's head back to your house. I'll tell you the rest when they get to your house."

His body language had changed. He turned full Guardian. His eyes glowed into the distance. Something was close.

Clay looked at Lucy and silently mouthed, "Trust me."

She nodded. Clay picked her up and carried her to the passenger's side of the truck. He put his finger over his mouth. She blinked, and the door was shut. Just like earlier, he was already inside of the driver's seat. Super speed must be a Guardian thing. He drove in reverse the entire way back to her house. What was just two minutes felt like much, much longer.

As soon as they reached the flat, he said, "The small black pebbles from the bottom of the lake protect you. They mute your vibration from being detected by Deminio. The strong ones can still feel you, but they do not know exactly where you are. They can't pinpoint your location."

"Good to know," Lucy said as she grabbed a handful of pebbles, examined them quickly before letting them fall through her fingers.

Lucy heard a car pull up to the front of her house and walked towards the door. It was Leon's Jeep, and to her surprise, another car pulled in next to Leon's.

Leon jumped out of the driver's side, and Lucy's dad easily stepped out of the passenger's side, no cane in hand.

Interesting. Lucy thought to herself.

She walked towards them, and before she could get to the bottom of the porch stairs, three more people got out of the back seat.

It was Talan, Dario, and Fazi.

The car next to them was all too familiar. Alika stepped out of her car and Omala out of the passenger's side. They collectively walked towards Lucy and formed a circle, Lucy still on the bottom of the porch step.

Right on cue, the roar of a motorcycle broke through the tree line. Everyone turned their heads. It flew down the road and skid to park next to Leon's car. His helmet came off, but Lucy already knew it was Emma. He walked towards Leon first, not looking at anyone else. They shook hands and brought each other close, eyes closed with their foreheads touching while their left hands hugged each other. Lucy had only ever seen Leon do that with Emma, a true sign of respect.

Emma walked towards Clay and did the same. They have a history Lucy didn't know about. She could feel the bond they shared. It was deep. He waved at the rest of the circle then walked up to Lucy. She thought he would shake her hand when he extended his hand to her, but he grabbed her forearm instead. He looked her in the eyes and bowed his head, taking a slight step back with his right foot.

Nobody else had said anything. They all just looked at her. All except for Emma.

Clay to her left and Leon to her right, Emma took her dad's place at Leon's right. Dario and Talan stood next to Clay, Fazi stood next to Leo. Omala and Alika were the ones to close the circle.

Just then, Lucy realized this was a ranking of some sort. She looked over at Clay, Dario, and Talan and could see they were all a part of the Guard. She didn't know how everyone else tied into this, but she knew they all belonged there.

"We all knew this day would come though we didn't expect it to happen like this," Clay went straight to the point. "There is more to this than we all knew. Lucy expanded and opened the Bloom. It is not the small micro-orchard it once was. The gateway to Mpiaron has appeared."

Lucy looked around and could feel everyone's air escape their lungs. Their faces paled.

"She has had dreams of it. Just different, she sees everyone in Mpiaron as human, just like she sees us. This has never been done before. There is no real way to know where we should go from here. I've decided to trust in Lucy to make the decisions she knows to be best for her. I can and will advise her. We all can if she asks for it, but nobody here-and I do mean *nobody*," Clay looked over at Lucy's dad, who was already fuming, "will demand her. Respect my terms or take it up with the Guard. The dream she had, led her to a destination. We need to go there. I will need the help of everyone here. We will take a vote. If we all agree, I will go with her to Mpiaron. If anyone disagrees, we stay and find another way."

He projected authority with the solidity of his voice.

"How do we know going to Mpiaron is the direction we should go from here? It would be safest if she stayed. The only reason to go to Mpiaron would be to help us figure out what to do. My concern, my only concern, is the effect it will have on her when she gets back." Alika sounded like herself but different. She had a thick Scottish accent.

Lucy smiled at her and received a small tight-lipped smile in return.

Alika spoke with force, not to challenge Clay's words but out of concern. Lucy wondered what Alika had meant by effect.

"We do not. We also don't have any information on moving forward with Lucy and her strengths or know how to battle the Deminio with her. I am putting faith in her dreams which guide her in the direction we all need to go in. The Angels speak differently to her than they do us. If anyone has anything else we can do or any input that could help, say it now."

Clay was a true leader.

Lucy wanted to speak out about the Angel she hallucinated the other day. Something inside of her told her to keep it to herself for now.

"If that's what you feel we should do, then that is what we do. Clay, *you* are her Guardian. One thing we learned is a Guardian's will to protect is more powerful than the strength they bear. Trust yourself," Emma spoke directly to Clay and to no one else.

"Lucy, do you feel okay?" Clay asked her.

"I am a little confused, but if you're asking how I feel physically, just a little lightheaded," she said.

"When you were younger, you showed signs of your gifts. You'd grow a flower, change the temperature of the water, call all the fish to the dock, create waves at the ocean when there were none, make a bonfire quadruple in size," Clay's voice and facial expression was full of amazement as he gazed into the past.

He looked over at Leo, Lucy's dad, and his face fell.

Lucy peaked a glimpse at her dad and could see he, too, was going through memories. Hard and painful memories.

"Lucy, when you would do these things, you would glow. When you glow, you attract the darkness, the Deminio. But you would also get sick. You'd faint, get nosebleeds, temporarily lose function of your limbs. You lost your sight for a day. That is when we decided," her dad motioned at everyone in the circle, "you would grow up living a life as close to normal as possible. We knew this day would come. We only hoped when it did, you would be stronger than you were before. We hoped when the day came, you'd be strong enough to face it. We don't know what will happen if you start using your gifts again. We do know if you don't learn to use your gifts, the Deminio will find you. They will find you, and they will kill you. Or worse."

"Mpiaron. Do you have any sort of inkling as to what it is?" Omala spoke up. Her soft voice was refreshing.

Lucy shook her head.

"It is technically a different realm within this one where most of us come from. It is where the Lemurians live, beings who are of Light. A safe place for all to go away from the Deminio," Omala spoke, and the warmth from her could be felt within the circle.

"Let's all go there, where we will be safe," Lucy said.

"You can't be there longer than three full days," Emma said.

"Why not?" Asked Lucy.

Emma didn't skip a beat, "You are too powerful. Mpiaron is concealed from the Deminio. If you are there, the Deminio would feel the Light coming from the Bloom after the third day. The Bloom is where the gateway is, as you've heard, and was made by you as a child. The carving was there, hidden from our side. But the Bloom being pulled through by you is a piece of Mpiaron that came through to this side. If you go to Mpiaron, the Bloom's portal stays open from this realm to that one and could be seen by any and all who pass. Even the Deminio. The longer you are there, the bigger the Bloom will get. If the Deminio see the Bloom, they will be able to enter into Mpiaron, putting every one of Light in danger. If you are there a second longer than three days, the gateway would open permanently. It will expand beyond anything we could conceal."

All of this information was a lot for Lucy to soak in, but every word was branded on her heart. She wouldn't forget any of it.

"Why am I so important? Everything before me was fine. If I stick to myself and live the way I was living without using my gifts, everything will stay as it was, and nobody would get hurt," Lucy said.

"That is not true. We knew when you turned twenty-two, you would evolve. There is a series of worldwide events happening, all caused by the Lemurians. There is also a series of worldwide events caused by Deminio, who grow stronger every day. Their strength is no longer balanced with ours. There is supposed to be a balance, but with you, we could slowly integrate more and more Lemurians around the world and restore it. More people to believe in magic and love, healing themselves and restoring earth. It sounds like a dream. With *you*, it is possible. Not just here on earth, but everywhere. The more Lemurians can spread light, the weaker the Deminio becomes. Not even that, if you take all of that away, right now they outnumber us in more than just the physical sense. Our numbers are low, our Light is dim, and our gifts are dying. Our people are dying, and the Deminio are thriving. Chaos fully upon us. We don't stand a chance without you, Lucy," Fazi spoke up.

His normally funny self was checked out. His straight-to-the-point attitude was not. Fazi was afraid.

"The Deminio feel you, but they don't know exactly what it is they are feeling. They aren't sure you really exist. They would just throw it out there every so often. They do know there is a shift in this particular area caused by you and the expanding Bloom," Emma said.

"How do you know what they feel?" Lucy asked.

Everyone looked around, looked down, up and at each other, just not at Lucy and not at Emma.

He looked at Lucy. With both pain and pride in his eyes, he stood tall. Leon put a supportive hand on Emma's shoulder and nodded.

"I was Deminio," Emma said.

She could feel how pained he was and how uncomfortable it made everyone else. He was close to Leon but not particularly close with any-one else, except maybe Clay by how they greeted each other. She knew she would have more questions for him, just not right now, not while everyone else was around. She smiled, "Okay."

"Take a vote. Who wants Lucy to go to Mpiaron?" Authority heavy in Clay's voice.

He looked to his side at Talan and Dario. They both put their fists to their chests. Alika did the same. Then Omala. Fazi hesitated and looked down. He took a deep breath and slowly fisted his hand over his heart. Her dad didn't move. In unison, Leon and Emma raised their fists to their chest and made a pounding sound.

Lucy looked back to her dad.

"I can't do this without your support or your vote. I will be okay. I can do this, dad," she said, truly believing every word.

He looked at her, eyes watering, but no tears escaped. He fisted his hand and slowly raised it to his chest.

Clay's voice was strong through the tension, "Lucy and I leave in ten minutes. Omala, help her pack."

Lucy was inside of her cozy flat with Omala while everyone else was outside discussing recent events. Lucy stood against the arm of her sofa bed. Her body Faced Omala, who was neatly going through Lucy's closet, picking out clothes to pack. She tried to focus, but her eyes couldn't help but wander outside.

She knew the conversation was going to become heated the moment she broke the circle and went inside. All were silent after the vote, clearly waiting for Lucy to leave, all eyes on her, and as soon as Omala shut the door behind them, heavy whispers broke through the door. It had been five minutes, and her dad's veins haven't gone back inside of his neck since. Leon was pacing back and forth with his hands on the top of his head. Clay's body was doing the shaking skin thing again. She finally let herself look at him. Wondering if he would ever look at her the way he did last night. She was hoping he would, even if it was just for reassurance. She was also hoping he wouldn't. She didn't want anyone to know.

"Did you hear me?" Omala said.

"Sorry, I didn't. I wonder what they are talking about," Lucy said.

Omala was sweet. She was also bold and honest. Lucy knew if she talked to her, their conversation wouldn't leave the room.

"Lucy, if you were supposed to hear what they're talking about, you'd be out there too," Omala assured her. "Now focus. I said time works differently in Mpiaron. You'll need different things there than you do here. I'm here to make sure you have everything you need."

Omala reached her hand out for Lucy to give her the crossbody leather bag she was wearing. It had a drawstring and a little flap that went over the top to close it. The long strap was a leather braid, and it was small.

There was a sweatshirt, a few bathing suits, a pair of jeans, a few shirts, and a dress. Omala waved her hands over the bag and the clothes, and Lucy half expected something to happen though nothing did. Omala held up the small bag and placed all of the items into the bag. Everything fit inside of it, it was impossible, but she did it. Omala held the bag out. Lucy walked over to retrieve it and was surprised at its weight. It didn't feel like she had anything in there at all. Lucy was in complete disbelief.

"Magic. I'm a witch," Omala said.

"Magic? Figures. You were always so sure of yourself. Magic suits you," Lucy said and extended her arms to hug Omala.

"Lucy, listen to me, please. To say it is important doesn't come close," Omala was serious and held Lucy's hands in her own. "This isn't a normal bag. It is connected to me. If you should need something, anything, focus on it and try to find ways to let me know. If you can write it down on something and place it in the bag, I will receive the message directly. I will do my best to make sure you have everything you need. Do you understand?"

"I do. Thank you," Lucy said and gave Omala another hug.

Lucy had a feeling, a warmth in the pit of her stomach. She turned her head and looked out through the window.

Clay.

He was looking at her, his face was stone, but his eyes were smiling. She couldn't help but feel even the slightest bit better. She relaxed her shoulders. He nodded to let her know not to worry. Lucy could feel it. The warmth within her body was coming from him.

Lucy walked outside and took another look at Clay. The smile in his eyes was gone. He wasn't just her neighbor or friend Clay right now. He was Clay the Guardian.

Her eyes soared the circle, and she was relieved when nobody saw the looks they exchanged. She looked at Emma, who was outside of the circle. He smiled and shook his head. He *did* see. He wasn't the type of person who would say anything, though he was Leon's closest friend. She shook her head and furrowed her eyebrows to let him know to keep it to himself. He looked away. He didn't know anything other than the look he saw, which wasn't much.

"What do we do now?" Lucy faced them all.

Clay spoke, "Now we go to the Bloom, and we open the gateway. We go to Mpiaron."

11

The moment they stepped into the Bloom, everyone had changed. They looked exactly like themselves and nothing like themselves at the same time. They were in their element and in their true forms. Everyone looked around and felt the trees and smelled the fruits. All seemed to have come alive with the energy of each other. The trees pulsed to their own rhythm, the butterflies and birds were full of life and neon colors displaying their wings and petals beautifully. The vines grew full in response to the energy they all brought. The scent of the fruits and flowers gave off a mouth-watering irresistible scent. Clay picked a mango, and another mango grew in its place. Everything was alive.

Clay, Dario, and Talan all grew over a foot taller. Towering over everyone else with their skin rippling and their two-toned eyes glowing. Though they all had different features, Talan with his blond hair, Dario with his ebony skin, and Clay with his natural glow, they all resembled in stance and mannerisms. They looked lethal. Lucy had never seen the Guard but would know a Guardian if she saw one.

Omala looked the same, except smoother. The way she walked was smooth. She could have been floating. Her hair *was* floating around her.

Leo and Leon had a slight glow radiating out of them.

Lucy didn't know what the other three were, and she wouldn't ask just yet. Fazi and Alika were the same type of being. Alika was usually much taller than Lucy, she had the same structure to her, but she was different, just a little smaller. She looked like she belonged in the Bloom. Her freckles glowed, her eyes were slightly bigger, and her fingers a little longer. When she walked, the flowers leaned in towards her. She might have been smaller, but her fiery essence was magnified. Fazi was the same. It made sense now. They both had much more in common than red hair and freckles. The way they looked as humans didn't take away from their natural charm of who they were.

Emma, on the other hand, did not look like he belonged in the Bloom. He looked chilling. His entire eyes were a deep onyx. It was like looking into a room void of light. His light skin pale, void of all color covered completely in glossy giant scars. The thought of the amount of pain he endured to get the scars made Lucy's stomach turn. Lucy couldn't place what it was about him, but something was still charming. He walked over to Leon and stood next to him.

That was when Lucy could see it. Emma definitely was not Enkeli, but he glowed just like them. Lucy tried not to stare. Nobody else got the memo as they all stared at each other wide eyed and happy.

"Besides the Guard, everyone else hasn't taken their authentic forms since you were born," Leon whispered so only Lucy could hear him.

"Why not?" She whispered back.

"They couldn't risk giving off even the slightest ripple of light. The Deminio would see it and be drawn to it. A moth to a flame," he said.

"What about now? Doesn't that mean all of us coming here puts us all at risk?" Fear struck every chord in Lucy's body.

She didn't know how to use her abilities yet, unable to protect any of them. Could they even defend themselves? What would happen when she got to Mpiaron? Is three days gone too long?

"Relax, Luc. Don't worry about us. Do what you have to do. Focus on why you're going. There is something there that you need, or else you wouldn't have had the dream. Our dreams are like a map. They often tell us where to go. Sometimes the story is irrelevant, sometimes it's not. Just trust yourself and if you need help, say it aloud. Answers will come to you. You have to go now, Luc. Love you. You can do this, and I will be right here when you get back." Leon gave her a hug and leaned his cheek onto the top of her head.

Her dad also gave her a hug, though not a word was said. He was strong, not tired or physically weak the way he had been the last few years. She looked at him again and noticed he even looked younger, a lot younger. He couldn't have appeared much older than her. His shoulders were broad and his head high, his skin smooth and wrinkle-free. Yet, his eyes were still the same. They held weight and fear and water. She knew he wouldn't let a tear fall. It wasn't in him to cry. Not because he wasn't sad, but because he had faith.

Clay had been giving orders since they entered the Bloom, not that Lucy had been paying attention.

Everyone took their places and looked at her and Clay.

"Ready?" Clay asked her.

She nodded, not trusting her voice. Everything in her was ready. All except for a small piece of her that wanted to go back to the night of the bonfire. When she was eating cookies on Clay's couch. When she was just Lucy, Clay was just her neighbor, and everyone else was just friends and family.

That wasn't the case. They were never *just* anything. They were always this way, only she didn't know. That very thought gave Lucy the boost she needed to keep going. They have all guided her this far and kept her safe for this long. It was now her turn to do the same. Whether they all did it out of love for her or out of duty and obligation didn't matter, they still did it. She wouldn't let them down.

Kona whimpered. It wasn't till that moment Lucy realized she couldn't take him with her. He would have to stay, and guilt flooded her entire body. All she could let out was one tear or else she wouldn't stop crying.

"Kona, Leon will take care of you till I get back, okay? I love you, and I will be back soon. You can sleep on the bed and everything. Be good, my boy." She looked from Kona to Leon. He nodded.

Leon understood that Lucy needed him to do this. She couldn't leave if Kona wasn't going to be taken care of. Kona somehow understood too. He rubbed his head against the tear on her face, walked over to Leon, and sat at his feet.

Lucy inhaled deeply and was ready.

"Alika, Fazi, get started," Clay commanded.

Alika and Fazi went to opposite ends of the Bloom facing inwards. Their palms outstretched in front of them. Though they were slightly smaller in size, they didn't seem small at all.

A low hum could be felt at their feet, just before the trees and vines started moving. They moved the same way they did at Clay's big house next to her dad's when the room turned into a spheric nest to protect Lucy.

The energy of every living thing in the Bloom grew, the butterflies collectively gravitating towards the tree with the carving on it, and the vines were closed in.

Clay began demands again, "Dario, Talan, take the perimeter. You two are not to leave this area at the same time until we return, one of you stays here at all times, and the other can rest at my cottage. Even when more Guardians come, nobody knows the area or Lucy the way you two do. Understand?"

They both nodded and took their places.

The vines continued to move and form a sphere. The more they moved, the thicker the wall of vines got and the darker it became.

"Emma, if you sense anything, no matter how small, let the Guard know. We don't want the Deminio to see you, not yet." Direct demands caused Emma to pull his fist to his heart and bow his head.

"Omala, stay available. If she needs you at any time, answer." Clay looked from Omala to the rest of the circle, "You may begin."

Omala closed her eyes and started whispering to herself. The air around her began to pick up and her hair lifted with the flow of the wind.

"Leon do not worry, or she will feel it. Do not spike any heavy emotions. Let her feel her own self while she is there, or she could wander in the wrong direction towards you or miss something too important to skip. Leo, you help Leon," Clay said directly to them.

He looked at Lucy's father and brother in the eye and said, "I will keep her safe."

Lucy knew he would keep his word.

Clay led Lucy to the tree where the spiral carving was with all of the butterflies. The sphere was absent of most light. She looked at Clay as he reached for both of her hands. He guided her left hand and his right hand to the carving. As soon as they touched it, everything turned black.

Clay focused on only Lucy, "Lucy, close your eyes."

She didn't hesitate.

Clay continued, "Inside, you have a light. I need you to turn it on. The best way to do it is to think of what makes you most authentically happy."

Thousands of memories came flooding her mind. Eating berries at three years old with Leon in the Bloom. Her dad's face when she stood for the first time on a wakeboard at five years old. Lying on the hammock outside her room on the balcony with her dad and Leon, listening to stories while looking at the stars. She thought about when she pulled

Leon's first tooth out because he was too scared. Hundreds of beach days with the people she loved most. She thought of riding the perfect wave. Climbing trees with her friends and staying in them for hours.

Lucy opened her eyes and could see a slight glow illuminating the air around her, the way her dad's and Leon's skin was.

"Good job. But if we want to get to Mpiaron, you'll need to search deeper. Think of the time where you felt most alive," Clay encouraged her.

She could see the glow in his eyes. The green and the blue. It made her think of the rush she felt when she faced him for the first time at the bottom of the cliff the evening of the bonfire. She closed her eyes and thought about that same night when she ate cookies at his house and how Kona had felt at home there. She remembered the blanket he laid out specifically for him. The carvings he made in her new home and the warmth that radiated off of his body when she fell asleep at his house and carried her home. When he confided in her and she was able to tell him her dream. His strength and ease when he faced the demon. The way the light of the fire hit his face when he told her how he felt about her. Then finally, she thought of the kiss. She had never felt more alive than in that specific moment when their lips touched for the first time. When every secret that has been kept from her had surfaced, she finally knew who she was and was no longer afraid of holding back. She let it all go, and the kiss happened.

That's when she felt it, the light inside of her.

She opened her eyes and couldn't believe what she saw. Everything in the sphere was glowing. Millions of iridescent specks of every color glowed throughout. The leaves were still leaves, but the moisture inside of them pulsed and glowed green. The pulsing fruit was lit by the juice inside. Every inch of the Bloom was magical.

Lucy looked everyone in the eye one by one before finally looking at Clay.

"One specific memory came to mind, and I knew." She let herself smile a little, only with her eyes.

"Your eyes are dancing," he whispered so only she could hear him.

He still felt it. Lucy was sure of it now. The moment wasn't over. What had happened between them wasn't a lapse for him. It wouldn't be the last of it.

She began to feel lighter. Her body eased and became less heavy. She glowed brighter. She continued to glow brighter and lighter until the light started blinding her. She closed her eyes and focused on her breathing. Lucy was going to faint. She couldn't hold on anymore. The light was too bright.

Then it wasn't.

She opened her eyes, and everything was back to normal. She was back in the woods again, next to the tree, standing beside Clay.

She had failed. Nothing happened.

"Can we try again? I think I can do it this time. Just give me a minute to catch my breath," Lucy asked.

Exhaustion flooded her body, but she was determined to keep doing it until she opened the gateway or passed out, whichever came first.

Clay was smiling.

"Lucy, we are here. We are in Mpiaron."

Lucy looked around and didn't understand. They were in the woods, in the Bloom.

"Where is everyone?" She asked.

"Back home where we left them."

Everything was the same. Almost. Lucy walked on the path out of the Bloom to show Clay and realized where the Bloom had been, was a natural forest, like the way it was everywhere else. It was reversed. The perimeter was the beginning of what the Bloom had been. All full of fruits, vegetables, flowers, and vines. The entirety of the forest was a

Bloom. Where the Bloom had been back home in Shadow Rock, only had trees. A piece of home within Mpiaron, as the Bloom was a piece of Mpiaron within the forest at home.

The butterflies and birds were everywhere. They somehow glowed in the daylight. There were colors in Mpiaron Lucy had never seen before. A tingle went down Lucy's spine. She looked up at Clay and found him smiling at her. Saying, *I told you so*, with just one look.

"Where do we go from here?" She asked.

"You tell me. What exactly did you do in your dream?"

He picked up some peaches from a nearby tree and gave them to Lucy to put in her bag. She placed them in there, expecting them to barely fit, and they fell, making a large thud. She looked down to see where they fell and realized they were still in the bag. Nothing fell, not on the outside, at least.

Clay was watching her reaction to the bag, "I asked Omala to charm your bag. Its weight and size will not change regardless of what is inside of it."

That made sense. All of Lucy's clothes fit inside of it, and Omala had told her it was magic. She now realized it wasn't the clothes that were made to fit in the bag but rather the bag itself was changed to fit the clothes inside of it.

"Good to know," Lucy said to herself more than to Clay.

"Clay, do you know your way around here?" She asked.

"Yes," he looked around.

"Where is the bridge? In my dream, it was over a river, close to the river mouth that leads to the ocean. The bridge at home in Shadow Rock is in a different location than the one here in Mpiaron," she said.

He nodded.

"If we can get to the bridge, then I will know where to go. We'll start there," Lucy's voice held no doubt.

Clay turned towards her, "It is about three miles from here. Follow me and stay close. If we run into anyone, do not say anything. We don't want anyone knowing you are here. They will start to worry about their safety. More than that, they would also want to help and protect you. If the Deminio feel it, and they would, they'll assume we are starting a war, and they will have confirmation of your existence."

"Okay, I'll wait for my cue. Don't just hint, though. Tell me directly. Otherwise, I won't say a thing," Lucy said.

She trusted him. She felt safe with him, more safe than she felt with anyone else except Leon. When Clay mentioned other people joining in on a war, bile rose in her throat. The thought of someone else risking their life for her made her uneasy. Lucy would never ask someone to do that. She knew her role in the grand scheme of everything was heavy. She just didn't know the weight she would have to carry.

The air here was a different kind of fresh than back home in Shadow Rock. The moisture in the air was fresh on her skin, smelling of salt from the ocean mixed with flowers from Mpiaron. It was hard for her to believe everything here looked like this. There was no definitive trail where they walked, but they didn't need one. The flowers looked the same as they did at home, just boldly different. They had a glow to them, slight, but it was there. Everything seemed so alive. The trees blew in the wind with sound, a light hum, or a whistle. They sang a song only they knew. The wind blew directly through them instead of around them, the way you would blow through a wind instrument. It was soft. Lucy knew she wouldn't hear it if she hadn't focused on it. The moisture in the air rapidly turned thick. A mist and concentration of salt grew in the air with every step they took. They were close to the water. She knew the bridge was near.

"Clay, what is Mpiaron, exactly?" Lucy asked.

She felt a tingle inside as Clay made quick eye contact with her before he continued to lead the way.

"Technically, it is a bubble or a pocket inside of earth's realm. A different dimension within this dimension. There was a time long ago where it was safe for all beings to walk the veil we live in. Slowly evil began taking over, still following the code we live by, except they found loopholes. Their numbers and strength grew with the fear among our people, the Lemurians. Humankind also grew, being fed darkness and sorrow. We tried to maintain the balance the best we could, but we needed a safe place for our kind to live and grow peacefully. When the day comes for a battle, we will be ready. Until then, it is best to keep everyone here in Mpiaron. It was its own village before, where Shadow Rock is now, on the other side of the streams and river made for Enkeli. A structure built for our people. A fortress like no other. The witches found a way to hide it within a tree, the way someone would hide on the other side of a mirror. It is exactly like Shadow Rock. The shores are identical as well as the lake and rivers. The only difference between the two is Shadow Rock has few houses around the lake, where we are now, and nothing on the other side of the river. Mpiaron has nothing around the lake. Instead, it has a whole village on the other side of the river where the bridge leads. Where your dream took place. We knew one day we would merge them again."

Clarity grew with every word Clay spoke, each a piece of a never-ending puzzle.

The trees started to thin out, and Lucy could make out the sound of the river close by.

Help me find where I am supposed to go, Lucy thought to herself.

"Where did you start your dream? At the bridge, or was there much more before it?" He asked.

"Does that matter? Aren't we just going where Adelaide lives?" Lucy wanted to get home soon.

Then she felt a tingle again.

What is that? She asked herself and looked over at Clay, who had quickly looked away.

"It always matters." His skin was rippling.

They walked through the last of the trees and were at the opening where the cliffs started by the ocean where the bridge was.

"This isn't the bridge," Lucy said quietly.

"This is the only bridge." Clay's skin rippled more. A steady vibration under its surface.

He looked around and had been scouting the area.

"I dreamt of a blue stone bridge, remember?" She said.

Clay thought to himself for a moment.

"A blue stone bridge?" He said to himself and shook his head, staring into the distance.

"A blue stone bridge?" He asked, to her this time.

"Yeah, that was the one in my dream," she said.

"The dream you had a couple of days ago, right?" He asked.

"Yes. Why?" Lucy grew uneasy with the questions.

"Lucy, that bridge was restored hundreds of years ago. It is now a wooden bridge." She could see Clay was trying to piece everything together in his head, "The timing of your dream makes more sense now. There was screaming in the distance, and the little boy needed help?"

"Yes, why do you say it like that?" Lucy asked.

"I thought your dream was a piece of history. Everyone in your dream was human because that is all you know. But your dream was a memory, which is a version of what happened. *Someone* called you here," he explained. "There was a time, right before we hid Mpiaron away here, where the Deminio were infiltrating the Lemurians security. The guards were dangerous, killing people because they were powerful. The guards were being possessed at rapid rates."

"The Guardians?" Lucy touched a flower with her fingertips.

"No, we are a type of being. The guards were human, protecting their people. Long gone in this area now, there is not the same kind of threat here." Clay continued to scout the area.

"What do you mean possessed?" She felt sick.

"Actual possession. The Deminio are dark creatures. Literal Demons. They can enter the body of any being and corrupt them, rotting them from the inside out," Clay explained with no emotion. "Want me to finish answering the question before we cross?"

Lucy didn't know why he'd say that until she looked up and took a good look at the bridge. She only noticed it was different but ignored the details until now. It was fifty feet high, which wouldn't be a problem if it wasn't as narrow as it was. She could stand on it, but there wasn't room for someone to stand next to her. She couldn't even take a step sideways, only forward. There was no railing of any kind, just the narrow wooden bridge.

"How could this be stable or safe? I am not usually afraid of heights, but this. This isn't safe."

Panic surfaced. All Lucy could think to do was sit down on the dirt floor and place her palms on the floor next to her.

Inhale, exhale. Inhale, exhale. Inhale, exhale.

Clay surprised her by sitting next to her.

"They made this bridge shortly after the memory of your dream took place. It is narrow without rails to remind us that we have to walk our path unique to us. Nobody can do it for us. It reminds us to trust ourselves." He smiled to himself and looked into the distance, "Let's take a break. Would you mind handing me one of the peaches from the bag?"

She took the bag off of her shoulder and handed it to him. He reached his arm inside, his whole arm, and pulled out two perfectly ripe peaches from the small leather bag. Clay handed one to Lucy. Lucy took a bite, and it was just the way she liked them, perfectly crunchy and ripe. The juice dripped down her chin.

"Almost every fairy tale and folklore you've ever heard of or read is real in some way. Fazi and Alika, for example, are witches from across the ocean in Scotland. Not the same kind of witch as Omala, but earth witches. Some would call them fairies, though fairies aren't what we think them to be. Fazi and Alika could technically be a combination because they work closely with fairies and sprites where they come from. Name any type of being, and I'll answer if they are real or not," Clay continued with their earlier conversation.

"Trolls?" She asked.

Clay paused for a moment to take a bite, "Not in the sense that you'd think. We call them Jinn, and they are not ugly and mean. I mean, yes, they can be, but that is with anything. There are good and bad in every species."

"So, if they're good, they're Lemurians? And if they are bad, they're Deminio?" She asked.

"Not necessarily. Lemurians have dedicated their whole lives to training and protecting. To following their own paths, each unique to them. They would sacrifice themselves without hesitation if that meant saving you. They could also be good and not a Lemurian, living amongst humans, hiding, or finding ways to blend in. On the contrary, they could be evil and not part of the Deminio. When you are Deminio, you are evil. Your soul is lost. There's no going back," Clay said.

"Emma did it. Right? Switched from being part of the Deminio to become a Lemurian?" Lucy asked.

She took the last bite of peach and sat with her thoughts for a moment. Clay hesitated to answer. She looked over at him, and his eyes were distant.

"Yes, he's the only one to ever do so. I'll let him tell you about it. It is not my place to share," he said and gave her a hard look.

Pain struck his eyes when Lucy mentioned Emma.

"Go on," Clay said, redirecting their conversation.

"Vampires?" She asked.

He nodded, and his jaw tightened.

"Sirens?" She went on.

He nodded and eased.

"Okay, can we stop there? I need to take this step by step. Let's stay on a need to know for the time being," she said, laughing through her nerves.

"In due time," he shrugged.

Lucy dug a small hole with her hands and buried her seed in the dirt. Clay smiled and threw his into the water, throwing it further than humanly possible, quickly reminding her he wasn't human.

Unease made its way back to Lucy with one glance at the bridge. It was their next step. She wasn't ready.

Clay stood up, offered his hand, and helped her to her feet.

When she looked him in the eyes, he smiled, *that* smile, the one that was only for her. He pulled her close and grazed her cheek with the back of his fingers.

She knew he felt the pull because she felt it. Lucy leaned into him and laid her head against his firm chest.

"I will always keep you safe. There is never a reason to worry or be afraid. Would you like me to carry you across?" Clay asked.

Lucy laid her head against his chest for a moment before she faced the bridge. She thought about taking him up on his offer when she realized it would be easy for her to get across. If at any moment she felt she couldn't do it, she could ask him for help. She knew she could do it.

They walked towards the bridge, and Clay stepped in front of her placing his foot on the first wooden plank when Lucy grabbed him by the arm.

"I'm going first." All hesitation was gone.

He stepped back and bowed his head. Just like that, the Guardian in him was back. Neighbor Clay was gone.

Lucy took a step forward onto the bridge. It was stable. She looked forward and took another step. Then another, and another, and another.

She paused for a second to let Clay know he could now follow her, but he was only a step behind her. When she took a step, he took a step. They moved as one.

A third of the way across, she had stopped and decided to look down. She was no longer afraid. The river was the same neon turquoise blue as the lake in Shadow Rock. It gave her comfort knowing that it was just calm waters beneath them and not the white rapids she saw in her dream. They continued across the bridge. She could see large and small fish glowing in the water. There were creatures she hadn't seen before though she wasn't close enough to identify what they were. They weren't mundane earthly things that resided on the other side.

When they crossed the bridge, all tension was released. Lucy was embarrassed for being afraid and hoped Clay didn't notice. She didn't want him to think she couldn't handle what laid ahead.

"It already looks different. The colors weren't as vibrant, there was a market right after the bridge, and I already don't see it. What do we do if I don't know where I am going? Where do we go from there?" Lucy knew the answer to her question but wanted reassurance.

"Lucy, if you ever feel like you do not know your way, take a deep breath. You have the answers within, all you have to do is still your mind, and the answer is yours," Clay assured.

It was the sign she needed. Leon said the same thing. Lucy remembered the dream of the angel she had and almost told Clay, but something inside of her told her to wait. The time wasn't now. She knew she had to learn to trust herself, or she wouldn't get far. She wouldn't realize what she needed to.

"Clay, who is Adelaide? She was who I was in my dream," Lucy thought back on her dream.

They stood at the end of the bridge.

"You never told me the full name." He took a deep breath and looked around for any sign of someone or something else.

Clay was patient with Lucy, but she knew he was waiting for her to make the next move. She pulled his arm to the nearby tree line and concealed them so they wouldn't be as exposed. Clay relaxed a little but continued to look around.

"Do you know of an Adelaide?" She asked again.

"Adelaide is a coven. It is like a last name. Adelaide is a surname and the name of the coven as a whole. Some of the strongest Lemurians are a part of Adelaide. It makes me wonder who was calling you, but I do have an idea. The only way they would call you from this side is if they knew you were in danger, or they could foresee the future and needed to let you know. If they are still in the same location when I was here last, then I know where they are. I've mentioned to you time works differently here. We could be here for five minutes, and in the veil we live in, it could be fifteen or thirty. A month here could be a year there or the other way around. It is completely unpredictable," said Clay.

Lucy tried her best to remain unaffected, but her heart started racing again, "What you are saying is my dream was a memory of someone who may or may not be alive and may or may not be useful now?"

Clay laughed to himself and said, "That is half true. Your dreams are always relevant."

Lucy looked at Clay, and his eyes were glowing more than usual. They matched the way Mpiaron was, as did everyone else back at the Bloom. She wondered why she looked the same. She had a slight glow to her before, but now she looked like her usual self. There was no type of glow or anything special about her.

"How will people know that I am from here if I don't look like any of you? They will know I am not from here," Lucy let her thoughts take over.

"Not everyone looks different, and everyone knows each other here. We aren't trying to fool anyone by making you blend in, we are trying to find something," Clay said as he scouted the area again.

They haven't moved since they went to the tree line.

"Back home, everyone looked different, and so did you. I don't know what the vampires or the werewolves look like, but I am sure they don't look like me," she said.

"Some of them do. If you are strong enough, like those on the council, the ones who you grew up with. They can take on human form for extended periods. It takes strength, but it can be done. That is partly why they were selected to help guide you because they can walk in the human realm without revealing their true form, and they're strong enough to change not just their form but their age. We do not want anyone knowing you are here, though. Too many questions will be asked, and like I said before, we need to stay under the radar. Grab the cloaks Omala packed in your bag. We need to put them on before anyone sees us," Clay looked repeatedly from Lucy to their surroundings.

"She didn't pack any cloaks. She only packed me necessities and clothes for a few days," Lucy said as she reached her arm in the small bag.

She found herself feeling around with her whole arm until she came across anything that could feel like a cloak and not her clothes. When she found what felt like a thin woven blanket, she pulled it out.

It was a dark forest green cloak. She reached her other arm in the same spot inside of the bag and grabbed another one. When she pulled it out, it was charcoal gray. Clay got the green one and opened it. With one swift movement, he had it around Lucy's body and was already tying it around the nape of her neck.

He was close enough for her to examine his face. Something she hadn't really had a chance to do, he focused on tying the knot, so she gave herself a few seconds to really look at him. He didn't look a day over twenty-five, and even that was pushing it. He had stubble on his face where usually he was clean-shaven. Lucy felt herself being drawn to him. The pull to him hit her in waves. They had a connection she couldn't understand, not yet. Clay had only given her a few small looks of reassurance. It had her wondering if he regretted their kiss.

"This is the color cloak of the Guard," he said, interrupting her thoughts.

He reached for the charcoal cloak and smiled a half-smile.

"What does the green one stand for?" Lucy asked.

"Nothing, it is a common color," Clay said.

Suddenly shy. She forgot he could pick up on her emotions, "Oh."

Did he know I was thinking about the kiss? She thought to herself and looked everywhere and anywhere, as long as she wasn't looking at him.

"We need to put this first." He motioned at both himself and Lucy, "You Enkeli and I, your Guardian. All other emotions aside right now, we do not have time, everyone is counting on us, and the longer we are here, the more dangerous it gets."

"I understand, Clay. Maybe not to the extent you do, but I'll learn. I am here to do what I have to in order to keep everyone safe and out of the Deminio's reach. I need to work on my thoughts and emotions. I know this. It's strange to me that you feel them. It's something I might never get used to," Lucy looked at him, trying to read anything he might give off.

"I can't read your mind. The only reason I knew you were thinking about last night is because of the way you were looking at me," Clay held back laughter.

Lucy was thankful she didn't blush.

"You've thought about it too?" She asked.

"Yes," Clay said after a moment.

His eyes were glowing, and his body gave off heat. He was right in front of her. He didn't move further away from Lucy after he tied her cloak.

In a moment's time, she felt the change, the pull. He wasn't Guardian Clay. He was neighbor Clay.

Without breaking eye contact, her hands found his. Clay intertwined his fingers with hers and pulled her closer to him, putting his arms around her waist. He closed his eyes and took a deep breath. Lucy could feel tension leave his body. He leaned down and gave her a soft, sweet kiss on her lips. The birds stopped chirping, the wind stopped blowing, the river stopped flowing. Lucy took a breath, and all things continued. She smiled before she opened her eyes. Clay pulled away and put his hands on each side of her face and kissed her forehead.

In one motion, faster than Lucy could see, Clay turned his body all the way around. His arm was suddenly outstretched. He was lunging towards the trees where the path from the bridge leads to the village.

Clay's eyes were glowing again, and his skin rippled. Guardian Clay was back. He was a foot taller than he had been only a moment ago.

She looked in the direction he yelled and saw a knife halfway into the tree. He walked towards it. Lucy trailed closely behind him.

As she got closer, she could see a leaf pinned to the tree by the knife. Clay grabbed the knife and returned it to its holster. He was breathing heavily, and his nostrils flared. He brushed his golden hair with his fingers moving it out of his face.

"That is why it is dangerous for Guardians," his words sharp. "When I let go even the slightest, my senses blur. When I feel whatever it is I feel towards you, I cannot do my best to protect you. This leaf that was falling wasn't a danger to you. I wouldn't have blinked twice at a leaf if I was following the code of the Guardians. This is why it is forbidden."

Lucy realized he had pinned the leaf with the knife against the tree because the leaf was falling. The accuracy was extraordinary. She could see how it could be dangerous. If that was actually someone and he was aiming to kill, he would have killed them.

"I'm okay, Clay. I am safe," Lucy said, her voice as gentle as it could be.

His breathing calmed.

"Let's focus on why we came here. Everything else will wait. In my dream, the marketplace was just past this tree line. Should we walk through it, or should we walk around it? If we follow the coastline, we could cut through the trees from the back of the village and hopefully avoid everyone altogether before we get to where Adelaide was in my dream," Lucy said.

"Good idea, though it would be best we go along the same path as your dream. We mustn't sever from what you did. We would not want to miss something," his voice strong, neighbor Clay had gone entirely.

It gave Lucy clarity for herself, too. She had to put her connection to him in the back of her mind, or else they'd both be in danger. She had to learn to compartmentalize her emotions the way he does. She didn't realize the threat before. Even thoughts she had could change his emotions and actions, it causes him to cross frequencies with hers. It would put him at risk as well as everyone else if Lucy didn't focus.

"Let's go. If you can, walk beside me at all times. I will follow your direction, but you need to feel my cues. Remember, you are not in danger here. Not at the moment and not with these people, but you can cause others to be in danger if they find out who you are," he said.

He opened his cloak and adjusted his knifes position displaying a row of small throwing knives, all ready to be used if need be.

"Okay, got it. I'm ready." Lucy understood what Clay was saying. She had to make sure nobody would see her for their sake, not hers.

12

Lucy and Clay walked in the direction of the trail that would lead them to what was the market before. If her dream took place hundreds of years ago, she only hoped not too much had changed since then. The bridge was enough of a surprise. She didn't need more obstacles added to her growing list.

Lucy could feel the ground beneath her pulsing. It wasn't moving or vibrating, but something about it could be felt. Blood running through veins. The water from the river was loud, and she could feel the trees absorbing fresh water with their roots. Everything was alive here, even the air. With each breath she took, she could feel jolts of energy within her. Every breath she took refueled her.

There weren't many trees between the water and the area where the town started in her dream. The moment she began to think the layout would be different, she saw the adobe houses through the trees. Almost exactly how they were in her dream, an orange cream color. Some roofs were rounded, and some had large palm leaves on them. As they grew closer, she could see how different they were. They didn't look like huts with holes in the walls for windows how they were in her dream. Instead, they were intricately detailed adobe homes. Some were individual houses, others were grouped together. Every window was a transom window, swung fully open with flowers and vines on every one of them.

When they reached the first opening, there was a courtyard. Lucy could see statues and bundles of flowers growing from the ground. In a row along the center of the courtyard were around a dozen or so small trees. They were much smaller than the other trees in Mpiaron. These were only double her height.

Once they entered the courtyard, Clay put his arm in front of Lucy and knelt on one knee towards the trees in the center. He gestured for her to do the same. He had his head down and both hands in his front knee. Lucy followed his lead but wondered why they were kneeling.

"We are entering sacred ground," Clay whispered.

"Thanks," she mirrored his tone.

They stood up and continued walking through the courtyard. Lucy noticed the houses on either side were all similar, but no two houses were the same. She still couldn't tell one home from the next. They all felt the same. All except for the doors. Each was painted and carved with different colors and textures. Most of them were bright and bold. She could see specific carvings on doors with the same colors. The predominantly red doors had a symbol that looked like a braid or sequence of knots intertwining throughout the length of the door. They were all different though, every red door felt the same. The primarily blue doors had feathers and wings, some had a bird, but all had the same theme. Different color doors brought the earth-toned village to life. There was a common theme between the same colors. Red, teal blue, different shades of green, orange, and royal purple, were all so beautiful and seemed to fit in with how Mpiaron felt.

Lucy turned around to look at the center of the courtyard with the small trees and statues. The flowers that grew around them were well-groomed and unlike the rest of Mpiaron she had seen, all grew wildly beautiful. These, on the other hand, were maintained by someone. The vines snaked around the trees, only connecting them weblike. The trees twisted in the same direction, small vortexes within them causing them to twist and turn and connect. Branches hung overhead, each tree having hundreds of colored ribbons and cloth tied to it in knots draping down just barely. All of the colors linked to the tree completed them. It was magical.

"What are these for?" Lucy asked as she reached up and grazed her fingers on the hanging ribbons above her head.

"They are oaths. Promises. Our people bonding themselves to the Light. As Lemurians, we each make an oath that sets us apart from others. We devote our lives to the Light. When we tie the knots, the oath cannot be broken without consequences. If we choose to aid Deminio or Darkness of any sort, we die a permanent death," Clay said.

Lucy could see his body shake at the thought of breaking the oath.

"How would they die? If you broke your oath, how would you die?" Lucy said.

"I will not break my oath," he said a little too quickly.

Lucy knew she struck a chord, "I am not saying you would."

"It is my duty," Clay paused, trying to find the right words. "It is my duty to exile anyone who breaks their oath."

He swallowed and looked ahead at the trees and ribbons. He wouldn't look at Lucy.

"Why is it your responsibility?" Lucy asked.

Clay looked past her and waved towards the sacred ground at a twisting tree full of ribbons.

She couldn't see anyone when she turned around. Lucy looked through the trees on the other side. Nobody was there.

Then she saw movement and looked closer. It was a small man, no taller than two feet. His skin was an earthy tone, greener than flesh-colored, allowing him to blend in seamlessly. His amber eyes were large and wide. They were aware of more than just what appeared to the eye. She could see that. He looked human, just a more animated version. His features were lengthy, his arms and legs were long in comparison to his body. His ears and nose were pointy and proportioned smaller than a humans would be. Lucy could see his skin was soft even without touching it, and on either side of his forehead, he had small black horns poking out of his long curly ash black hair.

"Clay, what are you doing here?" The little horned man asked him, looking Clay up and down repeatedly.

He was either shy or afraid. Lucy couldn't tell which.

"Hello, Jasutin, old friend. I am here because I need to find someone. We are just clearing out a slight mishap on the other side. All is well," Clay said.

He took a step in the direction they were headed before and guided Lucy along with him.

"*Lucy*? Is that you?" Jasutin said to her.

Lucy looked at Clay whose skin had started trembling the way it does when he is protecting her, the way the Guardians do when they are hyper-alert. Clay's face had flashed ice cold. He didn't reveal anything. Lucy reminded herself not to say anything until he asked her to.

"Jasutin, you must not tell a soul of our presence. Not even the flowers. They gossip. Do you understand?" Clay ordered.

Commands were heavy in Clay's tone, and by the look on both of their faces, he had the authority to do so.

"Yes, Clay, I understand." Jasutin looked down, "It is just, if I may, we haven't seen new faces in hundreds of years. Anyone here would recognize a new face, especially yours. Especially when you walk next to her."

He was uncomfortable and looked towards Lucy's feet but didn't look up at their faces. He was trying to help.

When Jasutin finally did look up, he couldn't stop staring at Lucy. Clay clenched his jaw and grew more irritated with each passing moment, though Jasutin was too distracted to notice.

"Are we in danger?" Jasutin asked, breaking the silence. He walked close to them, jumping over a few large roots.

"Not yet. We need to get to the Adelaide's without being seen by anyone. Much has changed since I've been here last. Can you help us?" Clay asked.

Lucy knew Clay had respect for Jasutin. He had the power to command him to help us and keep a secret. Two heavy burdens to bear.

"Yes. You will not be seen," Jasutin bowed his head. He smiled an awkward, pointy-toothed smile, "Let's go back the way you entered before anyone else sees or feels you."

Clay looked around, "No, we need to go through. She must not miss a thing."

"What is more important to you? Missing something or not being seen?" Jasutin asked and immediately looked down.

Before Clay could answer, Lucy stepped in, "Being unseen. We don't want anyone to know we're here."

Clay gave her a hard look but stayed quiet. He would have picked not missing something, but Lucy thought about the people of Mpiaron. She didn't want anyone getting hurt or being put at risk for simply knowing she was there.

"I get elixirs for the trees from them. Follow the willow trees around the outskirts, do not take the path along the water. Take the path along the forest. The willow trees will lead you to the Adelaide's. Nobody will be out in that direction. They'll all be by the water today. Every seventh day, we give thanks to the water, a ritual we all adapted to after the gateway was closed. The Adelaide's will also be gone. Make sure to get inside and wait, away from everyone else. I'd hurry though, it is quite a long walk, and our people will be making their way to their homes by nightfall," Jasutin said.

He pointed at the first willow and sent them on their way before he hurried back to his tree.

When they got to the first willow tree, Lucy remembered the words of the little boy in her dream. *Use the wood to find your way.* She could see the second willow tree in the distance, and they followed its direction. She smiled.

"What is he?" Lucy asked.

"Jinn. They are now limited to part of the middle eastern culture because they are the only people who strongly believe in them anymore. Many humans claim to have seen them or claim to be able to control them. If anyone thinks they can control Jinn they have gone mad. It is an illusion. Jinn are also known as Djinn, Dgenn, or Genie. Not the typical sense of a genie, though. They can be loyal as the Guard or as cruel as Deminio. They can ask for things you are attached to in order to have small power over you in exchange for a favor. They are smart and clever, fond of tricks and illusions. If you find one as loyal as Jasutin, you are incredibly lucky. The ones here in Mpiaron are Lemurians. Everyone here is. Amongst other things. That is part of being a Lemurian, being able to guide those in search of the Light with our Light without manipulating or explaining. We let people find us and follow our examples. We do not try to win anyone over. They find the Light in their own time," said Clay.

He reached for her hand, holding it face up, and pretended to cut her palm with his finger.

"Most Jinn ask for blood."

He was serious.

As Lucy looked into his eyes, she felt the pull, the one that connected them.

He must have felt it, too, because he dropped her hand and continued to walk to the nearest willow.

Lucy could barely make out the houses through the trees, just pops of adobe here and there. The trail Jasutin put them on was just like the rest of Mpiaron. Full of harvest. She was about to pass a blueberry bush when she crouched down and started picking berries. She looked up at Clay, who stopped a few feet in front of her, waiting calmly. His eyes looked around as he scouted the area.

"I would not usually rush you, but we don't have the time right now. If you are hungry, we can pick something easier to collect. We can stop and rest once we get back home. Right now, we have to continue, especially since we don't know where we are going and can be found at any time. Focus, please," Clay's voice was softer than usual.

"Yeah, okay," said Lucy.

She stood up. Sorrow filled her as she kept forgetting they were on a time crunch, but she also felt overwhelmed with the lack of information she knew. She didn't know much, and much of what she did know, she didn't understand. Jasutin, for example, how could Lucy know about Jinn if she had never met him? Clay could explain everything he knew in detail as much as he could, but Lucy would never fully understand until she saw or experienced whatever it was he wanted her to know. She would try her best, but for now, she had decided to keep all of her questions to herself. If there was something she needed to know, she trusted Clay to tell her.

They continued through the forest from willow to willow. Lucy still had a handful of blueberries and offered Clay a few by extending her hand to him. He shook his head. She shrugged it off and ate one. Immediately she felt a jolt of energy. Its juices exploded in her mouth as she gulped the juice of the blueberry. There was no way all of that juice came out of one berry, though it did. After eating a few, she was no longer hungry. Any weariness she felt had deceased.

A few berries remained in her hand. She offered them to Clay again. This time he didn't say no. Instead, he stretched his arm out, and

Lucy poured the rest of them in his hand. He ate them all in one bite, and she saw him smiling to himself as he chewed.

"Something funny?" Lucy asked.

"All of my existence, I have been around places like this, and I am still amazed every time. Gifts like these are treasures." He gestured towards the trees.

Lucy knew this was true, she could be around this place for the rest of her life, and she knew she would never grow tired of it. She admired Clay for that. He could still see beauty in the smallest of things, even after all this time and after everything he has seen. Clay was special in more ways than she knew. It wasn't just because he was her Guardian, it wasn't because of his oath bond to her, it was because of the little things like him smiling from a blueberry, or him choosing to make cookies from scratch, or the shy smile he has when he is around her. But she couldn't tell him. She wouldn't tell him, not yet.

Her eyes followed the trail, and she felt Clay looking at her. She turned to see him looking at her from the side of his eyes. Part of her wondered what he was thinking or if he could feel her thinking about him. His eyes glowed brighter and he smiled *that* smile.

They continued to walk for over an hour when she could sense they were almost there. The trees were thinning out again and had already begun to turn towards where the last houses were. They were on the complete opposite side of where the bridge was, close to the den Lucy saw in her dream.

She was looking closely at the structures throughout the walk. From what she could see in this distance, each house has been individual adobe homes since just after they began their walk. When they approached a cluster of homes connected to each other, she knew they had arrived. It looked exactly the same from the back. She could make her way there and would know exactly which door would lead her to the den in her dream.

13

Lucy could feel the energy from the side of the den. In her dream, she felt all of Adelaide's emotions, unable to rid of those so quickly. Lucy felt the memories of this place. She remembered how safe she felt in her dream when she got home to this den. The smells of smudge sticks and food cooking over the fire filled the air. When they reached the front, she led the way and went down the hall to a wooden door with a moon pendant on it. It was Adelaide's house.

Lucy pointed at the door. Clay knocked, staying between her and the door.

Nobody answered.

Clay knocked again.

Still, nobody answered.

"I'll go first," he said.

Clay pushed the door open and walked in, gesturing for her to follow and stay close to him.

When she walked in, the open space had looked almost exactly the same. The blankets were still on the floor next to the fire where she slept. The floor was now smooth adobe tiles instead of rough dirt. The herbs were hanging under the window on the wall like they did. There was a small table with chairs next to a bookshelf, which wasn't in her dream. Lucy looked at the books and could see they weren't books but journals. They were all in a language she didn't understand in unrecognizable writing. They were symbols going in different directions, not linear in up or down or side by side motions, but randomly placed characters.

"I have been waiting for you," Adelaide said as she walked through the door. A flash of memory from her dream that she didn't remember clearly, surfaced. When she looked in the mirror and connected with hazel eyes instead of her brown eyes. When she saw Adelaide, she looked into the hazel eyes of her dream.

"Owranoos?" Clay said before he looked at the beautiful woman who walked through the door.

"Hello Clay, Lucy," she looked towards them both and smiled a warm, assertive smile.

Clay walked towards her and extended his arm, "I knew it was you." They shook forearms, and Clay slightly bowed. Owranoos did no such thing.

"Where is Adelaide?" Lucy asked.

"I am Adelaide. Owranoos Norfali Adelaide," Owranoos said. "But you can call me Rani."

She smiled again and walked to Lucy, pulling her into a soft embrace.

"I called you here because I feel darkness. Nobody else can feel it, I am sure of it. But it is getting closer with each passing day. What is your age now?" Rani asked.

Lucy appreciated her bluntness. She also liked how she skipped any introduction. They were familiar strangers.

"I turned twenty-two a couple of days ago," said Lucy.

"Aah. Figures as such. They feel you now. I can feel them trying to get in through the trees, but they haven't found *the* tree." Rani looked into the distance, "Not yet."

"A scout came to the safe house in search of her. It knows more than they are letting on." Clay had a look in his eyes Lucy didn't recognize.

"Okay. Let us gather what we need, then we will be on our way. Make sure you change your clothes under your cloak. You want to blend in more than that. Though I don't know if it is possible at all for you to blend in." Rani reached into a woven basket and pulled out clothes, "These should fit."

Lucy changed underneath her cloak, as did Clay.

"What are we going to do now?" Lucy tried not to give much away, she truly didn't know how she felt.

"We need to trace your dream. I sent a calling for you but whatever you saw in your dream has value I don't remember. It was a long time ago for me and not so fresh in my memories. If there is something we need to know, it is on the path you took in your dreams. We need to follow it before heading back," Rani said.

"Let's go now," Lucy said and walked towards the door when Rani ran in front of the door before Lucy could open it.

"Wait. Everyone is going to be headed back home by now. Unless you want our people to know you are here, you need to stay unseen."

"We should not wait. Though we cannot have people see either of us. You have all been here for hundreds of years. Alone. No new people could come in. It makes sense why Jasutin recognized Lucy so easily," Clay was trying to make sense of what was going on.

"You saw Jasutin? What did he say?" Rani asked.

"He only told us how to get to you without running into anyone else. He said to follow the willows," Lucy thought back to anything else he might have said.

"Where did you see him?" Rani was curious.

Lucy could see the curiosity growing within Rani's hazel eyes.

"Templom. I am sure we weren't seen by anyone else. I would know if we were seen by anyone," Clay answered.

"What's Templom?" Lucy knew the answer as soon as she asked.

"Templom is the area of trees and statues in the main central courtyard when you first enter the village through the side of the bridge. It is sacred to our people. It is where we go when we want to reach anyone on the earth realm and where we go when we need to talk to the Angels. They leave us messages with the flowers. There have only been a few messages, but in times of solitude like these, those few messages make a difference. The statues represent some of our people," Rani explained in a gentle tone. She was open to any explanation and patient with her words.

Lucy didn't get a good enough glimpse at Templom when they were there.

"Okay," was all she could say.

At the mention of angels, she remembered the hallucination she had when she was half asleep and almost told the both of them at that moment, but again, something inside of her didn't allow her to say it aloud. She's been feeling that feeling more and more lately, listening to something inside of her. It was as if it was helping her, guiding her, a subconscious that has grown its silent voice.

Lucy looked over at Clay. He stood close to the windows looking out, constantly checking to see if anyone was listening in or if anyone was going to make their way towards Owranoos's home.

"Why can't we tell people? Let them know what is going on, tell them to stay calm, and let them know when we need their help, we will ask for it. I understand they'll want to help but isn't it better if we give them a warning?" Lucy asked.

"We are a loyal people. There will be an uprising in energy. Awakening magic we have laid to rest long ago. We know there will be a time when we need to awaken it, but we are here as Lemurians to *protect* you. We completely closed off Mpiaron the day you were born. Before that, we would rarely go to the other realm, only when absolutely necessary. The day you were born, we couldn't take any chances. If we were on the other side, the Deminio would know where we were by the energy we give off. Moth to flames, it would ignite the battle that has been building for eons. We couldn't take the risk with you so young. We need your power if we have any chance at survival. Telling our people now, with you undeveloped, would be sentencing them to death," Rani was sharp and wasn't giving Lucy direct orders, but Lucy knew that telling the Lemurians wasn't an option by the tone in Rani's voice.

"Lucy, let's get some rest. It is almost nightfall. Once everyone is asleep, we can trace your steps," Clay told Lucy.

She was about to say they should figure out something else, some sort of plan, when she saw Clay shake his head so only she could see. He didn't want Lucy to say anything else in front of Rani.

Lucy knew immediately she could trust Rani, this she was sure of.

What is Clay not telling me? She thought to herself.

They continued to make eye contact, and Lucy was trying to understand what Clay meant. She traced back every word from their conversations and didn't understand why he would want to hide anything. But, when she looked at him again, his eyes were focused and collected.

She knew Rani could tell something was going on because she turned around, awkwardly, towards the fireplace and mixed whatever was in the pot.

A few more awkward moments passed when Rani spoke up, "I will go to the bakery and get a few things. You two rest."

Her emphasis showed there was really something going on, something she didn't know. It was respectable of Rani to give them space in her own home.

Rani went to the door and got a large wicker bag from the floor next to the doorway. She turned around to made eye contact with Lucy and smiled with her eyes. When Rani turned to Clay, her face fell. The look was swift. Lucy was unsure whether it was intentional or not, but when she turned to look at Clay, she could see his face fell too. Rani was out of the door before she could look at her again.

"What was that all about?" Lucy asked Clay.

"I haven't seen any of these people since you were born, most since before. It didn't feel long to me until I realized it has been hundreds of years for them and only twenty-two for me. They've lived without loved ones and in total seclusion for the sake of Light. Rani has a history, and so do I. One you know nothing of. I wanted you to realize what they sacrificed before you said something you wouldn't understand," Clay spoke softly.

His eyes were distant as thousands of thoughts and memories flashed through his eyes.

"I understand," Lucy said.

She wondered if Clay and Rani had some sort of relationship. They were both awkward around each other. She couldn't look him in the eyes.

"Lucy, it is not what you think it to be. Owranoos and I were friends long ago. She has a history with a close friend of mine. They are soul-mates and haven't spoken since the day you were born. I have lived my entire existence knowing I could never be in any sort of romantic rela-tionship," his words were carefully crafted.

Lucy let out stress with a breath.

Clay walked towards her, "The only connection I feel and have ever felt is ours." He grabbed Lucy's right hand and put her palm on his sol-id chest. She could feel his heart beating through his clothes. Warmth radiated from his body. He reached out softly with his other hand and touched her chin, pulling it up so she could look at him.

"Do not forget it," Clay smirked.

He leaned into her and put his forehead to hers first, then put his nose to hers too. He closed his eyes and took a deep breath, breathing Lucy in.

Lucy thought he was going to kiss her when he pulled away.

"I won't," she said, only her voice was too soft for him to hear.

"Would you mind if I retrieved a few items from your bag?" He asked.

"Nope. Not at all." She took it off of her shoulder and handed it to him.

He reached his titan-like arm in the bag and pulled out a few blankets and two small pillows.

"I swear I only saw Omala pack a few sets of clothes in there," Lucy said and laughed to herself in disbelief.

"She could still put things in there. She put these in after you two packed. There is much more in there now than earlier. I told her to make sure you had everything you need. I even felt a tent in there," Clay laughed, too.

He made a bed on the floor in the corner of the room where there was nothing. Lucy wondered why he only made one bed and not two.

"I need to stay awake. If I get tired, I'll make a bed for myself," he said and smiled at Lucy.

Lucy took her cloak off and set it on a hook next to the door. She took her shoes off and walked over to her bed on the floor. When she laid down and covered herself, she was surprised at how soft and comfortable the floor was. Her eyes were suddenly heavy and more tired than she knew. The adrenaline from the day was fading. As she grew tired, her stomach grew uneasy, and she felt too far away from home. Too far away from Leon, she didn't realize how she could always just feel him even when they weren't close to each other. Being in separate realms felt like a bad signal, a bad connection. He *felt* far.

Lucy took a deep breath, "Can you sit next to me, please?"

She started to shake from the feeling of being far from Leon.

Clay walked over to her and sat on the floor beside her. He leaned back on his hands with his feet towards the fire. He put a hand on Lucy's cheek and stroked it with his thumb until she drifted to sleep.

She was no longer shaking. She wasn't nervous or overwhelmed or uneasy. She was okay. She was safe.

Clay was humming a familiar tune. While Lucy slept, she could feel the song's rhythm in her dream, a rhythm that kept her going.

"Has she shown any signs?" Rani whispered, trying not to wake Lucy.

Lucy kept her eyes closed and her breathing heavy, not wanting them to know she was awake.

"More than she knows. She expanded the Bloom. She has been building on the old barn where she currently lives and can carry triple what a regular human her size should be able to carry. Her balance is impeccable. She swims and can hold her breath for extended periods of time. When she writes and sketches at night, her skin glows so bright I could see it from inside of my cottage. She has no idea she does any of it. She was going to find out soon anyway, even if the demon wouldn't have shown up. Her gifts are strong, and she doesn't notice. It makes me interested to see how she will be once she starts exercising her gifts. What will she be then? What will be her true gift? She was placed here for a reason. She has to be strong. Know what I mean?" Clay said.

"I do. Why have you not tried yet? Why did you not tell her before? She could have been developing her skills her whole life. Why keep them from her? Her knowledge is that of a child," Rani said.

Lucy felt her heart pounding. If it weren't for Rani's soft tone, she would have been insulted.

A tingle covered her body, and she knew Clay's eyes were on her. He was checking to see if she was awake. Lucy breathed heavily and didn't move, too curious to know what his answer would be.

"When she was a toddler, she would get sick, too powerful for her young mortal body. We had plans to tell her as she got older, but Leo refused. I half agreed with him. Her body needed to develop in her own time without the force and pressure making her ill. I did not want her to wear her body down. The other half of me knew that if we trained her, she would be stronger than all of us, which is what we all want and pray for. But with the magnitude of her gifts, she would also attract Deminio, causing her to be unsafe, and if she wasn't fully in her power, she would die. A double edge sword with nowhere to go. Either way, there would have been consequences. We just had to do what seemed best for her with each passing day," Clay didn't whisper, but his deep tone was low.

The air grew thick with the mention of Deminio.

"I understand. You would be wise to remember I do not go gentle. If I am to go with you, I will help her on my terms. Not yours and not Leo's," Rani said after a few moments had passed.

"I know," pain clear in Clay's voice.

Lucy could only imagine what he looked like right now. She continued to breathe heavily.

"How is… *he?*" Rani asked.

Lucy knew she was referring to the soulmate Clay had told her about. Rani was curious. She was also eager. She couldn't even say his name aloud.

"He's, well, him," Clay said.

Lucy knew that tone. He didn't want to talk about whoever he was. Not to Rani.

"But he is okay?" Rani pushed.

Lucy opened her eyes to see Clay's response but made eye contact with him instead. She played it off and stretched. Naturally, she let out a huge yawn but dramatized it to make it seem as if she had barely awakened.

"Are you hungry?" Clay asked Lucy.

He didn't answer Rani's question.

Lucy nodded, worried her voice would betray her and give away the fact that she was spying on them when they thought she was sleeping.

Clay got up and walked over to the fireplace from where he was sitting. He reached for the ladle and poured whatever was in the pot over the fire into wooden bowls. He got a few pieces of homemade bread from the basket and walked over, handing them to Lucy.

The smell filled the room. Lucy could taste it even before she had her first bite. The bread was fresh and warm and the soup hot.

"It is a vegetable soup with fresh wild herbs and a sourdough bread also infused with wild herbs. We are going to need them if we are to remain unseen tonight," Rani said.

The spoon was warm and made of a pale stone. The wooden bowl kept Lucy's hand safe from the soup's heat. Lucy stayed sitting on the floor wrapped in her blankets. Clay and Rani both joined her on the floor when they finished serving themselves.

When Lucy took her first bite, there was nothing she could compare it to. It was like nothing she had ever tasted before. The soup was thick but smooth. The vegetables were full of nutrients. She could taste every vegetable individually. Carrots with broccoli and potatoes, the tomatoes popped with more flavor than a tomato should have. She could actually feel herself healing on the inside. She was numb to the everyday pain of being sore and exhausted. Everything hurt less and less until it was all gone. She could feel no trace of discomfort or unease.

The bread melted in the warmth of her mouth.

"What's in here? It's wonderful," Lucy asked between bites.

"The same thing all soup and bread is made of," Rani's voice was playful, and her eyes matched.

Lucy didn't understand. There were flavors in here she couldn't place.

"Mpiaron is all connected. That's why it glows the way it does. You could feel the water going in the trees and pulsing through every leaf. When you pick a fruit or a vegetable here, it doesn't stop being connected to the earth or anything else. What you are eating is giving you the connection. It connects you to the earth and to the people who are here. It connects you to the trees and the animals, even the water. Everyone here gives the same amount they take. You can see the light within Mpiaron. That is why it glows," Clay explained.

Lucy appreciated him doing his best to fill any gaps for her. Even if it was just because of his duty to her. She looked at him and smiled. His smile was slight just before he took another bite of the warm bread.

"Well, it is that, and I infused it with magic. I am a witch after all," Rani said casually and continued to eat her food.

Clay laughed unbothered, and Lucy didn't know how to feel.

Was she kidding? She thought to herself.

"No, she's not kidding," Clay answered.

"It won't harm you, don't worry. I would never harm you. You have my word," Rani said.

Her smile held promise Lucy trusted.

"Then why did you put magic in my food?" Lucy asked as she stared at her food, appetite gone.

"We need the aid of magic," Rani explained. "I put herbs in the soup and in the bread that will aid our mission tonight. I also charmed these necklaces for us."

She stood up and opened a drawer from a wooden dresser. Out of it, she pulled a small wicker box that held the necklaces she spoke of. Rani handed one to Clay and one to Lucy.

Lucy looked over at Clay's necklace. It was a pendant on a leather strand. The pendant was a raw blue opal, colors mixing blue and green, identical to his eyes. The opal was wrapped in a copper-wired cage. When Clay put it on, it was as if it had always been there. It was a part of him.

Lucy's necklace was identical to Clay's, all except for the stone. Hers was a white opal, much more manicured than Clay's as it was a flat circle, perfect and even. The copper was wildly wrapped around the stone, the necklaces matched their personalities. In a wave of awakening, she suddenly understood much more about her energy. She is the center of her Light that radiates within her. Like the stone, when Light touches it, it glows. When Lucy shines her Light from within, she glowed too.

"Wow," Rani whispered.

Lucy looked up at her and Clay. They both had the same strange look on their faces.

"What's going on?" Lucy asked.

Clay stepped forward towards Lucy and reached for her hand and held it up. When Lucy looked at it, she could see what they were seeing. Her skin was glowing. Not the soft glow that Leon and Leo had when they were opening the Gateway to Mpiaron from the Bloom, and it wasn't wild like the way her skin glowed before either. This was much stronger than that. It also wasn't a constant glow. It was waves of light on the surface of her skin, pulsing like the trees. As her blood pumped through her veins, the light traveled in and around her. This glow was much more obedient.

Rani came and picked up the necklace from Lucy's hands and placed it around her neck. When Rani removed it from Lucy's hands for a moment, Lucy had stopped glowing.

"These necklaces will help hide you when you need it. They can help neutralize your powers for the both of you." Rani looked back and forth from Clay to Lucy, "When we get out tonight, it will appear to everyone else as though I am walking alone. As long as you both focus and ask the stones for help, all should go as planned. No one will suspect to look further than what they can see with their eyes. We have become stronger at war and skill, but we don't think to look for danger anymore.

We do not expect an attack without warning, and we have not gotten a warning. This should work in our favor."

"Let's begin," Clay said.

He was in his element, and he was beaming. This was almost a game to him. It was infectious. Lucy felt the excitement. Finally, they could openly see the plan in front of them without entirely winging it.

14

Lucy, Clay, and Rani had all changed and got ready to start tracing the path from her dream and from Rani's memory. Lucy revisited her most vivid memories. She also hoped Rani would do the same with her own recollection of her actual memories. Though Rani had explained they couldn't rely on her memories as much as Lucy's because it was long ago for her, and selective memory had taken place. Lucy only hoped she could remember enough to find something useful.

"Could you try to remember, too? Just in case I forget something," Lucy asked.

"Yes, I will do my best. But I should mention, I sent a calling for you, not the memory of the dream. The dream was sent to you as the calling. Angels don't make mistakes when they intertwine messages. I, myself, don't remember that day so well, but I do remember those times. I could never forget them," pain seeped into Rani's eyes. "Trust there is reason behind the dream finding you. After all, nothing happens by coincidence."

Rani gave Lucy the same tight smile as she had earlier.

"We are going to start here and make our way to the location of the beginning of your dream on the other side of the bridge. After, we will come back here the exact way you did. Starting from here might show you something you didn't see the first time," Clay said.

Clay continued talking to Rani. He asked more questions from her point of view and was filling in any significant adjustments Mpiaron had since the last time he had been there. He was covering all of the bases. Lucy wandered off after that and stared at them both. She could see the connection between Clay and Rani. They were friends, not just acquaintances, but friends by choice. They've spent years knowing each other. Rani wasn't shy with Clay, not that she was a shy person, only reserved, but she had no reservations with him. None at all. Clay was also reserved and with Rani, he was not. His eyes were calm. He was spoke clearly to her, not assertive like he was to everyone else. The way he was when he directed them to open the Gateway. Rani followed his requests because she trusted him as a friend, not only as a leader. There was plenty of reason to believe they have more of a history than they will say. Lucy wouldn't usually snoop for information, but she did want to know more about who they were talking about earlier when she pretended to be asleep. It had to have been someone she knew, or did it? Lucy knew it couldn't have been Leon, that ruled one person out. She also grew up with most of their friends, but she assumed they were able to choose and adjust their ages according to what Lucy needed at the time. It could be any one of them as Lucy didn't know the actual ages of everyone. Even her father.

For a moment, she wondered if Rani had been with her father and couldn't see it. Lucy erased the thought immediately. Her father had appeared to be growing older and influenced poorly by his age, his health on the decline, but when the demon came, he jumped off the deck and ran like nothing was unhealthy about him. In the Bloom, before they left, he looked younger.

It was easy to believe everything she had ever known was a lie. Her friends were not her friends. They were oath-bound to protect her. Her dad and Leon lied to protect her, only to harm her in the process. None of that felt right. Those thoughts didn't sit well with her. She chose to believe her friendships were authentic. Friendships could be formed out of bonds and service. Lucy knew that. They could protect Lucy from a distance if they wanted to. Everything inside of Lucy told her they protected her because of the love they had for her.

If all was the way she thought it to be just a few days ago, if they were all human, not Enkeli or witches or Guard, she truly believed they would all still be friends. A part of her even believed she would have met Clay anyways, and somehow, they would still have the connection they do now.

Lucy's thoughts spiraled in many different directions. Clay and Rani continued to map out what they were going to do. They tried to find the easiest way around Mpiaron to run into the least amount of people. Though they would be hidden, it would take much less energy for them to go through without bumping into anyone. It would help them focus on the task. She didn't need to help them with this. She didn't know Mpiaron or the beings who lived there enough to have valid input. Lucy had no knowledge of what kind of beings they were or what any of them could do. All of this was new to her, yet somehow familiar.

"Okay, let's go," said Clay.

"Lucy, remember you need to focus extra on keeping your Light off and continuously tell yourself that you are unseen. The more you believe it, the easier it will be for me to shield you from others," Rani's tone was soft as she explained to Lucy what she needed to do. Lucy appreciated how direct Rani was.

"I'll do my best," Lucy smiled.

Readiness was all Lucy could feel. She hadn't been ready or prepared for much the last few days. Having all day to plan and rest made this easier for her to handle.

Clay's skin vibrated, and his eyes glowed. Lucy wondered how he could help protect her and still be shielded by Rani's invisibility spell. She might know the answer if she paid more attention to their conversation earlier instead of doubting her whole life.

"The moment we step out of these doors, the spell will begin. Are you ready?" Rani spoke to both Clay and Lucy, but Clay and Rani looked at Lucy.

She nodded.

Rani went to the wooden door and lit a white candle just to the side of the doorway. Whispering to herself something in a language Lucy couldn't place. She moved the candle in circular motions around them, then around the doorway before placing it on the small table next to the front window. Rani walked out of the front door and took a few steps before gesturing for them to follow her. As soon as Lucy and Clay stepped outside, the air around them shifted, and all sound was muffled. It sounded as if they were in a bubble. Lucy could still see Clay and thought it didn't work at first, Rani turned around to look at them, and her eyes looked into the distance. Lucy knew she couldn't see them, and they continued to trail closely behind her.

"What's going on?" Lucy asked.

Her whisper was hardly audible, but Clay answered.

"It is a part of the spell. Nobody can see us as long as Owranoos can't see us," he said, his voice normal.

He wasn't trying to conceal his voice.

"How will she know where to go?" Lucy asked.

"I told her the direction of your dream, where to go, and where you stopped. We will have to follow her the whole time, but if there happens to be anything you need to stop to see or get, we stop without her. It is slightly risky, but we will just have to catch up," he said.

"Okay."

She was going to continue asking questions until she looked away from Clay and took a look around. Mpiaron was definitely not the same as in her dream, partially because it was night. Mostly it was the same layout and concept, only not the same exact way. It had evolved. It glowed. The whole village was alive. They didn't need lights or torches or anything of the sort. When Rani walked, the floor beneath her feet lit up in small waves like a single drop of water hitting a calm, steady lake. The glow around the village was illuminated brightly by the moon and stars, which happened to be much brighter here. There was no light pollution. The essence of the vines and flowers also glowed. All were their own subtle neon lights against already illuminated surfaces. The trees surrounding the village glowed. The leaves had small freckles which glowed separately from the actual leaf. The flowers and petals had veins as thin as a single hair and pulsed with multicolored light.

It was nothing short of breathtaking. In the distance, the air had small specks of light, similar to that of a firefly, but it wasn't a bug, only orbs moving with the flow of the wind.

The path that they took was an alley or a small narrow street of some sort. The adobe homes were all soft in color, they did not glow, but their doors did. The colors Lucy saw earlier were still there, but the glow made the depth of the images dive. Mpiaron was the home of Lemurians, and she could now see they *are* the Light. They *live* in their Light. This was different than what Lucy had expected it to be, even though she hadn't thought about it too much. She just didn't expect it to be this magnificent.

As she continued to walk, she could see the small orbs moving around the alley. They seemed to have stopped in place, scattered and no longer moving around with the wind. One orb was floating towards them and manifested itself into a person. She knew he was a witch because he closely resembled Alika and Fazi when they changed forms in the Bloom.

"Ei there Owranoos," the witch said, his voice much more profound than she expected it to be by just looking at him. His accent was heavy.

"Leith, what a magical night. Isn't it?" Rani said to him.

"Ay," Leith nodded. "The uisge changed this evening."

"Uisge means water in Gaelic," Clay whispered quickly to Lucy. She nodded.

"Mpiaron is speaking to us, 'tis a night for us to pay attention. Keep an eye out, Owranoos. Somethin' is a brewin'," Leith said as he glided back into a floating orb with the rest of his people.

"Many thanks, Leith," Rani said.

Her tone showed no sign of the alarm Lucy felt.

"Leith is from a clan in Scotland. Out of the thousands of witches from there, only fifteen of them chose to be Lemurians. Two of which you know, Alika and Fazi," Clay said.

"They don't have as heavy accents," Lucy thought back to the last time she heard them talk.

"Not in front of you," he said.

Lucy remembered the accent Alika had the last time she saw her and nodded.

"They were hunted by Deminio before reaching a treaty where they wouldn't aid humans in any way. Before, they were here to help guide humans. Helping them heal themselves and helping them find their paths. The treaty sums up staying only to themselves and remaining hidden by all who are human and mortal. As long as they stayed to themselves, they would remain unharmed," Clay said.

His voice was still a whisper tinged with heaviness.

"Why did the fifteen of them choose to be Lemurians? That means they would have left their families and put their lives at risk. What would be worth that?" Lucy asked.

"You would have to ask them for the full answer. All I could say is what I know, this family, this strand of witches, they have been working side by side with Enkeli for eons. They are meant to be Lemurians. They were born for it," Clay spoke with honor, clear to Lucy that Clay had respected them for more reasons than them just being on the same side.

The narrow streets could have been alleys made up of cobblestone pathways that trailed off like veins. The map structure of Mpiaron was loose. You'd have to know your way around to not get lost. There were no cars. Everyone walked everywhere, and it made more sense to Lucy why the walkways were so narrow because there was no need for roads. When Rani took steps, there was the glow that rippled through the surrounding stones and the sand between them. Every step she took was magical.

"What other beings live here in Mpiaron?" Asked Lucy.

"Different covens of witches, some djinn, some Enkeli, some of the Guard. There are not many types of beings who live here," Clay said.

"Enkeli?!" Lucy yelled.

It was just loud enough for Rani to turn around and glare at them.

"I thought we were the last bloodline on earth," she continued.

"Yes, that is correct. On *Earth*. There are a few here not of your bloodline. All are men," he said.

They passed a group of people who looked normal, not fairies or djinn or witches.

"Them, there, they are Enkeli. Their bloodline isn't as powerful as yours. Still, they chose to help with what they could. There are three Enkeli families here, each with less than twenty men. They are Lemurians and help all of the time, just like your family. They are descendants of Angels. You are a descendant of one of the Archangels. There are few archangels though they are commonly known across several religions. Michael, Raphael, and Gabriel are most well-known," Clay's voice echoed throughout the bubble.

"Michael? That name is familiar. Where did I hear Michael?" Lucy said aloud to herself.

They passed a group of witches sitting around a table in someone's front yard space. There wasn't an actual yard, just a table. This house was connected to several houses, similar to the way Rani's house was. It was another coven. They all looked similar. Their hair was white and straight, and they were fairly tall with similar features. All had golden bronze skin. Men and women sitting around the table. When she looked inside, she could see a few of them inside of their homes. The food they were eating smelled rich and savory.

"This is where I got the bread dough from," Rani whispered and barely moved her lips so nobody else could hear her.

She waved as she walked by and got waves and hellos in response.

They passed a few more groups of people, rather, a few more covens. Lucy could see there were more witches here than any other being.

Michael. She remembered her half awake-half asleep dream.

"Michael. I had a dream of him. Well, I think it was a dream, or I was delusional," Lucy said to Clay without looking at him.

She made sure to step lightly and was interrupted by Clay. He reached his hand out in front of her, bringing her to a stop. He put both of his hands on either side of her arms and held her there in place.

"What happened? It was not a dream," Clay's energy shifted. Lucy did her best to shake him off and continued to trail Rani.

"He came and was sitting by my front window. He wasn't wearing a shirt, and he had scars all over his body. He also had weapons on him, and he shook his wings out. They were huge. He smiled at me, then I went back to sleep," Lucy said in short sounding much more disinterested than she was.

"When was this?" Clay drilled, body stiff.

Lucy had to think. It felt like such a long time ago to her.

"He came the morning of my birthday now that I think of it," she said.

"This was just before the demon made its appearance. This all makes much more sense now," Clay said. "The house held you with its vines was because it is guarded by a heavenly anchor of some sort. It is made to protect all who serve the Light. We have never needed it, not yet. He must have been there to aid us without letting us know. If Michael would have stayed, the Deminio would have seen him, felt him, they would have seen the Light coming from you and your family. The scout would have reported the presence of an Angel in that area, which to the Deminio would mean the Angel had more than just the Guard to protect. They know we can defend ourselves. The Deminio would know you were here. Who else did you tell?"

Clay explained all of this as they walked. He was speaking out loud to Lucy and sorting out the events in his head at the same time. He was trying to make sense of it all.

"Only you, just now," Lucy said.

"Do not tell anyone else, not yet. It'll cause chaos. Nobody sees angels anymore," he was saying much less than he knew. The only reason Lucy knew this was because he was no longer paying attention to the task at hand and what was going on around him.

Clay was in his thoughts for the remainder of the night.

The three of them continued to walk through the pathways in Lucy's dream. She was still amazed how every step Rani took came alive beneath her, Mpiaron was alive in a way it was not in her dream. Throughout the night, Lucy saw groups of Djinn, a few separate families, and could sometimes hear singing coming from the ocean. That was it. That was all she saw. Nothing stood out or nothing worth remembering, other than the enchanting ways of Mpiaron.

Clay talked about how there were more beings and creatures on earth that weren't here. They were forced to stay neutral, unable or unwilling to become Lemurians. He talked about folklore that was actually real, like the Menehune from the islands of Hawaii. He said they were the most talented builders he had ever come across and hoped to have aid from them one day. He'd also talked about vampires. When Lucy asked questions about them, he said they stayed out of the way and moved on to talk about other creatures.

They walked all the way to the bridge and back to the den before the night was over. They made a stop at Templom. It was where she met Jasutin, only this time nobody was there. The few trees that lined the center of Templom were beautiful. It was perfectly surrounded by flowers and vines. What stood out the most were the lifelike statues, each one representing someone important. Her dad was one of them. When she looked at him, she could feel the connection the figure held to her father. It made her miss him and feel him at the same time. He was young and healthy in the statue. He stood tall, the height was correct, and so was every line in his forehead and carved hair. She wondered why she never noticed how regal he was. Lucy was proud of him. She was proud to be of him.

That was the longest location they stopped before going back to Rani's den. Lucy laid in the bed Clay had made for her, unable to sleep while Clay slept in the bed on the floor next to her. Only he was sitting up, leaning against the adobe wall with his legs beneath the blanket. Rani was asleep in her bed by the fire. The silence and alone time gave her time to think to herself for the first time since she found out what she was. She missed her brother and father. It wasn't because she had never spent time away from them. It was because she felt so much had changed. She was changing, everything about her was evolving, they were changing, the world around them was changing, and none of them seemed to be changing together.

Suddenly Lucy had an idea, Omala had said if she needed anything to let her know through the small leather bag, and she would do her best to help her. So, Lucy reached over for her bag and rummaged through it. She found a notepad with a pen, amongst many other useful items, and wrote on a piece of paper.

Dad and Leon,

So much is happening. I am okay and doing my best to hurry back.

I am beginning to understand why you kept this a secret from me. We can talk more about that another time.

Please let everyone else know we are okay, and I am thankful for all of them.

Love you both 'til Niagara Falls.

Love, Your Lucy

She laughed to herself when she wrote *'til Niagara Falls*, Leon would say that growing up. When she finished writing the note, she folded it a few times and placed it on top of the notepad inside the bag. Lucy hoped they would get it before they made their return. A part of her believed they wouldn't. She laid down and closed her eyes for a moment before she heard something in her bag shift.

It was her notepad.

Lucy reached into the bag, and there was still the note on top of the notepad. She pulled it out and could see it was yellow paper and the paper she wrote on was white.

She opened the paper as quick as she could. A rush of excitement pulsed through her.

We love you too.

-Dad and Leon

Her heart was full. The note was not exactly the response she had wanted, but it was all she needed to continue after a night of not finding anything they needed to move forward.

Lucy turned over to look at Clay, who was still sleeping. She pulled his blankets over him, covering his body. It made her curious to know if he ever got cold. His arms were usually exposed. She finally laid down, read the note one more time, and folded it, holding it tightly to her chest before drifting off into a dreamless sleep.

15

Lucy was the first to wake, surprisingly. She laid in her bed on the floor and went through the events of last night in hopes something would stand out that didn't before. There was nothing.

Rani silently turned around in her bed and looked at Lucy.

"Does anyone know?" Rani said to Lucy, she was so quiet Lucy almost didn't hear her.

"Know what?" Lucy asked.

Rani looked from Lucy to Clay and back to Lucy, "About you two."

"There's nothing to know," Lucy said.

Truly, they weren't really a *thing*. They kissed twice and had a few moments of closeness.

"There is something to know, even if you won't admit it to yourself," Rani said accusingly.

"There really isn't," Lucy forced.

"I won't say anything. You don't have to tell me. You don't have to tell yourself. Part of being a witch is being intuitive, and you don't have to be intuitive to see what you two have. It is more than the bond of his oath to you," Rani said and started to turn back around to her other side.

"I don't know, I mean, I *do* know, but I don't. I know it doesn't make much sense," Lucy tried to open up instead of keeping to herself. It isn't like Rani knew anyone to tell.

Rani turned to face her again.

"It makes perfect sense. There are rules. You two are breaking them, but they were written long before you were born, and Clay has lived the entirety of his being training for this. There is going to be feelings, there is going to be chemistry, there is going to be a deep-rooted connection, and nobody else could compare it to anything. Just remember there is a reason it isn't allowed, but there is also a reason you two feel as connected as you do. Don't ignore it. You two will find your way," Rani gave her a hard look and got up.

Lucy understood what Rani was saying.

Clay yawned.

"Good morning," he said loud enough for both of them to hear, then turned to face Lucy. "Let's go to the stream and wash up?"

Lucy nodded and automatically reached for her leather bag.

Rani got up and checked to see if anyone was outside before they went to the stream.

"Would you mind staying here until we get back? I need time with Lucy." Clay said to Rani.

"Of course," Rani said and moved out of the way for them to pass, but not before giving Lucy a raised eyebrow.

Lucy laughed to herself and followed Clay outside to the stream. It was just behind the den on the other side of the tree line. They walked just past the trail that led them there, only she didn't see it then. It was small and easy to miss, so small Lucy leaped to the other side. Lucy took her shoes and bag off and placed them on the short patch of grass she was standing on. She sat down and put her feet in. Her feet didn't touch the bottom of the stream. She held her body up with her hands and scooted in towards the water until her feet touched the floor. The water was just above her knees. It didn't look that deep when she looked at it from above. But it was clear, and she could easily make out the rocks and sand at the bottom. She took a few steps until there was a smooth patch of soft sand and sat down in the water. The fresh water was cool against her skin.

Lucy looked up and saw Clay laughing at her. She immediately got up and reached for her bag, pulling out two toothbrushes and tooth-paste. She handed one to Clay, and they both brushed their teeth in silence.

Once they were both done and the stream had washed away any sign of toothpaste that lingered in the water, Lucy sat back in her spot in the stream.

"Why did you want to come out here alone?" Lucy asked Clay.

Clay smiled and said, "I don't know, I mean, I do know, but I don't know. I know that doesn't make much sense to you," he answered her question while also repeating Lucy's words to Rani when they both thought Clay was asleep.

Lucy was sorry but not sorry enough, "Oh, I'm not going to apolo-gize for saying anything. I didn't say much."

"I do not want an apology, Lucy. I do not want, nor do I need an explanation. I know nothing is clear right now, but it will be one day. All of this will be clear to us one day. Right now, we need to keep this-" he gestured with his hand at the both of them, "to ourselves. When the time is right, if you and I continue on this path, we will not *hide* anything. Whatever does happen, I am your Guardian before anything else. Al-ways."

Clay smiled the whole time he spoke. He was soft and warm.

Lucy didn't know what to say to him. All she could do was lay back and fully submerge herself into the water. She opened her eyes and looked up at the trees through the water. They were gigantic, vast pillars of earth towering over them. The fresh water pulsed continuously. She could feel the chill of the morning in the earth. She could feel the sun hadn't warmed it up yet and wished the water was a little warmer as she felt her skin get goosebumps from the coolness of it. A second later, the water heated up, that's when it hit her.

She sprung out of the water and yelled, "I got it! Clay, when I first got here in my dream, even before I swam across the bridge, I was at the back on the other side of the bridge. I was swimming. That's where we have to go. In the water."

In her dream, she was sunbathing and soaking up the sun *after* her swim.

Clay looked around, making sure nobody heard her. Lucy was too excited and forgot to keep quiet.

"Sorry," she said though her smile was too big for an apology.

"We need to go tell Owranoos," Clay said.

He submerged his body in the stream too, but only for a moment. When he did, the stream looked much smaller than it had a moment ago because he was huge. He never got out of Guardian form since Lucy's birthday. While he was in the stream, he almost didn't fit. He had to put his broad shoulders sideways to be entirely underwater.

"What is all this yelling about? Contain yourself as much as you can." Owranoos went to the stream and got a hard look from Clay before she continued with, "Please."

"Lucy remembered something," Clay was a little too defensive.

He stood up out of the water, and his face was hard. Guardian Clay was back, and he didn't appreciate Rani's tone. Lucy knew he wouldn't say anything, not this time. Rani has been helping them, and he knew how out of element they all were.

"My dream started in the ocean water on the other side of the bridge, but then I started telling my dream when I, or you, laid down in the sand soaking up the sun when I heard the screaming. The screaming overshadowed everything else," Lucy said, ignoring the both of them.

Rani and Clay were both acting out of instinct. They were keeping her safe. Rani was fast and to the point. She seemed to have thought out her words carefully and quickly. Clay is protective. He is her Guardian. It's in his nature.

"We will have to wait until the sun falls. It will be difficult for us to get there right now without being seen by anyone," Rani dismissed the idea.

Lucy could sense Rani was anxious about something.

"There is no time. We don't know how time is affected at home. We can't wait over twelve hours," Lucy whipped. She had to let them know she made decisions for herself and for her people too, "You said the longer we are here, the more difficult it is on the other side. Right?"

"Yes, you are," Clay said.

"What if someone sees either of you? What do we do then? The spell won't work nearly as well with the number of people who are out and could see or feel you. Some will feel you around. They already do after the way water responded to your presence yesterday," Rani asked.

"Then we tell them. If they see us, we tell them. Then we ask them to take an oath of secrecy, but we stay honest with them. They are us. We are them. They are *our* people. We will try to avoid them as much as possible, but if someone happens to cross our path and if someone sees us through your spell, then we tell them," Lucy said.

Lucy made her way back towards the den. She didn't care what they had to say. She couldn't waste any more time. She changed quickly into another outfit Omala had packed. It was a beautiful handmade floor-length white lace dress. Similar to what she had seen the other women wearing, she hoped it would help her blend in better than the t-shirt and jeans she wanted to wear. It wasn't something she would have picked for herself before, but it was beautiful, and she was happy to wear it. Wearing the dress felt right. She felt strong.

Clay and Rani still hadn't made their way inside. She had to leave. She couldn't wait any longer. Lucy walked out of the door around the alley that led to the back of the house and could see Clay and Rani in a heated discussion in the same place she had left them. Lucy went the opposite direction and walked on the cobblestones towards the rest of the houses.

Air, please help my sound not carry through. Sun, please shine your light away from me to keep me hidden. Earth, show me the path I need to take. Lucy said to herself automatically and took a few deep breaths.

She continued in the same direction as yesterday when she felt the wind blow heavily against her, and towards a different pathway into a narrow alley. An orange butterfly flew in front of her, with the way of the wind. The wind blew harder, and another orange butterfly flew in front of her along with it. Lucy looked down the alley at the butterflies and could see more butterflies gathering. They were flashing sun rays off of their wings. The one closest to her flashed, then the rest flashed their colors in order. Then they did it again.

They were telling her to follow them.

Thank you. Lucy said in her head and stepped towards the butterflies. She followed them a few blocks through the alleys they chose, not running into anyone. She could hear voices nearby. When Lucy thought she was going to cross paths with someone, the butterflies would direct her to a clear pathway. She followed them to the side of the houses where the trees were, only this time it was the opposite side, the side with the cliff trail on the beach. Through the trees, Lucy could make out the ocean and followed the trail that led there. It weaved in and out of the trees along the cliff.

When she walked to the cliff and looked down below, there was not a person in sight. The water was the same shade as the lake and water by her home, a clear turquoise blue. The depth was unclear. The sand was also exactly like home, and Lucy recognized specific landmarks and cliffs. This was a mirror of home. Its magic was just visible.

The path she walked on was beautiful and made her wonder why she hardly walked around on this side of the river at home. She always stayed close to the lake. A thought crossed her mind when she wondered what home looked like in this realm. If she went to where her house was, what would she find? On this side of the river at home, everything was just trees. She knew there were no houses this close to shore based on what Rani had said the day before when she walked them through the plan, there was just forest.

This particular trail she had been on once before with Kona. She put him out of her mind before she started spiraling down the guilt hole. When Lucy followed the trail to the side of the cliff again, she saw a narrow path going down to the ocean and could hear singing from below.

The song being sung was not one she could understand. It was one she could feel. She didn't have to understand the words to know what the song was about. It told a story, a beautiful yet painful story.

Lucy crouched down and looked below. The beach was not too far from where she was standing. Just below her were three beautiful women sitting in the sand along the base of the cliff. As they sang, she remembered singing she heard the day before. Only then it was just faint whispers. They matched their voices, the way they looked, and the way they carried themselves. They were magnets. A part of her was being pulled towards them, some sort of trance. It wasn't strong enough for her, but she knew it would be for some. The melody was sweet and deep, completely anchoring her thoughts.

She wasn't quite sure what they were, but they were unlike the other beings in Mpiaron. These were something different. Their skin was shining in the sun, natural skin colors only they shimmered as if water was on their skin. The first one she saw, directly below her, had a short auburn coiled afro and dark skin. Another had straight long jet-black hair to her waist with a lighter undertone. The last one had auburn hair like the first one, only it was long, and the front was in a braid. They could all be sisters. Lucy could barely make out their eyes, but it wasn't something she could miss. Their eyes were the color of the ocean.

The singing stopped. Lucy crouched down even further.

"Ocala sent a message to a few of our people and said someone is here, they crossed the water yesterday, and they were in the stream not too long ago," the one with black hair said.

"Could they hide from so many of us?" Another asked.

"Maybe they aren't hiding. Either way, we know something is happening. It is only a matter of time before we can go back to the other side. Ocala feels it. He feels more presence here the last few weeks."

Lucy peaked over to see who was talking. It was the one with the short afro.

The singing continued, and Lucy crawled backward and followed the trail. The conversation replayed in her head as she walked. Over and over again, *who is Ocala?* She thought.

A sound grew close, one she knew but couldn't place. The more she walked, the louder it grew louder. It sounded sort of like crickets or giant grasshoppers. She kept her stride, and the sound grew, multiple of whatever it was.

In a flash, chills covered her body. She remembered what it was. It wasn't bugs.

It was rattlesnakes.

She took another step, and the sound stopped. Lucy looked around, trying to make out where they were. She saw a nest of them to her left on the cliff in the sun. She walked backward slowly the opposite way. One slithered towards her. Then another. She turned and ran. They followed. Huge snakes slithered faster than she could run. Her legs sprinted as fast as she could.

The snakes moved faster.

Lucy was scared. Suddenly wondering why she had left Clay and tried to figure out what he would do in this situation.

They were at her heels. She was going to get attacked. They had caught up to her. Just when she thought they were about to strike, they passed her. They weren't interested in attacking her. She slowed down, and they surrounded her. Circles of snakes slithered around her. A few snakes got close to her heels. She naturally took a step away from them. They kept getting closer. She took another step and another. They were closing in on her. No, they were guiding her. She still felt afraid. Something inside of her told her she was in grave danger.

Lucy tried to go to the side when immediately one of them hissed. These snakes were not of Light. They all stopped and moved to the sides and back of her. She was surrounded by trees. There were steps made of stones and mud going down through a hole in the ground, leading to a dark cave in front of her. She couldn't see where it led. Something smelled foul coming from the dark tunnel. It looked like someone had dug their way down and placed large stones together to make steps.

The snakes grew closer. Lucy stepped away from them. Her foot landed on the first step. She didn't know what was down there, but she didn't have a choice. Some of those snakes were larger than she was. When she looked down, something was glowing.

Her whole body felt cold.

Eyes. Red eyes looked straight at her. Her whole body shivered. Evil was right in front of her. She took a step back, no longer fearful of the snakes.

Instead of snakes, she ran into something.

"Lucy!" Clay's voice said from afar.

She looked back towards the direction of his voice and down again at the eyes. They were gone. All of it was gone. The hole, the stairs, the snakes. Everything was gone. She was standing in the middle of the forest with nothing around her except trees.

She blinked once before Clay was in front of her. He crouched down eye to eye to examine her body. His heat radiated the warmth she needed. His hands were studying her. She fell in his arms, and they wrapped around her. She leaned heavily into his body, knees weak.

"Lucy, what happened? Are you okay?" Clay asked her and placed his hands on either side of her face.

He tucked a strand of her long dark hair behind her ear.

She shook her head, unable to speak and her eyes wide.

Clay was visibly in pain as he brought her closer to him, embracing her again. He held her tightly against his body. Lucy didn't know what had just happened, or how it happened, or how to explain it.

"Snakes. They were chasing me. They surrounded me. Then there was a hole… then there was… and now… it's all gone. You said my name, and I blinked, and it's all gone," Lucy trembled.

"I should have been here. Lucy, you could have gotten hurt, or worse," Clay said.

There it was again, *or worse*. Lucy brushed Clay off and took a step towards the trail.

He reached for her arm and brushed his fingers along her skin.

"I do not mean to control you, Lucy. Never. It is not about control. It is about keeping you safe. I cannot do that if we are not near each other. You are too valuable to disappear. Not only because you are En-keli or because I am your Guardian," Clay said. He stepped forward and closed the gap between them, "Lucy, I was scared. I felt you. You were afraid. There was nothing I could do but run towards wherever I felt you were."

"I understand. I do, honestly. I just can't sit down waiting for you and Rani, or anyone else, to figure out what is best for me without me saying what is best for me. I trust you, and I trust you will do what is best for me, and I know you will always do your best to protect me. But how am I supposed to learn if you don't *teach* me? I can fight too. I have gifts. Teach me to use them," Lucy said, surprised at how strong she sounded.

"Your training starts as soon as we get home. It is not safe here, not for our people. I will make sure you get proper training, not only in your gifts but also in combat. You have my word," Clay said.

The space between his eyebrows creased, and he held Lucy's hand up to his chest.

"Okay," Lucy didn't know what else to say.

Her eyes looked around in search of any trace of a snake. She found none.

"Lucy," he said.

Lucy looked up into his eyes. Clay was giving her the look. The one just for her, she swore she could feel him. Truly feel who he was.

"We need to do better, Clay. Let's do better," she said firmly.

"Agreed," Clay's eyebrows creased.

His eyes were glowing. She stopped shaking.

They looked at each other, knowing they shouldn't do anything but any reason not to seamed void. Holding back felt wrong. She couldn't. Not right now.

Their lips crashed, her hands traced his neck and his chest. His arms and hands fully wrapped around her body and lifted her off of the floor.

Lucy could feel his heart beating to the same rhythm as her own.

Everything else, at that moment, turned to nothing. She could no longer hear the birds chirping or the waves crashing on the cliffs. She couldn't hear the wind blowing through the trees. All she knew was Clay, and all she could hear was their heartbeats.

He slowed down too soon and pulled back slowly. She opened her eyes and looked at him, his eyes were closed, but he was smiling.

"I hate to do this, but we really do need to keep going. Time is too valuable while we are here," Clay said though Lucy could see regret in his eyes.

"Alright," she smiled tightly and pulled her body away from his.

Clay put Lucy down on her feet. She led the way and smiled as she took her first step. She looked back at him and laughed. He shook his head, wrapping his hands around the back of his neck, and laughed too. Two strides before he caught up to her.

Lucy experienced two totally different highs and lows within the last few minutes.

There was a struggle within Clay. He was juggling the way he treated her. He either treated her like a neighbor he had feelings for or like an oath-bound Enkeli when she was both.

It made her wonder if she really was both because she could see Clay was one or the other and hardly both at the same time. Could Lucy balance them the way he did?

"Clay, can I ask you something, and you answer without a filter?" She asked.

Lucy and Clay headed towards the trail that would lead to the bridge. The river mouth where the river met the ocean was nearby. The water was changing. Lucy could see the opening from afar. The bridge was near.

"I will do my best," he briefly made eye contact with her.

"I've noticed there are two sides to you. There is neighbor Clay, who I met at the beach and makes chocolate chip cookies from scratch and likes to watch movies and read. Then there is Guardian Clay, who is serious and assertive and, well, a Guardian. How do you do that, separate the two? Which one is who you really are?" Lucy asked.

She held her breath, a little unsure whether or not she wanted to hear his response.

Clay didn't skip a beat, "Most of the time, I am what you call Guardian Clay. That is me. That is who I was conditioned to be and who I have worked so hard to become. The other part, also me, but is who I have become through friendships and through you. You have brought out that side of me more in the last week than anyone else combined in my whole existence. It is nice to *feel*, to laugh, and actually *feel* it. Even to laugh, I do not usually do that. They go hand in hand. They are both me. They are one, and they are both who I am."

Lucy took in what he said. It helped her understand him more. She could tell laughter wasn't something he was used to. Hearing him say it made sense.

"I can see that. When I start training, will I have that too? Me, who I am now, and Enkeli Lucy? I just don't want to lose myself in all of this. I don't want to ever be lost," Lucy's voice shook with truth.

Clay didn't say anything. Lucy peered over at him and could see him weighing his thoughts as he tried to find the right words to say. He was good at helping her understand everything clearly.

"Lucy, you are Enkeli. You will learn how to use your gifts. I would be lying if I said it was an easy road you are going to walk. I can't even say that you won't change through it because it would be unnatural, inhumane even, for you not to change. I see the traits you have, and they are traits you have always had. You are truthful, you are Light to those around you, you truly care about the well-being of others, you take your time to show people their value and importance. All of those are parts of you that you have chosen to be and continue being. That is who Enkeli are. That is who you are. Those core qualities won't change, you will grow, you will become stronger than anyone you know, you will see things differently, but you will always be you," Clay said.

They continued down the trail. The blue of the sky reflected the most beautiful light through the trees and illuminated the path. It was clear the direction they were going was the one they should be on, in more ways than one.

"How do you know?" Lucy asked.

"Because I feel you. When you found out you were Enkeli, you questioned nothing. When you saw the Demon, you did not back down or become afraid or falter in any way. Instead, you maintained calm and listened with reason. You would have already begun to doubt yourself already. You would have planted that dark seed, and you have not. Instead, you are here asking questions to help yourself grow, just like you always have," Clay said.

He reached for her hand, put it up to his lips, and kissed her knuckles. Clay bowed his head and held her hand up high before releasing it. Lucy was thankful he didn't pass judgment or give harsh personal opinion. He could truly see her.

"Thank you," was all she managed to get out.

The bridge had come quickly, and Lucy walked towards it when Clay started taking off his clothes.

"What are you doing?" She breathed.

"We are going for a swim. That is what you did in your dream. That is what we need to do now," he smiled.

It was obvious. He knew Lucy was internally freaking out about him taking off his clothes.

Lucy looked at him and gestured with her finger for him to turn around. He smiled again before turning around.

She folded their clothes and placed them inside of her small leather bag. Lucy made a mental note to thank Omala for only packing her swimsuits instead of underwear.

The large rocks were smooth and easy to walk down. They had black sand in between them all the way down to the water. The water was not rough like in Lucy's dream. It was smooth and clear. It was inviting. Lucy put her feet in and was surprised by its warmth.

Water, please get us across safely and hidden from any eyes that might see us. Lucy thought to the water, the way she did in her dream.

Immediately, in response, the water made a visible current going from where she was standing all the way to the opposite side of the river.

"What did you do?" Clay asked.

He stood next to Lucy with his feet in the water. She couldn't make out his expression though it fell somewhere between amazed and concerned.

"I asked the water to help us," Lucy said just before she jumped in

It was warm and caressed her body with a different feeling when she was completely submerged. She could feel the water as a whole. It was alive.

She swam with the current through the glowing blue water, her body moved at a normal pace, but the water pushed her across the river three times faster than she should have gone. Clay trailed right behind Lucy and did the same. She saw a few of the multicolor fish she had seen from above the day before, some were larger than her, and they swam alongside her. One, in particular, stood out to her. It was the largest fish of them all. Its scales were deep blue and reflected every shade of water she had ever seen. It was long and thin. Its eyes were not the normal color of a fish but a deep blue to match its scales. Its eyes were human.

Lucy knew this creature was special. It nodded once before her body was lifted out of the water and onto the shore on the other side of the river. She thanked the water and dismissed it and could see the large fish from afar, making eye contact once before it swam away.

She had almost said something when Clay spoke up first, "Water responds well to you. Did you know you could do this?"

He was beaming, proud of her. He held out his hand and gestured at her purse. Lucy handed it over to him. He reached his arm in the small bag and pulled out two fluffy towels.

"Kind of, I guess. Subconsciously. I never really thought about it until I did it in my dream, then I realized once we needed to cross the water here, maybe I could actually do it," Lucy said.

She dried off and put her lace dress back on over her swimsuit. Clay smiled when he handed her his towel, he wasn't going to put a shirt on.

Lucy swallowed, making Clay laugh.

Then his face completely changed.

"This might be why we are here. Owranoos doesn't have any affinity with water. She cannot speak to it. There is permission you need to ask sometimes. Here in Mpiaron is where Ocala lives. He's the protector of the sea. He was the large creature in the water. If you were able to work with water here, he gave you permission to use it indefinitely. I already knew you had a connection with earth from the way earth responds to you with the Bloom. Now water does the same. I wonder if you'll have strengths with fire and air too," he said, half to himself.

"How do we find out?" Lucy was curious.

"When we get back, I will be there to help you, as I said earlier. You shouldn't try here, remember? It could be dangerous for our people." Guilt washed over Lucy as she remembered what he had said before. Clay went on, "Mostly, you will take lessons from all of the leaders on different subjects and topics. Your dad and Leon will help you most, as well as your cousins and uncles. They are Enkeli, after all."

Lucy grabbed her ear and shook it, trying to get the water out. As Clay talked, she could no longer hear him clearly. She was focusing on his mouth to lip read when her vision began to go in and out. The ringing in her ears grew unbearably loud.

Then there was nothing.

16

"Lucy… Lucy… Lucy…"

Why was the familiar voice so loud? Her ears rang.

"Lucy, are you there?"

"Lucy, can you hear me?"

She fell back into nothingness.

What was that sound? Something was bright. Then there was nothing but darkness.

"How long has she been asleep?" A voice asked.

Then there was nothing.

"Luc. Come on, Luc. I'm here. I won't leave you."

Leon.

Her head was pulsing.

She fought to respond to him, but it didn't work. She was too tired.

A dreamless sleep returned.

Roaring sounds filled Lucy's body.

Deep laughs. Flashes of lightning was all she could see through her eyelids. Sounds like thunder.

There was no storm.

There was yelling and bone-chilling laughs.

Then there was nothing.

"Lucy, if you can hear me. Know you are safe. I am never going to let anything happen to you."

Warm fingers stroked her face and her hair.

Big hands held hers.

Clay.

She felt he was there, always.

He never left.

She was tired.

Nothingness took over.

"Lucy, you need to wake up. We need you. I need my sister. Please wake up. I am trying my best to help you. Can you feel it? I am trying to help you," by the sound of Leon's voice, he was only holding on by a strand of hope.

She felt warm. She wasn't so tired anymore.

Her eyelids weren't heavy. The ringing was gone.

"Leon," she mouthed, her voice failed her.

"Luc?" Leon gasped.

"I feel it," she said.

He held her hand up to his face.

It was wet. Lucy opened her eyes to look at him. He was sweating. His face was red. His hands were shaking. His eyes were puffy and dark. He hasn't slept.

"What's wrong, Leon?" Lucy was lost.

"Nothing. Not anymore," Leon said.

She laid there on a bed, opening and closing her eyes because it was all she had the strength to do. This place looked like she had seen it before, she couldn't remember where it was.

The walls were bright, an off shade of white. There were huge French doors going towards what looked like outside. She couldn't see through the curtains from where she was. There were whitewashed exposed beams throughout the ceilings. She looked closer to see carvings. *His* carvings.

Lucy tried sitting up. Her body felt heavy, as if she had been lying down for too long. Leon guided her by the arm and helped her up. He stayed close and supported her weight with his arm around her waist. She stood up and stretched her body upwards, then she leaned on each leg separately, feeling the tightness of every muscle. She rotated her stiff ankles and sore knees.

Where am I? She thought to herself.

Lucy couldn't help but glare in a trance at the doors. The details on the wood were infinite. With her first step towards a door she assumed would lead them to the rest of the house, Leon reached for her arm again.

"Lucy, remember to breathe evenly. Okay?" He said.

Worry lines creased his brow.

"Well, yeah," she laughed.

How could she forget to breathe?

They walked together towards the door. When Lucy looked down, she saw she was barefoot and could suddenly feel the cool washed wood floor through the bottoms of her feet. It wasn't an ice-cool, but a refreshing and grounding cool. The floor was a shade darker than the washed beams on the ceiling. The room she was in was beautiful. It had only a bed with a wooden bed frame that seemed to be on theme with the rest of the room. A bed, white curtains, white bedding, and that was it. Just a bed and white walls. It didn't feel as simple as it was because of the detail in the wood. But it was beautiful, fresh, and comfortable. It was a place Lucy felt she could actually breathe. She felt safe.

Leon opened the door. Before it was fully opened, Lucy made eye contact with her dad, Leo. He stood just outside the door and said nothing but pulled her in for a gentle, heartfelt hug.

She walked into what was a living room with a spiral staircase just to her left. In the middle of the living room was an oversized gray sectional sofa that faced a fireplace as tall as her. Alika, Fazi, Omala, and Rani were all sitting comfortably on the couch. Each one looked directly at her.

To her right was a kitchen with more sets of eyes, Dario and Talan. Talan's eyes were heavy and rimmed with dark circles. Even his blond hair was dull. Both nodded at her and made eye contact before turning their faces and looking in a different direction. Lucy followed their eyes.

It was Clay.

He didn't look at her. He didn't move. He was facing outside, looking through a large glass door. Lucy looked outside. The lake was out there with Emma in the distance. She knew it was him because of his beanie and the way he slouched a little when he looked down.

When she looked at her friends again, she knew something was off.

"What's going on? What happened?" Lucy said.

Her voice surprised her with its fullness, unlike her unsteady noodle legs.

Nobody said anything, not a word. She didn't even see them breathe.

Air. I call on you to bring a calming breeze through us. Please stay with me and give me strength until I leave this room. Thank you. Lucy said to herself.

A slight breeze caused a current in the air. All of the windows and doors were shut.

"*That* is what happened," the silent roar in Clay's voice said more than the words he spoke. He didn't move, still facing outside.

Lucy looked around again. Everyone was looking at Clay. They were waiting for something.

"Dad?" She asked, and he looked down.

"Leon?" Lucy reached out to her brother. He immediately went stiff and turned his gaze towards Clay.

Leon's eyes burned to speak, though he said nothing.

Lucy looked over at her friends. Rani wasn't like them.

"Rani?" Lucy pushed.

Rani twitched slightly, the only indication of how affected she was.

They weren't looking at Clay because he was the last one to talk to Lucy. They were looking at him because he was the only one who could say anything to her. Lucy then realized they needed his permission.

"Clay, *speak*," Lucy demanded.

He whipped his head around. His eyes burned straight into hers.

Only this time, she wasn't going to falter or back down. This time, Lucy burned back. Lucy needed to know. She deserved to know.

"What is the last thing you remember?" Clay asked.

Everyone looked from Clay to Lucy.

"The last thing I remember is our conversation after we crossed the river in Mpiaron," Lucy said.

"That was the last thing you remember?" He said and huffed.

"Clay, what is your point?" Lucy's usually easy-going self was gone and replaced by strength and power. She could feel it just beneath her skin.

"My point is you used your gift once, and you passed out. You were uncontrollably shaking, your nose was dripping with blood, your ears were too. Your eyes rolled back. Your body couldn't handle it." Clay's stare hadn't changed.

"No, I didn't," Lucy said through blinks of remembrance.

"I saw you use your gifts, Lucy," Clay said.

"But you were wrong. I only half used them. I spoke to water and earth to help guide me. They did most of the work. And it wasn't just once, but four times I can recall," Lucy said.

The energy in the room changed, and everyone inside of it looked at each other. She could feel questions arising.

"When?" Clay paced towards her.

"Once when we walked outside before going to the stream. Another when we were in the stream. Another when I left you and Rani to bicker about what we should do next, I asked for help to remain unseen. Another was when I asked for guidance to go in the right direction when I got to the trails with no knowledge of where to go. The last was when I asked water to help us, and it carried us both across the river. So, five, actually," Lucy went on.

With every sentence grew more questions in everyone's eyes.

"Why did you not say anything?" Rani asked.

"I didn't think I had to," Lucy said.

"You put our people in-"

"Owranoos," Clay cut Rani off.

His tone a threat, plain as day.

"Do you remember any of what happened to you when you were a child? No, Lucy. You do not. Lucy, you almost died. I see what you were saying about having help and not doing it yourself, but you over-exerted yourself and communicated with water and earth without proper knowledge of how to do it and look what happened. It is my job, our job," Clay gestured at everyone in the room, "to protect you. You need to learn, and you need to have guided practice. We are all here to help you do that. We can't help if you aren't openly telling us what is going on with you. It is not just for your own personal safety either. It is for all of our safety. Because of what happened while we were on the other side, you using your gifts, pieces of Mpiaron came here. There are patches of land that came through. Several pieces resemble the small patch you call the Bloom. It puts everyone at risk Lucy, you need to understand this is much more than playing with the elements. There is much more to this than you."

With each word, Clay sent Lucy into her own spiraling thoughts.

"I didn't do it on purpose," she said. She had a lot more to say but didn't have the words to make them understand how she felt. Lucy was just as frustrated as Clay, even more. But she wouldn't let them know, not now.

Frustration visibly grew inside of Clay. His eyes were now glowing, and he took another step closer, almost closing the small gap between them when Leon stepped forward in between them and placed his hand on Clay.

"We know that Luc. What he is trying and failing to say is none of us really know how your gifts work, including you. You shouldn't use them without more knowledge of who we are and what we can do. Which is where we come in. I am your brother, and I would be here re-gardless. But them," Leon pointed at their friends, "they all have families of their own, families you know nothing of. They have whole cities of beings depending on them being able to help you. If you don't ask for help, it defeats their sole purpose for being here. Being away from family is difficult, but the pressure that lies on all of us is much, much worse. If we fail, Lucy, we die. Our families die, our people die, and the world will go down with it. So let us teach you."

Lucy didn't answer Leon. She had to soak what he said in. She was still frustrated, irritated, angry, and most of all, lonely. She didn't know how to tell them this. Lucy didn't want them to know she was struggling more than she was letting on. Leon's words helped, but Lucy still felt like she knew too little.

She looked around the room at their faces making eye contact with each one. Although she has known most of them her entire life, it was hard to believe there was a side of them she didn't know. It was even more challenging to think the part of them she didn't know was who they truly were, all in their true form with a family and a past she knew nothing of.

Something clicked inside of her.

"I thought that was the plan all along. When we got back home, you were all supposed to give me lessons-" Lucy said before getting cut off by Clay.

"Correct. *When we got home.* Not while we were still in Mpiaron," Clay said, still frustrated.

"We were safe there, and I didn't really know I was doing anything. It was all in my head, a *say it to myself* kind of thing," Lucy said.

The air in the room became stiff. The current was gone.

Clay's skin was rippling as he stepped between her and Leon.

"Lucy. How long, exactly, do you think you were asleep?" He asked.

"A few hours. I fainted, and you brought me… here," she grazed over his bitterness. She still didn't know where they were.

"No. Three days," he was bitter. Mad even. "Okay. How long do you think we were in Mpiaron?"

"A day and a half," Lucy said. She was sure of it.

Clay was filling with rage, and Lucy didn't know why. He still held his composure, but his face was cold. Lucy learned to read him well over the last few days.

"Lucy, you were gone three month's time here," Omala's soft voice spoke up.

Lucy couldn't stand anymore and sat in place, still by the door to the room. Lucy's mind went back to the few times when time was mentioned and was always told time was unpredictable. She took a deep breath.

Three months.

Lucy was trying to figure out how that was possible. There was no way a day and a half could equal three whole months. She thought of many things. Her first thought was of Kona. He wasn't with them. She thought of her dad, and Leon, and if they knew what was going on when she wrote them. Then she thought of what could have happened while she was gone.

Emma walked inside if the house through the giant glass door. She looked past him. The lake was close to the house, and the view was familiar to her.

"Lucy," Emma bowed his head then looked at Clay.

"I got word of scouts a few miles north. They went back to where they came from, but they were too close. If they would have kept walking, they would have walked right into a patch of Mpiaron," he said.

"Okay. Talan, take two of the wolves to check," Clay commanded.

There were no questions asked by Talan. He walked outside without so much as a glance.

Lucy's eyes followed Talan and remembered the boy he had always been. The friend he had always been to her. When he walked outside, Lucy saw the lake again and the view.

This is the view from the barn. Lucy thought to herself.

She looked around and wondered why it hadn't clicked before.

"This is my house? It is finished?" She stood up in awe.

It was much more than she had imagined it to be. Everything was simple and unique to her in a way she couldn't put together herself if she tried. The room she slept in was familiar to her because it was her own. To Lucy, just a few long days ago, this was still mostly a barn. The look of the barn was apparent in the frame and nothing else. She walked to the kitchen and placed her hand on the cool stone countertop. It wasn't a color she would have picked for herself, a deep sapphire blue stone with gold and silver specks in it. She loved it. When she looked next to her room door and saw the spiral staircase, it all clicked together. At the base was the spiral carving Clay had made when they first met. From this distance, she could see into the loft above her room. It was turned into a small library.

"Talan worked on the house when he wasn't guarding the Bloom. He told me your plans, and we all took turns getting it ready for your return. After a couple of weeks without you, it was a way for us to get out of our own heads and use our hands. Anyway, I hope you like it," her dad had a dad moment.

He was proud of himself and proud to show Lucy the craftsman-ship he put into it. The more she looked around, the more she could see bits of his work in the details. She was shocked he would be the one to plan it out when he barely stopped by. It made her home much more special.

This was her home.

"I hope you don't mind. I turned your old flat into a place for me to stay while I am here," Rani said.

"Not at all. Stay as long as you'd like," Lucy said.

Her smile was contagious. Everyone else was quiet and smiling as much as they could, given their circumstances. It was more from Lucy being awake and safe, but Lucy tried not to go too deep into her thoughts. She was afraid of what she would find if she dug too deep.

The tea kettle started whistling, and Rani jumped up off of the couch and took it off the burner. Omala followed Rani and smiled her gentle smile at Lucy before joining Rani in the kitchen.

Dario walked over to the large sliding back door and got out of their way.

Rani and Omala had different flowers, plants, and herbs they were mixing into the kettle of hot water. The house immediately smelled of flowers and mint.

"Thank you. Thank you all for doing this," Lucy had dual meaning to her words.

It wasn't just the house but the sacrifice they had made to protect her. Her eyes filled with tears. Not one fell.

Lucy could feel her body get warm. It tingled in a way it only did when Clay was around. She looked at him, just a few feet away. He was looking into her and took a breath before fuming out of the back door. Emma followed him.

Leon looked towards them and took a few steps to the glass door overlooking the lake. He shut it behind them and watched from a distance. He wouldn't leave Lucy.

Omala walked over to Lucy, still in the middle of her house, and gave her a sizeable steaming mug.

"Do not drink this. Only smell it. It is mixed herbs and root from a willow. It'll make you sick if you drink it, but it'll give you clarity if you inhale the steam," Omala said.

"Thank you, Omala." Lucy hugged her friend with one arm and held the cup with the other.

"Thank you," Lucy mouthed to Rani before she went to the couch and sat down with Alika and Jack.

Her body ached, and she was tired. Not the kind of tired you are after a long day, the kind of tired you are after someone dies, the kind of tired you are after you've exhausted all emotion.

Lucy sat and inhaled the sharp steam of the brew. A soothing wave of balm flowed through her every cell. It was chapstick for her soul, aloe for her body.

Everyone began small conversations. It was a nice sense of normalcy. Lucy didn't think she would have any normalcy when she returned. They were still themselves, except for Alika and Jack had heavy accents. Though somehow, they sounded more like themselves than they had before.

When Lucy looked at Omala and Rani in the kitchen, she could see they were both witches. They just didn't feel the same. Omala was warm. Rani was not. It wasn't that Rani was cold, she wasn't, but she also wasn't like Omala either. Rani was firm and much more intense. Omala was like an older sister who helped but wasn't too harsh, whereas Rani was more like a warrior. She had been through a lot and wasn't afraid to step on anyone's toes for their cause. It was clear she sacrificed much more than the rest of them.

They were different kinds of witches. Lucy was unsure whether or not there were several kinds. She just knew those two couldn't possibly be the same kind.

Lucy inhaled all of the steam, feeling refreshed and rejuvenated. Enough strength to get up and walk over to Leon by the glass doors. She looked outside and could see the deck was finished, and the two-lane lap pool she wanted was just past the deck's steps. It was perfect.

"I knew we had to build it," Leon said, referring to the lap pool.

He didn't look at Lucy. His gaze locked on Emma and Clay.

"Thanks, brother. So, what is it that nobody is telling me? What else has Clay so amped up?" Lucy said.

Her voice came off much more potent than she intended, and she was thankful. If she had faltered, Leon might have changed the subject.

"You already know. Pieces of Mpiaron came here. The Bloom is still here. Only now it is in patches all over Shadow Rock," Leon said.

"Okay. Translate, please?" She said.

"The Bloom is a Gateway from here to Mpiaron. Since there are now more pieces of Mpiaron here, it started merging. If you had stayed any longer, it wouldn't have been contained. What that means is instead of us having only one place to watch for the Deminio to go through into Mpiaron if they found it, there are many. Before, it was just the Bloom and only visible to anyone else while you were in it. But since you were *in* Mpiaron, you were technically in the Bloom the whole time you were gone." Leon paused and quickly glanced at Lucy, who was still piecing it together, "The Gateway was open from both sides the whole time. The minute you got back, we got in an altercation because a demon could feel your energy coming through one of the Gateways. Thankfully you ran into Jasutin. Because of him, we knew right away where the holes from here to Mpiaron were and where they merged. He worked from the other side and sent us messages through the different openings. While you were gone, we didn't just have one Bloom to watch over or one Gateway. We had fifteen quarter acre sized Blooms all over Shadow Rock. We had to call more Guardians and the wolves for help," Leon said.

He was still watching Clay and Emma outside.

"The wolves?" Lucy asked.

"A pack of wolves who are keepers of Light. They can protect us and send messages across multiple realms. You know one already," he smiled at her.

It clicked.

"Kona?!" She yelled.

"Yeah. Who would have thought? I didn't know they existed and still don't know much about them. Kona was reincarnated to come here as pack leader, meant to protect Light and Lemurians. His pack decided to reincarnate him through a magical process after their leader died. Once he incarnated, he was born a pure wolf. In his first year of life, his mentality flickers back and forth from animal to pack leader. After the year has passed, he is only pack leader but in wolf form. That's why sometimes he would act like a dog, and others you know he can understand you more. The catch is, as an alpha, you cannot change back and forth from wolf to human like the rest of the pack. So, he must stay a wolf in this lifetime. I'm sure Clay can explain it better than I can," he said.

"You explained it perfectly. Thanks," Lucy said.

She remembered her conversation with Clay about many supernatural creatures being real. Figures Kona played a part in all of this, just like everyone else.

"Are they closed now? The Gateways?" Lucy asked.

"Yes, thankfully. They all finished closing this morning. The only thing left is the carving on the tree, the actual rune of the Gateway. We have people watching over it at all times. Nothing goes in, and nobody comes out," Leon said.

The thought made Lucy fill with sadness. She wanted the people of Mpiaron, her people, to come back to this world again.

Leon hadn't taken his eyes off of Clay and Emma. Emma was talking the whole time by the looks of it, and Clay was just standing there, toes along the water. He was barefoot. It looked like he was actually listening to Emma.

"What's wrong with Clay?" She tried her best to sound uninterested.

It worked.

"He is upset there were too many close calls. Too many cracks in the plan. Everything we have done has had consequences we couldn't foresee. The Deminio are more powerful than we thought. He didn't want to have to call for aid. He didn't want to draw more energy and attention here to Shadow Rock. It's too close to you and too close to Mpiaron. At this point, though, we don't have a choice," Leon paused and studied Lucy's face. "A few days ago, when you got back, during the altercation, more guardians came. None that you know. Clay sent them to watch the Bloom north of the lake when you had just gotten back from Mpiaron. He had you in his arms as he yelled orders to all of us. He wouldn't leave you. Honestly, none of us knew if you were going to wake up. Anyway, a demon came close to entering Mpiaron. One more step, and he would have. Two Guardians stopped him. Two Guardians and one demon, they almost had him down when he cast one last lash of Darkness and pulled one of the Guardians along with it. If a Guardian or a Lemurian goes into the Darkness, it is spellbound to die instead of being tortured or stuck in a Limbo. Clay lost a brother while you were unconscious in his arms. He still didn't leave your side, three days, and the furthest he has gone is the back door of your bedroom. I think the only reason he is okay to go outside now is because you woke up. He is going through it right now."

"Oh." The only word Lucy could say.

She had to be careful with Leon. He knew her better than anyone else. He could feel her emotions if he tried.

She looked at Clay, and he was looking right at her.

17

Clay

Rage. Clay stepped outside, colliding with the fresh lake mist. It hit him with the last warmth of the day just before sundown.

Rage. A rare emotion for him.

Inside they had been talking about the house and filling Lucy in on what had happened when she shouldn't have been unconscious to begin with. He tried to understand why she didn't tell him she had been using her gifts. She was supposed to trust him. He was supposed to protect her.

Arsenio is dead. He told himself for the thousandth time and somehow found the strength to continue standing steadily.

"This isn't your fault. This is how it is, Clay. You know this," Emma said from behind him.

"I do," he affirmed.

His toes hit the water. He had clarity. He could breathe.

He understood what Emma said. He knew this is how it was. This is how it had always been. Only now, his connection with Lucy had opened parts of him, allowing him to understand the value of physical loss. He now understood what it would be to miss someone.

How was he supposed to tell anyone?

He wasn't supposed to feel this.

"Everyone was watching her like she was a flower made of glass. Beautiful, but could be broken. The strength she has is immeasurable. She's stronger than every one of them tenfold. They don't see it, not yet. You do. While everyone was watching her, I watched you. You *feel* her," Emma said. It wasn't a question.

Clay didn't respond. He looked at the reflection of the sunset skies on the glassy waters of the lake.

"If this is how you feel, trust it. Nothing happens by mistake. Nothing. Whether it lasts this way or if this is the way you two are supposed to bond, whatever that means, you need to trust yourself. Isn't that what a lot of your training was about? Trusting yourself, trusting your instincts? Follow that feeling," Emma said.

Clay understood what Emma was saying, but the feeling he felt deep inside was loss.

"Arsenio is dead," Clay said, words so short he cut himself off.

"It happens. You know that, " Emma's voice was softer than before.

"Yes, but I *feel* now. I know it happens, only now I feel Lucy. She opened part of me I didn't know I had. I feel grief. I feel his loss. I feel responsible. These are feelings I should not have. I am trained for this, to be a Guardian and a worker of Light, and we protect at any and all cost. A true Lemurian. That is what we do. That is what I am doing. Feeling clouds judgment. If my judgment is clouded, how can I protect her?" Clay said.

He knew Emma would keep this conversation to himself. As a Ska-ru, a Deminio who switched sides, he did his best to prove himself.

"Clay, there is nothing that can stop you from doing what's right. Nothing can stop you from doing what you were created to do. Cast doubt aside. Doubt isn't what you are made of." Emma put his right fist over his heart and pounded once.

As soon as Emma's words landed on Clay's ears, something inside of him clicked. The way it does when he knows what to do, he knew truth laid in those words.

"Thank you," Clay said.

He extended his arm to Emma, who reached out in return, palm to forearm, and they shook their arms.

"I do have a suggestion, if that's okay with you, that you two keep to yourselves for a while. Even if it's hard. Just until Lucy has a better grasp of this life and can protect herself without killing everyone else. We don't want anyone else to worry," Emma said.

His face was soft with a smile. He always hid behind his smile. His eyes, on the other hand, were complex and held seriousness and sorrow.

"I ask you to keep this conversation and any word of Lucy and me to yourself," Clay said.

They both knew the agreement they had. Emma was a demon before, but he was as loyal as Leon and loved Lucy as Leon did. He just didn't show it.

Emma nodded and turned to the lake.

Both of their toes were in the water. The water rippled towards them in response. Emma was right, and Clay knew it. They had to keep their bond, outside of what it should be, to themselves. Lucy might seem fragile to them, but everything inside of Clay knew just how dangerous she was. He could see she processed information clearly, without adding in her own judgment. She understood quickly as well and responds to situations too sharp for an Enkeli with no training. She is well-balanced and fair to herself. All of this is good until it is not. Until something happens that is too heavy for her. It is only a matter of time. That is when she will truly be tested, and acceptance would be difficult for her. He wasn't worried she couldn't control herself on the day-to-day, but for an event to take place in which it would be too difficult for her to process.

Demons were tricky. The Deminio aimed low every time. Clay had to watch from every direction, primarily where Lucy was concerned.

The thought of her name made him turn around to see if he could see her through the large glass doors.

She was talking to Leon. The orange glow from the sunset shone directly on her. She looked every bit the magic she was. Clay listened in and heard Leon telling her what had happened while she was asleep. Leon had a way of talking to Lucy. Everything he said, she received gently. It was true they all treated her like she could break at any given moment, but he could see Leon treated her like a gentle giant. Leon knew her strength. Leon didn't think Lucy was fragile like a flower. He knew she was fragile like a bomb. Constantly leveling out the conversation before someone said something that could tip her over. Leon was the soothing water to Lucy's fire.

Clay knew he was heavy with his words towards her. She needed to understand what was going on without filter or someone telling her half-truths. It was not his duty to tell her everything was going to be okay. It was his responsibility to *make* everything okay.

Nothing would stop him from fulfilling his duty.

When Leon mentioned Arsenio's death, Lucy's eyes fell. He could hear her heart speed up, and he could feel her intense sadness.

It registered with him. She was not sad because she lost a friend. She did not know Arsenio. She was sad for Clay. She felt for him too.

She looked up at him, her breathing shortened, and her eyes glossed over with sorrow.

With his eyes, he thought to himself what he wanted to tell her. *It is okay, Lucy. We will talk later. When the moon is up, and there are no ears around. When I can put a warm fire on and tell you how I came to peace with all I would ever lose, many years ago. Until then, know all is well.*

I'm okay, Lucy. He thought to her.

Her eyes widened, and she took a sharp breath.

Could you hear me? He thought to her again.

She nodded. She looked at Leon beside her to see if he noticed anything. He didn't. She looked back at Clay.

Lucy smiled her mysterious smile, where her eyes were dancing. Anyone could see it from any distance. Anyone could feel it from any distance. She was full of Light, even if she did not know it yet.

Clay smiled back.

Her eyes danced the way they do when she is deep in thought with no words to express herself. She never truly says how she feels or what is on her mind, but the way her eyes danced told a story words never could.

18

Lucy got the tour of her home from Talan. It was everything she wanted it to be and perfect for her. He paid close attention when she explained what she wanted it to be. He nailed it. It had one bedroom to the side, an open living room with a large fireplace that seemed to draw the room's attention. The whole house was as open as the barn had originally been. The only thing enclosed was her room and bathroom. The kitchen was open to the living room and dining room. Next to her room door between her door and the fireplace was the wooden spiral staircase. It led up to the loft over her bedroom, full of more books than Lucy owned. Outside was a deck overlooking the lake, a few steps down was the two-lane lap pool, and fifteen short steps from that was the lake. Last was the small pergola next to her house. It had vines growing all around it and a table under it. Her blue bug was parked just next to the pergola. Everything was simple and perfect for her.

The loft was where Lucy wanted to be. The whole house had large windows, but the loft had a large skylight above the entirety of the loft.

It was part of what used to be the roof of the barn. The stars above her. The windows on the wall were shuttered and open, inviting a fresh breeze inside the entire house. The loft had a desk by the rail that overlooked the living space. The wall was a floor to ceiling bookshelf.

Omala gathered a collection of books for Lucy. Some were old grimoires kept by their ancestors. Some were maps of places around the world marked safe for them to go. There were history books written by the keepers of Light. There were spell books. Hundreds of books covered the shelves on the wall. It gave the loft area a specific scent, old books, leather, smoke, oils, herbs, and hints of dried mildew.

It smelled of endless years of magic.

After her short tour, everyone left. Rani went to the flat. Some people went to the Bloom close by. Leo and Leon went to their home across the lake with Emma, who was now staying with them. Everyone else went to the house next to Leos, the one Lucy thought was abandoned. It wasn't just Clays bigger house. It was a safe house for all Lemurians to go in times of need.

Lucy was sitting sideways at the bottom of the spiral staircase and looked across the room through the glass doors. They were both open. She could see the stars and the reflection of the moon on the lake. The water looked like glass from where she stood. Clay was still standing with his feet in the water. Lucy contemplated walking over there many times. She wanted to talk to him. Only something inside of her told her when he was ready, he would come inside.

A memory of his voice echoed through her mind. *I'm okay, Lucy.*

She walked to the bathroom and turned the brass knobs to the rainfall showerhead. The water was almost too hot. It was perfect. Lucy showered off the last few days of being unconscious and let the water run over her stiff skin. Down the drain, along with the hot water, went anything negative she might have been holding onto. She took deep breaths in and out, and envisioned her entire body was a giant water bottle filled with dark, murky and muddy water. With each breath in, she pictured fresh water entering through the top of her head. With each breath out, she felt the murky water leave through her fingers and toes. She did this for countless breaths before she finally felt clarity. The clear water filled her, and she had a clear mind. When she turned the water off, she felt refreshed and much lighter than when she stepped in. She brushed her teeth and hair, putting it into a long braid. Moisturized her body with a mixture of oils Rani had made for her and put on her most comfortable pajamas, always an oversized t-shirt and shorts.

Lucy walked to her room and looked at the large bed with a fluffy comforter and pillows. It should look inviting, but she spent the last few days laying on it and couldn't bring herself to lay down. Instead, Lucy got a pillow and the large white comforter from her bed and walked out of her room, up the stairs, and into the loft.

She placed the pillow and blanket on the floor over a fluffy rug in the middle of the loft and turned around at the wall of books she now had. Many books were interesting, but one made her skin buzz when she looked at it. Lucy pulled the small ladder over and retrieved the book.

Lachfll 331

There were many Lachfll books. This one was the only one she felt the need to read. It had a gold script on it and looked much more used than the other Lachfll books. She pulled it out and got comfortable on the floor with her fluffy comforter and pillow. The stars shone through the skylight, and the moon was the only light she needed.

She read the first page. It had small details of the archangel Michael.

The pages that followed are what mattered most.

I knew he was different by the way he walked. We were on the battlefield, through the smoke, I could see a man walking. Men were in the dirt dead. Men were on the floor dying.

A man walked to me, he had no shirt on, and his body covered in scars of silver. Not a drop of blood on his skin.

He was so close I could smell him. He smelled of fresh water and earth.

He looked at me. Light shined from inside of him.

I was safe.

I was dying. Struck by an arrow while hunting, my father didn't know I followed him, and he shot me, his only son. I was eight years old and wanted to be just like him. I laid on the floor, cold. I heard shuffling in the leaves next to me. It was a man. He was not wearing a shirt but cloth. His scars on his body had a glow to them. He was warm. I could feel his warmth.

He picked me up. I fell asleep in his arms.

I woke up on my bed with not even a scar.

The bottom of the ocean was beautiful. I was stuck to the anchor of the ship. Nobody knew I was down here. I could not untie myself as my full dress held me down. Water filled my lungs. The colors were bright. My heart slowed.

A man was walking on the ocean floor.

His eyes were warm. His body was full of scars. He was beautiful.

He gave me breath. I rose to the top of the water.

The plague was killing all. My whole family was dead, all but my newborn son and me. I ran with my son in my arms. I had nothing. I was running from the disease. My son needed to live. I needed to take care of him.

It was dark, the wolves howling. Closing in on us. My son was screaming. I didn't know what to do. I tried to help him, he was cold, hungry, and scared.

Death was calling us in more ways than one.

I heard growling behind me.

Then I felt light on my feet.

I was flying. My baby was in my arms.

I felt arms on me, warm and strong.

A man with wings full of scars carried us. My son slept comfortably, and the heat from the man's body carried on to both of us. Hunger was gone.

We fell asleep and woke up in a new safe home. Crops were in bloom, and the well was filled with clean water.

We lived.

I was in a car accident. I died. I could see my body on the floor in front of me.

A man came to talk to me.

He was bald with a scar on his face.

He smiled, and I felt warm.

He touched my bloody hand.

I blinked, and I was back in my body.

I was alive.

Lucy felt a warm arm around her. An arm pulling her close and fingers tracing her arm.

Clay.

She would know him anywhere. Her smile was faint in the light, eyes still closed.

"Did not mean to wake you," he said softly.

"You can always wake me," Lucy's voice was a whisper. She meant it. "Sorry for the sacrifices you have to make. I'm sorry you have to lose so much for me. I'm sorry about Arsenio."

Lucy swallowed back tears.

Each word held depth in her heart.

"It is the way it is supposed to be. It isn't a sacrifice. I learned long ago, it is the life of a Guardian. I knew what I signed up for when I made the oath to you. Arsenio gave his life for the Light. It is the greatest honor for us guardians," Clay said.

Lucy could feel the vibrations of his deep voice in her chest.

She rolled in towards him and lifted the blankets to cover him at the same time. When she looked at him, she noticed he was wearing pajamas, too.

"I understand, but I am still sorry," Lucy's voice still a whisper filled with exhaustion from sleep.

"Thank you."

Clay was lying on his back. His eyes looked up at the sky through the sunroof. The moon shined on his face and his eyes glowed. Lucy could see his lips part as if he was going to say something. Instead, he closed his mouth and smiled to himself.

Can you hear me? She heard his voice in her head.

"Yes!" She said. "How are you doing that?"

"It is rare, but it is known to happen with oath-bound Guardians. I wasn't sure if it would work at first. I hadn't tried though, when I did try earlier by the lake, you heard me," he said.

"Will it work if I try to speak to you?" Lucy asked.

"I am unsure. Give it a try," he looked at her.

I love you. She thought to him.

His face didn't change. He didn't hear her.

She took a deep breath and focused.

Thank you for protecting me. Lucy changed her words and felt sure of them.

Always, Lucy. His voice was strong in her head.

"That is amazing," Lucy couldn't help but smile.

"Yes, it is. With practice, we could communicate from a distance. Always for your safety, of course. I do not hear anything you do not wish for me to hear," Clay said.

That explained why he hadn't heard her the first time.

"We have to keep this a secret, don't we?" Lucy asked as she leaned into his chest.

"Yes, we do. Emma and Owranoos both know. They won't say anything, but I am not sure anyone else would keep it a secret if they were to find out. Everyone else is Council and doesn't see many things the way Emma and Owranoos do," Clay's voice was smooth, completely unbothered.

"Won't they know if you are here?" Lucy hid her irritation.

"They won't suspect anything. It is normal for a Guardian to have a room in the house of who they are oath-bound to. You don't happen to have an extra room. They'll think I am on the couch, or I could easily go to my home before any of them get here," he said.

Lucy felt his smile, and he kissed the top of her head. Clay's arms wrapped around her, her hand laid on his chest over his heart, and she could hear his heart beating.

He turned her body for her to look up, too. They both laid on their backs, Lucy still in his arms.

"Look at the stars," he said to her, the hum of his smooth voice could have soothed her back to sleep. "What do you see?"

She looked up through the large skylight. At first, she only saw stars, hard for her to focus over the heavy beating of Clay's heart.

The more she focused on the stars, the more she let go. Once relaxed, she could see them moving slightly. Some stars grew brighter, some flashed.

Lucy breathed, "I see water, the bottom of a body of water. When you lay at the bottom of deep water and look up towards the sun."

"Hold onto that. Remember that feeling, that picture you have in your head. The stars tell stories. They help us like a map would. They are our Light when we cannot find our way. They are a gift to us," Clay's voice was distant, his hands mechanically stroked her hair while he thought aloud.

The stars moved back to normal. From the corner of the skylight was a large shooting star, it went from one side of the skylight and arched its way to the other side.

"The angels heard you. Water is where we start tomorrow," Clay said.

That reminded her of the book she was reading before she fell asleep.

"Oh yeah, speaking of Angels, I found this book in here. It's called Lachfll 331. I started reading it and fell asleep," she said.

"Michael," Clay reached to the other side of her to get the book.

"Yes, how do you know?" Asked Lucy.

"I wrote it," his voice unchanged.

"You wrote the book?" She turned towards him to see his face and not the sky.

"Over the millennia, I wrote down stories of the angels told by humans. Legends of the angels who performed miracles, I tracked them. Lachfll 331 was about the Archangel Michael. The beginning of the book is all testimonials. The rest of it is what he has done that mortals do not know of," Clay said.

His eyes looked up at the stars, his mind elsewhere.

"You were there?" Lucy asked.

He said angels don't appear anymore.

"For some, yes. Others are just stories passed down," he said.

"So, you've met him?" Surprise was in her voice as she propped up on her elbow so she could look directly at his glowing eyes.

"Yes," his voice longed for better words. "He raised me. He trained me. He chose for me to be a Guardian."

"How come you've never told me?" Lucy asked.

He didn't move.

"I knew you'd find out one day. In the right time. It isn't something I bring up," Clay said.

"The whole Guard is trained by Angels? That's amazing." Lucy said.

"No. Not the whole Guard. Just me," his tone was smooth, his eyes glowed, focused on the night sky.

"Oh. How does that work?" Lucy was trying to piece everything together.

"I was created and trained to build the Guard. I was created to lead them. The angels wrote the rules and guidelines for me to follow. With that, I did as I was told. I built a strong immortal army. I chose mortals who had what it took and made them immortal. We walk the earth and protect the Light. Angels stand out and tip the scales, we were intended to do so in a less obvious way where we could still aid humans in making their own decisions. I was specifically trained to protect you when the time came. The angels made it clear, Michael made it clear," Clay turned his body to place his hand on her leg, his eyes still on the stars.

"Wow, Clay. That explains so much. You do everything in ways nobody else can. You being their leader is easy to see. You were created and born to lead. It's who you are, and I see it now," Lucy said.

She did see, and she did understand. Clay wasn't just in charge of the people she knew. He was the leader of the entire Guard.

"I get that from my father." He sat up a little.

"I didn't know you had a father, only because you never mention him. I didn't know how that worked," Lucy said.

She didn't want to push him too far.

Clay sat up and finally looked at Lucy, his face inches from hers. His eyes glowed bright blue and green. His skin began to ripple the way it does when he's on high alert.

"Michael. The Archangel Michael, he is my father."

19

Lucy hadn't been inside the safe house since her birthday, the day she saw the demon, and the house created a sphere-like nest to keep her safe. Her whole life she thought it would be dark and dusty on the inside, abandoned even. She believed the inside of the fence would be unkempt and full of weeds. It was the opposite.

The yard had a garden with rows of nothing but vegetables and herbs. Every kind of herb you could think of. There was a chain-link fence along part of the wooden fence where the garden was. The fence was full of different types of berries. A fire pit was on the back of the house, the same side the lake was on. Which might as well have been the front, every home around the lake had a front door nobody used. Around the fire pit were different types of seating. It had a large log, two benches, a few Adirondack chairs, and two hanging hammock chairs. The back door had a large porch, much larger than Leos.

Lucy walked through the freshly cut grass, between the garden and the fire pit to the porch stairs. They had carvings on them, the same as the rest of the houses on the lake. The door was the same color, dark wood as the rest of the house. It had an abstract stained-glass panel in the middle of it that shined a colorful pattern on the floor just before the door. The whole house was made of dark wooden logs, even the walls. It had the same feel as Clay's house across the lake. Even though the entire house was made of dark wood, it felt much bigger than she thought it would be. The layout didn't look the same as the last time she had been in there. There were much more pictures on the wall. The living room was definitely bigger, twice the size even. When she looked at where the stairs were, they felt further than they did before.

Kona stayed by Lucy's side since their reunion this morning. Since she found out about him being a wolf and since her return from Mpiar-on, he was the alpha of his pack. He was still Kona, only now he was on high alert, and every time someone's voice was within earshot or every time the house creaked, he scouted the area. Lucy could tell he was a warrior in a wolf's body, but also a friend to her.

A memory of a conversation she had came to mind. The house changed depending on how many people it needed to host. She looked at some of the pictures on the walls. They were pictures of people she didn't know. All of them were taken at the lake or places around it, some of them looked familiar, but she couldn't place any names. Yet, there was something about them, few people smiled in the pictures, but each one of them looked happy. They were calm and relaxed. Lucy felt the peacefulness through each photo.

She continued to walk around the house and could see its age. The lamps were old, in excellent condition, but old. There was no overhead lighting either, just lamps of all shapes and sizes. Most of them were the same abstract stained glass as the front door only the colors were much softer and gave the home a lighter feel amongst all of the dark wood. The only overhead lighting was in the oversized kitchen. Lucy was surprised at the size of the kitchen. Usually, older homes had smaller kitchens. It was fully stocked with fresh produce she assumed to be from the garden outside. In the cabinets were dehydrated fruits and meats, flour, several types of dried beans, a whole cupboard dedicated to dried herbs, and always had been by the smell of it.

The whole house was made of wood, but it was nice and open. Every breath Lucy took was fresh. The old, paneled windows were opened and let in a cross breeze. Not one thing was out of place. She could find not one speck of dust. There was only a clean living space and tons of plants all around the house. Some hung from the dark wooden ceiling. Some were on shelves. There were small trees in some corners of the house. The fluffy sofas she saw in the living room were the same as before, only each one was much longer, they could easily fit fifteen people comfortably, and all faced a ridiculously large fireplace.

Something felt familiar about it. Lucy had never seen a fireplace of this size before. She could walk inside of it without ducking her head. On the border of the fireplace were tiled stone carvings, and each tile was different. Some had feathers, some had leaves, some looked like they had waterfalls.

Where have I seen this before? Lucy asked herself.

When she touched the carvings and got to the one with feathers on it, everything registered, and she remembered. The doors on the houses in Mpiaron mirrored the tiles. Each door had different colors. Lucy noticed the textures varied, making them appear different in color when they were all the same exact stone.

The fire was burning, too small when you compared it to the vastness of the fireplace. Nevertheless, the radiating warmth and crackles were soothing. Omala had been steadily throwing herbs in there to make the smoke of the fire blue. When the smoke went out of the chimney, it was a royal blue and easily seen by Lemurians from a distance. Blue smoke meant council meeting. It protected the house and all who were on their way.

Everyone else was there before she was. Alika, Fazi, Omala, Rani, Dario, Talan, Emma, her dad, Leon, and a few people she didn't know filled the room. Her uncles Silas, Colton, and Mikael were also there, each one happy to see Rani and greeted her like an old friend.

Separate conversations echoed throughout the living room and kitchen. Lucy was the only one who didn't engage. Instead, occupied with her surroundings and observed the interactions between each person.

Alika, Omala, Fazi, and Rani stayed together. When she passed them, they talked about different journals Alika's father had written that could help them. Her uncles stayed with her dad, Leon, and Emma, who never left Leon's side. Dario and Talan went back and forth between talking to Emma and Leon and the group of people she didn't know.

"All here?" Clay's voice echoed every bit the warrior he was.

Within a minute, everyone either sat on the large sofas or stood behind them. All looking toward the fireplace where Clay stood.

"In Mpiaron, they could sense our presence," his voice roared throughout the room. "Thanks to our old friend, Jasutin, we are safe, and none of the Deminio were able to cross through or find us. The Deminio could sense the open Gateway. You did your best guarding it and keeping it safe. Still, we need to do better. What happened with Arsenio is unacceptable. We cannot underestimate a demon, they have evolved as we have. We have become strong. They have become stronger. I also received word from the wolves," Clay gestured outside. "The Deminio have more beings swaying in their direction. Not Lemurians nor Deminio, but aids. Beings are trading their safety for information and favors. We do not know who is on our side or if anyone truly is. We do have to find out. I am hopeful that bringing Owranoos over from Mpiaron will bring hope to those who have family there. Soon they will stop living in fear and choose our side and be reunited with their loved ones. It is their decision to make, we don't work like Darkness does. When people choose Light, it is because it is what they want. That being said, the carving has not left. The Gateway isn't secured and can be opened again. It is our duty to ensure everyone within Mpiaron stays safe at any and all costs. We are here to vote. Everyone in Mpiaron is trained and ready for battle. Our vote is whether or not we should integrate Mpiarians. They can help train Lucy and help anyone who is now worthy and hadn't chosen a side when we closed Mpiaron. The downside is, them being here will have a concentrated amount of Light in one area. It will attract more Deminio and eventually reveal our location. We all vote now and if there is anything anyone wants to add, do so now. I want to bring a few here to help Lucy train. I believe every race can give Lucy the education necessary. I do not think we should bring them all until she learns to protect herself. That being said, my vote is no. Not yet. All in favor of opening Mpiaron and integrating our people?"

Clay addressed the room. Nobody raised their hands. Nobody except for Lucy. Everyone else agreed with Clay, though Lucy was unsure whether it was because they trusted his judgment or their own.

"They deserve to know," was all she managed to say.

"Clay, if you feel we need to leave the Gateway shut until Lucy is ready, that is what we will do. You know, inside, what is right for her. What is right for her is what is right for all of us," Emma spoke up.

Emma was a sounding board and the only one to speak up to Clay.

"Lucy, if the Mpiarians know what is happening, they will want to come and help. I won't stop them from coming back. They are not prisoners there. If they come back, the attack of the Deminio won't be a few months or years from now, but days. They *will* attack. Without you and your gifts, this will all have been for nothing. If we train you first, even a week of training, and gauge what you can do, and if we test your physical limits, we could let them know where we are and have them base their decision on that. Not on what ifs or fragility. Can we compromise on a week of training?" Clay asked.

Lucy nodded. She didn't want to say too much. Lucy didn't trust herself when it came to hiding how she felt, especially not in front of the people who knew her best.

"Everyone stay close. The house will accommodate anyone who wants or needs housing." He looked at the Guardians and outside, then he turned to her uncles, "Anthos, call your sons. All of them."

He called them by their last name.

"Are you going to call the Guard?" Talan asked.

"Not yet," Clay said, every bit in charge. "I stay with Lucy unless I check posts and patrol. Other than that, I will not leave her. All of her training will be done under my watch and with my approval. If she emits too much energy, I will be with her if any demons show up. If at any time she weakens, she goes straight to Owranoos. Owranoos, stay within reach," he spewed commands, and all Lucy could think of after he spoke of demons was how she felt when darkness showed up the last time she was in this house.

Every hair on her body stood up.

Are you okay? Clay's voice inside of her head.

She looked at him, and he was looking at everyone else.

Yes. Sorry. Lucy thought back to him.

His eyes flashed neon, the only indication he heard her, and he continued to give commands towards everyone else. Lucy zoned out and stared at the fire with the blue smoke.

"Leo and all Anthos. You're up," was Clay's last command before dismissing them.

Lucy's uncles stood next to each other close by and faced her. Leon was next to her, and her dad was in front of her. They decided to stay outside the fence in the middle of the safe house and her dad's house on a patch of grass. Everyone else watched closely instead of going to their stations. Clay didn't seem to mind, he was with the Guardians, and they were watching too.

"Okay. Lucy, everything you think inside is exactly the same as you saying it aloud. Be careful with the things you let occupy your mind, for the things you say to yourself inside are much more powerful. If you wouldn't say it aloud, don't think it. For example, if you think to yourself, 'I wish the water was warmer,' the water will warm up. If the water is cold and you ask it to heat up, it will respond. We now know you have allied with water and earth. They are their own element and allow you to be heard by them. Have you tried anything else?" Leo, her dad, was Enkeli, his voice different than what Lucy was used to.

"Not that I'm aware of," Lucy said.

She wiped the sweat of her palms on her jeans.

"Let's start with this." Her dad set a small glass of water on top of a stool in between them.

He gestured for her to do something.

"Water, lift out of the cup," Lucy's voice shook, and the pressure of everyone looking at her was where her focus was, not with the water.

"Lucy. Try again," her dad said, expression and tone emotionless.

"Focus Luc," Leon whispered and encouraged her.

She let it all go. She let go of the pressure.

Immediately she sat down on the grass and crossed her legs. Her hands at her sides and palms down on the earth. The grass under her was cool from the morning dew. She focused on that. She closed her eyes and breathed.

In and out.

Inhale, exhale.

She breathed until all she could focus on was the grass beneath her and the air in her lungs.

With her eyes closed and her mind clear, she said, "Water. Up."

She felt it. The water rose. Something inside of her knew.

She held onto that, the state of knowing it responded without visually seeing it.

She held on to the feeling.

Gasps echoed around Lucy, and she opened her eyes to see the cup of water was empty. The water was in a perfect sphere and hovered directly above the cup.

Moisture was in the air. She looked around and could see water begin to come up out of the grass and float all around her in tiny drops. It slowly rained upwards until it got within eye level to her, then it stopped.

"Thank you, water." Lucy bowed her head and closed her eyes, and she could hear the water splash inside the cup. The droplets wet the surface of the grass.

Everyone cheered. Her dad helped her up and hugged her. Leon gave her a high five. Her friends clapped and wooed for her.

She looked over at Clay, who beamed a smile at her.

Well done. His voice in her head.

He turned around and directed the guard towards their posts around the lake.

"How do you feel?" Her dad asked.

His brows furrowed with concern, Leon's face mirroring Leos.

"I feel fine. Let's keep going."

They continued for hours. Throughout the training, Rani insisted for Lucy to drink a special elixir in between exercises. The elixir was supposed to help her.

Lucy worked with only the cup of water for some time before she moved on. She boiled the water, froze it, moved it from one cup to another, she dumped it out into the grass and put it back, and sat on the floor the entire time.

"Clay, are you ready for her over there?" Her dad yelled from the back porch of his house.

Clay nodded once. Leon gave Lucy a hand to help her up, and they walked down to the lake.

Her nose began to drip. She wiped it with the back of her hand. Blood.

"Lucy, sit down," Leon's voice was stern, a rare occasion for him.

"I'm okay. It's just a bloody nose," she said but sat down for his comfort.

"No, it isn't. Sit down." Their dad was at her side and held her by her elbow.

"Seriously. I'm fine."

Everything inside of her felt normal.

"Until you're not. This is how it starts, a bloody nose, then dizziness. When you were younger, you'd faint often," her dad's voice was distant with the memory.

"I don't remember that." She looked up at him.

"You were too young. You wouldn't remember," Clay said as he walked up and looked closely at Lucy, he evaluated her temperature and pulse.

Are you okay? Really? His voice in her head.

Yes. If I wasn't okay, you'd know. She thought to him and gave him a tight nod.

"She is okay. Keep going," his words written in stone.

Her dad clenched his jaw and squeezed his eyes shut. In that moment, Lucy understood the rank and demand in what Clay said. He had a say in everything, the final say. What he says goes, without question and they all honored his decision.

Clay walked up towards the porch of her dad's house and leaned on the railing to watch from a distance.

"Okay, what are we doing now?" Lucy continued to push herself.

She directed her attention towards her family in front of her. Her dad, Leon, and her uncles.

Her uncle Mikael stepped forward into the lake and turned around to look at Lucy, "Now you make waves."

Lucy took her shoes off and walked into the lake. She stopped when she was knee deep next to her uncle. The water was the same temperature as her skin. When it wet her jeans, she didn't feel it.

"Feel the water," he spoke, "breathe and feel the water. The water will tell you where the fish are. It will tell you about the tides. It has been here for millions of years. Pay attention to it, work with water. Now talk to it and see what you can do."

Mikael was much softer than her dad. He had always been the one to surf with them, teaching them to surf and to snorkel. So it made sense he had close ties to water. Not only because he was always in it, but because of his personality, he was strong, clear, and didn't have to yell to be heard.

Focus and breathe.

Focus and breathe.

Focus and breathe.

Lucy repeated this mantra to herself before she spoke aloud, "Water, I call on you to guide me. Please let me know you hear me."

The water around her legs got warmer, and flashes of memories came in a rush.

She could see her and Leon learning to swim in the lake as toddlers. The first fish she had ever caught. Her and Leon sneaking the boat when they were ten to pick up their friends around the lake. Them jumping off of a rock at Cove Black on the other side of the lake. She saw herself fall off of the wakeboard when she was first learning. Her doing laps as an adult. Her first kiss.

So many memories flashed in just a moment's time.

Water was showing her memories they shared. What Lucy didn't know at the time of these events was that water was listening and soaking these memories in too. Water had always helped her. She didn't just feel the warmth of it on her feet but in her entire body. She was happy.

She felt happy memories.

In between the good memories were a few not so good ones, like when she broke her arm. The countless times she fell off of the boat. Every time she went for a swim so she could cry. Her crying for her mom after every dream she had of her that she didn't want her dad to know about. The feelings she felt when those memories surfaces weren't sad, surprisingly. It was more of a release and her being washed clean.

Lucy felt lighter.

Let's make waves. She silently said to the water.

A second passed, and she could feel the ripples before she saw them. A small wake. Then another, and another, and another.

Until they weren't wakes anymore. They were small waves. Perfect barrels.

Thank you.

The last few waves rolled, and the water softened.

"Okay, that is enough. Lucy needs to eat, and she needs rest." Rani walked towards her and helped her out of the water. Lucy didn't move with her. She stayed in the water.

The sun was setting.

How could that be? She thought to herself.

"What's going on?" She asked aloud.

Everyone was in different places than when she first walked into the water.

"Water took you back to your memories. Its own way of showing you it is present and always has been. It has been hours of you standing there. Are you tired?" Mikael asked.

She was. The moment he asked the question, it hit her. Hard. Lucy was exhausted. She felt if she laid down right there on the shoreline, wet and all, she would sleep until tomorrow morning.

"I am taking her home. Owranoos made an elixir for her to take when she gets there. We will be back at the same time tomorrow. Nobody bother Lucy until then," Clay's voice echoed around her.

Lucy didn't trust her legs to walk back up to the house, but she didn't want anyone to know she felt weak. She did the only thing she could think to do. She sat down. Her jeans made her movement in the water stiff, the water at her chest.

Water, please give me the strength to get up and walk to the car. She took a deep breath, immediately, she could feel the water moving around on her skin. A small current washed through her entire body. The water chilled shortly after and electrified her energy.

Standing up was easier than it should have been.

"Didn't get enough water?" Leon joked as he helped her out of the water and wrapped her in a large plush towel.

"Thanks," Lucy said.

It was all she had the strength to say.

Clay must have felt it, too, because he pulled his truck down to the water. Lucy said a quick goodbye to everyone and thanked them.

She plopped in the passenger's seat of the car. Leon shut the door and smiled at her as he tossed her a bag of dried mangoes through the window just before waving bye.

"Well done today," Clay said once they were past the tree line and away from earshot.

The Guardians and the wolves could hear from a far distance.

Clay reached over and opened the bag of dried mangoes, handing a slice to Lucy.

Lucy smiled at him and took it.

"Is this normal? For me to be this tired?" She asked.

"There hasn't been a woman Enkeli in millennia. From what I can remember, they all reacted differently towards their gifts. You become physically drained, which seems normal considering the strength it takes. A few became mentally weak, forgetting who they were and losing any grasp they had of their sanity. You will find your balance," Clay said.

He usually wasn't soft with her. She must be tired.

"How do you know? You know. That I'll find my balance," she asked.

"You have many teachers. You have several witches aiding your health, and you have your family. Family by blood and family by choice. They all love you and can teach you the way you need to be taught. You have me. I will make sure you come first," there was no trace of doubt in Clay's voice.

They pulled up to her home, and she was overwhelmed with fatigue. Her clothes were wet, sweat beaded on her face, and dripped down the sides of her neck.

A shower was all she could think about. It was what she needed, despite being around water all day.

Clay opened the door to the truck and helped her out. He guided her inside and made sure to catch her had her legs failed.

"I made pasta and fresh bread. Drink the tea in the refrigerator. I also drew you a bath and made an elixir to put in there. It will help you get a good night's sleep. Bath. Eat. Sleep. You got it?" Rani spoke directly to Lucy.

"Yes, thank you," Lucy said.

Rani smiled and slightly bowed her head. Lucy took a moment to really look at her. Rani was beautiful, her light brown hair was wavy and fine. Framing her soft face perfectly. Her lips were the perfect shade of red, naturally, and matched her hazel eyes and rosy cheeks. She was small framed but had softness to her.

"Rani, I appreciate you," Lucy said just before Rani walked down the stairs and passed them. She walked to the flat and closed the door.

"Bath?" Clay asked.

Lucy nodded and squirmed a little under his grip. He picked her up and carried her inside to the bathroom.

Does he really think he's going to take a bath with me? Lucy asked herself. She couldn't look him in the eye.

"No, I don't," he laughed and put her down. He placed a bathrobe on the hook next to the bath before he walked out and shut the door.

She thought the highlight of her day was working with water. That was before she peeled off her cold, wet clothes and submerged herself into the bath. The smell was exquisite. She knew it well, fresh jasmines and sea salt. The tub was in the ground and spacious enough for her to stretch her body out and float. Her original floor plan had a small claw foot tub with a separate shower, this was an in-ground bath large enough for four people with a waterfall shower head up above the tub. She was thankful for the change and reminded herself to thank Talan later.

The tiles had shells in them, the stone used for the bathroom was once sand, and shells turned into rock. The entire bathroom was covered in this tile, the walls, the ceiling, the bathtub. It glittered with depth instead of feeling uniform. Although it was all the same material, each tile was different. Some were grayer, some were more sand toned, others were slightly blue, and most of them were marbled with every color combined. The way the shells varied and the way the sand gathered was all different. In them, she felt the ocean.

Her eyes were closed, and her body was completely submerged underwater as she washed her hair. Lucy knew she had to hurry. If she took too long, she would be too tired to eat.

When she took her first breath after being underwater, her lungs filled with air, and her nose filled with the smell of fresh bread. Her stomach growled. Lucy rushed out of the bath and went through the door that leads to her room. The other door leads to the open kitchen and living room where Clay was. Quickly, she brushed her hair, moisturized her body, and got into her comfortable pajamas. Always an oversized tee shirt and shorts.

When she went to the kitchen, Clay had their food on the coffee table next to the couch.

She walked over and sat on the floor next to him, thankful for the comfort of the ground.

"Drink this first." He handed her a cup of iced tea.

She took a sip, jasmine with a few herbs she couldn't place. Her body filled with a warm tingling sensation even though the tea was chilled. Rani knew what she was doing. She knew her herbs well.

"Yes, she does," Clay said through a bite of pasta.

"You can hear my thoughts?" Lucy asked.

Her face fell with concern.

"You are screaming them at me. It is your exhaustion. You can't filter out what you do and do not want me to hear. Like you not wanting me to see you in your bathrobe," he said jokingly.

He smiled but didn't look her in the eye.

"Oh my gosh, how embarrassing," Lucy said and leaned her head in one of her hands to hide her face while she ate with the other. She wondered what else she had said.

"Do not worry. It will not happen once you have had enough rest. Eat so you can go to sleep." She could hear the smile in Clay's voice.

She ate her food and drank her tea until she couldn't have another bite or another sip. A crackle sounded in the distance. She had just realized the fire was on in front of her. Lucy looked up at Clay and smiled. He knew the fire was her sign to her dad she was okay.

Clay got up and took their dishes to the far side of the room where the kitchen was. Lucy reached for a few pillows and threw them on the plush rug next to the fireplace. Under the coffee table was a crate full of throw blankets. She wrapped the fluffiest one around her body and laid next to the fire.

The warmth on her face was medicinal. The food settled in, and exhaustion was gone, soreness replaced by ease. Clay made his way to her and sat on the floor beside her, placing her between him and the fire.

He put her legs on his and had begun to massage them.

"Clay, can I ask you something?" She said through heavy blinks.

"Anything, always," he said.

"What kind of life are you supposed to live? Can you have a family? A wife? What is in the cards for the life of a Guardian? Not just as a part of the Guard, but the rest of it." She didn't know where it came from, though she was glad she asked.

"Go to sleep, Lucy. You need your rest for tomorrow," he said.

"You said anything," Lucy said.

"It is our choice. Many Guardians have families, wives, do normal human things. Though we usually don't because we can't truly feel the way humans do. We weren't made for it. Humans live such short lives. For us to fall in love and have them die is trying. All is allowed as long as it doesn't change our ability to guard," he said. "Dario always finds love. His wife reincarnates, and he can feel her every time she is reborn. It is beautiful, truly. Talan, on the other hand, prefers to have short relations. Though it is frowned upon, he has been much the lady's man through-out the years. He finds a thrill in it. He is quite fond of you."

"Talan has flirted with me since we were kids, or I guess since I was a kid. It is all fun and games for him, though. He never means what he says." Lucy closed her eyes, unable to fight it before continuing, "Dario, that suits him."

"He does mean it, Lucy. I can see it in him, and I know him well enough. He falters around you, much like I do. You have a light that attracts us to you, similar to the draw of the Deminio. All beings will find themselves drawn to you the more you use your gifts. You do have to be careful. People will be drawn to you because of the way they see themselves when they're with you, not for who you are," irritation taint-ed his voice.

"Have you ever been married? Or had… partners?" The question she had been wondering finally escaped her lips.

He paused and took a deep breath. After a few moments he let it out, "Long ago, not in the way you might assume."

"You've been married?" She pushed.

"No, never that. I have known love before," he said.

Lucy figured he kissed like he'd done it his whole life and the way he was massaging her legs made her feel his hands knew what they were doing.

"It isn't what you think. You are who I have been waiting for my entire existence. My hands know what they're doing. My lips know you. My hands know you," his words struck her, lightning in her veins.

"Oh," was all she managed to say.

"I feel you on a level nobody else could comprehend. It is more than a bond, much more than being sired. When I took my oath to you, everything inside of me changed. Everything. When you marched towards me the day we officially met at the beach, I felt you. When you were standing on my front porch, barefoot and waiting to come inside, I knew this was not just a Guardian and Enkeli bond. I *feel* who you are," his voice wasn't more than a whisper, but his words were loud.

Her eyes shut, too tired to say anything back to him.

I have never loved anyone other than my friends and my family. I don't know how to do this, Clay. She thought to him.

"Do not rush, whether it be me or someone else. When you love someone, you will know. When you are in love with them, you will know," he whispered.

His hands stopped massaging her legs, and she felt him lay next to her. She opened the blanket for him to get under with her. He scooted in and pulled her close to him. He was warm and smelled like water and trees.

"Clay, what did you do today? While I was with Water?" Curiosity beat her need for sleep.

"I was ensuring your safety," he said.

She could feel the vibration of his voice throughout her body.

"I am safe, even without you. I didn't realize until right now, but I feel Michael around. I don't know why all of a sudden I feel him, and I know he's been present. I feel it," Lucy said in a daze.

"He ensures my safety," Clay said.

His fingers brushed through her hair.

"Do you talk to him?" Lucy asked.

"Every day." She could hear the smile in his voice.

"I would, too. If he was my dad," she said.

"You can still talk to him even though he is not your father." Clay turned his head to look at her.

She was too exhausted to look up, "I wouldn't want him to think I am a burden. Him being an angel and all. He's probably too busy for me."

"He would not have shown himself to you if you weren't deserving of it. Nobody is a burden to angels. Even those who walk with Darkness, with the Deminio even. If they call on them, the Angels will listen. Talk to him. He is here to help. You need to rest now. Goodnight, Lucy." He kissed her forehead, and she drifted off into a deep, dreamless sleep.

20

Kona whimpered. Lucy's eyes were still closed. Kona pawed at her pillow, not in the way he used to do. It was more humanlike.

She turned around.

Kona pushed the pillow, and Lucy remembered who he was.

The space next to her was empty. Clay was gone.

Lucy sat up and looked around the room, the fire was crackling, and there was a log freshly placed in the fireplace. It was still dark outside. She had only been asleep a short time.

Lucy reached out to touch Kona, and he pounced away from her towards the back door. He let out a soft growl towards the outside. She got up and walked towards the back sliding door to let him out.

When she got to the door, Kona was waiting for her. He stared outside and made a deep rumbling sound. She looked out and could see movement through the light fog by the lake.

For a reason she didn't know, she felt the need to hide. She hid behind the curtains and looked out, there were two figures. One she immediately recognized as Clay. The other had a black beanie on and a flannel shirt. She'd have known it was Emma by his stance, even if she couldn't see the beanie.

Everything inside of her told her to go back to sleep. She took a few deep breaths and closed her eyes. She pictured herself in a bubble. A bubble wrapped around her body where nothing could get in, and nothing could get out. Clay couldn't feel her, not her emotions or sense that she was awake. She hoped it would work, though she had to actively envision the bubble.

Her hand reached for the sliding door and cracked it. Their voices carried through the wind and straight to her.

"They know, Clay. We aren't ready for a battle," Emma was furious.

"We will be when the time comes. I will not start a war, if they choose to, we will figure it out," Clay's voice was much calmer than Emma's.

"You don't understand. There is someone out there who can see us. Someone or something we can't see. There is someone out there who knows this land like we do. They're giving the Deminio updates," Emma said, growing impatient.

"How do you know?" Clay asked, indifferent.

"It's hard to explain," Emma said and turned towards the house.

Lucy pulled herself back and ducked down in hopes they couldn't see her shadow through the curtain.

"You need to try. We cannot base anything off of a feeling this time, Emma. Not while we are dealing with the Deminio. Not with her," Clay pointed his chin towards the house.

"I try to fight it. But I still feel them sometimes. I know I am not supposed to, and I haven't felt them this way in years. It's getting stronger. The larger they get, the more I feel them. My brothers and sisters. I felt eyes today while she was in the water," Emma put his head down.

"There was nobody there, we had the lake checked multiple times, and we surrounded the lake the entire time. The wolves sniffed out the area and didn't find any new scents," irritation grew in Clay's voice with every word he said. Not with Emma but with the lengths they took and the possibility of cracks in their security.

"That is exactly my point, Clay. There were no *new* scents," Emma pushed.

Clay turned towards the lake. He ran his hands through his hair and inhaled deeply.

"What you are saying is someone or something is here and can somehow see us, and has this whole time? Something we haven't picked up on?" Clay asked.

"Yeah. If they can do that and someone can easily get by, what don't we know? We have grown and evolved tremendously, even within the length of time she has been born until now. How much have they grown too? We can't pretend they haven't changed since I left. They are worse now. I feel eyes, Clay. I know it. It doesn't feel like Deminio, but it isn't Lemurians either. Don't take this lightly," danger in Emma's voice.

"I take nothing you say lightly," Clay said. "I will ask the witches to aid us tomorrow. Alika and Fazi specialize in earth ties, they will find the cracks, they will find out what is going on."

Emma's shoulders eased.

"I will bring this up to Council tomorrow," Emma said.

"No. We speak of this to no one," Clay forced.

"They need to know, Clay." Emma took a step closer to Clay and looked up at him.

"No, they don't. I will see what the witches come up with tomorrow. We bring it up if necessary. Not before then. Lucy barely started her training and doesn't need more pressure on her, and we don't need to instill fear in everyone else right now. Not until we need to. Fear-based decisions are the worst ones to make. We move in Light and in power. Understand?" Lucy felt the order in Clay's voice.

Emma extended his hand, forearm to forearm. Then he turned around and disappeared through the tree line to the left, towards the Bloom.

Lucy hurried to shut the door as silently as she could and crawled back to her makeshift bed on the floor next to the fireplace. Kona was no longer inside of her house. She slid under the covers and focused on her breathing. As soon as her breathing softened, Clay opened the sliding door. Lucy closed her eyes and pretended to be asleep. When Clay shut the sliding door, he also closed the curtains so nobody could see inside. He walked all around the entire house, even up to the loft, and closed the curtains and shutters from every window and door until everything was covered and nobody or nothing could see inside.

She continued to fake being asleep and focused on her breathing.

His footsteps grew near, and she heard him take off his shoes and walk towards her again. He laid down and went under the blanket, putting his arms around her. Lucy could feel his body relax a little, now that he was next to her. Only he didn't relax fully. He didn't plan on going back to sleep.

Lucy immediately began to drift off.

She wondered why Clay hadn't woken her up. She wondered if Clay had any intention of telling her what Emma told him. She hoped he would, even before he talked to the witches. He always does what he feels to be best for her, but that doesn't mean he always does what is best for her. Only what he thinks to be.

Lucy's eyes closed, and all she could remember of her dreams was a familiar tunnel and a warm honey voice.

"Good morning." Clay was in the kitchen, his usually light hair was dark and wet from a shower, and he was dressed for the day.

"You're up early," Lucy said as she rubbed the sleep from her eyes.

"And you are well-rested," he said.

He was slightly sarcastic, more playful than usual.

"What's so funny, Clay?" She asked.

Lucy got up out of bed and stretched her body.

"Nothing," he said and looked at the clock on the wall next to the table.

Lucy looked outside, then at the clock.

"Oh my gosh, how is it noon already? Why didn't you wake me up? Everyone is waiting for me!" Lucy said.

She rushed to the bathroom to go brush her teeth, then to her room to change her clothes. She put her hair in a French braid when she paced to the kitchen to let Clay know she was ready to go.

"Now that you are ready sit down and eat," Clay said. Unlike Lucy, he was not in a rush, and it irritated her.

"There is no time to waste. We need to leave. I have to train," she said as she reached for her small leather bag that holds everything and slung it over her shoulder.

Lucy had just made it to the door when Clay said, "You need to eat."

His voice was still too calm.

"What about everyone else? They are waiting for me," Lucy said.

"They are not. They are training, just like they did before you found out. When you are ready to join them is when you join them. They wait for nobody. Just as I do and just as you do," he said.

She took off her bag and placed it on the island as she sat.

"Here you go. Eat," Clay said.

He placed a plate of blueberry pancakes in front of her with a side of berries and more of the tea Rani had made. Lucy ate every bite of her food and drank every last drop of the tea without saying a word. She was waiting for him to bring up his conversation with Emma last night while also contemplating whether or not she should ask about it.

"How'd you sleep?" Lucy asked him.

She eyeballed him to see if his face changed. It didn't.

"Comfortably," he said.

"Did you fall asleep shortly after I did?" She pushed.

"I don't sleep much, but I did sleep last night," he said through a bite of his second stack of pancakes.

Clay didn't answer her question.

"I slept like a log. Only woke up once." Lucy looked at him.

"Great. You needed it after your first day of training yesterday," he said.

Clay wasn't going to say anything, and Lucy knew it. She didn't know he would keep secrets. She only knew he wouldn't lie to her. Those were two completely separate things. It had her wondering what else he knew and was withholding from her. What wasn't he telling her? If the chance came for her to talk to Emma, she was going to.

"Are you ready?" Clay said after his last bite.

"Always."

21

"Who are they?" Lucy asked as she studied their faces.

"More of the Guard. A little past them, hidden in the trees, are the wolves," Clay told her and gestured towards the forest.

"They're like Kona? How many of them are here?" She asked.

"Yes, most of them, at least. Except they can shapeshift as where Kona cannot, he is alpha. There could be hundreds in each pack. We only have a few from twelve different packs," he said.

Somehow, she wasn't surprised.

"I don't know why, but I thought wolf packs were small in numbers," she said. A part of her was putting his conversation with Emma in the back of her mind. She was distracting herself.

"Some packs make up whole cities. All rural and untraceable to humans, that is why they only sent a few from each pack. They need to protect their people," Clay said.

"Wow. Are there any close by?" Lucy wondered how big this can of worms was. It keeps getting bigger and she felt she would never get to the bottom of it.

"Kona's pack, this is their territory. It is part of the reason we chose here for you to grow up. They could protect you. He spent twenty years of his life preparing for this, from the day you were born when they offered to keep you safe, till he reincarnated and was placed into your life as a wolf pup. It was to help him remember and create the bond with you," Clay said.

"I'll thank Kona next time I see him," Lucy took a few deep breaths. "What are we going to work on today?"

"Today, we will work on listening to yourself. You will also be educated on Deminio," Clay's voice changed a bit. He was becoming Guardian Clay.

They walked to the water instead of the trail. Emma sat on a small rowboat at the end of the dock with a cooler. She looked at the boat where there was only one other seat in it.

"You ready?" Emma said as he looked Lucy in the eye.

"I thought you were bringing a larger boat," Clay forced more than he asked.

"I was going to, but Lucy and I have been friends for almost her whole life. I know she is best asking and receiving information when someone isn't there to cut in and answer questions with a filter," Emma directed the statement at Clay.

He was too passive for Clay's liking. Lucy wondered if this was Emma's way of disagreeing with Clay's decision to withhold information from Lucy.

"I will be safe with him. We will just circle from here to my dad's house across the lake and back. You can watch us from here the whole time," Lucy said.

She looked across the lake and made out movement on the other side. There seemed to be more people today than yesterday.

"Actually, I planned on taking her to Cove Black. You can meet us there. Take the trail from your house all the way there along the lake. You can see us the whole time," Emma said as he helped Lucy into the small boat.

"Okay. Stay safe, I will meet you there," Clay said to Lucy. He then directed his attention towards Emma, "I am watching you."

His voice ice.

Emma didn't seem to care. He pushed the boat away from the dock and hopped in with perfect balance. Without missing a beat, he began to paddle.

As soon as they were out of earshot he looked from Clay, who was visibly watching them, to Lucy.

"He stayed the night with you?" Emma asked.

"How would you know?" Lucy said.

She caught him. The only way he would know is if he was there last night.

"What do you know?" He said, not changing his face. If he has adjusted his facials, Clay would be able to read them.

"Kona woke me up, and I heard you guys talking last night. I didn't hear the entire conversation. I don't think I did, at least. Just the part where you said you know eyes are on us that we don't see," Lucy's words spilled out of her, unable to hold them in.

"Does he know?" He pointed his chin towards Clay as he rowed.

She thought for a moment about what she should say. Emma was easy to talk to. He never held judgment.

"No, I was fishing for information this morning and he gave nothing away," she said.

"He is protecting you," Emma's tone was defensive. He sided with Clay.

"I know," Lucy said and looked at the water beneath them. "I don't want Clay feeling guilty or anything like that, which is why I didn't bring it up. Normally I would have, but Clay has had a lot going on and much more on his mind than he says."

"That's true, but in my opinion, he should stay open with you if he wants to protect you." Emma paused for a moment, choosing his words carefully, "By the looks of it, Kona agrees with me if he woke you up."

Maybe he didn't agree with Clay.

"Can you elaborate with me on what you said last night?" She asked.

"I mean, what you said is what I know. I feel eyes. I feel the Deminio closer and closer every day. I just can't see beyond that. I can't see any-thing else. I am never wrong about this. Never. It is a part of who I am. I was born of Darkness. As much as I try to get away from it, it finds me. It is a drug," Emma explained.

"If what you feel is true, what can I do to protect us? To protect me?" Lucy teetered between annoyance and determination.

"Lucy, you will see that protecting yourself will be the least of your worries for now. But it is also all you can do. The Deminio know you are hard to kill. They are cheap and easy and want the easiest kill that will hurt you the most, even if it's just for fun. They will come for everyone else first to leave you vulnerable. You will be the last one they kill. If they target you, they know everyone else will come between you and them, and that is what they want. They don't know your strengths, a good thing since you are not as developed as you could be."

Lucy's body was covered in chills, and she could feel Clay's eyes on her. Clay not getting in her head showed her the importance of the conversation.

She looked into Emma's dark eyes, they were hazel, but they were dark. A small glimpse of light in them, one star in a black night's sky. As he rowed, he didn't work up a sweat, they were going fast enough to make wakes in the water. Emma's breathing was even. His strength was extraordinary.

"They will go after your family. They will hunt your friends and everyone you have ever known. They will find the Gateway to Mpiaron. It is only a matter of time now. You need to push, Lucy. Stop listening to everyone else. Push Clay. Push Leo. Push Leon, and most importantly, you need to push yourself. Everyone keeps saying you'll be ready when the time comes, and I'm telling you. The time is here," Emma was full of frustration as equal as he was empathy.

He didn't tell her anything to scare her. He told her so she could best prepare herself to save everyone else, ultimately. It wasn't just about her saving her own life. It was about her saving everyone else's.

"What should I do? If you could tell me what to do, what would you say I do?" Lucy was hesitant but couldn't ask anyone else.

"Find tools that can help you. Do not stop your training, even if you pass out. Do it until you pass out, then when you wake up, you need to keep going. Push yourself. Your physical body will heal and learn to catch up. If it doesn't, then you will die, and so will everyone else eventually. But if you don't push yourself now, then you won't ever get the training you need, and we will all die anyway. Open your eyes. There's a lot you don't see," Emma's eyes burned into her.

She felt truth in every word he spoke.

"Okay."

She understood the depth of his words, clearer than any other thing she knew at this point in time. Every person she loved and cared about depended on her to keep them alive. Her heart was racing. Fear. She felt fear. For the first time since she found out what she was. Lucy was afraid.

"Are you okay?" Emma asked.

"Yes, why?" She said, putting on her best face.

"I sense fear. It is part of being a demon. We could sense fear. We feed off of it. Now that I am Skaru, a demon who is Lemurian, and no longer Deminio, it is something that stayed with me. Lucy, you can talk to me. I am not like them. You've always known that. I wasn't built to feel obligation or duty, or guilt. So if you tell me something, I don't have the urge to talk about it with someone else or measure everything you say. I speak without filter, and I'll always tell you the truth. That's another thing to know. Deminio cannot lie. They can change visuals, trick you with your own words, but they cannot lie. So tell me what is really on your mind," Emma had a way with words, but his energy was neutral.

"All of you will die if I don't figure this out," she decided to be open with him.

"I mean, yeah, most of us will. The rest of us will be damned for eternity," he laughed.

"That's unsettling." Her breathing grew heavy, and she adjusted her body in the seat. The boat suddenly felt small.

"There is nothing unsettling about it. I feel the same way sometimes, undeserving of the Light inside," Emma's body language grew hard.

"I've never thought of it like that." She looked at him directly.

His eyes sparkled, different than before.

"You have all of this weight on you because of the Light you have inside. The strength you have is equal to the weight you carry. Like me. I was given a chance to make things right, but I always question why. Why am I deserving of the Light if I was created a Demon?" He asked though she knew he wasn't expecting an answer.

Lucy answered anyway, "You *are* deserving. You are warm, protective, fun, loyal. You can make anyone laugh. You disappear randomly and always find your way home. Leon would be lost without your friendship. He looks at you and sees all things good. He doesn't see the demon you see or your inner demons. He looks at you and sees a fun surfer who is always up for a laugh and an adventure. He looks at you and sees the only other person he can hang out with when he is having a bad day. He looks at you and sees his brother. There is absolutely nothing undeserving about you."

"Thank you, Luc. I mean that." He bowed his head.

"So did I," she smiled.

"Have you ever thought that you hold fear because you care? In all of my years, even as a demon, I've never met someone who loves the way you do. You look at everyone, and you can see the good in them. You understand their flaws without changing the way you see them, and you focus on what makes them good. You focus on what makes them beautiful. When you walk into a room, everything lights up. You make people want to be better. You make them better. You were chosen for this. You can't forget that. There's a reason it's you and not Leon. I know you think of it sometimes. Things are easier for him, but there's a reason it's you and not him. I know there is a reason I am here, and I know that one day I'll have to pay for it," Emma's voice was firm. It was weird for Lucy to see him so serious. Especially now, with her. She wondered what he meant by paying for it one day. She didn't understand why he felt that way.

"Those are nice words, but you give me much more credit than I am worth," she said and laughed, trying to lighten the mood.

"Don't be so hard on yourself. Demons can't lie, remember?" He said.

"Thank you."

"Are you going to tell Clay you heard us talking last night?" He brought them back to their current situation.

"I was going to wait for him to tell me if he chooses to. I know he tells me most things," she said as she looked towards the shore and could see Clay jogging.

"You're lying to yourself, and you know it," he said between rows.

"I'm giving him the benefit of the doubt," Lucy said.

"He isn't hiding anything from you that could harm you if that makes you feel any better. It is all things you could know, he just doesn't want to overwhelm you," he said.

"Thanks," she said under her breath, and rolled her eyes to look back at Clay.

"All I'm saying is, he is trying to do his best to keep you safe. I know I said that I believe the best way to keep you safe is to be open with you, but that's not how he feels. He knows what is best for you more than I do. He was trained for this, and he feels you. If he isn't telling you something because he thinks it's what's best for you, trust that you don't need to know. But he *will* tell you if you ask him," Emma said.

Lucy hadn't taken her eyes off of Clay, but Emma's emphasis had her thinking.

"This just makes me wonder what else he is keeping from me, what else isn't he telling me? What secrets does he have that I don't think to ask about?" She couldn't blame anyone for trying to keep her safe, she was beginning to understand.

"He doesn't really have secrets. He has information. There is a difference, but if you ask him, he'll tell you. If you asked him about last night, he would tell you more information than he told me. He knows more than I do now. I told him my information, and he spent the morning talking with the witches. If there was something to worry about, he would have told you already," Emma was confident in his words, he believed what he was saying, and Lucy did too.

"Okay," Lucy said.

"I still have to teach you a few things about the Deminio, and we're halfway there. There's a lot I need to tell you before we get there." He changed his body language, a little uncomfortable to be so serious with her.

His rowing picked up speed, and he adjusted his form.

"I'll let you know if I have any questions," she said and motioned for him to go on.

The water below them rippled, and the fish seemed to be closer to the surface than usual.

"Cove Black was made by the Deminio thousands of years ago.

They have forgotten about it since then. They would use it as a place to go without being felt by anyone who belonged to the Light. When they go in the water the rocks make them mortal and human for the time they are there. They don't need it anymore because they have witches who have joined the Deminio and can help them blend in. The Enkeli found it and used it to silence their gifts or as a resting pool. When you go in there, I need you to tell me what you feel. Or what you don't feel. When you go in there, you won't be able to control water or earth or any other gift you might have. That will help us find out if you have any other gifts without wasting your energy by having you try to work with random elements or by testing your abilities. Are you catching my drift?" Emma made eye contact with Lucy for the first time since he started talking.

"You're saying when I get into the water, I need to tell you the changes I feel with myself. You can target what I need to work on or what I can potentially do by me telling you what I feel is missing? Or what I feel, period," she said, brows raised.

"Okay, you're lost. When we go in the water, you will feel different. I know you will. You might be short of breath. If you are, then that means you could have the gift of air. You will automatically feel heavier because you use water more than you know and we already know water works with you. The earth will feel far away. Just tell us anything and everything and leave it to us to figure out. This will save useless training and a lot of your energy," Emma explained.

This made sense to her now, more than before, at least. Lucy was thankful Emma thought to do this. When Lucy looked over at Clay, he was still jogging, but he was looking at her. She couldn't make out his face very well, but she could tell by the shadows on his face he was looking at her.

"Okay, I get it now. I haven't been there in the water of Cove Black in years. We would dive off the rocks that made the pool of Cove Black and into the lake, remember? But we never got in the water of the pool because Leon said it had huge leeches." She squirmed at the thought.

"Leon lied to keep you from going in there. If you had gone in there as a teenager and got out, you could have had a splurge of energy flash through your body. That is also a risk. You would have started your gifts back up and rebooted them. Like a rubber band being snapped, you're going to have to work to control it when you get out. But we will figure it out as we go," he said.

His confidence in her and her abilities was refreshing.

"What made you switch sides?" She asked out of nowhere.

"Love," Emma said so smoothly. It was an easy answer.

Lucy remembered hearing something of it a few days ago.

"Love is that strong, huh?" She laughed and looked over at Clay again.

"You don't realize you've been missing something in your life until you have a piece of it and wonder how you ever went without it. I wasn't supposed to fall in love. I wasn't supposed to know how to love. I was incapable. As soon as I looked into her eyes, I knew. I was supposed to kill her. I pretended I didn't see what I saw, and I let her magic slide, passing her off as human so she could live," Emma spoke as if he was reading a story.

His stare was out past Lucy and into nothing. He was watching it happen in his mind. His rowing was mechanical. His body was a machine, separate from his soul.

"Do you still love her?" Lucy asked.

"I've never stopped. I'll always love her. I haven't spoken directly to her in a long time, but I do love her. We both have to put duty before love, something you seem to struggle with," he redirected the conversation.

Lucy stopped herself from rolling her eyes again.

"Our love is forbidden," she said. Her heart started beating faster, and she had to work to slow it down again.

"Clay can change the rules. He is really the only one who can. I mean, the rule was set for a reason. It puts you at risk. Not to mention Clay can't differentiate the difference between love or the oath. As rebellious as he has always been, he always walked the fine line between breaking and following the rules. It's only a matter of time before everyone else finds out. Anyone with eyes and a brain can see it if they just paid attention. I'm actually surprised nobody else has said anything," Emma's insight on Clay was more than she thought to notice.

"Rani knows, she sensed it right away," she said.

His face fell with the mention of Rani's name, "Of course she did. She's good at that."

"Good at what?" Lucy didn't know Emma and Rani knew each other.

"Knowing things."

He stroked the oars even faster. They would be there shortly.

Visions from her dream rushed to surface. Emma said he was in love with someone and passed her off as a human so she could live. That is what happened with Adelaide, or Rani, and Rowan.

"Rowan?" She asked Emma.

His face changed. His eyes darkened, and the veins in his neck stuck out. When he looked at Lucy, he couldn't look for long. Shame.

"Smart girl. But you're kinda wrong, and your kinda right. I was Rowan when I first met her. Owranoos was magic, fierce. She was a storm. I knew she was a powerful witch even before I first laid eyes on her. I could feel her magic the whole day. My demon blood could sense her close by." He was somewhere else entirely, rowing at a steady pace and looking out into the distance of the past, "You see, I possessed Rowan. The Deminio were attacking the Lemurians. Witches and Enkeli in particular. We told the leaders of the human race they were possessed with darkness, and we would kill them on the spot. We started the war and got the humans involved so we could do it openly. No trial, just death by hanging or beheading or torture. We made all leaders, Kings, and Queens believe us. We possessed some of the strongest warriors and shamans. I happened to possess Rowan. He was the best human warrior anyone had ever seen, and his father was a commander of the cavalry. We started the separation between humans and supernatural beings with this war, killing everyone we could. When Rani walked towards the bridge that day and saved the little boy by helping him cross the river, something about their innocence and her will to help him live had ignited a warmth within me I had never felt before. I knew I had to protect her from anything that would harm her. As demons, we have a strong will for darkness, but a strong will, nonetheless. I wanted to know her, so I followed her. The weeks that followed were hard. I could feel Rowan fading, my time in his body was limited. I told her the truth. She didn't see a demon, she saw *me*. I left Rowan's body that night. He had hours left to live. My demon soul had caused decay and rot to his flesh. As demons, we wouldn't leave a body unless it was dead, but I wanted him to say his goodbyes to his family. Guilt and shame were my first emotions, making me want to stay in the dark. Then Owranoos hugged me when I was in demon form, and I felt love. She loved me. After that I came clean and told the Lemurians what was going on, and with some help from everyone who could make it happen, we made Mpiaron to keep the Lemurians safe." He looked up at Lucy.

A few moments passed as Lucy processed what he was saying. She didn't see him as a demon. It was difficult for her to imagine him doing anything to hurt someone.

"Possession, is that a real thing? Like what you see in movies?" She needed clarity for her imagination before it ran off thinking nonsense.

"It is a lot worse in person. The human's soul is trapped inside of their own physical body. They watch themselves do crazy things. Kill their families, torture, contorting their bodies to move like creatures of the dark, and there is nothing they can do about it. People perform exorcisms but they only work sometimes, and demons can latch on if the person can't let go of the fear. I am ashamed to have done it, but I can't take it back." Emma looked lost, still looking forward.

Lucy trembled. A chill crawled up her spine. It was difficult for her to think of anyone capable of surviving being possessed, like tar on your soul, having to share your body.

She changed the subject, "So you and Rani?"

Lucy intertwined her hands.

He laughed, "Always. Just are at odds right now. Owranoos stayed in Mpiaron to be with the other witches."

"Instead of being here with you?" Lucy asked.

"Right. Don't get me wrong, I see why she did it. Especially feeling obligated to help everyone in Mpiaron because if it wasn't for me, or demons, they wouldn't have needed to hide away to begin with. It's just I couldn't go to Mpiaron without consequences because of my demon blood. It would make the signals go off. Her going there meant no contact with me at all." His eyes trailed off again.

"She would choose the Light over anyone. Just like I would, just like you would and any other Lemurian," Lucy tried to comfort him.

"We'll see. I will always choose her. Anyways, that only scratched the surface, but at least you know more about why Mpiaron was created and more about demons. Don't trust a demon or any being of Darkness. Ever," he said, his focus was back on her.

Lucy wasn't ready for their conversation to be over, she had so many more questions, but they had reached the shore by Cove Black.

"All good?" Clay asked Emma from the shore as he walked in the water to help Lucy get out of the boat.

"She knows everything she needs to know for now," Emma said.

Lucy caught him. He said demons can't lie. Emma wasn't telling Clay that Lucy knew about their previous night's talk, but he said enough for Clay to not ask. It was sneaky of him but also clever. Emma would keep his word, and Lucy would pay closer attention.

22

"Lucy, when you get in the water, make sure to communicate as best as you can, okay?" Clay spoke slowly.

"You got it," Lucy looked down as she spoke and stepped on the rocks that surrounded the natural pool of Cove Black.

The rocks were bigger than she remembered. She had to climb a few to get to the water. Cove Black wasn't really a cove. It was a rock pool made of several rocks above the lake, with a small waterfall going down the rocks into the lake. Every stone was a deep black, only illuminated by the sun when they were wet. It formed a kidney shaped small pool just big enough for about seven people to fit comfortably and was too deep to stand. Each rock was smooth and rough, it was smooth enough to walk and sit on, but it would cut you like sandpaper if you fell on it. The water was clear but looked black because of the rocks, and there was not one living creature inside. It was a pool of nothingness. No life inside, no algae, no bugs, nothing.

Lucy didn't wait for them to give her the okay to get inside of the water. She wanted to feel the water and provide an authentic explanation of how it felt. She took off her dress and jumped in the water.

It was fresh. That was all it was.

"It's fresh and warm. That's all I feel. But, I do feel heavier," she said out loud.

"Good job. I'm right here if you need me," Clay assured her.

"My head doesn't feel full. I don't feel too much air either. I do feel thunder in the water," she thought to herself as she felt the cool water. The water almost felt like it was shaking, "Shaking, it feels like it's shaking. My hands feel like they're getting swollen, and my feet too."

"Don't worry, it's all of your energy being muted. Your body is fighting back. Just take a few deep breaths and keep going," Emma said and crouched down to be closer to her.

"I can't see the same, my vision is blurry, and my body is starting to ache," Lucy said.

"Push past that," Emma encouraged her.

"I can't. All I feel are weird minor discomforts. My body is super sore all of a sudden." Lucy felt like she needed to stretch her body out.

"Emma, listen to what she is saying." Clay smiled at him.

"She's human," Emma smiled back.

"We thought this whole time her body was human and rejecting the powers of the Enkeli. When in reality, her powers keep her physical body healthy, her body is catching up. She is a healer, too, like Leon," Clay said to Emma.

"So, what does that mean?" Lucy said as she floated in the middle of the pool, face up towards them.

"This means your training is going to change. We need to find your limit and aid in your healing capacity. We need to see how it changes when we continue to push you," Clay said.

"Why does she get sick then?" Emma asked Clay.

"I don't know, not yet. I'll figure it out. Maybe Michael will have some input," Clay said.

He put his focus back towards Lucy, "What else do you feel?"

She took a moment to close her eyes and float. Excitement was building, despite the aches she felt. The smiles on Clay and Emma's faces were enough to keep going. Feeling their eyes on her, she began to feel heavy. As she breathed in and out, she floated, something she was good at even in Cove Black.

The heaviness of their gazes began to pull her underwater. *This couldn't be normal*, she thought to herself. She had to paddle to stay up. The air in her lungs wasn't enough, she sank.

Imaginary weights pulled her down, and she began to panic.

"Relax, Luc. We are right here," Emma said, much calmer than she felt.

She couldn't keep herself above the water.

With one last breath, she sank. Quickly going under twenty feet to the bottom of the rock pool. She could see Clay dive in, but she reached the bottom before he was even in the water.

She fought and felt she wasn't alone. She looked down, and between two large rocks, she saw eyes. Red glowing eyes. All of the air released from her lungs as she tried to scream. She tried to kick to push herself up, and it was useless. Lucy was a magnet, and the floor was steel. The same red eyes she saw at the bottom of the cave's staircase in Mpiaron that disappeared when Clay called out for her. She looked up at Clay, and he grabbed her hands, pulling her up. She kicked, but it was useless. When she looked down, the eyes were gone, just like last time. The surface couldn't come fast enough, and with one stride, Clay had them both out of the water and on a giant rock.

He held her up as she choked over water and fear. She threw up. Her shaking hands pointed at the water because she couldn't say a word through her vomiting.

Clay and Emma knew something was wrong by the way her eyes

bulged out of her head towards the water.

"What is it?" Clay asked.

Emma's intense gaze towards the water had Lucy believing he felt it too.

Lucy leaned over and looked, she could easily see the bottom of the water, and there was nothing down there except rocks. There was nothing there, just like before.

"Nothing. I thought I saw something, but I think I just panicked," she said.

An inner struggle was building inside of her. She wasn't sure what it was she saw, and it could have easily been a reflection of the sun or trees.

It wasn't a reflection. An inner voice said.

Then like a rubber band, she felt ease snap over her. The wind blew fresh air filling her lungs with the scents of the forest. A small stream of mist blew right through her, and she could smell the night-blooming jasmines though it was midday. The color returned to her face. She no longer felt weak. Clay still didn't let go of her.

When Lucy looked up, she made eye contact with Emma. He knew something. She could tell by the look in his eyes.

"Did you see anything?" Lucy asked out loud to both Clay and Emma.

"No, just you getting pulled under. There was nothing else I could see. Are you sure you are okay?" Clay asked.

She nodded.

Emma didn't say anything. It made her wonder whether he saw something and was keeping it a secret. She knew now that Emma couldn't lie, but if he didn't speak up about what he saw, he was keeping his own secrets.

They all were.

23

They made their way back to Lucy's house on foot. Lucy went over what she learned about demons with Clay while Emma walked on the other side of Lucy and continued to stay silent. When they got back, there were more people than before. Her cousins had made their way into town as well as more Guardians. There were also two more witches with Alika and Fazi. They looked like they could be related.

She made conversation with them outside in between her house and the lake. The new witches were from the same coven as Alika and Fazi. The Guardians all told her where they came from and legends they had with Clay. More and more people scattered from her house all the way to the safe house, all through the Bloom and the forest. Some were training, and some were setting up camp. Tents lined the forest. She learned the safe house could adjust itself as needed. If one hundred people needed a home to stay then the doors would change inside, and there would be one hundred individual rooms for each one, all fully equipped for each person and their specific needs. All without changing appearances from the outside. Each door in the hallway led to another hallway of more doors. The basement was even a room full of doors, there weren't enough people to fill every room, but the house knew when people were coming. If more doors appeared, there would be more people arriving soon. Lucy was amazed at the extent of magic surrounding her and wondered how she had never seen it before.

Night came quickly, the sky was filled with a cotton candy sunset, and the air was crisp from the dew of the lake. The trees reflected the colors they did during golden hour, always most beautiful as the sun set. Lucy took a seat next to Leon around the makeshift fire pit consisting of large rocks in a circle. Leon had his guitar out, and he was playing under the moonlight. It seemed as if everyone stopped what they were doing and gravitated around him.

Lucy looked closely at her twin brother. He was the way he had always been. He was Leon. People always gravitated towards him, and they loved to be loved by him. He had a way about him that made everyone feel important. His song was a happy one, and for the first time in a while, as he played, Lucy felt the way she did before everything happened. The way she did the night of their birthday beach day when they were all playing games in the water. Everyone was together and happy. They smiled and laughed as the evening went on.

Life had taken turns the way life paths do, and Lucy couldn't imagine being here with anyone else. Everything had been so uncertain, and still, she felt happy. Their entire family was gathered around the fire, her dad, his brothers, and their sons. Her friends and their families and all of the witches, wolves, and Guardians gathered around.

Then she looked at Emma, who was sitting on the other side of Leon. He didn't have anyone. It was just him. Nobody else of his kind existed.

He was the only Skaru.

Leon's song ended, and everyone was silent around the massive fire, a huge thick circle of chairs and blankets with over fifty people gathered around.

Lucy looked at Emma and said, "Emma, I'd like to thank you for today. Thanks for taking the time to teach me about demons and Deminio. Thanks for being brave enough to choose this path."

She spoke softly, but everyone heard.

Leon puffed up and slung his arm around Emma, who had smiled shyly at Lucy, not wanting to take any credit.

"This guy right here is my best friend. He is my brother. There's nothing I wouldn't do for him," Leon said.

"Thank you, thanks," Emma nodded his head quickly as he adjusted his black beanie with both of his hands and pulled the collar of his flannel shirt up.

"You two are the definition of brothers if I've ever seen any. To do what you did for him, Leon, that was brave," her uncle Silas said.

Lucy didn't know what he was talking about.

"Yes, I'm thankful to know you both, and it is a privilege to stand next to you during these times," Dario said and bowed his head towards them. He was always respectful in a way only Guardians could be.

"What are they talking about?" Lucy asked.

Leon and Emma looked at each other, and Leon took his arm off of Emma.

She turned to Clay, who was sitting on the other side of her.

"They can tell you. They can explain it better than I can," Clay gestured towards them.

Lucy redirected her focus back to Emma and Leon.

"I am a demon, you know this. Even though I changed sides, demons can't be Lemurians. I couldn't be a part of council or make any decisions as my word held little value, and my blood is the blood of Darkness. Everyone treated me fairly, I couldn't talk to the Angels the way you guys could, and I couldn't ask for help either or enter Mpiaron. The Guardians above couldn't help me or communicate clearly with me like they can with you guys. I was devoted to the Light for millennia and was still only a demon. Rules are rules, I understood and accepted it. Then, I was chosen to help protect you two when you were born. Leon came around, and we grew close as you two grew up. He found a way for me to join the Lemurians and be an equal. I can do most things you all can do now," Emma said.

"How did you do it? What did you do?" Lucy asked Leon.

"I gave him a part of my soul so he could be a part of us," Leon said, unphased. He looked at Emma with a smile.

"Because of Leon, I was able to take the oath of Light and was able to become a Lemurian. I can feel him at all times. A part of him is within me," Emma said.

"We are connected in a way that's kind of like the way you and I are connected as twins. I can't really explain it, but I can feel it," Leon said to Lucy.

Lucy always knew there was more to them than she knew. Leon always kept Emma separate from her. Not secretive, just separate.

"I will forever be in your debt, and just so you all know," Emma turned and spoke to everyone, "I live my life to protect and carry on the duties I was given and carry the oath of Light. I will never take for granted the gift Leon gave me or the acceptance all of you have given me. I don't deserve it."

"It's no gift. It was always yours to begin with. It's yours to keep. We have no debt. You are my brother, and that's what brothers do. I'd do it again, over and over if it meant keeping you here with us," Leon said, his voice cracked.

"I'd give my life for you," Emma said and reached out his hand to Leon.

"I'd give my life for *you*," Leon returned. He extended his hand, shook forearms, and put their foreheads together while they hugged with opposite hands.

Lucy looked over at Clay, who stood up and put his right fist over his heart and pounded to the beat of his heart. The Guardians stood up and pounded their chests one by one. The wolves joined in, and then the Enkeli. Lucy could distinguish the different heartbeats.

They all stood up and faced Leon and Emma, all showing their fight for them. Chills waved over her body as the beats of their hearts became one.

They were all one.

Leon joined in and raised his right fist up high, "AAH-OOH!" He rooted.

"AAH-OOH!" Roared everyone else.

At that moment, the fire roared, and the already high flames doubled in size, well above Lucy's head.

The fire is responding to them. She thought to herself.

Cheers came from all around, smiles and laughter echoed from everyone. Their magic was tangible.

Kona howled from beside her, and you could hear wolves howling in the distance.

As she breathed, she felt happiness and pride. She was proud of who she was and who she was surrounded by. The strength and love she felt were incomparable. There was no way the Deminio stood a chance. The Lemurians had something the Deminio would never have.

Something to fight for.

24

Lucy walked through a large hallway. The walls were made of dirt, and roots weaved their way in and out of the dirt walls. It smelled of earth. She was underground. Deep underground. There were no lights, yet somehow, she could see.

"Lucy, can you hear me?" A deep voice said in her ear.

She turned quickly to find nobody there. She couldn't see anyone. Something told her she had nothing to fear. The voice didn't make her feel at odds, it was comforting.

"Yes, I can. Who's there?" She asked.

"There is no time. You have eyes on you. Emma is right. You need to tell the head of the Guard. I believe his name is Clay. You need to tell him they are watching. Tell the witches to pull Mpiaron through and to be prepared. There is no time to wait. You have three days before they start the attack. Three days before they come for you. They know everything. They see everything. You have more people who will fight for you. Call on the Clans," the voice said, sounding further and further with each word.

"Who is watching?" She asked as quick as she could.

"If I can slip through and talk to you, if I can get in your dreams, they can too. You need to tell Clay, Lucy. I will find you. Meet me at-" the voice was nothing but *an echo, and she couldn't hear it clearly anymore.*

The cave became darker until she couldn't see anymore.

She couldn't see or hear anything. She was lost in the earth.

Her breathing grew shallow.

There was no more air.

Lucy screamed.

"What's going on? It's okay! I am here. You are safe!" Clay rushed towards her from the fireplace.

She grabbed at her chest and peeled the suffocating blankets off of her.

"You are home safe. I carried you in. You fell asleep on your chair outside around the bonfire." He brushed her wet hair out of her face.

She was dripping with sweat.

When she looked around, she realized she was home on her couch and tucked in with blankets. There was a book next to the fireplace and a pillow on the floor beside it.

"Clay, I heard your conversation last night with Emma," Lucy said in a hurry.

"I didn't want to worry you. There is much going on, and there is no need to tell you everything. You have your own burdens to bear," he said.

There was no touch of defense in his voice or no sense in explaining himself. He was completely normal.

"You weren't hiding it from me?" She asked.

"No, I would have told you if you asked. I always do," Clay said as he sat at her feet and pulled her feet onto his lap.

"I kind of did this morning, but I guess I kind of didn't." She thought of her conversation and knew her indirect jabs at him went over his head.

"You know how it works, Lucy. If you ask, I will answer. If you have a question, you can always ask me. It is never too much, and you never intrude. You could have walked out and joined the conversation. I would have filled you in." He looked her in the eyes as he massaged her legs, "Now tell me what set you off. You screamed when you woke up. What was your dream about?"

His voice changed, he was Guardian Clay.

"Okay, well, it started a few days ago, in Mpiaron. Not just my dream tonight," Lucy said.

"So *you* are the one keeping secrets?" He said, his eyes hard.

"I mean, I guess. Let me go on. Okay. When I went on my own and you found me, there were snakes that I thought were chasing me, so I ran from them. When they passed me, I realized they weren't chasing me, but they were guiding me instead. They took me to a cave with stairs that went down. They were trying to get me to go down the stairs. I looked at the bottom of the stairs, and I could see glowing red eyes. My skin felt cold immediately," Lucy explained.

"Did you go down the stairs, Lucy?" He didn't change his expressions or his breathing.

"No. I barely saw the eyes, and I heard you yell out my name. I turned to see you, and when I looked back, the eyes weren't there anymore. None of it was," she said as she took a deep breath to continue. "I didn't think much of it until last night. Emma said there were eyes on us. It immediately made me think of the glowing red eyes in the disappearing cave."

"Go on." He maintained all poise. The only hint of change was the way his eyes began to glow.

"Then today, in Cove Black, I thought I didn't see anything in the water. I thought it was only my imagination, but something literally told me it wasn't. I saw the glowing red eyes again at the bottom of the rocks when I was pulled under. It didn't feel like a hand, but I was pulled," she said.

"Why didn't you say anything when it happened?" Clay asked her.

Emma's face flashed through her mind suddenly, the way it looked when she made eye contact with him. He knew something was down there, but there was no proof.

"I mean, I was going to, but-" she didn't want to finish the sentence.

"But Emma didn't say anything, and he knew what you had seen?" His face didn't change.

"Yeah. How'd you know?" She asked.

"He told me when we got back, he just wasn't sure what you had seen, and since I haven't been wanting you to worry, he wanted to run it by me first," he said.

Lucy wondered what Emma had said.

"Okay, either way, my dream was the real message. I was underground. A voice said Emma was right and to tell you there are eyes on us. That they see everything," Lucy was trying to explain her dream to Clay, but it wasn't coming out the way the deep voice had said it.

"Whose voice was it?" His hands stopped massaging her legs.

"I don't know. He also said to tell you he knew who you were. He said we only have three days to get ready, then the witches need to pull Mpiaron through." Lucy looked into the distance of nothingness as she tried to remember what he had said word for word.

"Lucy, is there anything else you can remember? I really need you to think." He sat up.

"He said to meet him somewhere, but then his voice became distant like static, and I couldn't understand him anymore. He said if he could pull through and see me in my dreams or get to me, then so can the Deminio." She took a deep breath, "He also said to call the clans. Whatever that means."

Clay got up and ran to his phone. He dialed a phone number so quick, Lucy couldn't see his fingers move.

"Gather everyone... yes, let them know... right now... see you outside of the safe house in ten minutes." Clay hung up the phone.

"Lucy, go change. It is cold out," he ordered.

"I need to shower, I'll be fast," Lucy said. She turned and walked away before he could say no. She knew he would say there was no time.

She needed to sort out her thoughts, and the only way she thought to do that, privately, was to take a shower.

Once she was in the shower, she closed her eyes and took a deep breath as the hot water washed over her.

She imagined her body was covered in mud. The mud to her was the weight of the dream. It was unease and an unclear mind. As she breathed and as the water went over her body, she imagined the mud, the heaviness, the clouded mind, all of it going down the drain.

Lucy did this for a few minutes until she no longer felt the "mud" on her body. Until she could take a deep breath and no longer feel the weight of the day.

"Lucy had a visitor in her dream. We all know dreams from Enkeli can be prophecies. This was not one of those dreams. This was a visit. Neither of us knows who it was, and she didn't see him, she only heard his voice. We are all aware there have been eyes on us, but we have underestimated the power of the Deminio and the depths they'll go," Clay's authority roared over everyone outside of the safe house.

He stood at the top of the porch steps as he overlooked the small crowd. Lucy was two steps below him, looking at both Clay and everyone else. Leon was at the bottom of the steps. Emma and her dad flanked him. Owranoos and the rest of the witches, including Alika, Fazi, and Omala, surrounded the perimeter. Clay had them search and secure the safe house before he and Lucy got there and continue to do so until they were done. He didn't want to take any chances being heard by unwanted ears.

"The man, whoever he was, wanted to meet with her. His voice cut out before she could hear when and where. Before she could no longer hear him, he said to have the witches begin to pull Mpiaron through."

Everyone had suddenly stopped breathing. Time stood still for a moment. Everyone looked eagerly at Clay, waiting for his demand. The energy had changed, from the night they had around the bonfire to a few hours later dealing with such a weighted decision.

"He said we had three days before the Deminio come for her," Clay continued.

As one, everyone sucked in their breath, and a hum of whispers was born.

"Quiet." Clay wasn't wasting any time, "They said to call the Clans."

Those words changed everything, a total uproar. Lucy even heard someone hiss. They took steps forward and shouted. She could feel the wolves giving off heat, even in their human form. Kona howled from the gate.

Within seconds one of the wolves who Lucy had met that night, Dyami, changed. She hadn't seen any of them change form. It only took a second, and his clothes were in scraps on the floor. His head towered over theirs, much larger than a wolf should be. He was showing teeth. Steam rose above his body, and a low growl escaping his raised lips. His black and gray fur twitched with unease.

He had caused a ripple effect. Ten more wolves changed and were almost as tall as the Guardians.

Nobody seemed to mind.

"I need to know if anyone has seen or felt any of the Clans?" Clay asked.

Everyone looked around. Lucy was confused. She reached for Leon's arm and walked down the steps to him. Clay looked at her quickly. His eyes flashed their glowing colors and went back to how they were when he wasn't in Guardian mode.

Nobody said anything, the night's air stagnant.

"Her dream was underground. My guess is he called to her from one of their old underground hideaways nearby. We do not know much about the Clans, except they are neutral. We need to decide what to do. Do we trust him? Do we find him? Do we pull Mpiaron through? Is he just saying all of this to help them kill us all?" Clay was calm and collected, his usual facade.

"He won't hurt us. He won't hurt me," Lucy said and could feel everyone's attention shift from Clay to her.

"How can you be sure?" Clay asked.

Lucy, if you can trust him, how come he did not come to you in person? Clay's voice echoed in her head.

Would he have been able to reach me if he tried? She thought and looked up at him.

"Because he couldn't get in my head and be part of the Deminio without you knowing. Feel me out. I wasn't touched by Darkness," Lucy said aloud.

"I have felt them around, the Deminio. Just eyes, but I know they've been watching us without being seen by us. We need to do more," Emma said, his voice low but loud enough for everyone to hear him. He looked at Lucy, "No, you haven't been touched by Darkness."

"What about pulling Mpiaron through? That takes days of effort from both sides. It will weaken every one of us for days after. Do we trust him with that decision? We might not even have enough time to pull it through if we started right this second," Rani said from the fence, still on the perimeter.

"So, what do we do? What are our options?"

Lucy addressed Clay and Leon, but it was her dad who answered.

"You need to listen to yourself. You need to train. You need to be educated. We need more time because three days isn't enough, not even close."

"We don't have a choice, Pops. Whether this guy is lying or not, we have to be ready at all times. If we pull Mpiaron through our new numbers and strength will make the Deminio pause before they try anything. Lucy needs more practice, and there is no way she can learn from us if we are more focused on protecting her from what has been watching her. We would have all of the Lemurians here. If he is lying, it'll rush the Deminio towards us. They'd know exactly where we are at, and they'd know about Lucy, and we would probably all die anyways. If he is telling the truth, then we need to come up with a better way to teach Lucy, or else we will die. I don't know about all of you, but I don't want to die this way. If we are going to die, I want it to be because we gave it all we've got, not because we weren't ready. Let's be ready," Leon said.

With every word he spoke, Lucy grew anxious.

"Everyone can take the next few hours to scout the area and make a decision. At sunrise, we decide whether we call the Clans and begin to pull Mpiaron through, or find another way," Clay said just before he walked through the crowd to his truck.

Lucy, come with me. There is something I need to show you before we come back to vote. Clay's voice was in her head.

I'm going to sneak out. I'll be right there. Lucy thought back.

She told Leon she would be back in a few and walked through the crowd when everyone began talking. As soon as she cleared the gate, she took a deep breath, the energy of everyone there was overwhelming, and she hadn't realized it until she got in Clay's truck.

"So, where are we going?" She asked.

"For a drive." He smiled.

25

They drove down to the beach and across the bridge that leads to the other side, where Mpiaron is. It was just trees. Lucy would have thought it was only forest if she wouldn't have been to Mpiaron. Certain trees looked familiar to her, landmarks she remembered from when she was there. There was a smell, too. The scent on this side was as if Mipiaron had a leak. She could catch slight scents of herbs and oils. They stayed along the coast while they drove, slowly swerving around the trees as there was no road.

When they came to a stop, they walked around, and a rush of familiarity surfaced. She remembered this exact place when she was in Mpiaron. It was the shoreline where there was a dip in the earth. Cliffs were leading down to the water with a small bay or even large pool of water between them. It was a strip of land, or ridge, on the other side. Underneath the strip of land that enclosed the large pool of water were small holes where you could swim from the pool of water to the ocean in multiple areas. The pool stretched about the length of a football field but only half the width.

Even in the dark, it looked the same as it did when she was in Mpi-aron. Exactly the same. The placement of trees on the shoreline was the same. She couldn't forget it. This is where she saw the snakes.

"Clay-," Lucy could have vomited.

"I knew you would know where we were. Do you have an idea of what we are doing?" Clay asked her.

"No, but the thought of evil snakes and the red eyes is unsettling," Lucy said as she looked around the dirt for any sign of a snake.

"Snakes should be the least of your worries. Listen, we don't have much time. If I am right, this is where they started being able to see you. I will go in the water below. Water neutralizes energy so they won't know I am with you. We can communicate silently. It will take me one second to get back to you. This is the only place I can think of with access underground. If there is a chance he is here, I want to take it. I want to know who he is," Clay's eyes glowed, and his skin rippled.

"Are you asking me to walk around in the dark, alone, looking for a scary secret cave that may or may not have dark red glowing eyes and walk towards it? Alone?" She grew cold just thinking about it, her body shook and the hairs on the back of her neck stood up.

"Yes, that is exactly what I am asking you to do," Clay said as he leaned into her and reached for her face.

"No, you will be down there," Lucy pointed at the water below and pulled away, "and I will be up here scared out of my mind."

"Lucy, I would not let anything happen to you. I am closer than you think. Watch." Clay leaped off of the cliff, and in a second, he was next to Lucy.

She looked him up and down. He was drenched, and his long hair dripped. He went in the water, fully submerged, and leaped out fifteen feet up in only one second.

"How did you do that?" She asked.

Lucy looked down off the cliff into the water again and could see the calm waters rippled from Clay jumping in. The moonlight shimmered in the small wakes.

"Practice. I am a Guardian. There is much about me you do not know. Trust me, Lucy. You will be okay. I wouldn't do anything to hurt you, and if I thought you were in any real danger, I wouldn't be doing this. Are you ready?" He said as he reached for her hand.

Lucy thought for a moment, really feeling out the situation. She felt no unease around it. She was safe, and it wasn't because he said she was. This time she didn't pull away when Clay reached for her hand. Instead, she gave it to him, and he put it up to his heart.

"I am ready," she said.

Part of her was sure of herself, sure of Clay's duty as a Guardian to protect her.

Then there was a part of her that wasn't. The thought of snakes and red eyes wasn't going away. The fear she felt the first time was still too fresh.

He smiled and jumped down. This time, Lucy heard the splash.

Her hands shook, and she didn't have any light to guide her. Once she took a few deep breaths and calmed down, she looked around and realized she didn't need one. The moon and the stars lit the path. It was a ways away. She remembered being chased and running for what felt like a long time.

Are you okay? Clay's voice echoed in her head.

Yes. Lucy thought as she took another deep breath, comforted by his voice.

Lucy, you can do this. I am here with you. His voice was soft yet held the same amount of certainty it did earlier.

She continued to walk in the direction the snakes chased her. Clay was right, now that she gave it a thought. There was still so much about him she didn't know. She didn't know anything about him being a

Guardian, other than him actually being a Guardian. She had no clue what it entailed. Lucy didn't know what he was good at, what he liked, who his friends are, what are his strengths and what else could he do? Other than him talking to her about Michael being his father, she really knew nothing about him.

Whether she would still feel connected to him if she knew him better hadn't crossed her mind. However, the pull she felt towards him was one of the things she was most sure of.

Lucy stopped and looked down at the base of the tree. Right next to her was a tree she remembered from when she stopped running. She looked around for a cave or the stairs. She felt it before she saw it. When she turned around, the staircase appeared.

Clay was right. It did work.

I found the staircase. Lucy thought to him.

Okay, remember I am here. I can be with you in seconds. Clay thought back.

Lucy took a deep breath and took her first step down the makeshift stairs made of stone, wood, and mud. It was somehow illuminated by invisible light. No shadows were present as a wave of relief washed over her. The stairs went far down with vines on either side of her climbing the dirt walls. That was it, stairs, dirt, and nothingness. When she reached the bottom of the stairs, she looked back up and could see the trees with the moon's glow touching their leaves.

The path was still dirt, compacted, and claylike. The walls rounded at the top, forming a tunnel. As Lucy walked around, she realized she didn't know what she was looking for.

"Hello? Did you call for me?" She yelled down the tunnel, hearing only her own echo and waited a moment before she continued to walk through the dark dirt tunnel.

It was the same as her dream. The roots of the trees were all around.

"Hello, Lucy," a voice said to her.

Her whole body got cold. Chills covered her skin. The voice was cold and raspy. It wasn't the voice of the man she heard in her dream. This voice was evil.

CLAY! HELP! She screamed in her head.

Trust me, Lucy. Clay said in her head.

The thought of her running into any sort of Darkness was at the back of her mind before she heard the voice. She didn't know what to do, and Clay didn't come.

Red eyes glowed in the distance. Whatever it was inched closer. She grew colder as it grew near. With every step it took towards her, she took a step back, making sure to keep it as distant as possible.

It was either she ran and waited for Clay, or she stayed and fought. She didn't know how to fight it, because she didn't know what it was. She only knew it was dangerous.

She turned around and ran. Lucy ran as fast as she could. She could feel Clay was near, but he wasn't there. Not yet.

Her back was cold. That thing was chasing her. As her back continued to get colder, she knew it was closing the gap.

She could feel it right behind her.

In an instant, its rough hand grabbed her arm and swung her around. It forced her to look at it.

A man. He had red eyes. His hair was a colorless white and fell to his shoulders. It looked dirty, greasy. His face was pale and veiny with black circles under his eyes, inhumane. His grip was ice cold and sweaty. Everything about him was rabid.

Lucy was scared to blink, afraid of what would happen if she closed her eyes. There was nothing she could do. His speed was much quicker than hers and the strength of his grip was unbearable. She wanted to scream for Clay, but she couldn't make a sound. She couldn't breathe. The man's other hand wrapped around her neck. Her body paralyzed with a fear she had never felt before. The only thought in her mind was if she died right now, everyone she knew would die.

He smiled. His teeth were rotting and sharp. A vampire.

"You are going to die, and your family is going to die. I've been watching you-*we've* been watching you," he said.

He opened his mouth and licked his lips. He laughed and took a deep breath in. He was smelling her. He was tasting her through the air.

Then he froze. Suddenly his smile disappeared, and he didn't move.

"Put her down and take your hands off of her," a familiar voice said. Lucy couldn't see him.

"Ha! Why should I? You can't stop me," the vampire said.

"She is *mine*," the smooth voice declared. He spoke slowly.

The vampire let her neck go but kept his other hand on her wrist.

"No, she is not. You haven't tasted her blood," the vampire grew sour. He was impatient and temperamental.

"Yes, I have. She tastes of chamomile and lavender. Occasionally, chocolate chip cookies and too much pasta. Always tastes of salt water. Now take your hands *off*," the voice said.

With every word, the vampire's grip eased before he finally let go and threw her arm down with such force she fell back.

She should have fallen on the floor, but instead, fell into someone else. All she could see were large hands around her body. He was warm. He had a gold ring on with some sort of crest on it.

"I'll be watching you," the vampire said without taking his eyes off of Lucy.

As he ran off, she saw him move more like a creature than a man with two legs. The coldness on Lucy's body eased but not by much.

"Are you okay? Did he hurt you?" The man said as he helped her find balance.

Lucy looked up at him. His hair was black and curly. His face was fair, his dark pink lips were bold and full, as was the rest of his face. His eyes, they also glowed red. Not the same blood red as the monster who just left. His were a warm amber red.

Relief overcame her, and she started shaking.

"I'm okay. Thanks for saving me," she said and took a step back.

She couldn't stop shaking. When she looked at him, she felt safe, but the cold grasp stained her wrist.

"Thank you for taking the time to meet with me, Lucy. Though I am sincerely sorry for my brother," he said.

He was the voice from her dream, the man from her dream. She was so close to him she could smell his sweet breath and the scent of him. Something inside of her wanted to inch closer to him.

"You haven't tasted my blood," she said as she thought back and tried to remember any part of her life she could have missed.

"He doesn't know that. He's too ill. A healthy vampire would have known, yet a healthy vampire wouldn't force feed from you," he said with a smirk.

"You're a vampire?" Lucy asked.

"Yes," he said.

She looked into his amber-red eyes and could see herself in them.

"How did you know what I taste like then?" She was pushing it, she should go find Clay, but she didn't want to leave just yet.

"You're easy for me to read. You like to swim by the color of your hair. I smell chocolate on you from a distance." He sniffed as he moved closer to her neck, "You've also been drinking a lot of tea, and I sense acidic fruit. Mangos."

"How do you know?" She asked.

He tasted the air, "I can smell your blood. I wouldn't feed on you even if you begged me to. And you *would* beg."

Her stomach turned with his deep voice, and not in a bad way.

"Don't say that. That's sick. You don't know me at all," Lucy said, she should be disgusted. She wasn't.

She turned around and walked towards the stairs.

When she reached the stairs halfway point, he yelled, "Wait," he reached gently for her arm, "vampires, like me, aren't like him. You smell my scent, my face, my smile, my voice. I was made to be irresistible. Everything about me attracts you to me. The touch of my fingers on your arm." He stroked Lucy's arm with his fingertips, goosebumps surfaced, "When my breath hits your face. The way my eyes look at you and see only you." He put his chin down and raised his eyebrows, eyes full of intent, "I didn't mean to sound arrogant before. When we bite, it feels good. Pleasurable, even. That's all I meant. I don't know what you know of us, you are new to this, but we wouldn't harm anyone," his voice was relaxed.

Lucy did her best to keep calm. She knew nothing of vampires, nothing at all.

"How do you know? That I'm new to this?" She asked.

The weight of her body leaned towards her front foot, a few inches closer to him.

"Many of us know you are here. It's hard to keep secrets in our world. Whispers travel fast. I've been watching you. Many of us have." He let go of her arm.

Lucy resisted the urge to word vomit. If she said something, she might say too much. She didn't know if they could trust him.

She understood what he meant by irresistible. It was unnatural yet felt natural.

Chills resurfaced at the thought of being watched. He stepped closer, only one step below her on the stairs, and he was still much taller than her. He inched closer. Their noses almost touched.

She thought he was going to try to kiss her when he looked her in the eyes and said, "Call the Clans. Pull Mpiaron through. Start today. If not, it'll be too late. We will be there when you need us. You have my word." He reached for her hand and flipped it palm side up, then kissed the center of her palm.

"Now go before anyone else can see you. Stay with your Guardian at all times. Stay safe," he said and retreated, walking down the steps.

When he reached the bottom step, he turned around and said, "Lucy, I'll be seeing you."

He smiled, showing a perfect row of white teeth. Not pointed like the other vampire. His smile held promise. She turned and walked up the stairs and looked up, then looked back towards the bottom steps, and he was gone.

When Lucy reached the top and her foot touched the grass, Clay was immediately next to her. She looked back to show him the stairs and the cave, but they were gone. just like last time.

"Lucy, I could hear two others down there. I felt it more beneficial to stay up here. I knew you'd be okay. I couldn't hear past the opening for some reason. What happened?" He pulled her close and kissed her forehead.

After a moment, he held her at arm's length and examined her to see if she was physically hurt.

"Vampires. That is who has been watching us," she said.

"Did they try to bite you?" Clay checked for any sign of blood or punctured skin.

He wasn't fazed at all with the mention of vampires.

"No, almost, but no. I walked down the stairs like before and the tunnel was all dirt like in my dream and like the first time the snakes led me there when we were in Mpiaron. A vampire, a bad one, came and chased me. He was disgusting and horrifying, and I was terrified. He smelled like old blood and rotting flesh. His hair was dirty and un-washed, his skin was translucent and full of veins. Everything about him was evil. His voice," Lucy shuttered, "was bone-chilling, and he was going to kill me. He actually told me he was going to kill me and took pleasure in telling me."

Out poured her word vomit. The thought terrified her all over again. She felt so helpless at that moment. She didn't want to feel like that ever again.

"You weren't in danger," Clay said.

He moved his hands up and down her arms to warm her up. She hadn't realized until right now she was shaking again. She didn't have the nerve to tell Clay she was warm, and it wasn't him that made her warm. Amber eyes flashed through her thoughts.

"Another vampire came. He saved me." She remembered his face, and something inside of her tingled. The thought of him being nearby gave her comfort.

"What did he do?" Clay asked. He was fishing for something.

"He claimed me. But the other vampire didn't know he was lying. Why?" Her voice dense with defense.

"They are a different sort of being, vampires. They do not follow the same moral compass or code we do. They have their own rules and their own way of living. Neither good nor bad. They lay low in terms of fighting the balance we fight to keep," Clay said.

"He, the one who saved me, was the one I heard and talked to in my dream. He made the other one leave by telling him he drank my blood," she said and walked towards the shore where the truck was.

It was still dark out, the path only illuminated by the moon.

"I would know if you were bit," irritation tainted his voice.

"He said it to get the other one to leave me alone, he was going to kill me, remember? The good one said to call the Clans, and they will help us when we need it, but that we have to pull Mpiaron through, and we need to do it today or else it will be too late." Lucy remembered.

"What did he look like? Can you remember?" Is there anything significant on him that you can think of? Any tattoos, jewelry, anything at all?" He asked.

"No, not that I can think of. He had curly black hair, amber eyes. He was about as tall as you when you are in human form. He wasn't like the other one. He was trustworthy. He was good," she said.

She trusted him and she didn't know why.

"There is no such thing as a *good* vampire. They can be righteous, they can be kind, but they cannot be trusted. The way they work isn't like us. Their loyalties aren't the same as ours. Even if they agreed to fight for us, they would ask for something in return, something larger in scale than they gave, and I couldn't guarantee repayment. It would start a whole other war," Clay said.

Lucy could see him weighing options in his own head. He touched the small of her back and guided her back towards the direction of his truck.

"He had a gold ring on. That's all I saw that stood out. I saw it when I almost fell, and he caught me. Only his face and his ring, it had a crest on it." Lucy looked into the air as if the ring was right in front of her.

"You said his hair was black, did the crest have a triangle on it?" Clay asked a few minutes later when they arrived at his truck.

"It did," Lucy thought back for a moment.

She knelt down and traced what she remembered of the crest in the dirt with her finger as best as she could recall.

"This changes things. We need to get back." Clay helped Lucy get in the truck and drove off, away from the Darkness and back to the safe house, "Lucy, the Clans are vampires. Known to be families of vampires who live underground and have been unheard of for centuries at a time. They very much live in a different world than we do, hardly ever crossing paths throughout all of history. The one you spoke to if I am not mistaken, is a royal of some sort. We need to find out more about him from someone who knows more about them."

Lucy's eyes widened. She touched the palm of her hand where the vampire had kissed her, and it still tingled. She could feel him close by, and she didn't know how. She wanted to see him again.

"Do you trust him?" Clay asked.

Without hesitation she answered, "Yes, Clay, I do."

"Okay. It is decided, there will be no vote. We will work to pull Mpi-aron through, and I will call on the Clans."

26

Clay, are you close by? Lucy thought to Clay after she laid down in her bed. It was the first time she laid in her bed since she came back from Mpiaron and was unconscious for days.

I am reading by the fire. Do you need something? Clay's voice in her head was soft and full of patience.

No, I just haven't been alone in a while. It's strange. She laughed out loud, overly tired.

Go to sleep. He laughed back.

What if I see him? What do I do then? She thought, worry in her inner voice.

Whatever you feel is right. Ask him who he is, though I doubt he will come to you tonight. It takes power to be able to visit in dreams. If he has any honor and you do not want him in your head, he will stay out. Clay thought to her.

Okay. Thanks for being here. I'm sorry I scared you today. Lucy thought as she closed her eyes.

Clay didn't say anything in return but, somehow, she knew he was smiling.

Lucy was almost asleep when she heard footsteps coming towards her room. Clay opened the door, walked in, and gave her a look that made her smile.

He was in his pajamas. Sweatpants and a tee shirt. His hair was a handsome mess from lying down reading.

She opened the blankets for him to get in.

"Lucy, I've lived for what feels like forever. My whole life falls short when I compare it to the last few weeks," he whispered.

Clay opened his arms for her to lay in his chest.

"If it counts, I've never let a boy in my bed before or sleep next to me. Besides Leon, but he doesn't count."

"I'd hardly call myself a boy," he laughed.

"He's in there somewhere," Lucy poked his hard chest.

"I doubt it. You could still say you've never let a boy in your bed," Clay looked at her and winked.

"You know what I meant, jerk," she said playfully, this was the first time they had banter.

"I never have either," he said.

"Never what?" She asked.

"Had someone in my bed," Clay looked at the ceiling.

"Really?" She tried to keep calm.

Lucy propped herself up so she could look him in his eyes.

"Yes, I mean, I've lived my whole life to build the Guard. Romance or love wasn't supposed to be part of it for me, not really," he said, looking at the ceiling.

"Love?" She said, still looking at him.

It was all Lucy had caught from what he said.

He laughed, "Go to sleep Lucy."

He poked her forehead as if pushing her to lay back down. She did and looked up at him. His jaw was relaxed, and he had a smirk that reached his eyes.

"What's so funny?" She asked him.

"Of all the things I say, you catch the *one* slip I have," he said and looked down at her.

"I mean, you said you've been in love before," she said.

Lucy couldn't help but look anywhere except directly at him. She held her breath.

"Not how you think," he said. He was looking at the ceiling.

"But you said you have known love before," Lucy did her best to even out her breathing.

"When we become Guardians, it happens different ways for all of us. When we officially become a part of it, we see things. Visions of what could happen, the different roads you could take depending on what direction humanity goes. I remember every vision I had, and I had countless. I saw you. I saw us living a life together, I saw us in love. I never thought it would happen, not for me. I thought when you came, if you ever did, we would have the oath to bond us and nothing more. Two powerful people, two warriors, a strong duo who would lift humanity. When I saw you at the beach, the first time we formally met, at that moment the oath solidified, a rubber band snapping back to form. I couldn't resist the urge to have more than the oath. I wanted to be your friend, your confidant, just yours. My world began to gravitate around you," Clay said.

He was composed. Even as he laid his heart out in words for Lucy to hear, he seemed to have it all together. He was sure of everything he said.

Lucy didn't have a response for him.

She didn't know what to say.

Instead, she had a confession, "I can't stop thinking about him. The vampire. Not the scary one but the other one."

Clay laughed, "I would be worried if you didn't. Vampires are known for their charm."

He stroked Lucy's hair.

"He said something about that." She gulped and replayed their conversation in her head.

"He will come back. I smell him on you. He will see you again. I am sure of it," Clay said.

"That's what he said. I'm drawn to him. Not in the way I am drawn to you. I hardly know him," Lucy said, and surprised herself with how open she was being. This was new to her.

"You hardly know me," Clay's voice was empty, full of air but not yet a whisper.

"But I *feel* you. Goodnight, Clay," she said.

Lucy tucked her head into his chest and finally resisted any urge to fall asleep. He kissed the top of her head.

She let go.

Morning came and went. Clay had explained to everyone everything that happened with the vampires and Lucy. He wasn't the same leader as he was the night before when he was willing to listen and be reasoned with.

He was assertive. No questions could be asked about what they would do.

Omala had her opinion on the witches using too much magic and drawing too much attention while also draining themselves. She said they weren't strong enough, and the other witches agreed, even Rani. Clay said he would help and dismissed their worries. It wasn't usually like him to be dismissive, but he didn't seem to be worried about it.

Leon was biting his nails. Their disconnection still intact, she had never felt so distant from him. It was unlike them.

They spent the rest of the morning making plans. No two people had the same role, whether it was scouting the forest, gathering herbs, reading old journals from their ancestors. Some even dove to the bottom of the lake to gather rocks to place around Shadow Rock.

Lucy wasted no time with lessons. By the end of the day, she was able to lift parts of the water off of the bed of the lake. She was able to help some of the divers walk to the bottom of the lake in large bubbles of air instead of diving to the bottom. Her cousin taught her how to take water out of a tree and put it back in without killing it. She nearly killed a werewolf by taking the fluids out of its body. Leon had to heal him or else he would have died. He tried to show her how, but she was more concerned with the wolf's health and making sure he would live than she was about learning how to heal him. She didn't want to risk his life.

Growing a large tree from just a seed was one of her favorite things she did. With help, she called all of the fish in the lake to jump out of the water at the same time. Anything she tried, she was able to do, even if just barely. Some better than others, but everything responded to her in one way or another.

When it was time for her to call on air, it didn't respond. So she blew as hard as she could in the direction she wanted the wind to blow and could feel it blowing in the same direction, but barely.

Lucy then realized the elements would only work if she put in the effort, met them halfway and understood they were their own beings, gifting her with the ability to manipulate them. If she didn't put in the effort, they wouldn't help her. It made her wonder what else she could do, as she was unsure of the extent of her power because there was no way she could save them with the exercises she had been practicing. Surely lifting fish out of the water and blowing wind couldn't save them. She also wasn't tired or drained like she was before. Everything she did was playful. Lucy felt deep inside of herself, this wasn't what she needed to be doing.

What power did she hold that she didn't know of? She wasn't sure what she had in her that could save them all or what made her sick. A part of her didn't want to ask because she was unsure whether anyone knew the answer. If she asked Clay, he would tell her as much as he knew in the best way he could explain it. She didn't want to hear it from him, she needed to hear from an Enkeli, from her dad. Even her uncles could help, her cousins had affinities for elements, Leon could heal, her dad went from limping and getting old, to looking a few years older than Lucy. Her dad and his brothers, her uncles, could pass as her siblings. The younger her dad looked, the more he looked like Leon. It was how the Enkeli worked. They could heal themselves, and what that entailed was their bodies regenerating themselves. Lucy wondered how old her dad actually was.

All of her cousins had helpful advice, and all seemed to be fully educated on who they were. Each one had their own way of being Enkeli, each one of them was strong. Whether they had affinities for the elements or could adjust someone's emotions, heal, speak to animals, cause tornadoes, hear someone else's thoughts, many different abilities.

Her cousin Sawyer called animals to him, and they understood him. He could ask them to do things or ask them for favors. They would honor him by doing so. He could also communicate with spirits who have passed on. He said there are ways animals communicate that is similar to spirit.

Sawyer's brother, Sanford, talked to a wild wolf and asked him to sniff the area for demons. He was able, with permission from the wolf, to go into the wolf's mind and share it with him while they scouted the whole lake before he was snapped back into his own body. He amazed all who saw, especially the Guardians who were on watch as they haven't seen something like that in centuries.

Mateo, another one of Lucy's cousins, didn't need to come up for air when he was underwater. He was favored by air and water. They both aid him whenever he needed them. His brother, Max, could create fire within his hands. If the fire was already aflame, he could make it grow and manipulate it to take on different forms.

They all seemed to be well trained in whatever craft they wielded. Most had claircognizance, a way of knowing. Those with lesser ability to connect with spirit, whether an element or animal, were warriors and worked closely with the earth. All were knowledgeable of the history of the Enkeli and did their best to remember the women Enkeli before Lucy, though it was long ago. Lucy was educated on the other Enkeli families in Mpiaron and what their functions were, each family was different.

Rani had made her way to Lucy by the safe house early in the morning and gave her tea to drink throughout the day. She finished all of it by the time night fell upon them. Rani, Omala, Alika and Fazi left to call on other witches who they could trust to help pull Mpiaron through. Not a word was heard from them since they left.

27

Lucy

I laid in bed, exhausted. As much as I wanted and needed to sleep, I felt terrible my friends were out scouting for our cause while I was resting.

Naturally, I did what I would have done before all of this happened. I got out of my bed with a pillow and the comforter and went to the kitchen for dried mangoes and iced tea. I put them on a tray and headed up the spiral staircase to the loft. This was, without a doubt, my favorite place in the whole house. The fireplace came at a not so close second.

This felt weird, being alone. I was alone for months at a time before all of this happened, and I was fine. Now, it felt strange. I was kind of scared something was going to happen and I wouldn't know what to do.

Clay said he was going to help Emma tonight. He wouldn't leave me unless it was necessary. I knew he was in his house, close enough to get here in seconds if I needed him, but he still felt far away. Dario was placed on duty to protect me and was on the back deck laying on the hammock. Most of the Guard preferred to sleep outdoors.

I felt guilty for thinking about the vampire. My body heated just thinking about him. I wondered throughout the day where he could be and if he was close. The tunnels underground were not explored or known by our kind, he could be directly under me, and I wouldn't know. I wondered what he saw if he had been watching me. I wondered whether this was compulsion or connection but didn't have clarity when I let it sit.

Guilt struck every time I thought about the vampire. Clay wasn't my boyfriend. He was my Guardian. Yet, he was also much more.

Clay is gentle with me and assertive when necessary. But something about him I can't place, it's like I can't get close. He shows me all of him, but there is still so much of him I don't know. I wonder if I try hard enough. Should I ask more questions, or should I ask him to be more transparent? Is he allowed to tell me everything? There were many questions I had, and I don't know if there will be enough time for answers.

All else aside, I was impressed with myself today. My energy was filled and alive. Using my gifts was easier than I thought. The question still stood, what gifts weren't I using? I would get tired and sick as a child. What gifts were I subconsciously using to make me feel that way? Especially as a child, the gifts I had were raw and untamed. Even when we were in Mpiaron, I went unconscious for days after. Whatever it was, I know it is what I need to find in me. Those gifts will save everyone. Something inside told me it would save everyone, even if it didn't save me.

How do I tell them that? That I had a feeling saving them would kill me? I would do it, over and over again, I would. I see how everyone works together and helps each other. Selfless and always giving, it reminds me of the way everyone was in Mpiaron.

I wondered how they would pull it through and how it will affect here. There will be reunions. The beings it will draw to us, to our side, to the Light. Rani and Clay had mentioned most beings in Mpiaron had family on earth and hadn't talked to them since they separated this realm and the one Mpiaron is in. Will their families help them? Or are they now part of the Deminio? We were about to find out.

So much was going on, and there wasn't a way to slow it down.

Clay, is everything okay? I thought to him.

A few moments passed. I didn't think he would answer when his deep voice filled my head.

Yes. Get some rest. I'll see you in the morning.

His voice was kind, but I couldn't help but hear the rush in it. He was too busy to talk.

I laid down, ate the last few bites of my late-night snack, and my eyes seemed to have closed before my head hit the pillow.

I thought I was in my loft. Where am I?

The tunnels. That couldn't be.

"You're dreaming," a smooth, familiar voice said.

The hair on my arms stood up, and my palm tingled. I couldn't see him through the darkness.

"You're in my dreams, so easily," I said.

I took deep breaths. I didn't want Clay to worry while he was busy.

"It's much easier to do when you are thinking of me. Even easier when you are alone. Where is your Guardian? I thought I asked you to stay with him," he said.

The pit of my stomach dropped. Why would he ask about Clay's whereabouts? Would he harm me?

"He is close by. A few of them are," I was honest and did my best to keep my heart rate even.

"You're heart races when you think of him. It's forbidden, you know. Your," he paused for a moment and looked up, "relationship."

I didn't like the pause between words. I turned around to see where he was.

"We aren't in a relationship. What's it to you?" I clarified and immediately regretted it. I didn't want to let him know anything about any of us.

"It's nothing to me. I said nothing of romance. You assumed I meant a committed relationship. I don't believe in the same definition of a relationship as you do. We have consorts of sorts. Some are temporary, but when we find our mate, it's forever," he said.

His voice was annoyingly taunting.

"Isn't that what relationships are?" I asked, still turning.

"You said you weren't in one. Your heart rate says otherwise."

He didn't answer me.

His breathing was nearby. He was close to me.

"Show yourself," I said.

"What's it to you?" He was mocking me and laughed.

"Leave me alone. Now," I did my best to sound authoritative and remembered how Clay showed his strength with only his voice. I closed my eyes and tried to wake up.

"But I haven't told you why I came to you in the first place," he teased.

I opened my eyes and waited for him to say something. Some part of me wanted to stay, though I'd never say it aloud.

"If you insist," he said, his voice growing further.

"Wait! Tell me," I said.

"You asked me to leave you alone. Now you want me to stay. You need to stop being so indecisive and make up your mind. It isn't a good look for someone like you," he continued to play.

My heart started beating faster.

He laughed.

"Someone *like* me? You don't know me," distaste heavy in my voice, I tried to give nothing away.

"You enjoy reading, art, and swimming. You eat too much fruit and not enough of anything else. You are a twin. You get annoyed when people try to make decisions for you. You talk to yourself more than you're willing to admit. You also wrinkle your nose when you smile, and lately, that hasn't been enough. When you laugh, you snort sometimes, even though you try to hide it," he said.

Everything he said was the truth.

"How-," I said before he cut me off.

"Oh, how do I know? I told you I've been watching you. Other people dream about you too. I see their dreams and pick up on loose thoughts and conversations. You'd be surprised at how they all really see you," he said.

All flirting was gone. He was telling the truth. I knew it.

"Are you taunting me? If you're not going to tell me anything useful, then you need to leave," my curiosity and annoyance both grew at an even pace. I spoke into the air as I still couldn't see him.

I don't know why I was more curious about him than I should be. He knew what he was doing.

"Think of it as less daunting and more fun." He stepped into the light and continued, "You see, unlike you, *I* am not in any real danger. Now here's the deal."

I couldn't help but stare at him. He was just as beautiful as the first time I saw him.

"There's a deal? Clay was right. You guys really don't work like we do," I huffed.

It made him smile, "We don't. We are vampires. Let me drink from you."

I instinctually took a step back as Clay's face flashed in my mind.

"It isn't for me. It's for you. If I drink from you, I can protect you," he said.

"You are absolutely *insane*. Help protect me? What does that even mean? My Guardian can protect me better than you ever could," with every word I felt regret for being here, I need to get back to Clay.

How do I wake up?

He took a step forward.

"As much as I'd like to say it would be for me, it wouldn't be. Yes, your blood would probably be the best I have ever tasted. Yes, your blood would make me stronger because of your Angelic roots. I just wouldn't want the ties that come along with it, like feeling your emotions. You call, I come. Always. I can protect you against demons in a different way than Clay can. He can kill them, he will kill them, and more will come in their place. I can kill them, too, but that would mean I have chosen a side. If I drink from you, you are mine. If they kill you, then they start a war with us. We are too many for them, the Clans and the Lemurians. They wouldn't kill you just yet. It would buy time," he said.

Everything he said made me feel like he was digging a hole I couldn't get out of.

He looked up towards the surface as if he could see it and took a step forward, closing the gap between us. Something was going on up there.

"Why do you care? Why go out of your way to help at all?" I said.

"So many questions. So little time. When you have your answer, call on me. I won't be too far. Right now, you need to be with your Guardian," his voice was soft. His voice held secrets.

"What's your name?" I asked.

He reached up and tucked my hair behind my ear. He then traced my jawline with his fingertips. I could feel his authenticity. I could barely breathe.

"Massimo," his voice echoed in my head.

I blinked once, and I was back in the loft lying down on the floor. It was hard to catch my breath. Part of me felt out of control, and that part of me was growing by the minute.

The fireplace made a cracking sound. New wood was put in there. But by who? Nobody else was in my house.

I sat up and saw Clay standing at the top of the staircase, eyes burning into mine.

28

Clay

"Lucy has been thinking about him. The vampire. His compulsion is strong, and he hasn't even compelled her. Of all my time here on earth, vampires have never crossed my path before," I said.

"Until now." Emma jumped down from a willow tree, branches in hand.

"Until now," I couldn't hide the bitterness I held inside. "Let's go back inside of my house."

I looked at the windows to Lucy's house. She was no longer in her room.

Clay, is everything okay? Her enchanting voice in my head.

"She's calling for me," I said.

"We have to get your part of the ritual ready for the witches before they get back. This is the only way," Emma said.

Yes. Get some rest. I'll see you in the morning. Was all I had managed to think back to Lucy. If I said anything else, I wouldn't be able to stay away.

"It's for her own good and yours. Separate it right now, her and the duty you have. You keep slipping, and I don't know how long I can cover your ass anymore," Emma said.

We walked back inside. He had eucalyptus branches, willow vines, and pinecones in his hand from several large treetops and placed them on my table.

"I know. I feel drawn to her. Even right now, I feel her in the loft. Everything inside of me tells me I need to be with her and not leave her alone. The crazy part is, I *can* separate it, being her Guardian and being with her. I just do not want to," I looked over at Emma.

He rolled his eyes and smiled.

I still do not understand the sense in rolling one's eyes.

"Have you told your dad about all of this?" He said as he took a second to look up at me. He then looked back down at the leaves to separate them from the branches he had just cut down from the trees.

I cut the palm of my hand with a sharp knife and let the blood drip into a large glass jar.

"No. I have told my father nothing. He has been close by. I can feel him. I wouldn't be surprised if he already knew. He would advise against it, but he wouldn't tell me no-,"

"Shh. Do you hear that?" Emma cut me off as he crouched down.

He still moved instinctually, like a demon.

"No, I do not," I said, still standing at the table with my palm dripping blood into the jar.

He looked up and placed his finger to his mouth, ensuring my silence. He crouched down and crawled on the floor. Though he was no longer dark, I still felt uneasy when he crawled like the demon he was. I could feel my eyes glowing and my blood changing.

Instinct took over. Even my open cut healed completely and closed, leaving no trace behind. I had to relax and cut it open again to get more blood.

"What is it, Emma? Tell me," I tried to ask but it sounded like a command.

"There are echoes underground. We haven't sent anyone to the tunnels. Is Lucy okay?!" The urgency in Emma's voice set both of us on alert.

I felt her. She was still in the loft.

Lucy, are you okay? I thought to her.

She was sleeping. I could feel that.

"She's sleeping," I said to him.

"How did he contact her last time?" Emma said.

He pushed more than he usually would. I was thankful it was Emma who was here. He's one of the only people who spoke to me like an equal and not a superior.

"Her dreams," I knew what he was getting towards. I said it more to myself than to him.

"I know how they work. She is okay, but you should go check on her," he said and went back to separating the leaves from their vines.

"He won't harm her. I told her not to let him taste her. She won't let him. She will be okay," I said.

I felt it. Lucy felt no fear or alert, only questions, and doubt.

"A part of her was with him today. She was as present as she could be, but I mean, if that was my… person whose Guardian I was, I wouldn't let her stray. Especially with a vampire. I told you how they work after living with them for so long, similar to us but they have their own ways," Emma tried to sound passive, but he does not have it in him. It isn't who he is. His demon qualities were visible. He was possessive.

"She is not mine to claim. I do not want her with a vampire without being in my presence. It bothers me how he thinks it is okay to intrude into her dreams, to insert himself where she should have privacy. There is something he wants, and the trade might be worth it. That is the only thing stopping me from ending him," I said.

I filled one jar with blood and began filling another.

"That and a war with vampires," Emma said.

"We would win," I had no doubt.

"At what cost?" He looked up at me.

"The Guard can take them, but the wolves would find pleasure in it. I am not worried about the vampires." This was true, though I was concerned about Lucy wanting to spend more time with them.

I pushed the thought out immediately.

Lucy was recently introduced to a whole new life and way. She would not know what she was getting into if she began to form relations with a vampire. It would change everything. Our dynamic would change, hers and mine as well as hers with our people. Nobody trusted vampires. I would have to be her Guardian and protect her while watching her possibly walk us into danger.

Would that be such a bad thing? Not her and the vampire, that would be doom, but us merging with the vampires. They can be dangerous, but not all of them are untrustworthy. Having them on our side could help us. That is the true reason why I am okay with him talking to Lucy. She could do what she wants either way.

I will not tell her how I feel. I will not let myself get into it again. It is too dangerous.

"Can you finish up? You know what to do," I asked Emma as I finished filling the last jar with my blood.

"Go get your girl." He clapped and smiled. Always teasing.

"Shut up," I said through a laugh.

I walked towards the door and out into the brisk night air. Emma was one person I didn't always have to be assertive with. He was a demon before, he wasn't going to judge me. I felt human with him most of the time. I was able to tell him my thoughts, even ones I wasn't proud of. Everyone else saw me as Clay the Guardian. That is what I intended, and that is my purpose. That is who I am. But, since I have known

Emma, I would say he has been a good acquaintance.

Emma wasn't afraid of me. Demons do not hold fear. It is what makes them ruthless. Nobody else would ever admit to being afraid of me, they respected me, they obeyed me, some admired me even. I could sense part of them was afraid of who I am, who my father is. I knew it was not how I was towards them. It was their own emotions and judgment. That is also what made them all great at what they do. I often wish they could see themselves as I see them, even if for a moment.

They are strong, unique in their own light. They would not be here if they were not superb in their own abilities. I wouldn't have chosen them to be council if they had any trace of a crack in their craft.

As I approached Lucy's barn house, I could feel her heart racing. She was uncomfortable, yet she was still safe.

I walked up the back porch stairs next to her pool. There was steam coming out of it. Dario was lying on the hammock right in front of the back door.

"You are dismissed for the evening. Go get some rest," I said to him.

"Thank you, Clay." He put his fist to his heart and ran to the safe house. Not a sound was made.

I slid the back door open and could see the fire was dying. I walked over to the fireplace and placed a wooden log inside of the fire. It took immediately.

Lucy's breath was sharp. I raced up the stairs and was at the top quicker than a human could blink their eyes.

Her hair was wet from sweat, her brows furrowed in her sleep, her hands in fists, and beads of sweat covered her entire body. I wanted to wake her. I knew if she needed me, she would call for me. All I would have to do is wake her up, and she would be here.

She rolled over and kicked the blankets off of her body. Her heartbeat slowed to its natural rhythm. Every time it picked up, I could hear the fire roaring and crackling louder.

She has not worked with fire yet. She needs to.

Demons are close. Everyone stay alert. Clay, shield her. Talan's voice was in my head.

All Guardians. Prepare and conceal yourselves. I let out an alert to all Guardians close by.

Lucy's eyes opened on cue. I watched her look around, full of light. Her body glowed just barely. I sensed she was unaware of it. She was using her senses to catch up with the energy around her.

When she looked at me, I saw her take a deep breath. She was relieved, and her light dimmed down to nothing. Lucy knew she was safe.

29

"His name is Massimo," was all Lucy could say to Clay as guilt flooded down to her soul.

"Just as I thought. I will have the witches on it first thing in the morning. You need to rest," Clay said to her as he walked towards her.

Lucy wanted Clay close by. She wanted to feel him close to her.

"Can you stay with me?" She asked him.

"I can," he said.

Lucy looked up at him, unable to look anywhere else. He took his shoes off and crawled into the blankets next to her. They laid side by side, Lucy on her side to face Clay. He was on his back looking up at the stars through the loft's skylights.

"You said last night I hardly knew who you are. Tell me about yourself," Lucy's voice was soft.

"What do you want to know?" He said.

"Everything."

"Give it a go."

"Who is your best friend?" She said.

Almost immediately, he laughed, "I do not have friends."

He turned to look at her.

"You have been alive for who knows how long, and you don't have even one person you could call a friend?" Lucy knew he wouldn't lie to her, the thought of him not having friends gave her a weird sense of loneliness.

"No, I guess I don't," Clay said.

She noticed his eyes were glowing and haven't stopped since he got there.

"I am your friend," Lucy said and smiled at him.

She suddenly felt too cold and covered herself with the blanket.

"I am your Guardian," he said.

"You're cutting me short of our friendship. Are we friends?" She asked.

Her smile faded.

"Is that what you want to be? Friends?" He asked.

Lucy was unsure what context he was referring to. After tonight she was uncertain of many things. Clay wasn't one of them.

"If we were both human and we didn't have the weight of everything good in this world on our shoulders, then I would say friendship would be on the table. We might have fallen in love and gotten married like mortals do. We would live right here on the lake and have ten children. Or we might have been together our whole lives, traveling the world just us two until we grew old and passed away in each other's arms. Or we might have been the best of friends who baked fresh cookies and watched movies together." He thought to himself for a moment, "Lucy, we will never know what would have been if it were that way. What I do know now is I feel who you are. I feel most myself with you, and I want to be close to you."

The last few days, Lucy hadn't felt much connection with anyone.

She felt it now, the pull she had to Clay.

"Lucy-," Clay tried to speak before Lucy cut him off.

"Wait, you said I hardly know you." She was going with the tactic Massimo used on her, "I know more than you think. You speak to everyone on an equal level, regardless of who or what they are. You don't usually use your authority even though you easily could. They respect you more for it. You are their leader by nature and by choice. You take your time to enjoy all things great and small, and you really take the time to listen. You are someone people can count on. You have it in you, just like your father. I only saw him for a minute, and I felt towards him what everyone else feels towards you. There is no one more fit to lead than you. Guard aside, you care deeply for those around you. Your brothers in the Guard are your brothers. You do what's best and what's right. You see everything as something that can be accomplished. There are no roadblocks or mountains in your eyes. When you smile, you mean it. You do this thing with your eyes when you are happy, and you like to touch the leaves when you walk by anything that has them. Water isn't your favorite, but you love to swim. You'd rather read than do just about anything else, and as much as you don't want this, this power and duty, you wouldn't place the weight on someone else. A part of you doesn't trust anyone else with it. You don't trust anyone else to protect me."

Lucy laid her head down on his chest, listening to his steady heartbeat. She felt him smile. He kissed the top of her head and squeezed her body closer to him.

"He asked to drink my blood," the moment was gone. Lucy couldn't hold it in. She couldn't keep a secret from him. All she asked of Clay was to not keep secrets.

"I would know if you did. You didn't let him," he said. His arm around her shoulders stiffened, "Lucy, you must not let him drink from you. Not ever."

She turned her head and looked up through the skylight at the stars and the glowing moon. She knew he was right. She wouldn't tell him Massimo's reasoning for him wanting to drink her blood. Not unless she thought it could help them, but she couldn't see that happening, not yet anyway. The Guard was strong, the Lemurians equally strong. Massimo was charming, but she didn't know anything about vampires or whether or not she could trust his people. When she was near him, she felt she could trust him. When she was distant from him, she questioned her judgment. It wasn't like her trusting Clay, which was as easy and natural as blood pumping through her veins. Trusting Massimo was like trusting yourself to hold your breath beneath the water for extended periods of time. You know you can, but not for how long. Or trusting your parachute to work when you've just jumped out of a plane. It works thousands of times, but there is a chance it won't.

Part of her wanted to give into Massimo today. Lucy didn't know why. But she knew she would soon find out.

Lucy sat up a little to see Clay's face. His eyes were closed, and he was content. With one finger, she turned his head towards her and kissed his lips.

He kissed her back and made her thankful it was a cool night as it began to get warm between them. Nothing could ever amount to what she felt for Clay. It made her want to be better, to try harder, and train harder. Lucy wanted to earn the right to stand beside him when the time came. Lucy wanted to fight the war as his equal.

With every emotion, their kiss grew deeper, equally eager and passionate. Not knowing where her body ended and his began. Under the moon and under the stars, time stood still.

"Morning, Luc."

Leon was the first to greet Lucy when she arrived at the safe house.

"Good morning," she said as she hugged him.

Lucy greeted everyone else there, including her dad. The greetings were short. Omala, Fazi, and Rani were not there, only Alika. Their attention was directed towards her.

"There have been many possessions throughout the world in the last three days. Demonic possessions over humans. We don't know if they are trying to send a message to scare us. A few of us have been preparing elixirs for us all to keep everyone safe. We need everyone to drink at least one cup a day and more if you get physically injured. It is hard for demons to possess humans and much more difficult for them to possess us, but it is being done and has been done before. We are exercising every option, and at the very least, we can take the elixirs." Alika passed around what looked like tea bags and put the rest on the countertop for everyone to get as needed.

Alika's accent was an easy adjustment for Lucy to get attained to. It was difficult for Lucy to remember what she sounded like before because it suited her well.

"What happens to humans?" Lucy asked.

"We are doing our best to help them, but we need to stay focused on the test at hand. The Vatican had been notified, most of them are dark, but there is a light sector that performs rituals to separate the demon from the body," Alika said.

"What if they aren't catholic? I thought the Vatican only did exorcisms on approval to those of Catholic faith?" Lucy asked.

"That is only in movies. This sector is sworn to secrecy, no religion specified, like us. They work closely with us in tough situations like this and use rituals we have provided as well as copies of the Lachfll books which hold tools of their own," Alika said.

"The humans will be taken care of. We need to take care of ourselves. If we fail to protect ourselves against demons, we also fail to protect humans from them. Is everyone clear of their tasks today?" Clay wasted no time.

Everyone nodded and went to their posts. Lucy was unaware of where everyone else was and what their duties were. Apparently, they talked about it prior to her arrival.

Clay walked to the kitchen and asked Alika to join him. Emma and Leon followed.

"Change of plans. There are a few places we need to go. We have to get out of town. Emma and Leon, go pack camping gear. Food, tents, blankets, whatever can fit into my truck and your jeep," he gestured at Leon. "First, we need to pull Mpiaron through. Owranoos found a loophole and a way to do it quickly. The witches are waiting for us outside. Immediately after they're finished, we need to leave. Now let's pull Mpiaron through to Shadow Rock."

Alika was radiant and smiled with excitement. Lucy was suddenly reminded of Alika's family in Mpiaron, which she hasn't seen since it closed.

They all walked outside. Nothing was different.

"What do we do?" Lucy asked.

"*We* don't do much, Luc. We sit and wait for instruction. The rest of the witches and Guard are on the perimeter of where Mpiaron is hidden. Alika is here to conceal all of us here on this side," Leon said as he walked outside and gathered a few Adirondack chairs for all of them to sit on.

Lucy followed and sat down. She got as comfortable as she could get. The sun on her skin was warm, and the cool breeze was refreshing. She could feel the pulse of magic in the air.

"They have begun," Alika said.

Alika stood facing south, the direction where the rest of the witches were. She mumbled to herself, and Lucy felt like she had to be quiet.

Lucy looked around and could see everyone watching Alika closely. Emma and Leon instinctually took Alika's sides. Clay stood next to Lucy. For the next hour, time didn't seem to exist.

She is muting our energy. We are all powerless right now. Clay's voice echoed in her head.

What if demons come? Lucy looked at him.

She will stop shielding us and we will fight. Those odds are fairly high. He thought to her.

What can I do to help? She asked.

"It's time for us now. Is everyone ready?" Alika asked.

Everyone else but Lucy nodded. She was just following along. Clay handed Lucy a sharp needle and gestured for her to follow his instructions. He pricked his finger. Lucy looked at Leon, who did the same. As well as Emma and Alika. Lucy followed and watched as the drop of blood pooled at her fingertip.

"Together now, just one drop on the soil, in three, two, one," Alika said.

Every one of them let their drop of blood fall to the first at the exact same time. A pulse hit Lucy's body. The ground was alive. She could feel it. The water from the lake was feeding the soil she was standing on. The grass beneath her feet rippled. The house creaked. It was expanding, intuitively adding on rooms to itself for more to fit inside.

Lucy felt it, the exact moment Mpiaron was pulled through. Her eyes closed as she sat in her chair. She could feel the breeze hitting her face and could smell the salt of the ocean and mixed smells. It didn't smell how it usually did in Shadow Rock. She could smell fresh produce, smoke from hundreds of chimneys and much more fresh air. The floor pulsed in small waves and ripples of glowing light.

"Thank you, Clay, for your help. Your blood changed the way this was originally planned on being reversed. The way the magic works is different than its intended way. Much has changed since we made the choice to conceal Mpiaron. There are many ways of doing something, and that goes for both sides, not just ours," Alika said to Clay.

Lucy looked at Leon and whispered, "Clay's blood?"

"Clay and Emma gathered a branch from the top of the tallest trees surrounding Mpiaron and Shadow rock. They are the anchors of the perimeter of it all, the anchors that keep us safe. They soaked them in Clay's blood. His father is an angel. His blood is sacred. They're doing a ritual in the location of Templom, burning all of the branches. It protected all of us today and hid the impact Mpiaron has here," Leon whispered back.

Lucy nodded at her twin then looked over at Clay. He didn't look drained or phased.

"It's done," Alika said to all of them.

"You all said it would take days. That was much faster than I thought," Lucy said.

"Thanks to Clay's blood," Alika said.

Clay nodded, "Pack the trucks. Lucy and I are going to pack our bags, and we will meet you all back here in thirty."

Leon looked like he was about to say something when he turned and patted Emma on the shoulder. Emma nodded, and they both walked to their dad's garage. Alika went inside the safe house and smiled softly at Clay before she opened the door.

Clay and Lucy got in his truck and drove their way to the other side of the lake where their houses are.

"Sometimes, the other side of the lake feels far, but a good far. Just far enough to not be so close to everyone," Lucy said as she looked out of the window.

Clay smiled and let out a low laugh, "I agree."

"Where are we going?" She asked.

"To our houses to pack," he said.

Lucy knew he was being sarcastic, which wasn't like him.

"Clay." She looked at him with knowing eyes. He didn't want to tell her.

"There are ruins, hidden by magic and spells. We need to tap into the raw organic energy there. It will help us when we need it. Pack up and meet me in five minutes back here," he said.

Clay parked the truck, and Lucy went inside her house and watched Clay as he walked straight into his garage. She waited for him to be out of sight before she walked into her home and went straight to her closet for her little leather bag Omala had spelled for her when she first went to Mpiaron. She opened it to see if it still fit everything she would need it to. When she reached her hand in, her arm went straight in. It still worked.

"Perfect," she said to herself.

Kona ran into her closet.

"Hey there, you've been busy lately helping everyone out. Thank you for all you've done and for your sacrifice. Being an alpha must not be easy," she reached out to touch him on his head. He stopped next to her and laid there as she laid out the clothes on her bed.

He didn't seem the same, he was still Kona, but he was also much more than a wolf and a pack leader. He was a friend.

Lucy didn't know how long they were going to be gone or where exactly they were going. She didn't know what to pack. Jeans, tee shirts, and a few sweaters were what she settled for.

Her stomach growled. Lucy walked to the kitchen and got a few things they might need. Snacks, a few canisters with water, tea Rani made. When she gathered everything she needed from the kitchen, she headed over to her linen closet and got some blankets, pillows, and towels.

She was ready.

"Are you coming with us, Kona?" She asked.

He grumbled and looked outside, then back at her and walked over to her and put his head to hers before he ran outside.

"Okay. I'll be seeing you soon," she whispered to him even though she knew he wouldn't hear her.

"You'll be seeing who soon?" Clay asked from the doorway, "Are you packed and ready to go?

Lucy tapped her full leather bag housed across her body.

"All good here. Let's go," Lucy walked over to him and instead of walking outside, she pulled him inside and shut the door.

"Lucy, we really have to get going," Clay said with his eyes shut, pained to turn her down.

She wrapped her arms around him and waited till he did the same a few moments later. She took a few deep breaths and rubbed her hands up and down his back. Lucy took a few deeps breaths before she let go.

"Okay, I'm ready now."

She reached for the door and walked outside.

Clay smiled and let out a breath as he ran his hands through his long hair. Lucy looked back and smiled at him, knowing it was her that made him feel that way.

"I packed as well as I could with the amount of time given," she said, proud of herself.

"Well done." Clay walked towards the driver's side of the truck.

Lucy peaked at the truck's bed before getting in and couldn't believe the number of things he packed in that short amount of time. There was a tent. Half of it was firewood nicely stacked and cut, a few duffle bags, and a few axes.

They both jumped in the cab of the truck and headed back towards the safe house.

"That's a lot of wood to take camping. You know, in a forest full of wood," Lucy said as she tried to keep a straight face.

"It is all carved and spelled to protect our path," Clay said as he looked over at her. "It doesn't smoke either, nobody could track us, and we will stay warm."

"Oh. Well done," she repeated him.

When Lucy looked outside of the window from the passenger's seat, she could see the Bloom. Tents and makeshift cots lined the road the entire way to the safe house. She found it strange not everyone wanted to stay there. Some people preferred to sleep outside in the forest. Lucy felt the same when she thought about it. She would rather have her own tent or space in the forest than share a home with countless other people.

Nobody was around. Usually, she could see people around the lake or surrounding the house.

When they arrived at the safe house, Leon's Jeep was packed and ready. Leon and Emma were outside talking to each other. Owranoos was there with Alika and Omala while Fazi was talking to Dario and Talan.

"They're all coming?" She asked Clay.

"I insisted it be just us, Emma and Leon. They insisted otherwise," he pointed his chin towards the group as they parked.

Her dad paced down the stairs of his house and helped her out of the truck.

He brought Lucy close to him and held her tightly for a moment before he said, "Listen, Lucy. Be careful. Trust yourself, and I'll see you soon. I love you." He kissed her forehead before he let her go.

Lucy couldn't speak through the ball in her throat. Something about his tone worried her. She settled for a smile, and her dad nodded knowingly.

"Let's go," Clay's voice echoed.

Emma and Leon hopped in the Jeep. Rani, Alika, and Fazi rode in his back seat. Lucy got into the truck with Clay and felt it shake a moment later. She looked back and saw Dario and Talan standing right behind the window on the bed of the truck, they both helped Omala up, and she stood in the middle of them. One of them tapped the top of the cab to let Clay know they were ready.

Lucy could see Kona on the top of the porch stairs with her dad in the rearview mirror. They would be okay.

Protect them. Lucy felt the words in her head and closed her eyes.

She waited for a sign. Unsure if she would ever get one when she felt a slight buzz in her body before sending it off to them, something she had never done before, but it felt right. There was an unknown feeling. They had two days before Deminio came, according to Massimo. If anything were to happen to anyone while she was gone, she would never be able to forgive herself. Her family was there, everyone she had ever known. All of the Lemurians in her rearview mirror.

30

"Clay, do you have siblings or a mom?" Lucy asked.

"Not in the sense that you do. I have the Guard. They are my brothers. Though they are my brothers, Michael is only my father. Not theirs. The Guardians are my brothers by bond and by oath," he said. His openness about his family was refreshing.

"What about your mother?" Lucy looked over at him.

"My mother was human and died long ago. I remember her but her life was short lived, in comparison to my own."

That resonated with Lucy. Her shoulders released tension she didn't know she carried.

"Do you see him? Your father?" Lucy wondered this often but never asked.

After a moment of thought, Clay answered, "Yes."

"How often?" Lucy knew this was a topic he wasn't open about.

He studied her for a moment, his eyes off of the road too long, but he bobbed and weaved through the trees as if he was paying attention.

His eyes narrowed, a soft warning. It was slight, but his intention was clear. No more questions of Michael.

Clay reached down and picked up a small basket with a linen cloth over it. He gestured for Lucy to take the basket. She could smell them the whole time, but she couldn't place where the smell was coming from. Chocolate chip cookies filled the large basket.

Lucy picked one up and got a mouthful of soft chocolatey deliciousness.

"These are heavenly," she said.

"Well, my father *is* an angel," he said.

They both laughed.

She got three more with her other hand and reached up out of the window and handed them to Dario above her. One for each of them.

She noticed Clay looking around and driving between trees and rocks.

"How do you know where we are going?" She tried to find any sort of road, but there was none.

"There is a stream close by. I am following the stream," he pointed to their right.

The stream was small. It looked like the stream they would go to when they were children where they would innertube all day. Though this stream was too far, it did look the same. The memory made her smile.

When she finished the cookie, she was surprisingly tired. The views were beautiful. In all of her life, she had never come this way, not through the forest with no roads. A half-day came and went. They followed a stream going off the river and upriver.

They came to a stop. All of them got out of the car and walked together towards the water. It was a waterfall over a hundred feet tall. The water was the same color as the lake. A bright clear turquoise with no rocks in the pool of water that formed beneath it. She had never been there before.

"It is enchanted, people can't find it unless they are with an Enkeli," Clay said.

"Thanks," she nodded, making eye contact with him. He reached for her hand and brushed it before releasing it, ensuring it stayed between them.

The pool of water was large enough for all of them to fit, and somehow Lucy knew it was exactly what they were going to do.

Together they went from the cars to the water and walked right in. Exactly the way they did in the ocean, they held hands. They've been doing this since before she could remember. When the water was too deep for them to stand, they turned to float on their backs. In a circle, feet out and heads inside of the circle, breathing and floating in unison. Lucy felt the magic in them doing this. She could feel the water pushing them up from below, both wanting and helping. This time the circle was slightly bigger, Clay was holding her hand joining them for the first time, which changed the dynamic. A pulse was felt throughout. He brought the circle to life. Lucy hadn't known the extent of Clay's power until now.

This time was different. Their thoughts were exchanged, hopes flooded their minds, and allowed Lucy to understand how they worked and why they were chosen to be there with her. They all had the same sense of determination and optimism. They were chosen and also chose to be here with her, for the sake of all they love, for the sake of her.

Lucy didn't understand why they had faith in her, when each of their abilities was much more developed than hers. Clay was strong. They all were. They played a crucial part in the circle they had and in Lucy's development as a child. Anything she could do, they can do. It might not all be from one person, but they all could come together and amount to what she could do.

It made her wonder, again, what they are choosing not to tell her.

What power did she have that she didn't know of, the power that takes from her? The day when Lucy worked with water and nearly fainted, having to drink the elixir. It had to have been the same as when she was a child and would lose consciousness. What made her different and not like them, and why was she not strong enough to wield it?

The question lingered over every conversation though nobody could tell her. Lucy was starting to believe they didn't tell her because they didn't know. She had to find out on her own.

As Lucy stared at the sky, she could see clouds begin to heavily roll, it was mid-day, and the sun was illuminating everything around them. She tilted her head slightly to look towards shore to find Rani still there. She didn't get in the water. Instead, Rani was burning a log and chanting. Something in her hand was on fire, and she was making symbols in the air towards them.

Rani was protecting them.

Can anyone hear me? Lucy thought to everyone as they were in the circle.

Yes. WOW! Woah. Yeah. Sweet! She heard their voices in her head.

I'm going to try something. Don't break the circle. Lucy thought again.

Water, please bond us closer together, turn this circle. Lucy thought to water this time.

She closed her eyes and focused on breathing. The water answered after a pulse. She could feel the current under them changing. Then, while still holding hands, it picked them up almost fully out of the water. Each of them was on their own water platform, and the water turned them clockwise.

Cleanse their hearts of doubt, fear, any darkness they may be carrying. Illuminate every shadow. Help them feel love, happiness, and hope. Give them the strength and will you have. You have moved mountains and carved rocks with grace and persistence. We shall do the same. Lucy wasn't expecting what happened next.

The water turned warm beneath them and curled up, softly running a continuous current over their bodies and cleansed them with the intent of the water.

Whispers of cries, doubt, and anger were washed away. Traces of loneliness were washed away. Fear of failure, dark thoughts washed away. Lucy knew they weren't only her own thoughts and emotions, but feelings of those within the circle. They all did a great job concealing these thoughts from everyone else. Subconsciously, Lucy knew they all had human ways about them. It was normal to have these feelings, even for them. Now they were gone. Those seeds of darkness and clouded thoughts were gone and washed away with the water. They were the way Lucy had always seen them.

The feelings of everyone rushed towards her and left her in a heart-beats time, leaving her winded. Lucy blinked vastly. Her vision grew blurry and out of control. Her head started pounding, and the ringing in her ears became so loud she could feel her ears getting hot, and the rest of her body got cold. Popping sounds came from inside of her head. Her hands were suddenly full and swollen, feeling like her fingertips were going to burst if she didn't pull them close to her chest, break-ing the circle. She could no longer keep her body afloat. Her body was heavy, cold, and pulsing vigorously.

The air escaped her lungs, the water was turning red, then black. She couldn't see anything.

She almost gave in to the silence and relief that was sure to follow. She would have if the arms that wrapped around her body didn't knock her awake again. Air struck her face, unable to breathe as she clutched tightly to herself. Her eyes were wide open, and she could see nothing.

Sand was at her back. She could feel only the pounding on her chest. The ringing in her ears was deafening.

Air. I call to you. Fill my lungs and help me breathe. Lucy formed thoughts through the numbing pain.

Then everything went dark.

The grass felt nice. It wasn't the grass that made her itch, it was the kind of grass that was fresh on her skin. The air was fresh and alive. She could feel cool moisture in the air. Everything was several shades of green. The trunks of the trees were covered in vines, and all connected through the vines in some way. Vines were everywhere. Some had purple flowers, some were just leaves

She looked up. The sky wasn't blue. It was a glowing fog. In front of her was a hillside made of rock with vines hugging every surface. There was a narrow stone staircase carved out of the hillside and lead to an opening in the rocks. Above and around it was more rock and vines creating a wall going so high it went above the glowing fog. She couldn't see how high it went.

"Lucy." She heard from a distance behind her in the trees.

The stairs were magical. She walked forward towards them.

"LUCY!" She heard louder but still in the distance.

The stairs were small and steep, full of cracks. The rock was shiny and reflective in some spots making the stairs look slippery.

A strong hand pulled her backward. She was falling on her back.

SWOOSH. She heard a strong gust of wind. Wings.

LUCY! Wake up, can you hear me? Wake up. I'm here. Clay's voice was muffled, an echo from underwater.

She was coughing. Her throat was raw. Everything was dark.

Finally, she didn't struggle for air.

"I can't see," she croaked.

Her eyes were wide as if she could open them just a little bit more, she would be able to see, but there was nothing.

There was mumbling.

Lucy, can you hear my voice? Clay's words in her head.

She nodded.

More mumbling.

"What?" She forced.

She could hear Leon's muffled voice, but she couldn't hear what he was saying. His voice was distorted.

Then she heard Clay's voice. It was also distorted.

It is okay, Lucy. Just focus on breathing. Deep breaths. I am here. His voice in her head, she could feel his fingers rubbing her arm. She was lying in his arms.

Her hands felt around. There was water, wet sand, and dirt. They were still by the waterfall.

"I can't see. I can't see anything," her throat was made of sandpaper.

More mumbling.

Lucy, drink this, please. Clay's voice was smooth as she felt liquid at her lips.

It was sour and chunky like a smoothie that had been in the sun for days. It tasted fermented.

She gagged.

She felt it at her lips and drank till she gagged again.

"I can't drink anymore," she said as she sat up to gag again.

Her eyes were watering, and she could feel her whole face getting wet with tears, but she wasn't crying. She blinked rapidly to get rid of the excess water. But the water wasn't going away, so she kept blinking.

She could see. First it was just color blotches. The more she blinked through the water, the clearer her vision got.

There was mumbling. Lucy looked up and could see all of them having a conversation.

"Clay, I can't hear."

She looked at him. He was rubbing her back.

I know, Lucy. Keep breathing. It will come back. Your ears were bleeding. The elixir will help. Do you think you could stomach a few more sips? His voice in her head.

He reached for the cup and swallowed the chunky elixir. Right when she thought she was going to throw up, there was none left.

The ringing had stopped. Lucy touched her ear, and it was wet. She thought it was from her tears, but when she looked at her hand, it was red. Her ears ached as they began to pop. She screamed from the pain. She could feel the stream of blood dripping down her neck.

"When Lucy is okay, we have to keep moving," Rani said.

"Lucy moves when she says she moves. You don't make decisions for her Owranoos," Leon's voice struck. Lucy could feel his anger.

What are they talking about? Lucy thought to Clay.

Good, you can hear them. Owranoos wants to keep going. She says you will be fine. Leon doesn't want you to make any sudden moves until you are okay. He thought to her.

His transparency when she asked him questions was the only thing keeping her from losing it.

I know we have to keep moving, but I don't know if I can stand. Something doesn't feel right, something is off, and I'm not talking about me. I feel cold. Lucy thought to Clay.

Do not tell anyone. I sense Deminio close by. I will stall, and you tell me if and when you are ready. Is that okay with you? He thought to her.

"If something happened, we need to stay here. There is no such thing as coincidences. Set up a fire and the tents. Get the food going. We are staying here," Clay demanded. His voice harder than it was in her head.

Rani was frustrated but didn't say anything and didn't walk away. She stood there watching them. Nobody else said anything, either. Dario and Talan went straight for the equipment and started setting up. Emma grabbed Leon by the arm and pulled him out of earshot. Alika and Fazi started on the food.

Clay picked Lucy up and carried her back into the water. Lucy held on with what little strength she had left, a little hesitant of the water after what had just happened.

"Trust me," he said.

He was only about knee-deep when he knelt down. Lucy looked up at him, dripping in anxiety, tears, and blood.

"It's okay. I'm just going to wash you up a little," Clay whispered in her ear.

Alika came up next to them with a small glass bottle of soap and handed it to Clay before she left.

Clay adjusted Lucy to sit between his legs with her back to him, facing the waterfall. He put soap in his hand and rubbed it into Lucy's hair, taking the blood out. Small circles over her temples, ears, and neck. Massaging it into her shoulders and arms. The soap was warm, tingling over her body. It melted into her skin and seemed to have washed her from the inside out.

"Alika works with the earth. She only creates mixes when they call to her. She felt the need to make this yesterday and said it was for you. Now is the right time. Like I said, there is no such thing as coincidences, only synchronicities." Clay whispered.

It smelled of lavender and jasmine, and maybe some sandalwood. Lucy closed her eyes while Clay washed her face.

Her body didn't feel so heavy anymore. She sat up on her own and looked at the clear water. The sound of the waterfall was roaring and mute at the same time. Nothing about the water was dangerous.

"I feel better," Lucy said, turning to him.

He smiled, and his brow furrowed in the center.

Lucy laid in the water to get all of the soap out of her hair and off of her body. It left a smooth residue and reviving scent. As she laid in the water, she felt the return of the water, the warmth, and the tingling. It never left her. It caressed her hair, twirling it under the water and she could feel it pushing against the parts of her skin that still had blood. The water was helping her.

Thank you. I know you didn't harm me. Lucy said to herself. The temperature of the water cooled down as the presence of water left.

"You are learning much more than you let on. Well done," Clay said to her, soft so no one else could hear.

"Well done? I thought you would be upset with me," she said to him as she sat up.

"I could never be upset with you. If there are eyes on us, we need to ensure they don't see what you can really do. Today you pushed yourself. Look at the outcome," Clay said as he gestured towards the group.

Lucy looked over at them. The first thing she saw was Emma smiling, a full and happy genuine smile. His skin had more color than it usually did, and he was laughing. Leon was with him. He looked bright and was subtly glowing the way Enkeli do. Omala, Alika, and Fazi were making food and something about them was different. Omala didn't have her reserved face on. She was more vocal. Dario and Talan were both setting up tents so quick she almost couldn't see them, they were tall, and their skin was vibrating. Their eyes glowed so brightly she could see the blue and brown from the water. They glowed different colors than Clays, yet both eyes were different.

"They are the same, but they are different," she said.

"The qualities that make them unique are shining bright. You illuminated any shadows they had and magnified what makes them special. You hurt because of it. You could have died because of it. Now, just an hour after your heart nearly stopped, you are healthy and back to normal. If they went to battle now, they would never be more prepared than this moment right now," Clay's was gentle as he spoke to her, he branded every word onto her soul.

Lucy knew he spoke truth. She felt the weight of every word he said. She knew part of her gift, even if she didn't know how to use it. It wasn't water or air. It wasn't making things grow or being strong. None of that could kill demons.

To Lucy, they all seemed to have a handle on whatever it was that made them strong. Only because she didn't know her potential. When they were in the water, she could feel every emotion they all concealed. They didn't want to show her the struggles they had. They didn't want to discourage her.

"Are you ready to get out of the water?" Clay asked Lucy.

"Yeah, I guess I am," she said.

Clay stood up and extended his hand out to Lucy, helping her to her feet.

I am strong enough. I promise. She thought to him.

He rubbed her hand with his thumb before letting it go for her to walk on her own. Lucy looked up at Leon again. He was looking at them. His smile was gone.

They both walked up towards the rest of the group, the tents were set up, and the food was laid out on a small table.

"Lucy, over here," Omala called out for her.

She walked over towards one of three tents, where Omala was.

"Your bag is on top of the bed we made for you in your tent. I put lotion in the bag as well and an extra brush just in case. Grab a blanket on your way out, it is starting to get cold, and we need you well," Omala said with a touch of love in her voice, as always.

Lucy could make her bed out. It was the only one with a small bag on it and a colorful quilt from home. It was next to a bed she knew to be Leon's. She recognized his bag at the foot of the bed. Emma also had a bed on the other side of the tent. The only reason she knew it was Emma's was because there was a black beanie on the bed.

She opened her bag and reached for thick leggings and an old hoodie. She quickly changed out of her wet clothes, put comfortable socks and shoes on, brushed and braided her hair, and headed back out, blanket in hand. Afraid if she laid down on her blow-up mattress, she would fall asleep.

"Here you go." Leon handed her a bag of dried mangoes and a burger.

"Thank you," she smiled at him.

"I knew you'd be okay. It was a close one though, don't scare me like that again," he said. His smile was faint, but it was there.

"I'll try to keep the almost dying to a minimum next time," she said, and they both laughed.

Leon sat down and pat a log next to him for her to sit close. She sat and devoured her food.

Everyone except for Clay sat around the fire and ate. Omala was sitting on the other side of Lucy, talking to Emma. They were talking about making ice cream from scratch, which seemed silly to Lucy because of their circumstances, but it was refreshing to hear them speak of something mundane. Fazi was telling jokes to Talan and Dario. Alika was sitting on her chair lying back, looking at the infinite stars above them.

Rani was sitting across from Lucy, eyes on the fire. She looked different, overly tired, bags under her eyes and somehow much thinner. The stress must be getting to her. She has been supplying everyone with various elixirs and doing spell work since she crossed over from Mpiaron. Pulling it through this morning must have taken its toll on her.

Where are you? She thought to Clay.

Just on the other side of the tree line. I can hear you all. I am just scouting the area before everyone goes down for some rest. I will be keeping watch while we are away from home. His voice in her head.

Okay. She thought back.

She was going to say something else when Leon interrupted.

"What's going on with you and Clay, Lucy? Don't say nothing. I've noticed it for a while," he said.

"I don't really know, to be honest with you," Lucy looked her brother in the eye.

"You don't know? Or you don't want to know?" He huffed.

"Both. Leon, if you're going to judge, then I won't talk about it," Lucy said softly and turned her body towards the fire.

"I'm not judging," Leon said.

"Sure," she tried closing the conversation, fully aware Clay could hear them.

"Do you know who he is?" He asked.

"Yes, I do. He's the leader of the Guardians and council," Lucy said.

"Is that what he told you?" Leon asked.

Lucy turned her body towards Leon and adjusted her blanket tight around her body.

"That and who his dad is," Lucy said.

"Lucy, it's not supposed to happen. He isn't just their leader, but our leader. He maintains the balance of the Light. He is the leader of all Lemurians. He doesn't talk about what he has done, and he doesn't show his strength. You underestimate him," Leon told her.

"I knew he was our leader but didn't know he was the leader of the Lemurians," Lucy said.

"His dad is an angel. Lucy, he has fought battles with his dad in the other realm. He has killed more demons than all of us on earth combined," Leon was quiet, whispering so nobody else could hear him.

"If he is so powerful, then what is the problem?" She said.

His brows furrowed, "Putting aside it's dangerous for you both. If his dad is an angel, we can't mess with him. It's dangerous."

"I am not messing with him, Leon. It is more than that. I don't even know how to explain it. I know our bond is different because he is my Guardian, but there is something else there. I don't know if it's love but it is some type of energy. I feel like I have known him for my entire life, longer even. You know more than anyone that I've never truly connected with anyone. I have always felt like I couldn't be myself with anyone except you and dad. But I can be myself around him, and he under-stands what I am feeling without me having to say too much. I think he can relate to my position better than anyone else. So, say what you want. It isn't just me having a crush on some guy I met. I can't say I know what I am doing, but I've never felt like this. Ever," Lucy said to him, louder than she should have.

She looked around to see if anyone heard her. They were all still engaged in their own conversations.

"Just be careful. Rules are set for a reason, and there is a lot you still have to learn about all of this. It has never happened before, him being with someone. You're still my sister, I know how important you are to everyone else and for obvious reasons, but I still see you the same. I've always known the strength you have, but you are still you. I don't want anything to happen to you," Leon said.

Lucy nodded and understood. She truly did.

"I'll figure it out, and if I need help with anything, I will come to you. You have my word," she smiled at her brother.

"Are you ready for bed?" Leon asked her.

"Finally. I thought this time would never come."

31

Clay

Clay heard Lucy go to sleep an hour ago. She was exhausted after today and she was getting closer to unlocking it. But he wasn't sure if she would do it in time for the war.

After his talk with Emma today, he wondered what the plan of attack was for the Deminio. They always worked differently than how they have been lately. They aren't as obvious as they have been in the past. It is like they are adapting to the energy of the balance.

Clay received word there has been sickness spreading around small countries globally. There has been a release in low energy making its people weaker. Therefore, more susceptible to demonic attacks, entities harvesting energy. He had a hard time believing they had grown so quickly and how structured the Deminio was. They have never been this good at being quiet or organized. Even the way they were with the tunnels, they were secretly built by the Guardians millennia ago as a passage without showing too much Light, forgotten about, and then adopted by vampires. He didn't know they knew about the tunnels. Somewhere within the time of Lucy's birth till now, they grew in strength and knowledge. He hadn't run into a demon since the day when one showed up to get Lucy. Almost as if they were avoiding him.

Clay stood on top of the tallest tree he could find and could see the entire camp and waterfall. Its beauty hasn't been seen in hundreds of years.

It gave Lucy the strength she needed to overcome the inner battle she was having with herself. Not finding her medium. He could feel it, the Light. She almost had it tonight before her body shut down. There is no way of him finding the right words to help her get to where she needs to be. It was about her feeling it herself and working with it once she had a grasp of it.

Time was running short. Pretty soon, it was going to be all or nothing. Clay has been in enough wars to know how it worked, though he did know this time was different. More beings were involved from all over the world. It was an eternal battle that was going to tip the scales forever.

Clay felt his skin ripple.

Something was growing closer.

He ran in its direction. It wasn't moving very fast, and it wasn't getting closer to them. It was going around them. He could feel its exact location. His senses told him it wasn't Deminio, but it wasn't of Light.

As he approached, he felt his eyes glowing, and every cell in his body was ready to fight.

"Clay," a male voice said from a distance.

"Who is there?" He asked, alert.

"It is I, Massimo."

Clay heard as he approached him.

"What business do you have here?" Clay's voice was ice.

"I knew she would ask you for permission if she agreed to it. But I have come to speak to you about why it would be best for her," Massimo said.

"What would be best for who? You do not know what is best for Lucy if that is who you are talking about. You are not our kind. You do not understand our ways," Clay's tone reflected his Guardian physique.

"Clearly," Massimo said, too smooth for Clay's comfort.

"You didn't answer me. What would be best for who?" Clay asked.

"She didn't talk to you about it. Maybe she should," Massimo paused for a moment. "I want to drink from her."

"Of course you do, and she did talk to me about it," Clay torched his words.

"She might have told you, but I can tell she didn't tell you why I want to." Massimo waited for Clay to respond. When he didn't, Massimo continued, "It isn't about the blood for me. You see, I drink only donated blood from someone who agrees to it. Only drinking as little as possible and eat normal food to curve my appetite. It will be hard for me to stop drinking from her, but I will. Do you know the outcome of blood-drinking?" Massimo 's voice was as powerful as Clay's.

"I do know it is on the brink of evil, inhumane even. It is not something anyone should ever volunteer to do," Clay said, he was becoming too defensive. He took a deep breath.

Massimo did the same, "That depends on the vampire. Clay, I can protect her. If I drink from her, I can protect her. I can know her moods, some thoughts. I can help, even just for a little while. My clan will have chosen a side. Other clans will follow once they meet her. It will protect her in its own sort of unspoken oath. That's what you guys all go by, correct?"

Clay knew little about vampires, though he didn't take the time to speak to any of them. They have never reached out like Massimo has.

"You cannot drink from her. That gives you a claim to her in your people's eyes. The answer is no," Clay said.

He looked closely at Massimo. Massimo could have been one of them, his build was similar to their human form, and something about him was familiar.

"All she has to do is call out to me, think about me. I will hear her. I hear her thinking of me sometimes. She's skeptical of me, too," Massimo closed his eyes as if the thought pained him. "I am on your side, Clay. Times are changing. It is time we change with them. It might not be within the next few days or even months, you guys might not need me *yet*, but if the day comes that she should need me, I will be there. *We will be there.*" Massimo's last few words were said from afar before he disappeared into the abyss of the forest.

Clay didn't want to believe they would need to call Massimo. But he also knew he could trust him. His intuition said he could trust him with Lucy's well-being, which confused him as to why Massimo would want to drink from her when most vampires would stake their claim.

Massimo was of true vampire blood. He could see by looking at him that he was born of vampires, not created to be one. Massimo was of royal descent, not just from his ring but his features. He wondered what Massimo meant when he said, *"we will be there."*

There could have been more like him. Clay was unsure. He had questions for him and would have demanded Massimo to stay, but vampires weren't under his command, and he couldn't make him do anything.

Clay? Lucy's voice in his head was tired and soft.

Yes, Lucy? He smiled.

Massimo is close. She echoed.

Go back to sleep. You need your rest. He thought to her.

I feel Deminio. They're close, too. Her voice was full, no longer tired. Clay's skin started rippling. He could feel his muscles adjusting to the darkness and his flesh changing.

Wake up Emma and Leon. I will be right there.

32

Lucy wasn't cold, but she had icy chills covering her body. It was the same as when she heard the demon on her birthday, outside the safe house's fence. She didn't know where it was, but she did know it was close. Massimo's voice filled her head at the same time.

"All she has to do is call out to me, think about me. I will hear her." Echoed in the air around her.

She still felt Deminio. It was a strange sense of knowing. Massimo, Clay, and Deminio were all close by.

Clay? She called out to him, not wanting to alarm him.

Yes, Lucy? His voice in her head not a moment later.

Massimo is close. She thought to him, her body no longer carried warmth. Feeling Deminio as it inched closer.

The thought of them being so close to a demon made her angry. The thought of Massimo close by without protection worried her.

Go back to sleep. You need your rest. Clay's voice was balm to her soul.

Fear swept over her in a wave, she didn't know where it was coming from, but she was sure she did feel Deminio.

I feel a demon. It's close, too. Lucy couldn't hide the fear in her voice.

Wake up Emma and Leon. I will be right there. Clay said.

Lucy got up without making a sound and crouched next to Leon's bed.

"Leon. Wake up."

She tapped his shoulder.

He sprang out of his blow-up mattress. Lucy covered his mouth with her hands.

"We need to be quiet," she mouthed.

He looked her in the eye and whispered, "What's going on Luc?"

His whole attention was on her.

"Deminio is close. I feel it," she said.

Without responding to Lucy, Leon reached over and touched Emma's arm. Emma opened his eyes. They were all black. No white was showing.

"A demon is close," Emma said, his voice nearly inaudible over the sound of Lucy's heart.

Lucy and Leon made eye contact before looking back at Emma.

"I feel it, too. That's why I woke you guys up. Clay is on his way," Lucy updated them just before she heard the zipper being opened.

"It's me, Clay. Stay in the tent," Clay's voice said through the tent door before he could finish opening it.

"If Deminio is close by, we have to alert everyone and be ready for it," Leon's concern was making him glow. His Enkeli blood was glowing.

"The tents are spelled. They only smell of human to Deminio. They won't harm humans so close to the safehouse," Clay said softly. He put his finger to his lips, signing for them not to make a sound. He pointed outside.

We waited to hear something.

Nothing could be heard except for the blowing of the wind through the trees and the sound of the waterfall nearby. Everything else was silent.

Lucy's hair stood up on her entire body. She focused on breathing and could feel herself getting cold from the inside. Beads of sweat covered her face. It was close.

That is when she heard it. It was faint, but she knew it was there. Barely a sound of leaves ruffling. It could have been a squirrel if she went based on sound.

Lucy, what is your favorite thing to eat? Clay asked her in her thoughts.

She raised her eyebrows and opened her eyes wide at him.

In complete disbelief of Clay's question, she chose to ignore him and focused her attention on the demon. She could hear sniffing and started feeling colder except for the demon's direction. Her skin was ice-cold.

Lucy, when's your dad's birthday? Clay's voice was normal, not nervous or any sort of emotion other than normal.

Clay. This isn't the time. She thought to him.

Answer. He said, giving Lucy a smile with his eyes.

A tie between pasta and dried mangoes, and his birthday is on April twenty-second. She thought and her inner tone was impatient.

Where is your favorite place to go swimming? He asked her.

She ignored him and looked over at Leon and Emma, who were both standing back-to-back.

Remember our first kiss. Lucy could hear the smile in Clay's voice and exhaled, not knowing she was holding her breath.

I remember the first time you came over to my house. You forgot your shoes at home, and I knew things would be different between us. I knew we would be Guardian and Enkeli, but we would also be just Lucy and Clay. You make me feel normal. You were standing there, picking at your fingers and waiting for the perfect moment to knock. Your hair was freshly washed and smelled of jasmine. You would have turned around if Kona didn't corner you into staying. He thought to her.

She smiled and relaxed. Not understanding why Clay chose to bring that night up in the midst of a demon's presence.

There have only been a few times in my life where I sat and thought about how someone made me feel. I feel that with you, you make me feel. Not exactly how a Guardian feels, I feel protective and feel honored to be your Guardian. But I also feel thankful to have you in my life and grateful to have the opportunity to be as close to you as I am. It is an honor. The bond we share is far beyond what is expected.

She found it difficult to think of anything other than him.

Lucy's thoughts went from Deminio to Clay and back again, over and over. She could no longer feel the cold on her skin, and she wasn't sweating anymore.

Leon looked at Lucy and whispered, "Good job. Keep it up."

"Keep what up?" She said.

"Whatever you're doing, keep doing it," Emma spoke up.

Your skin started glowing and was attracting them. I needed to sidetrack you. We will all be okay. I promise. If it knew we were here, it would have approached us already. Clay was calm.

How do you know? She thought to him.

Evil isn't good at waiting. Lucy looked up at him and had a smile that wasn't his typical smile. His cheekbones were more pronounced. It was a half-smile. His smile was a face of conquering. He wasn't worried about a demon. This was the first time Lucy felt who he was, what he was. He was lethal. He was Light.

When Lucy woke up, her entire body was sore. Her ears rang, and her stomach turned. The sun was hitting the tent through a gap in the trees making the air too warm for comfort. Lucy looked next to her to find Leon and Emma were not in their beds.

She wanted to get up and go outside, but the ache in her muscles wanted otherwise.

Naturally, the thoughts that rushed towards the front of her mind were from last night. Darkness loomed over their camp. Lucy peeked outside through a window of the tent by unzipping the tent zipper next to her bed. There was a trace of Deminio. It felt as if it was made of tar and rolled all over their camp. They needed to leave.

Soon.

Lucy stretched her legs and her arms. Rolling around to her stomach to stretch her back and center. She rolled her neck and every joint she could while laying down, one by one. Nothing felt normal. Nothing felt comfortable. Her body was unfamiliar to her, new wounds surfaced, and she didn't know if this was the end of her discomfort after yesterday or if it was the beginning of what would be her new normal.

"Lucy, I know you're awake." His voice was loud and a bit obnoxious. He was always so full of energy and happiness in the morning. Something she would never understand.

"Leave me alone to die in peace, Leon," Lucy grunted.

Laughs echoed throughout their camp, and Lucy felt a rush of embarrassment, forgetting they were not alone.

"I made breakfast," Fazi said.

He always was a good buffer.

"I'll be right out."

Lucy reached for her small leather bag and pulled out her toiletry bag. She stretched a little more and took a few deep breaths before going outside.

Everyone made small conversation about the day and what had happened the night before. They all had their own take on what they felt.

When Lucy opened the zipped door, the first person she laid her eyes on was Talan. She hadn't talked to him much since the beach day. But he smiled his warm smile at her, and she couldn't help but smile back.

"Lucy, I served you a plate," Fazi called out from the picnic table where the food was.

"Thanks. I'll be there soon," she said.

Everyone was sitting in their seats around the morning fire in the same places they had last night. All of them except for Talan, who was standing close to the water, which is why Lucy saw him first.

She looked up at him and shifted her head to the side, calling him towards her as she walked to the stream that followed the pool of water in the opposite direction of where everyone was. The stream would eventually lead to the lake by her house.

Talan followed her. The dirt was moist and compact, with small bunches of greenery here and there. She looked up at him as they walked, and he peaked at her quickly from the side and chuckled.

"What are you looking at?" He was still him. Still Talan, the guy she grew up with who lived five doors down.

She smiled, "You."

"You've always been weird," he teased.

"You've always been an ass," she laughed and pushed him with one hand.

"You know you love me," he teased again.

She laughed an actual knee slapping laugh. It had been so long since she felt like this, like herself.

"Alika use to tell me you had a crush on me growing up. Now that I know what I know, you were always just a little extra protective of me. Even more so than anyone else, other than Leon. It is your duty," she said.

They got to the stream, and the water was just below her knees. Talan helped Lucy in the water, so she didn't slip. She went in her bag and got her face wash, toothpaste, and toothbrush.

After a moment, he said, "That's half true. You've always been intriguing to me. You live and think in a way that's almost backward."

"How old are you? I've watched all of us grow together. How is that?" She said.

"I'm not as old as Clay. I'm the youngest Guardian in the Guard, actually. I'm two hundred and thirty-four years old," he said.

She kept brushing her teeth.

"We all vary in age and have all come from different places. Once we are chosen, we go through an initiation and training period for just over one-hundred years," Talan said.

"You feel younger than that. You feel like you're my age. Clay and Dario feel much older, now that I think of it. But you, you feel youthful," she spoke her thoughts aloud.

"Have you ever thought that your soul isn't your age?" He said, raising his brows.

"No. I-," she said before Clay cut her off.

"Talan." He was within earshot and when Lucy looked back at him, he was shaking his head.

"I've got to go. Talk to you later, Luc." He winked at her before getting up and walking away.

"What was that all about, Clay?" Lucy said when she knew Talan couldn't hear her.

"It is his turn to patrol the area," Clay said soft enough so only Lucy could hear him.

"It had nothing to do with him talking to me?" Lucy asked.

"If you take me for a jealous person, you've got it all wrong. I am not a child, and you aren't a toy," Clay said as he sat next to where she was standing in the water with his arms hanging over his knees.

Clay narrowed his eyes at her and smirked.

"You are definitely not a child," she said under her breath as she washed her face.

"Try calling water. See how you feel now that you are in shallow waters," he said.

"I need my strength. I need food and water," she opposed and suddenly felt queasy.

"The strength you seek doesn't come from food or water. It comes from in here." He pounded his chest once with his right hand.

"Then why did I feel better yesterday after drinking that disgusting drink?" She asked.

"Because it was not just a disgusting drink, but an elixir made for you. It was spelled and medicinal," he said.

She stood in the water and was nervous to call upon it. Even though she did yesterday evening, she was uneasy. There wasn't much water here.

Water, please get warmer. She thought, and it replied with skin temperature water where just moments ago it was fresh to the touch.

"Well done, but that is not what I mean when I say call on water. I know you can manipulate it, but can you call on it? The *essence* of water," Clay said softly.

"I don't know how to do that," Lucy's doubt could be heard in her voice.

"You did it yesterday. I'm trying to figure out how." Clay looked up and looked around.

Her skin was warm. The right side of her face got cold.

Deminio.

Clay was now towering over her on his feet. His skin was rippling, and his eyes glowed.

"Ssshe issss here!" The voice-*its* voice snarled.

Her entire body went numb. She wasn't sure whether to feel scared or angry, and she couldn't bring herself to look at it again. Not after the last time she saw a demon. This was a different one. It was weak and didn't sound as scary as the first one did.

"I haaave been waiting to meet you. Everyone will know of you, Lucy," it said. Voice raspy and rough.

"You won't live long enough to relay the message," Talan's voice was much more playful than it should have been.

In one second, she heard a sound that was like putting water over hot coals. Then she heard nothing.

"You are safe." Clay picked Lucy up out of the water. "Talan." Clay nodded at him, giving approval.

Lucy felt the world shaking. The clouds were growing heavy.

"Pack. Leave no trace. We need to leave. Now," Clay gave orders.

Lucy couldn't feel anything. She couldn't move. Her ears were ringing.

She blinked. All of the tents were up.

She blinked again and could see one tent.

She blinked and could see the table with food.

She was tired.

She tried to stay awake, but her eyelids were too heavy to stay open.

Nothingness took over.

The sound of its voice echoed in her head. It was all she heard until she heard nothing.

33

Lucy woke up in the passenger seat of Clay's moving truck. She lay with her head in the middle seat and her legs propped up on the passenger side door. It was dark out.

It couldn't be. Lucy just woke up.

She looked around and felt Clay's hand on her arm, his thumb stroking her skin. She could *feel*, which was an improvement to how she was earlier.

"Here is something to help. Drink." Clay handed her a canister full of liquid. Lucy braced herself for the disgusting drink she had before.

As soon as it touched her lips, she felt a wave of rejuvenation over her entire body. It wasn't distasteful at all but refreshing and fruity. It was sweet and smooth. Lucy went from her whole body feeling like she broke every bone to her having a slight headache in a few heartbeats.

Lucy sat up to see where they were and could barely see in front of the car. It was pitch black outside.

"Where are we?" She looked over and asked Clay. He put his hand out of the window, making a thumbs up, then there were flashing lights from behind them. Lucy looked back. It was Leon's Jeep. Clay was letting Leon know Lucy was okay.

"We have been driving for ten hours up the stream. We will be there soon," Clay said.

"Pull over," Lucy said, feeling compelled to not go any further.

"We are almost there, Lucy," Clay said as he took a deep breath. He knew this was coming.

"Tomorrow is the third day. We don't have time for this. We need to go back," Lucy said, looking back at Leon's jeep.

"Massimo said, '*You have three days before they come for you*' Right?" Clay asked.

"Yes, that's right. Clay, we have to go back," Lucy said, her voice held power.

He continued to drive through the darkness, "They won't start a war if you aren't there. They will come for *you*. They won't start a war when they see Mpiaron is pulled through and you are not there. Pulling Mpiaron through the way we did, in silence, is enough for them to pause."

"What about our people? My dad? They are all in danger," Lucy couldn't contain her frustration.

He looked over to make sure she was finished speaking and said, "It was your father's idea. Everyone here was in on it. They knew you needed to get away."

"Then why are we going to this location? What is the real reason?" She asked.

"The reasons are the same. There are sacred ruins with untapped energy that could help us," Clay looked over at her again.

"Pull over, Clay. I mean it," she ordered.

Clay looked at her for a long second and stopped the truck. She jumped out immediately and ran towards the driver's side of Leon's car.

"How could you leave our dad at home when you knew he would be in danger?" Lucy yelled out to Leon before he could get out of his seat.

Leon walked towards her and looked at Clay, who now stood a few feet behind Lucy.

"Answer me!" Her rage couldn't be contained.

She was scared for her dad. She had to protect him. Her heart grew angry at them for keeping this secret. They always seemed to have secrets. Always appearing to be open and honest but with half-truths and hidden agendas. Lucy had enough.

Leon put his hands up as if he was taming a beast and slowly walked backward, away from her.

Her skin hurt. It burned and grew sore like a sunburn mixed with a bruise.

Everyone else was out of the vehicles and surrounding them. Lucy thought she was going to explode with rage, then she saw the look on their faces.

Fear.

They were scared.

"Lucy," Clay called from behind her.

She whipped around. "We camp here for the night."

And so it was.

It took less than three minutes for Talan and Dario to pitch Lucy's tent and set up her bed. Before they could put Emma's and Leon's beds in there, Lucy picked up her small leather bag, went in, and zipped the door shut.

She wanted to be alone. She needed to be alone. There was pain in her heart where love usually was. It was becoming more difficult for her to rely on them. Half-truths are lies in her eyes. There was nothing they could say or do that could fill the void that grew larger with every secret. Their people were relying on her to save them, and she didn't know how.

Something inside of her was doubtful. Somewhere along the timeline of the last few days, a seed of doubt was planted. Every time she found out something was hidden from her, the seed was watered.

It also occurred to her they couldn't tell her everything all the time. They have all been alive for so long. There was no way they could tell her everything they knew with the time they had. They all told her what she needed to know. She understood that. What she didn't understand was why they would find ways around telling her the truth.

She should have known they wouldn't be back in time. She should have known she was leaving her father there in danger. She should have known about the Deminio looming around from Clay himself, not from Emma coming to her house in the middle of the night or from Massimo.

Massimo. She thought of him. If he was here, would everything be different? She wasn't sure, she wanted to see him. She had questions only a third party would be able to understand and give unbiased information.

The only way Lucy knew to see him was to go to sleep. She didn't feel like talking to anyone outside of the tent.

Her head hit the pillow, and her body ached. She was sore. Her body felt awful again. It was unclear what she was doing to make her body feel this miserable. She took a few deep breaths. Even the blankets hurt her skin, feeling rough and heavy. She was cold, the blankets were to keep her warm, but she couldn't put them on through her exhaustion. How was she supposed to go to sleep?

Her bag made a slight sound, like something being set on a table. She reached her arm in the bag and found a small canister with a note on it. She took it out and read the message.

Lucy,

Drink this. It'll help. Nobody knows I made it and gave it to you.

I'm with you, and I am here for you.

Yours,

Omala

The elixir was red and smelled sweet. It was the same one as earlier. Lucy's mouth watered at the thought of it. She drank it, sip by sip. When she had the last drop, she still felt uneasy but not half as bad as she did. Her stomach was queasy, and her head hurt, but everything else was replenished with the drink.

She laid her head down, got under her covers, and closed her eyes. She could feel Clay close to her, right outside of the tent. Unsure whether he was guarding it so she would be okay or so nobody would come in and bother her. Guilt. She wanted to see Massimo when Clay was right outside of her tent.

Massimo was a vampire who she knew nothing about. She knew nothing about vampires. Perhaps it was time to learn.

Massimo. Massimo. Massimo. Her voice echoed his name in her head.

Sleep felt far away.

"Lucy," his voice echoed around her.

Lucy opened her eyes, and she was underground again. But, this time, it wasn't dirt around her but brick and stones. The only reason she knew she was underground is that she felt earth around her more than air and sky.

"Lucy."

No longer an echo, he was right behind her. Guilt flashed through her.

"Massimo," her voice was cool and collected. She greeted him by bowing her head slightly.

"You call for me, yet your Guardian told me to leave you alone," he played with her.

"My Guardian?" She was surprised.

"He didn't tell you of our talk last night?" He asked.

Of course he didn't. Nobody tells her anything. She was no longer guilty. She was fuming.

"We've had an eventful day. We ran into a demon, and I fainted just after he was murdered. I woke up just a little while ago to find myself here, too far away from home, when Darkness will be storming over Shadow Rock tomorrow, and we will not make it back in time to fight. So, no, to answer your question, he didn't tell me of your little talk last night," Lucy said in one breath.

Massimo laughed. She looked up at him in disbelief. He actually laughed at her.

"You fainted after a demon was killed? Some Enkeli you are," he laughed again.

"This is pointless," she whispered under her breath.

"Nothing is pointless. If it was, we wouldn't be here right now. Why do you call to me? Have you called to accept my offer?" Massimo said.

She hadn't thought about it at all since the last time they had talked. But the thought of him drinking her blood was distasteful.

"Hardly. I call you because it seems like everyone lies to me and I have a feeling you won't," she told the truth. Feeling more like herself at this moment than she has in the last few days.

"Clay wouldn't lie to you," he said.

His words flipped the guilt switch back on.

"How would you know?" She asked him.

Lucy walked towards the wall. The tunnel was dark. She sat down and put her back against the cool stone wall with her legs crossed in front of her.

"Your Enkeli, he is a Guardian. They wouldn't lie to Enkeli. I'm a vampire, even I know that to be true," he said as he sat down next to her on the floor.

He put his hand on her knee. She didn't move, but her heart started to race, unsure how to feel.

"I know everyone up there," he pointed up with his index and middle finger, "is doing all they can to make sure you are safe. It's about more than you, Lucy. Don't forget they all have family and their lives on the line too. People are counting on *all* of you."

"They keep things from me," she said.

"You also keep things from them," he fired back.

"You don't know that." She looked at him.

"Am I wrong?" He asked as he looked back at her.

She could feel his hand putting pressure on her thigh, his thumb stroking her leg to comfort her.

"No," she said, breaking eye contact. "Why am I talking to you about this and not them? You're a stranger, and I feel more comfortable talking to you than them."

"I will listen to everything if you choose to tell me. Vampires have compulsion. I won't use it on you. Ever. So many people feel at ease around us, I'm not proud of it, but it is how humans are drawn to us for us to feed," he said, still looking at her. Every cell in her body believed him. She could feel him looking at the veins in her neck, moisture in his words.

"Why wouldn't you use compulsion on me?" She asked.

"Because when you ask me to bite you, it will be because you want to. Not because I made you believe you wanted to, and I never want you to question it," he said.

"I won't." She looked over at him.

"Okay," he said, the corners of his mouth twitched up as if he was laughing at a joke only he knew.

"I'm serious. I won't," she said a little louder, looking forward across the tunnel.

"Okay," he repeated.

"I don't know how to protect them," word vomit spewed from her. She didn't know why she said that.

"There it is. That's why you came." He pointed at her.

"Okay," she mocked him and rolled her eyes.

"You do know how to protect them. It is inside of you somewhere. If you let go and let instinct take over, it will come out. You just have to trust yourself. Trust them, too," he said, pointing up again.

"What about you? Can I trust you?" She said looking over at him again, his face inches from hers.

"You tell me," he said. His eyes had light in them.

"I don't know why, but I do," she said.

His smile was small and one-sided. He leaned in towards her. She thought he would kiss her when he stopped just before he met her lips. His warm fingers traced the veins on her neck and down the skin on her arm.

"Be careful who you trust. Don't drink anything in the cave, Lucy. I'll be seeing you," was all he said, before disappearing into the tunnel.

Lucy blinked, and was back in the tent, under her covers.

"What cave?" She whispered under her breath.

Only Massimo wasn't there. She could still feel his fingers on her skin and his breath on her face.

Light flashed the front of the tent, and she could see the shadow of Clay's body directly on the other side of the door.

The sound of them still setting up tents and their space was quieter than their voices. Small arguments took place outside of the tent, Lucy stayed quiet to eavesdrop.

"She won't like it," Leon said, aggressively.

"I think what you're forgetting is, it's not just about her," Emma's voice carried through.

"I have my entire family who I haven't seen. The last of my bloodline is depending on us. So, she has to understand," Alika said, her voice as fiery as ever.

"That is a lot of pressure. She hasn't found it yet, her Light. I mean, she has, just not knowingly. None of us know how to show her because she doesn't know what she's looking for. We need to find a back-up plan," Leon said to deflect focus away from Lucy.

"She is still Lucy, you guys. When has she not come through for us? When has she not found a way? Since they were kids, she has always found her own way. Look at tonight, when she was upset. She wanted to protect everyone at home and her skin was pulsing with Light. Give her time, she almost has it," Talan stood up for Lucy.

She could hear by the direction of his voice, he was standing next to Leon.

"We don't have any more time. Lucy has to figure it out," Omala said. Lucy was surprised at her words. Omala usually was more opti-mistic.

"Or we die. That is our other option. We die, our families die, hu-manity crumbles, the end comes. Lucy will damn us all-," Rani said be-fore getting cut off. Something was off about her voice. It was a different tone, one unfamiliar to Lucy.

"Owranoos. Next time you speak like that, I will drive this spear through your heart before you are able to finish your sentence. Do I make myself clear?" Every sound stopped, Lucy stopped breathing, and the sound of her heart beating was so loud she thought everyone else could hear it too. The tents stopped being built. The fire even seemed to stop crackling. Clay's words were cold and deadly, killing their conver-sation along with the thoughts they all had about what they should do.

Lucy assumed Rani nodded because she didn't hear her say any-thing.

Clay was their leader. He was *the* leader of the Lemurians. At that moment, Lucy knew he had thousands of lifetimes full of defending the Light, which also meant killing anyone who threatens it.

"That isn't circumstantial to Owranoos. If any of you speak ill words, it only invites Darkness in. It plants seeds. I have zero tolerance for poor judgment," he continued. The energy changed. Just moments before, it was full of rage and uproar. Not anymore, chills filled her body once more, and it wasn't because Deminio were close by.

"We continue to the ruins at dawn. Eat and rest, though none of you deserve it. Talan, Dario, you two have cover tonight. Darkness is near. We need to be ready. Witches, secure and protect the grounds and our trail ahead before anything else," his commands were just that, commands. Clay wasn't anything less than the leader he was born to be. She had assumed this was the side of Clay they all knew, not the relaxed self he was around her and definitely not neighbor Clay.

"Omala," he said.

Lucy heard soft footsteps come closer to her tent, just feet away from her head.

"Secure her tent for extra security. No sound can come out of it. If Deminio comes, they will be blind to the space," he pressed.

"You got it," Omala said too cheerful. She was nervous. Lucy knew that tone.

A few moments later, a rippling wave of energy went over the tent, then it was gone.

"Done," Omala said, walking away from the tent.

A few moments passed before Clay called out, "Omala." Her footsteps stopped. "Thank you." Clay said, softer than he had been. Lucy could hear the sincerity in his voice.

He let out a sigh that only she could hear.

A few moments later, Lucy could see the zipper of the tent opening. Clay walked in and immediately made eye contact with her. He didn't break eye contact as he closed the door and put a small bag of his own on the other side of the tent.

"I thought you were asleep," he sighed.

She didn't say anything and watched as he set up a blanket on the floor with a pillow.

"How is Massimo?" His voice was ice.

"How did you know?" She asked in a whisper.

He looked at her for a moment. She had no clue what he was feeling or thinking.

Clay didn't say anything. Lucy felt alone. She suspected he did too. She opened the blankets for him to get under and lay with her.

He walked over to her, stood next to the bed, and closed the blankets over her.

"Goodnight, Lucy," he said just before turning around and going to the other side of the tent. He laid his head down on his bag and pulled a book out.

Lucy took offense in Clay's actions. She didn't know what to do other than turn around and face the other side of the tent so he couldn't see her.

"If you don't want me to see him, then say so. You said not to let him drink from me. I didn't. I listened to you," she said to him.

He took a breath like he was going to say something, then paused before saying, "I honestly do not care who you are friends with. Do you not find it alarming that he shows up now? Of all times in your life, he shows up now."

"He helps," she said.

"Lucy, did you hear any of what went on outside?" He asked.

"I heard *you*," a dagger to a tender spot, she said it anyway.

"It is my duty to keep you safe, to keep you *all* safe. It isn't to be your boyfriend, or their friend, or to have friends. It is to keep you all *alive*," the rumble in Clay's voice would have been frightening to her if she wasn't connected to him the way she was.

"Would you really kill Rani for saying those things?" She said, still facing the tent wall with her back to him.

He sighed. A moment passed, and he didn't say anything. He was choosing his words carefully.

"I do not function the same way you do. If you are Light, everything else is Dark. Everything else is intolerable. We were trained to eliminate any and all sources of danger. A thought plants a seed. To answer your question, yes. Yes, if Owranoos spoke honest words threatening you, I would kill her," he said, his voice was calm.

"Have you killed many beings?" She asked as she turned around to face him.

He looked at her with glowing blue and green eyes.

"You already know the answer, Lucy," he said.

She stared at him, wanting him to say it.

"Yes, I have." He didn't blink.

"I couldn't do that. I couldn't kill someone, especially someone who was good," she said.

"Just because they are good doesn't mean they aren't a danger to Light," he said.

"That is completely unfair," she snapped.

"That is not what I said. You said someone good, and I said just because they are good doesn't mean they are Light. I wouldn't kill someone who had any trace of Light in them, whether they knew it or not. I would kill someone who had seeds of Darkness. What happens to seeds that are watered? They grow."

"Killing is wrong, Clay," she said.

"I know. It is also my duty to kill and to protect. I killed that demon earlier. If I would have left it to live, it would have killed one of us or warned the Deminio. You would have done the same for anyone else," Clay said.

He was right. Lucy would have killed a demon to save someone's life.

"How do I do it? How do I kill a demon?" She asked.

"I can't tell you how to do it. You will know when the time comes for you to do it. It isn't a skill but a craft. Not everyone is capable," he said.

"How do I protect everyone?" The question she's been too cowardly to ask.

"You do know how to protect them. It is inside of you somewhere. If you let go and let instinct take over, it will come out. You just have to trust yourself. Trust them, too." He tilted his chin towards outside. "Isn't that what Massimo said?" He turned over.

Clay was bitter about her talking to Massimo. It didn't feel like he was jealous, more upset that he didn't know Massimo. She wanted to tell him he had nothing to worry about. If she did, then she would be lying. Lucy didn't know anything about vampires. She really didn't know anything about Massimo. She didn't know how Clay knew what they had talked about either and wondered if he heard their entire conversation.

Clay was so easy to talk to before. Now she could barely talk to anyone. Massimo listened to her. Nobody else listened to her anymore, not even Clay. Could she blame them? They were on the brink of war, and she was getting nowhere. Still, Massimo listened and offered his help.

34

"Lucy, pack your belongings. We leave in five," Clay said without looking at her as he packed.

She could hear noises coming from outside of the tent. She folded all of her things and changed as quickly as she could. She put everything in her bag and went outside. Everyone was packed and ready. They stared at her, waiting for her to get out of the tent. As soon as her foot hit the floor, Talan and Dario took the tent down. It was folded and in the truck before she was.

Eye contact with any of them was impossible. She was still annoyed by them hiding information from her.

Today is the day Deminio would come for her in Shadow Rock, and she wouldn't be there.

Lucy stepped into Clay's truck, and they drove. When she looked back at where they camped, there was a huge willow tree over where they set up their tents under the walls of leaves and vines of the willow, and she hadn't even noticed.

An hour passed, and neither her, nor Clay had said anything to each other.

"Lucy, there will come a moment when everything clicks. You will come into your Light. You will know what to do. He was right," Clay referred to Massimo, though he didn't say his name. He was still full of frustration and unspoken words.

"What if I die before then? We all die with me," she said.

"I won't die. I am immortal. But yes, most of you will die. Just do not give up and do not stop fighting. Ever," he said.

"I will try."

He looked at her for the first time, "There is no try, Lucy. There is either do, or don't do."

When they first approached the ruins, it was easy to spot. Even before they parked and got out of the car, it looked beautiful and enchanted. Maybe even a little haunted. A flashback of her dream when she fainted the day before clicked. It was where she was now, the side of a mountain with stone steps covered in vines leading to a doorway. She didn't say anything to anyone, not about her dream or about this being familiar. Something made her keep this to herself. It was a sign. She could feel it. A sign from the Light to know she was exactly where she was supposed to be.

Clay parked the truck, and Leon parked next to Lucy's door. She still hadn't talked to any of them after yesterday. Nobody got out of the car. Lucy went to open the door when Clay instantly reached over and held the door shut.

Do not make a sound. We are not alone. His voice in her head.

She nodded and looked over at Leon, who was looking at her through the glass of the window. His eyes had dark circles under them, his shoulders slumped. The weight of what happened the previous night was visible in everything about him. Lucy couldn't be upset with him.

Never in their lives had he ever done anything other than love and protect her.

Lucy smiled at Leon. It was soft and just enough to let him know she wasn't angry with him. He smiled back and took a deep breath.

"You okay?" She mouthed to him.

He nodded and mouthed, "Are you?".

She nodded back and smiled again. She could breathe after receiving the sign. Leon's shoulders relaxed a little, and he took a deep breath, too.

Dario and Talan jumped out of the back of the truck at the same time, making the slightest *thump* on the ground. Clay motioned a few different signs with his hands. They exchanged motions few times before they both disappeared.

Where'd they go? Lucy thought to him.

They are checking the area. Deminio have been here recently. Even in her head, Clay couldn't hide the alert in his voice.

Lucy's body became warm, too warm, then ice cold. Although not sure what was happening, she did know Deminio were near. Her blood told her so.

It's coming from our left. The left side of my body feels like ice. It's close. Lucy thought to Clay.

He gave her a questioning look and got out of the truck, gesturing for her to stay. He looked at Leon and back to Lucy, telling Leon to keep her safe.

As much as Lucy wanted to follow Clay, she didn't know how to fight a demon, let alone kill one. It would put everyone else at risk.

Clay, Talan, and Dario all went to the left and disappeared behind the heavy forest.

Fear struck every chord in her body. Lucy's right side got cold. There was more than one. Of this, she was sure.

Suspense wavered in the air over them. Lucy looked over at Leon and knew he felt it. He was looking out of the other window instead of at her.

She heard a shrieking sound coming from the direction the Guardians were. The only thing Lucy could think of to do was to get out of the car. She opened the door as quietly as she could and tapped Leon's window once. He turned and jumped in his seat.

"Get back in the car!" He mouthed and pointed at the truck.

Lucy, where are you? Clay's voice in her head.

I'm still here. She said.

An ear-piercing shriek roared over any other sound. She ducked down and covered her ears. Shivers overtook her body. She had to fight to keep her teeth from chattering. She could see her breath in front of her, and it wasn't because of the weather.

Clay? She thought to him.

No response.

Clay? I felt another demon. I am not sure how many there are. She thought louder.

There was nothing. She couldn't hear him.

She knocked and tried to open the door to Leon's car, and it was locked.

"Leon, get out of the car!" She began to panic.

He looked at her and said, "Where's Clay?" He mouthed through the door, still not opening it.

Omala, Rani, Alika, and Fazi were in the backseat with their eyes glued to the outside.

"Why aren't you opening the door?" She asked.

"Too much energy, if we step foot on the floor, the demons can find us. They haven't secured the grounds yet." He gestured towards the back seats.

"Why didn't you tell me that before I got out of the truck?" She said. Her back could have been made of snow.

A demon was close.

She turned around and could only see the trees of the forest. Lucy would go back in the truck but found it pointless as she had already stepped foot on the ground.

Clay. Are you there? She thought to him.

She waited a moment and still she couldn't hear him.

The staircase on the mountainside in front of them was warm. Lucy could feel heat radiating from it. There was nowhere else to go, back in the truck or towards the stone steps.

"Something isn't right. I can't hear Clay," she said to Leon.

"None of us can hear Clay," Leon said with a confused look on his face.

Lucy forgot she'd never explained hers and Clay's ability to communicate. Emma looked at her, and she could see in his eyes he knew what she was talking about. His whole demeanor changed, and he got out of the car and walked around to be closer to her.

"Try again. Try to get a hold of Clay again," Emma whispered and gestured with his hands to try again.

"I've tried a few times, and I don't hear anything," she said as she moved the dirt around with her foot.

"Lucy. Try again." He looked her in the eyes.

She nodded and closed her eyes to focus.

Clay. Just let me know you're all okay. She thought to him.

There was nothing but silence mixed with her own thoughts screaming at her.

When she opened her eyes, Emma was waiting for an answer, she shook her head.

"I don't hear him, Emma," her voice shook.

Lucy's back was cold again. This time she could feel it in her bones. Emma looked behind her, and his face changed somehow. She couldn't place it at first. Then he blinked, and his eyes turned black. His skin lost all warmth, and his mouth grew thin. He was the demon he had always been.

What was different about him, what made him not scary, was her own skin wasn't cold where he was. It was warm. It was the Light within him that was different from the other demons. She could close her eyes and know it was him. She would know she was safe with him.

"Hello, Emmanicko. I *see* you," a voice said from behind her.

She wanted to run, at least put Emma between her, and whatever it was that was behind her, he'd know what to do. But something inside didn't let her. She couldn't move. Not sure if it was because she didn't want to see it or because she was afraid. The voice of the thing behind her was the voice of a demon.

"I see *you*. Leave or die," Emma said.

"Give me Enkeli, and I leave with no problem," it rasped.

Lucy looked Emma in the eyes, and he didn't break eye contact with the demon behind her. He didn't trust it.

"I won't give you anything," Emma didn't change the tone in his voice. He might as well have been talking about the color shoes he was wearing, but his body language slowly changed to a defensive post.

"Work with me, brother," it said.

Brother? She thought to herself.

"We stopped being brothers long ago, Darahnzo," Emma snapped.

"We will never stop being brothers. We are the same," Darahnzo inched closer to her with every word. His rotten, cold breathe blew Lucy's hair.

"Yes, that is right. We are brothers," another demon said from behind Emma, it walked towards them. He was outnumbered. The demon resembled Emma. It walked strange, though. Lucy looked down and could see it had hooves in place of feet. As it walked, she observed its features, and it had the same facial structure as Emma did. They really were brothers.

"Farnazae. You dare challenge me?!" Emma had fire in his voice, and his eyes changed from pitch black to the black of night, still not breaking eye contact with the demon behind her.

"No, Emmanicko. *You* dare challenge *me?*" The demon behind her reached for Lucy, its hand barely grazing her arm before Emma pushed Lucy down and leaped towards his demon brother.

Lucy's head hit the truck before her body slammed against the floor. She turned her body and felt heat on her head. Emma was getting attacked by a demon, and Clay wasn't responding. Leon wouldn't get out of the car.

The shrieking sound echoed over them had forced her into the fetal position.

Light, help me. She thought within. She could feel the wind blowing and the earth-shaking. That was it. That was all that happened. Emma was pinned down by two demons who were too occupied in torturing their risen brother to pay attention to her. They took fighting with Emma personally.

She looked up at Leon, who was only feet away and realized, the demons didn't know Leon was there. Or the witches, for that matter. This was her fault.

Not knowing what to do, she jumped on top of the demon to try to pull it off of Emma. As soon as her body hit the demon's body, it felt like a rock and sand at the same time. Ice cold and hard, though not all the way solid.

It laughed and threw her off. She couldn't let Emma die. By the look on Leon's face, he was only staying inside to protect the witches from harm. His face was a sight she will never forget as long or short as she lived. He was physically in pain too. It wasn't just him feeling bad for not helping Emma. He was experiencing the pain Emma was being put through.

Emma drew a large dagger and in one swift movement he stabbed one, knocking it to the ground before it dissipated. The other one was still on top of him. It was strong. Emma closed his eyes and pushed as hard as he could. He couldn't move.

Emma was going to die.

Lucy was up off of the ground and on the other side of Leon's car in a second. Her stomach turned from the motion.

"Get in," a familiar voice said.

She was too worried about Emma to do anything when she heard another shrieking sound. It was deafening and paralyzing. She dove to the floor and held her hands to her ears and her knees to her chest.

Then she heard nothing, nothing at all.

She looked under the truck and could see Emma lying on the floor and a set of feet next to him. The nothingness in her ears turned into a loud ringing as she watched the two sets of feet walk to Leon's side of the car. Leon got out and ran around to check on Lucy, followed by Emma and the other person. Before they could get to her, arms wrapped around her body and pulled her close.

She would know those arms anywhere.

"Lucy, breathe. Focus and breathe," Clay's voice was soft. She could hear him.

"Where were you? Emma almost died," her words escaped her mouth before she had a chance to think about what she was going to say.

"I'm okay. It was close, but I've had closer calls," Emma said like it was no big deal. "My old friend Massimo here helped out."

Lucy looked from Emma to Massimo. He was the one who saved Emma's life and told her to get into the car. Leon patted Massimo's back in thanks.

"You all know each other?" Lucy asked.

"I know him, from... before. I've never told anyone. We're old friends. Leon feels how I feel and can sense the fondness we share," Emma said and gave Massimo a smile one last time.

Clay tightened his jaw, "We were ambushed by a troop, I couldn't respond without taking my attention off of them."

Dario and Talan stood close to the stairs, breathless.

"Sixty-eight of them, gone and-"

"Talan," Clay cut him off before Talan could continue.

"We need to move before more find us," Alika said from behind Lucy, her Scottish accent heavy.

"You are right. Massimo, you are welcome to join as long as it is clear where you stand," Clay told Massimo directly.

Lucy's heart raced as she waited for his response. She looked over to Massimo and could see in his body language he wasn't going with them.

"I will be here if you need me," Massimo said.

"Then so be it. Let's go," Clay said as he dismissed Massimo and headed towards the carved stairs.

Everyone followed except Massimo. Lucy looked back, and he was looking right at her, into her with his amber eyes. He didn't smile or wink how he does when he makes her nervous. Instead, when nobody was looking, he put his fist over his heart and bowed his head to her. She smiled at him and tilted her head before she followed everyone up the staircase.

Lucy looked over at Clay and knew he saw the whole thing by the look on his face.

Clay smiled at her and put his hand at the small of her back, "Looks like you have made an ally."

35

The staircase etched from the side of the mountain was steep and much higher than it looked. At the top of the stairs wasn't a door but a tunnel through the mountain's base. Stone and dirt at their feet with stone and few vines on the walls. All trickling their way up to meet each other at the top from either side. It smelled of fresh earth. The break of the tunnel was met with the sky above them, full of indistinct heavy clouds mixed with a glowing fog. It wasn't of this world. They walked on a white ash stone trail. Every stone was a different size and shape. No two were the same and somehow fit together perfectly. Each stone was smooth, evidence of being walked on for thousands of years. There was a smell looming in the air, a familiar one she couldn't place. It was partially stagnant air, but it also had the scent of running water and stagnant water combined. Mildew and moss, it smelled of old and new.

Lucy could breathe. Something about where they were had shifted the weight she was carrying. They were in the middle of a collection of mountains in a pocket of earth and sky. The stone path was made with stone pergolas guiding them through a meadow in the mountains. The blades of grass grew short, unkept but organized. Small collections of white and blush flowers were everywhere. Waterfalls of every size etched the mountainside and made their way through the meadow without overflow. Water springs formed on stones and bases of the trees. Vines connected everything, merging the winding stone path from pergola to pergola. Hundreds of moss-covered statues and rocks throughout. Lucy stepped off of the stone path and onto the cool grass to get a closer look.

They weren't statues or rocks. They were tombstones and memorials.

This was a cemetery.

The names she read were unfamiliar, and somehow, she felt connected to them. As Lucy walked and read the names, she knelt down and touched each one on her path. When she looked around, she could see thousands of them. The stone path wound around and through the sacred ground, guiding them to where they needed to go.

When Lucy turned around to walk back to the stone path, she saw everyone else standing along the stones looking at her. Each had been there before. They watched her closely. Small smiles on their faces, all except for Emma. He wasn't smiling, he was nervous, and nobody but Lucy seemed to notice.

"We need to keep pushing forward," Clay said.

The path was squared, and the turns were sharp. Most were open to the cemetery except where the vines were too thick as they draped down the sides of the pergola. There was an occasional giant gong hanging between pillars, the sound of their footsteps hummed off of the metal and rang in Lucy's ears. She wondered how loud they'd be if someone hit them and what force they'd have to use to make the proper sound.

There were carvings of demons and angels throughout every pillar. In some, the angel would be the creature of Light, and the demon would be the creature of Darkness. In others, the angel would be Dark, and the demon would be Light. Lucy understood there was much she didn't know and much she would possibly never know if she were to die. The balance between Light and Dark was not black and white like she once believed.

They came across a large gazebo in the center of the meadow through the grove along the stone path. The stones at their feet spiraled to the center where all the paths met, and there was one single round stone.

Lucy walked to the center stone and stood directly on it. She looked up and saw the rest of them near what appeared to be an altar. All except for Leon and Emma, who were underneath one of the archways. It was suited for them. It was the only arch that had an angel and a demon carved both under the same light. One wasn't Dark, and the other wasn't Light. They were both the same. Clay knelt down at the front and center of the altar. Everyone else knelt behind him at his sides. She didn't know what to do, kneel down alongside them, go stand with Leon and Emma or stay put.

Lucy looked over at Leon when he gestured with his head for her to go over to him.

"This is the Lighthouse. Where all beings of Light can come and feel connected to each other. It hasn't been used since before the Lemurians created Mpiaron many millennia ago. We suspect they will try to make their way here soon. No creature of darkness or Deminio can enter here," Leon said softly.

Emma looked around in awe. Lucy couldn't help but stare at him.

"I could be in here every day for the rest of my whole existence and never get tired of how it makes me feel," Emma said as he looked around. She could see his eyes lighting up, when only moments ago his eyes were pitch black. The skin on his face still looked flush, but she could see some color returning to his neck.

Lucy took a deep breath, then another. Tension released throughout her body, and she understood what Emma was speaking of. Lucy felt a wave of heat only a moment before Leon hugged her.

He hardly ever hugged her anymore. Lucy could feel the love he had for her through his warm touch. Physical touch seemed to bother her the last few years. She thought she could somehow feel the emotions of the person she made contact with. Now that Lucy was here and knew more about what she was, it made sense. She wondered what other gifts she had, ones that were always there but not consciously aware of.

"We should be heading out soon. Deminio has already been close by. We should hurry," Emma said quietly, and his voice still carried an echo throughout the gazebo.

"He is right. Gather your thoughts and your spirit, meet me when you are all ready," Clay said as he stood up and walked out of sight on the other side of the gazebo behind a large pillar.

Lucy took a step towards him to follow, and Leon reached for her wrist, "Stay close to me, please. Something feels off."

Lucy nodded and walked to Clay.

When she reached him, they were both out of sight and just out of earshot.

"Are you sure we're safe from Deminio here?" She asked him.

"Somewhat. They've changed. Just stay close," Clay said, clutching his spear. Lucy didn't believe him. His eyes were everywhere except her.

He leaned in and kissed her, long and hard. Clay's large hands wrapped around the nape of her neck and covered her lower back, pulling her body close to his. He was hot and his skin rippled. He pulled away, taking two steps back without breaking eye contact.

Lucy didn't want him to pull away. She almost took a step forward when the group walked out of the gazebo. From where they stood, it looked as if they were having a conversation and nothing more. Almost as if it never happened. Almost.

"Everyone stay close. We won't break up into groups unless danger comes, and we have to save Lucy. I will not leave her again, neither will Leon," Clay said as he looked for Leon. Leon knew what to do and took his place next to Lucy.

They walked through the cemetery and stayed on the stone path.

"When we get to the ruins, you all do exactly as I say," Clay said without turning around to look at them. "But if you should see or feel something, communicate it with the rest of us. We can get through this together."

"That wasn't part of the ruins?" Lucy asked.

"Not exactly," Clay said.

There was the bottom of a mountain on the other side of the meadow. Lucy followed Clay through the rest of the vine-covered path and stayed close to him. She could feel darkness lingering like it was watching her from a distance. Unsure as to whether it was from the recent attack or something new. As they walked and approached the base of the mountain, Rani had everyone drink from a canister. When it was Lucy's turn, she took a sip. It was only water. She could hear Rani whispering something as she walked past her.

Rani looked at her, and Lucy blinked, but before she could blink, she saw Rani's face, something about it looked different. Her eyes were dark when they were usually light brown and hazel. Lucy blinked, and Rani was normal again.

"Hallucinations. This water is to clear the mind," Rani said to Lucy.

Nobody else saw or said anything. Hallucinations are the road she's in for. She had to trust herself.

Lucy thought they were going to hike up the mountain, by the looks of it. Clay began walking to the left on the mountainside and counted steps. She knew what he was looking for before he got there, a boulder perfectly shaped as if the Gods handcrafted it themselves and placed it there for them to find. Perhaps, that is precisely what happened. Clay rolled it over with ease.

A cave awaited them on the other side, into the mountain.

Leon sensed Lucy's hesitation and placed his hand on her shoulder.

Once they passed the threshold, she thought it would be dark, but somehow light struck through cracks in the mountainside and into the cave. She couldn't see twenty feet in front of her with the way the cave was. It wasn't straight and narrow, but it wound with winding sharp turns and went steep into the mountain. It looked as if it had been eroded by a small stream of water for hundreds of thousands of years. There were even shells in the layers of compressed sand. It was cold and wet with some dry patches, and she could tell by the smell nobody had been in there for a long time.

"Stay close, Lucy. These tunnels can be unpredictable. They see things and hear things we can't. We have to be mindful of their space and their offerings," Clay whispered to Lucy.

"Offerings? What does a tunnel have to offer us?" She said.

He didn't answer and looked around.

Information and desires, confusing the two and binding them. Being both poison and saving grace. His voice in her head.

How do we know what the cave will offer us? She asked him.

It depends on our intentions. Its offerings are only as pure as we are. If your intentions are good, you should have nothing to worry about. It could give us the answers we need. It could help us figure out how to help you. Clay said.

They made another turn in the cave. The curves of the path and walls were sharp. If Lucy didn't tail Clay, she wouldn't see him in front of her. If the cave was what they said it was, she made sure to stay close so she wouldn't have to find out the hard way. Something inside didn't feel right.

"Clay, I feel eyes," she whispered to him.

He nodded and didn't turn around. His skin rippled. Lucy could see the glow in his eyes whenever he turned his head to the side. He was on full Guardian mode. She looked behind her quickly. Dario and Talan were on the same wavelength as Clay. Every part of them was Guardian. She had to look up at Clay after he took form. He was the height Guardians are and towered over her as if he didn't already. The freckles on Alika and Fazi were also glowing. It looked like someone had splattered glow-in-the-dark ink on their faces. Omala and Emma seemed no different. Rani, on the other hand, looked unquestionably altered. Her face looked longer, sharper, from her chin to her ears and her nose. Her eyes were large and wide.

Rani looked at Lucy, making direct eye contact, and Lucy felt the urge to look away instantly. The pit of her stomach churned.

Clay looked at Lucy, sensing her unease, "Are you well?"

She thought for a moment about what to say. *Rani looks scary?* Wouldn't necessarily fly. What if what she saw was Rani's natural form? None of them looked human. Why should Rani be the exception?

Lucy settled for a nod at Clay, not trusting her voice. Lucy was glued to Clay's back as he continued to walk through the cave, making sure to not turn around again.

Leon's heat radiated from his body heating, Lucy's back. She reached her hand back towards him and felt his warm hand touch hers softly before letting it go. They would do that before they went to bed as children. They both had night terrors growing up and would touch hands briefly before bed to remind themselves they were not alone.

Right now, was the perfect time to reach for Leon. Lucy needed a reminder her brother was at her side and not just literally. Nobody understood Lucy like Leon did.

"Clay, I feel the walls peeling," Leon said to Clay from behind Lucy.

"Peeling?" Lucy asked.

"The walls will transform direction from person to person because everyone's wants, needs, and intentions are different," Clay said and stopped. "Stay close," he demanded of the group.

Clay reached out his hand to Lucy, she happily took it. He gestured for Leon to do the same, and she extended her arm out to Leon. His hands were always warm. Holding their hands prevented her from shaking.

There wasn't much for her to do other than follow in Clay's footsteps. She paid close attention to the walls of the cave. The light shining through invisible cracks from above. She couldn't see the sky when she looked up, only the random sun rays. The way the light hit the floor was magical, streaking the air in front of her and lighting the floor at her feet.

Clay's hand pulled her closer, squeezing her and locking her in. His stride slowed until it came to a stop.

He looked back at Leon, "You were right." Then pointed with his head to look behind him.

Talan, Dario, Fazi, Omala, and Alika weren't there anymore.

"Alika!" Lucy yelled.

"It won't help. They know what to do, they will wait there for us. It's not that they have disappeared or are lost. They just couldn't move forward. They will wait in the same place until they can keep going and catch up. We should do the same," Emma said to Lucy. His eyes were sparkling onyx.

"Lucy, drink this. It'll keep you safe," Rani said, her voice matching her features. She looked at her and quickly looked away at Leon and Clay to see if they could see in Rani what Lucy saw. They didn't seem to notice. It must be how she looks when she's not in human form.

Rani's, now thin and pointy hand, was in front of Lucy with a small gold cup filled to the rim with a silver liquid.

She took the cup. All eyes were on her. When the cup hit her lips, a voice echoed in her mind.

Don't drink anything in the cave, Lucy. Massimo's words were strong in her memory. She didn't know how he knew about the cave or about the drink. Lucy just knew she had to trust him.

"Can you all turn away? The last few times I had to drink anything, I gagged, and it's embarrassing," she said, trying her best to sound normal.

Clay stepped in between her and everyone else. Even though they turned their heads, Lucy turned around, so her back was to them. She reached into her bag as quietly as she could and dumped most of the liquid in a different jar that was in there. She left a few drops and picked them up with her finger, placing them at the corners of her mouth for appearances.

"Done. Thanks, Owranoos. I appreciate you," Lucy said, handing Rani back the cup. She called her by her full name, unsure why.

Rani took the cup and smiled as she put it in her own bag.

Clay went back to the front of the line and reached for Lucy's hand again. Lucy put her hand back for Leon, who grabbed it immediately. She squeezed Leon's hand gently.

"I won't let go, Luc," he whispered to her.

"Thanks." She looked back at him and smiled.

Rani's face caught her eye. Rani was staring at Lucy. It almost looked like she was on her toes. Something was off. Her stomach felt uneasy.

"Hold on. My stomach hurts," Lucy said. The corners of her mouth felt numb.

That's where the elixir was.

Lucy sat on the floor, grabbed water out of her bag, and gulped it down.

"Leon, will you go with me to check ahead? If Lucy doesn't feel well, it might mean something is there. The caves do not lie," Rani said.

Lucy wanted to tell him not to go, to send Emma instead, but Leon nodded and went anyway.

When they were out of earshot, Lucy couldn't help but say something now that Rani was gone.

"Does Rani always look like that? What kind of witch is she, exactly?" Lucy said to Clay and Emma once Rani and Leon were gone.

They looked at each other, then back to Lucy.

"What do you mean?" Emma said.

"Her eyes, her face, even her voice and hands, all were sharp and different. The black in her eyes gives me the chills. I've noticed her being a little different the last couple of days. I thought it was because of Mpiaron, but when we got in the cave, she changed, and it didn't look natural for her. I've never seen her out of human form, though, so I wouldn't know," she said, then looked over at Emma who currently had few demon features, "No offense Emma."

Emma shrugged.

"Lucy, Owranoos doesn't have a different form," Clay said with his eyes moving as if he was reading something in hyper speed.

"AH!" Leon's scream echoed through the cave.

Emma fell to his knees, his body and face in agony though he didn't make a sound. Demons were used to pain.

Lucy sprung to her feet and started running towards the direction Leon went when Clay's arms swung and caught her torso before she could get anywhere. He extended a hand to Emma, helping him to his feet.

Emma nodded and took a deep breath, letting them know he was okay.

"Lucy, these caves were made to aid us or send us to our demise. We do not know which is which. We move together," Clay said, holding her hand and moving swiftly.

Lucy reached her hand back. Emma took it without question.

Clay picked up speed, testing Lucy to see how fast she could go. Her body didn't fail her this time. She moved as fast as Clay and Emma.

Clay slowed down and had put his finger to his lips.

"Lucy didn't drink the elixir, or she would be here right now instead of you. You will have to do, we don't have much time. Cooperate, or you will die for nothing," Rani's voice said though it didn't sound like Rani was alone. It was multiple voices at once, both higher and deeper than her own.

"If you kill me, you break the barrier. War will start when the first drop of my life's blood is drawn," Leon threatened.

Rani laughed, "We plan on it. I kill you, I kill Emma. You are weak. Your sacrifices will balance out. An Enkeli dies and a demon dies."

Lucy looked over at Emma, who was sweating. Clay came to a corner and looked over slowly. He moved back fast, hiding behind the cave wall that separated them from Rani.

"That is not why you are here," Leon said.

"Shut up, you fool," the voices of Rani lashed, and a whipping sound struck them all.

Leon screamed again, and Emma arched his back.

Everything that happened to Leon also happened to Emma. Emma's back dripped with blood even more black than his eyes.

"Kill me then. You can kill me. I will *never* be Lucy. You will *never* have her. You've tried for centuries to rid of Enkeli and the Light, you've waited millennia, and each time you fall short. This time is different. This time, you die," Leon's words cut deeply into Lucy's soul.

Leon was her brother, her twin. He couldn't die, not for her, not for anyone. His life was too valuable to her.

He will not die.

Her spirit roared.

She was full of heat.

Clay's arm touched Lucy's body and pulled her close. He was trying to comfort her. But why wasn't he doing anything?

Emma stepped forward and entered where Rani and Leon were. She could still see him, but she couldn't see the others.

"Rani. You are still in there. Fight! You can do it," Emma said.

"Ha! She hasn't been here for days, and none of you noticed," the voices inside of Rani spoke.

"I did," Lucy said. Clay pulled her close again to remain out of sight. She pulled away, walking towards the direction the others were.

"I noticed," Lucy repeated and looked up at Rani, who immediately took a step back. It wasn't Rani. Lucy didn't recognize her eyes. They were black and soulless, not like the warm hazel of Ranis. "Rani is kind, warm, overwhelming with opinions, and she isn't negative. She might overanalyze everything, but she wouldn't doubt anyone's path. I knew from the start," Lucy said, her voice much stronger than she felt. The demon took a step back.

"Either way, she is no longer here," the beast inside Rani said in multiple tones.

"Oh, she is there." Emma walked towards it as if talking to a friend, "Rani wouldn't go without a fight, even after her heart stops beating. I know you feel it, her forcing you out."

"I haven't felt her since last night, Emmanicko," it said, moving closer to face him.

Emma moved swiftly, reaching for the demon in Rani when we heard a loud "boom" noise. It was as if he hit a thick glass wall.

Lucy looked down, and there was a circle drawn in the dirt surrounding the demon and Leon. Leon was standing in the center.

"Leon?" Lucy said.

"I can't break the circle," Leon said.

"Do not worry for us, Leon. Step out and let me kill this beast," Clay said from behind Lucy, placing a hand on her shoulder before reaching for a throwing knife with his free hand. His other housed his spear, mirroring his father. As she looked at Clay, she could see his stance was of Michaels, as were his facial expressions.

"Tsk tsk, Clay. You should know better than that," it laughed.

Chills covered Lucy's body.

"*I will kill you,*" Clay warned. His skin rippled so fast he was blurry.

"Not before I kill him." The demon touched the back of Leon's neck.

Leon crouched from the burn of its hand, his knees giving in. Emma fell to his knees.

"Fight back, Leon!" Lucy screamed at him.

"If I fight, the war starts now. It is different for us as Enkeli than it is for the Guardians to kill them. It goes both ways," Leon choked.

The demon let him go, throwing him on the floor. He bounced up right away.

"If *it* kills you, the war starts. Either way, it starts here and now," Clay said.

He was tapping the boundary of the circle with his spear and making eye contact with the demon. He was on to something.

Leon went close to Lucy, his face inches from hers.

Boom.

Leon tried crossing the circle boundary and bounced back, hitting the invisible wall.

"You try to fool me! The only reason I possessed Owranoos is for the strength in her magic, I can wield it," the demon shouted and laughed.

Clay looked at Lucy and then back to the demon. He wasn't taking his eye off of it.

Leon turned around to face it just in time to catch a knife in his abdomen. The sound of his flesh being sliced will haunt Lucy forever.

"No! Leon!" Lucy screamed, hitting the boundary. She kicked and screamed. Her face wet from tears.

Lucy began to panic.

Leon didn't move. He stayed standing. He was a healer. He could heal himself.

It gashed his abdomen again. Then his leg, then his other leg, and his arm. All in three swift moves. Leon fell to the floor, Lucy and Emma fell with him for different reasons. Leon wasn't strong enough to heal himself of wounds of that size and amount. He was going to die.

Lucy was shaking, hot, and sweating. She had no idea what she could do.

The demon laughed and held his blade up once more. It was going to stab his heart, and there was nothing any of them could do to stop it. Finally, it paused and looked up at them, and smiled.

"Now!" Clay yelled.

If Lucy blinked, she would have missed it.

Emma leaped into the circle with his arm aimed at the demon. In his hand he held a dagger. The demon swung its blade and hit Emma right in the heart. Then, as Emma fell down onto the demon, he dug his own dagger into the demon's heart.

A second later, the circle was broken, and Clay caught Leon just before he hit the floor. As much as Lucy wanted to tend to her brother, Emma needed her, so did Rani.

She pulled Emma off of the demon. When she saw its face, it was no longer the pointy featured, black-eyed, hollow-skin-looking creature. It was Rani.

Lucy pulled both the dagger and knife out of their hearts. Rani immediately gasped for air, alarming both Lucy and Clay. Clay's spear was at her throat in a second. She coughed and blinked a few times, staying on the floor. Her wound closed immediately.

"What happened?" Rani asked.

It was her. Lucy grabbed the spear and pushed the pointy end away from Rani, nodding at Clay that it was okay.

"How's Leon?" Lucy asked.

"He has a pulse." He didn't look up at Lucy. Instead, he put his hands over the wounds and whispered to himself. She couldn't understand what he was saying.

"Oh no. Emma!" Rani cried, pulling his head onto her lap.

They were in love, and they stabbed each other in the heart. Emma turned his back on Deminio for her, and he was willing to kill her for the Light. He knew what would happen if he went into the circle, he was willing to die at the hands of the one he loved most for the Light.

Lucy checked him for any kind of life. He was gone. His features weren't of a demon anymore, but as the human she always knew him to be. He didn't look troubled how he always did. His eyes weren't dark. His face was relaxed.

He was finally free.

"By the Gods," Talan's words slipped.

Dario and Talan were the first to get there. Immediately picking up Emma's body and helping Rani up onto her feet.

"We need to get out of here," Dario said as he looked around.

"Where is everyone else?" Lucy asked.

"We had them go back outside. They couldn't help us if they were dead," Dario said softly.

Lucy winced at the word *dead*.

Her eyes were heavy, her face wet. She had been crying this whole time. Emma was gone. He battled demons his entire life, and this time he lost.

This can't be it. Lucy thought to herself as she shook her head.

Clay picked Leon up with ease. "Let's get out of here," he said to everyone while he looked at her. Although his voice was gentle, he was pained, too.

Lucy walked behind Clay, who was carrying an unconscious Leon. Clay was behind Talan, who was leading them out, Rani was behind Lucy, and Dario was behind her, holding Emma. Nobody said anything the entire way. There were no words.

Once they got outside, Clay laid Leon on the grass of the cemetery, and Dario spread Emma's body inches away from Leon. Alika and Omala rushed towards them, asking questions about what happened, but they didn't get too close. Leon's wounds were beyond repair, even for them.

"What do we do?" Lucy asked, her voice shook.

Clay was kneeling down next to Leon and took a breath of relief. He looked up at Lucy and nodded, smiling slightly at her. Everything was going to be okay. She sat at Leon's feet with a hand on each shoe. She wanted to stay out of the way. Everyone else formed a circle around them.

She heard whispers and could see Clay's mouth moving. He was chanting the same chant as he did inside the cave. First, he placed his hands on either side of Leon's head, kneeling down, so his face was inches away from Leon's. Then his hands went over each leg where the stab wounds were, he continued to chant. He then went to Leon's abdomen where his deadly injuries were and chanted as he held down his hands, pressing firmly on Leon's stomach. He stayed there the longest. He was sweating.

The clouds opened up and shined only on them two. A stream of light giving life and color back to Leon's skin. Last, Clay went back to either side of Leon's head.

Leon opened his eyes. He blinked a few times before consciousness hit him.

Without hesitation, he remembered everything and clutched to his stomach, his body curled like he was holding himself together. He screamed. It was an ear-piercing, heart-wrenching, helpless scream.

He turned to his side and crawled to Emma, gravitating towards him. He grabbed Emma's hands and put his forehead on Emma's. He took deep sobbing breaths, tears covering them both, spit spilled from his mouth.

He screamed, and screamed, and screamed.

Leon looked up, up at the clouds in the sky, and screamed. Still holding on to Emma's hand, he threw his body back, so his chest was facing up and screamed again.

"Have you no heart? Help him!" Leon screamed at the clouds.

Just then, the clouds roared, thunder and lightning struck. There was no rain, just moisture in the air.

A siren sounded. It was like a horn or the sound a large shell makes when you blow into it. It was the most alluring, grand, beautiful, horrific, eerie, frightful, and breathtaking sound she ever heard.

Clay stood up and held onto Lucy's hand, standing next to her. They formed a complete circle around Leon and Emma.

Lucy could barely stand. She could barely look at her brother and Emma, but she couldn't look away either. Sick to her stomach, she couldn't save him. She couldn't save any of them.

The sound was on repeat, like an alarm. The clouds changed. They moved quickly. Forming a dark circle over the mountain.

The clouds were heavy with a darker circle, but it wasn't a circle of clouds. It was an opening.

Clay dropped to one knee and bowed his head. Everyone else quickly followed, Lucy hesitated. Leon didn't follow them. He stayed looking straight up at the opening. Lucy got down on her knee and bowed, peaking at Leon through her fallen locks.

Warmth was the first thing she felt. She knew what it was they were bowing to. Or more like *who* it was.

She knew it was him before she looked up, his spear being the first thing she saw.

"Son," Archangel Michael said, speaking to Clay.

Clay put his hand to his heart and bowed again, "Father."

"You all have been doing your best alone. It is time you do your best *together*," Michael said as he flew down to them. His smooth deep voice was a sound of its own.

"Emma is *dead*!" Leon cried.

"What makes you say that, Leon?" Michael said, turning to Leon. His voice carried both grace and authority. He landed in the middle of the circle, his wings still outstretched, breaking the circle. They were even more majestic than Lucy remembered. He tucked them close to him as he overlooked Leon and Emma.

"He was a demon! Demons die. They don't go to the afterlife or reincarnate. He died for me. He died for nothing!" Leon cried.

"He didn't die for nothing. Because of him, there is no war. He bought you time. A demon killed a demon. That isn't uncommon. On the contrary, he was also a Lemurian and in turn part Enkeli, because of you," Michael said.

Leon wasn't picking up what Michael was saying. Instead, he cried, unable to process anything through his pain.

"Leon, he was also a Lemurian and in turn part Enkeli," Lucy said through a cracked voice.

She understood.

Leon looked up at her, still not aware.

"Anyone who is of the Light, especially a Lemurian, goes to the afterlife. He was Enkeli, like you, because of you," Michael said, putting a hand on Leon's shoulder.

Leon looked down at Emma's lifeless body. His tears slowed though he was still pained.

"Emma. If you can hear me, I am sorry I wasn't able to save you. I will be forever in your debt for saving me, not just today, but many times. Your charisma, your laugh, the fight you had in you against your demons inside, it saved me. You inspired me in more ways than I will get to explain to you. You made me want to live. Not just be alive, but truly *live*. I'll never know the battles you fought on the inside, but I do know that the Emma I knew was every bit the Light we all need to find. Thank you for honoring us with your friendship and thank you for honoring me by choosing to be my brother and choosing for me to be yours. Whenever I catch a wave or see new waters, I will think of you. I already miss you. I will never stop missing you. Love you, brother. Aah-ooh." Leon pounded his chest at his heart as tears streamed down his face. Gulping away at the ball forming in his throat.

Dario, Talan, and Clay responded in unison as they pounded their right fists over their hearts, "AAH-OOH!"

36

The ride home was quiet. All eight hours of it were mostly silent. Talan drove Leon's car. Leon rode in the back of Clay's truck with Dario and Rani. Emma's body was lying in the bed of the truck on a few blankets with flowers Rani had carefully picked before they left the ruins.

Lucy couldn't look back without crying. Guilt was the only emotion she could feel. If she was strong enough, she could have saved him.

But she wasn't.

"Lucy, breathe," Clay said, reaching out placing his hand on her leg.

She did as she was told. Defeat was all she felt.

"What's going on in that head of yours?" Clay asked, his voice gentle. He felt her sorrow.

"Nothing," Lucy lied.

"I cannot help you if you keep to yourself," he pressed.

Lucy thought to herself for a minute. Going back and forth on whether she should tell him or not, she didn't know if it was grief or how she really felt.

"What's the point? What's the point in me having this extraordinary gift if I don't know how to use it? I can move water, call wind, start a fire, feel other's emotions at times, even my dreams. None of those could have saved Emma today. None of those could kill a demon. So why me? Leon should be the one with the power. He was brave today. I was helpless," Lucy said.

Clay waited a minute. Lucy couldn't catch her breath as frustration surfaced.

"Could I have saved him?" Lucy asked.

Clay thought for a moment, "Today? No."

"So, you're saying if I knew what I was doing, I could have?" She asked and looked over at him.

He didn't answer and focused on the road.

"Clay. Please, answer me," she said. Her voice cracked, and tears flooded her eyes.

"Trust your timing and trust your path. It is the way it is supposed to be," he said.

"What if it was Leon and not Emma? What if the demon would have killed Leon instead? His life would be on my hands, my brother would be dead because of me. Emma is dead because of me," she could barely speak through her sobs.

Clay thought for a moment, then he spoke words she will never forget, "Lucy, learn from this and soak it in. There will come a day when the only person who could save our kind is *you*. That is when it will count. No part of me doubts your ability. It is a burden and a curse, and you are the only person with a heart pure enough to hold it. Yes, Emma died. Yes, you could have saved him. *Make that mean something*."

37

When they pulled the cars up through the back of Lucy's house, Leo was already there waiting for them. Leon jumped off of the bed of the truck and went straight to Leo's arms. Lucy couldn't join in. She wanted to crawl into a ball in the dark and stay there forever. Leon cried, and his body trembled. After a few minutes, they went into Lucy's house and told their dad what had happened. Lucy stared at the fire the entire time from across the room, away from everyone. Other people joined in, her uncles, some wolves, her friends, and a few people she didn't recognize.

The tension grew in the room mid explanation, and Lucy couldn't stay there. She got up and walked out towards the water onto the dock to put her bare feet in the water.

Everything felt different.

She looked around. There were fruit trees on the tree line. Vines and berries and vegetables and more butterflies than she could count. It looked like the Bloom, only it wasn't.

It looked like Mpiaron.

Lucy gathered herself after a few minutes and stood up, her feet heavy as she walked towards the road. There weren't just a few tents along the sides of the road but small teepee-like houses lining the entire road. She looked along the water towards her dad's house, and the small homes didn't stop.

More people were here, more than just Lemurians.

Lucy still had her bag on her and hoped she still had her keys in there. She stuck her arm in. They were in there.

As she drove, she looked in her rearview mirror and could see Clay standing on the porch of her house with his glare straight at her. He smiled.

When she reached the road past the tree line, people walked closer to the road, wanting to see who was coming. They all knew who she was.

She drove slowly.

The entire way to the bridge over to Mpiaron was covered in fruit trees and different kinds of homes, tents, teepees, and RVs. The longer she drove, the more she could see just how big all of this was.

The bridge came quickly, and she could see Mpiaron from where she was at. It was there. In all of its glory, it was there. Chimneys were smoking, and people were outside. Tons of people were on the bridge.

A man looked at her and smiled, then proceeded to walk across the bridge. He picked up speed and started running. Lucy looked past him and could see another man running towards him. Once their bodies touched, the warmth and love they gave off was immeasurable. Lucy got a good look at both of the men. They were identical twins. Reunited after years of not seeing each other or communicating.

She sat there for over an hour crying and watched thirteen different sets of reunions. Some were families, some were friends, some were lovers. Feeling the love and warmth in every hug and every kiss, she understood now more than ever the importance of what she had to do.

Lucy knew she couldn't let them down. Not again.

Lucy got to her house with no one left inside. It was clean, and there was food in the oven waiting for her. She knew because Rani left her a note letting her know. Lucy showered, got comfortable, and ate.

After hours of her lying there, someone knocked on her bedroom door.

"Come in!" She yelled and sat up.

It was Clay. He looked at her and took a deep breath. His shoulders relaxed, he raised an eyebrow. He was waiting for anything, any sign from her.

Lucy laid back down and buried her face in her hands. Her sobs continued.

He walked over and laid down, not touching her. She was too frail.

"I know you have had a long few weeks, specifically the last few days, but something is going on outside you won't want to miss," Clay said, a glimmer of hope in his blue and green eyes.

Lucy got up and started walking towards the door.

"Wait, you're going to want to change. Wear your favorite color," he said.

She gathered strength and walked into her closet to put on her favorite orange dress. It was a long wrap dress, with long sleeves, light, smooth and soft. She slapped on some makeup in an attempt to cover her puffy eyes and brushed her already straight hair, parting it in the middle and tucking it behind her ears out of her face.

Lucy went into her room, and Clay wasn't there. She walked out to her living room. He wasn't there either. She looked over through her glass doors and found him waiting outside with an outstretched arm. Lucy looped her arm through his.

When she looked down towards the water, she could see the dock had a small wooden boat docked to it. Leon stood on the edge.

Her dad, her friends, and family all stood at the waterline. Lucy walked up and passed them all before going up to Leon for the first time. Clay waited at the waterline next to Leo. Her dad put his arm on Clay's shoulder and smiled.

Lucy looked onto the boat. It was Emma. He looked so peaceful as his body rested on a bed of wood and flowers. It was his pyre.

Leon crouched down and untied the boat, setting it free.

As it floated away, a sense of peace hit her. One she hasn't felt since before he died.

"Luc, will you?" Leon said, voice too raw to say anything else. It was the first time they spoke since he died. Lucy had a hard time looking him in the eyes. He held no blame towards her.

Lucy stepped to the very end of the dock and closed her eyes. When she opened them, she felt warm and whole. Fire was already inside of her.

"Fire," was all she said, and the boat went up in flames. As soon as the fire was lit, Leon pulled out a long candle from his pocket and directed its wick at Lucy. She touched it with her fingertip to light it, the flame took immediately. He walked over to their dad, who had another candle, and lit his. Leo lit Clay's candle, who lit Dario and Talan's candles, and so on.

It didn't stop with the people who were close to them. As the candles lit, a wave of small flames surrounded the entire lake. It wasn't hundreds. It was thousands of small flames from thousands of candles being held by thousands of people.

Across the lake, she could see the dock in front of the safe house and her dad's house. Massimo was there, and he wasn't alone.

Clay and her dad walked over to the end of the dock with Leon and Lucy.

"Vampire clans took the Oath of Light. Jinn, the rest of the witches from Scotland and Ireland. Every werewolf, too. They are all a part of us now. This is it," Leon said.

As Lucy looked around, she could see the faces of everyone who was there. Somehow, she recognized them all. She could feel them, she could feel their heartbeats, she could feel their memories. They all believed in her and in the Light. As her eyes made their way around the lake and back again, she felt warm. Her heart overflowed with love and determination. The fire in her burned everything else.

Clay let out a soft laugh. She turned around and could see him, her dad, and her twin brother smiling at her.

She looked down at her hands. They glowed. A glowing aura surrounded her entire body. Her hair and her dress blew in the wind. The water rippled.

This was what she was waiting for.

This feeling.

Lucy looked up, shoulders back, palms up, proud. When the time comes, she would be ready to fight the Deminio.

Leon saw her Light, as could everyone else. He pounded his chest with his fist over and over again to the beat of his heart. Clay joined him. Then their friends, the Guard, the wolves, the Clans, the witches. They all joined in. The beat roared, causing the lake to ripple. They kept going until their hearts beat in unison. Until it was one solid rhythm.

"AAH-OOH!" Leon shouted and raised his fist up in the air.

The next sound she heard was thousands of reasons she couldn't fail, thousands of people who believed in her. Thousands of fists in the air as the army of Light roared together, "AAH-OOH!"

EPILOGUE

Lucy was woken up early to the *sound*. The same sound she heard when Michael came to see them at the cemetery.

She ran out of her house to find Clay and Leon already out there.

"He died, in turn, a part of you died. This is my gift to you for choosing to give him part of your soul," Michael looked up.

They followed and looked up towards the roaring opening in the sky.

It was Emma. He didn't look like a demon or a human with a dark past. He was healthy. His eyes had a sparkle in them. He stayed up there, up above looking down on them.

"Leon, I'm okay. You'll be, too. You saved me from darkness, from Deminio, and from myself. You could always see me, who I truly am, in here." He pounded his fist over his heart, "There isn't enough time to tell you all I know now. Just trust yourself. Thank you for being my family. Thank you for being my brother. When you catch a wave or see new water, I will be with you. Love you, Brother. Until we meet again,"

Emma smiled and laughed a little.

"Aah-ooh!" He pounded on his chest before disappearing into the hole in the sky, but not before he stood up proud with his chest held high. He rolled his shoulders, and wings bloomed from his back. Emma had wings. Only his wings were black, the same sparkling black as his eyes when he was a demon.

Leon and Clay responded together, "AAH-OOH!".

Just like that, Emma was gone.

"He has wings. Only angels have wings. How?" Clay asked his father.

"There is much about him you all aren't aware of, but like you, Leon," Michael extended his hand to Leon, connecting forearm to forearm. "I gave him a piece of my soul, giving him a second chance for his sacrifice. We are with you all," Michael said as he jumped, shooting his wings under him and going through the opening in the sky.

When they looked up, they could see a group of Angels. They were warriors, holding hands in a circle on the perimeter of the opening. The moment Michael flew through the center, the hole closed, and clouds filled the space.

Leon stayed there, looking up, his face wet with tears and his heart full of pride.

ACKNOWLEDGEMENTS

Writing this novel has been such a dream. In the midst of all the craziness life seems to throw out, I found pieces of me in a series of dreams. Those dreams became a story and it's one I never thought I would share. Since I was a child, I always understood things in a different way. It could be isolating at times, because there were times where no matter how hard I tried, it didn't seem to be enough. But with the help of certain people in my life, I was able to mold and remold who I was into who I always wanted to be. I can only hope that this dream turned book can be an escape but also something people can hold onto, to help you find connection to others but most importantly, connection to yourself. Nobody can tell you who you are, that is something only you can do.

First, I'd like to thank my husband, Adam, who has loved and supported me unconditionally. I know that without you, I wouldn't have experienced the love and connection I was able to write so easily about. Without your support I wouldn't be here today. Thank you for building a foundation of love with me for us and for our boys. And thank you for being my number one cheerleader and celebrating every step of this journey with me. To my sons Nico and Zeek, you are extraordinary human beings. Nico, your kindness and ability to be true to yourself is something that truly allowed this story to unfold as I couldn't finish it until after you were born. Zeek, your soul is sweet and optimistic, and although this book was written before you were born, you are all the magic and love that I wrote about.

My brother, Nico, I truly couldn't have written this without you. You inspired this whole thing. You inspire me. There are parts of this book I know only you will know references to, and things that happen in here only you and I have experienced. It was an honor to be able to write a piece of our story. Erika, my big sister, your support in every aspect of my life has been one of the things to keep me going. You've showed me different ways to be strong and I knew that in any moment when I was overwhelmed, you'd be there with a kind understanding heart and any big sister feels in this book are all from you. My little sisters, Mia and Remy, you two asked more than anyone else how my book was coming along or what it was about. Thank you for fueling the fire. My mom, thank you for all you do and for always encouraging me to keep going. Thank you for your love. Dad, thank you for your support and for being present in my life. Not just for the big things, but for all the little things too.

Ari, my beautiful cousin, playing witches for hours on end and creating spells and all things magical really let me express myself in ways I couldn't with anyone else as a child. Thank you for going along with it. Pisha, thanks for being a sounding board and for always being there to cheer me on. Apa, I have you and Ama to thank for this, your love is something I cherish and hold onto forever. Ama, you listened to every one of my dreams and every story I had, you really understood me and never shut down my imagination or my stories. Your story telling was always my favorite, you brought every story to life and if I am half as good as you were at it then I know I wrote a masterpiece. I know you're proud of me always.

Rani, your friendship is one my most treasured. You have showed me what unconditional love from a stranger is. Thank you for your feedback, for being a muse and for always being open to every idea I had and helping me run with it.

One of my favorite people, Courtney, thank you for being the cheerleader and the shoulder I needed depending on the day and for helping me understand the value of self-love and determination. Joe aka Tiff, if you wouldn't have walked into our office when I was writing my dreams down and said, "Are you writing a book?" I wouldn't have ever thought to write one. Jackie, every time I said anything about my writing you always had a vision bigger than anything I could ever think of and the faith you had in me is something I hold close to my heart.

My friends, Max, Nanj, Andrea, Nallely, and my college girls, Fern, Hillary, Moose, Mariann, and Nayeli, each of you have shown me sisterhood through bonds and connection and have showed me family is who you choose.

Fern, you are an angel, and have been without a doubt, one of the best friends in my life. You've built me up and have been a sister from the moment we met. We are cut from the same cloth, and I am so appreciative of the lengths you've gone to be present in my life.

There are a few other people who have inspired this novel, some are no longer with us. But if you read this book and a memory with me sparks, you are a part of this magical book as much as everyone else. Love you all and thank you so much for reading.

Made in the USA
Middletown, DE
01 October 2021